Graveyard
Dust

Also by Barbara Hambly

A Free Man of Color

Fever Season

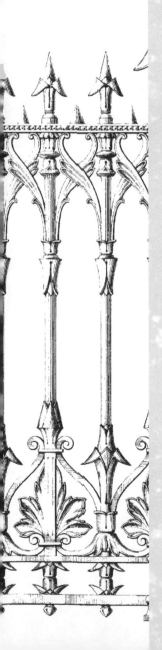
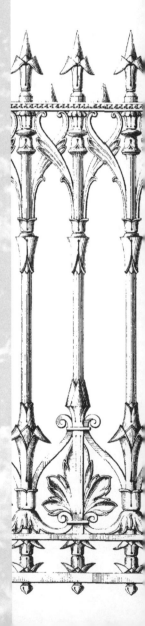

BANTAM BOOKS
New York
Toronto
London
Sydney
Auckland

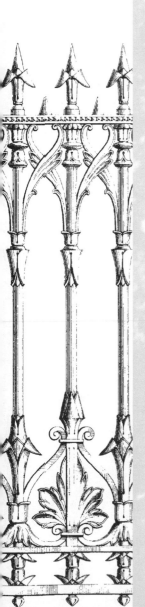

Graveyard
Dust

⟨⟨⟨⟨⟩⟩⟩⟩

Barbara
Hambly

GRAVEYARD DUST

A Bantam Book / July 1999

Library of Congress Cataloging-in-Publication Data
Hambly, Barbara.
Graveyard dust / Barbara Hambly
p.   cm.
ISBN: 0-553-10259-1
1. Afro-American men—Louisiana—New
Orleans—History—19th century—Fiction.   2. Free Afro-
Americans—Louisiana—New Orleans—Fiction.   I. Title.
PS3558.A4215G73   1999
813'.54—dc21   98-43456
CIP

Published simultaneously in the United States and Canada

Bantam Books are published by Bantam Books, a division of
Random House, Inc. Its trademark, consisting of the words
"Bantam Books" and the portrayal of a rooster, is Registered
in U.S. Patent and Trademark Office and in other countries.
Marca Registrada. Bantam Books, 1540 Broadway, New
York, New York 10036.

PRINTED IN THE UNITED STATES OF AMERICA
BVG   10 9 8 7 6 5 4 3 2 1

For Mary Ann

Special thanks to those, in New Orleans and elsewhere, who have helped me with this book: to Paul Nevski of Le Monde Créole; to the staff of the Historic New Orleans Collection; to Tim Trahan of Animal Arts in New Orleans; to Priestess Miriam of the Voodoo Spirit Temple; to Greg Osborn of the New Orleans Public Library; to Adrian and Victoria; to Kate Miciak; to Diana Paxson; and always, to George.

T E R M I N O L O G Y   O F   V O O D O O

Since voodoo terms were originally transliterated from various West African languages through creolized French, spelling is a matter of guesswork. I have in most cases used the modern Haitian spellings and names as found in Métraux's *Voodoo in Haiti,* the starting point of much of my research.

The shape and structure of voodoo in Louisiana in the 1830s is something that can only be guessed at. Refugees fleeing the uprisings in Sainte Domingue (the island now divided into Haiti and Santo Domingo) brought extensive voodoo beliefs with them to a land that already had its own variants of these same practices, and much depended on the religion's interaction with its immediate surroundings. In Haiti, after the black revolution, voodoo became an accepted religion; in Louisiana its evolution was marked by external pressures from the prevailing Christianity and culture. In addition, the voodoo *loa* tends to proliferate: There are dozens of variations of the spirit Ezili (or Erzuli), of Ogu (Ogou)—Ogu Feray, Ogu Badagri, Ogu Osanyl, and Sen (or San) Jak, Maje and others—of Baron (or Bawon) Samedi or Cemetery, also known as Baron La Croix. I have simplified as much as I can without doing violence to what I understand to be the basic tenets of the religion.

Some *loa*:

Ogu (or *Ogou*)—warrior spirit of justice, often depicted as a soldier; frequently identified with Saint James the Greater

Shango—blacksmith spirit, also warrior; a spirit of iron and fire

Ezili (or *Erzuli*)—spirit of womanhood, in various incarnations a mother and an Aphrodite flirt

Baron Samedi (or *Baron Cemetery*)—lord of the dead, often depicted as an obscene trickster, lord of the Guédé

Guédé—family of dark and dangerous spirits, spirits of power and death

Papa Legba (or *Limba*)—ruler of the crossroads, of doorways and bridges, and of transition states; he is the first *loa* petitioned in Haitian ritual, that he may open the doors for the other *loa* to pass through

Damballah-Wedo—the sacred serpent, spirit of the rainbow and of water; called also the Zombi-Damballah

Bosou—bull spirit of potency and strength

The *loa* may possess worshipers of either their own identified gender, or the opposite, and may possess them to various degrees. Some "horses," as the possessed are called, do not remember things said and done during their possession; the woman I talked to who had been possessed by Ogu said she was perfectly aware of herself, but observing: craving cigars, for instance (which Ogu loves, though the woman possessed was a nonsmoker), and rum.

Other voodoo terms:

vèvès—complex designs drawn on the ground to focus or summon the *loa*

hougan—voodoo priest or "king" in old New Orleans terminology

mambo—voodoo priestess or "queen"

gris-gris—an amulet or charm

tricken bag—amulet made of several ingredients sewn together in a bag, usually a gris-gris of ill luck or malice

wanga (or *ouanga*)—spell

wangateur or *root-doctor*—magician, sorcerer

congris—mixture of black-eyed peas and rice, a favored food of the *loa*

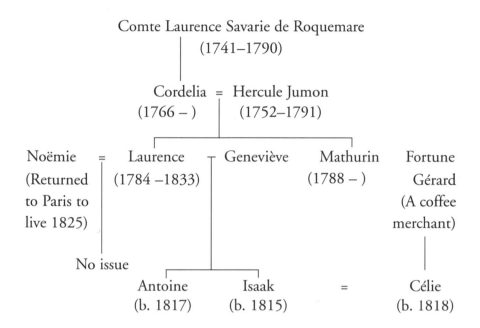

Comte Laurence Savarie de Roquemare
(1741–1790)

Cordelia = Hercule Jumon
(1766 –)   (1752–1791)

Noëmie   =   Laurence   ┬   Geneviève   Mathurin   Fortune
(Returned   (1784 –1833)   (1788 –)   Gérard
to Paris to   (A coffee
live 1825)   merchant)

No issue

Antoine   Isaak   =   Célie
(b. 1817)   (b. 1815)   (b. 1818)

Graveyard
Dust

———◦◦◦◦———

African drums in darkness sullen as tar.

Rossini's "Di tanti palpiti" unspooling like golden ribbon from the ballroom's open windows.

Church bells and thunder.

Benjamin January flexed his aching shoulders and thought, *Rain coming.* Leaning on the corner of Colonel Pritchard's ostentatious house, he could smell the sharp scent in the hot weight of the night, hear the shift in the feverish tempo of the crickets and the frogs. The dim orange glow of an oil lamp fell through the servants' door beside him, tipping the weeds beyond the edge of the yard with fire.

Then the air changed, a cool flash of silkiness on his cheek, and he smelled blood.

The drums knocked and tripped, dancing rhythms. *Fairly close to the house,* he thought. This far above Canal Street the lots in the American suburb of St. Mary were large, and few had been built on yet. Ten feet from kitchen, yard, and carriage house grew the native oaks and cypresses of the Louisiana swamps, as they had grown for time beyond reckoning. January picked out the voices of the drums, as on summer nights like this one in his childhood he'd used to tell frog from frog. That light knocking would be a hand drum no bigger than a vase, played with fast-tripping fingertips. The heavy fast thudding was the bamboula, the log drum—a big one, by the sound. The hourglass-shaped tenor spoke around them, patted sharply on both sides.

One of the men on the plantation where January had been born had had one of those. He'd kept it hidden in a black oak, back in the *ciprière,* the swamp beyond the cane fields. Forty years ago, when the Spanish had ruled the land, for a slave to own a drum was a whipping offense.

"Not meaning to presume, sir." Aeneas, Colonel Pritchard's cook, stepped from the kitchen's gold-lit arch and crossed the small yard to where January stood at the foot of the back gallery stairs. "But I'd be getting back up to the ballroom were I you." A stout man of about January's own forty-one years, the cook executed a diffident little half bow as he spoke. It was a tribute to January's status as a free man, though the cook was far lighter of skin. "Colonel Pritchard's been known to dock a man's pay, be he gone for more than a minute or two. I seen him do it with a fiddle player, only the other week."

January sighed, not surprised. The kitchen's doors and windows stood wide to the sweltering night, and the nervous glances thrown by the cook, the majordomo, and the white-jacketed waiter toward the house every time one of them cracked a joke or consumed a tartlet that should have gone on the yellow-flowered German china told its own story. "Thank you." January drew his gloves from his coat pocket and put them on again, white kid and thirty cents a pair, and even that movement caused bolts of red-hot lightning to shoot through his shoulder blades, muscles, and spine. He'd been a surgeon for six years at the Hôtel-Dieu in Paris and knew exactly how heavy a human arm was, but it seemed to him that he'd never quite appreciated that weight as he did now, after an hour and a half of playing quick-fire waltzes and polkas on the piano with an injury that hadn't healed.

A shift of the night air brought the smell of smoke again, the knocking of the drums, and the hot brief stink of blood. His eyes met the cook's. The cook looked away.

Not my business, thought January, and mounted the stairs. He guessed what was going on.

The air in the ballroom seemed waxy and thick as ambergris: one could have cut it in slices with a wire. Pomade and wool, spilled wine and the gas lamps overhead, and—because at least two-thirds of the guests were Americans—the acrid sweet sourness of spit tobacco. January edged through the servants' door and, behind the screen of potted palmettos and wilting vines that sheltered the musicians, sought to resume his seat at the piano as inconspicuously as it was possible for a man six feet, three inches tall; built like a bull; and black as a raw captive new-dragged down the gangplank of a slave ship from the Guinea coast, and never mind the neat black coat, the linen shirt and white gloves, the spotless cravat.

Hannibal Sefton, who'd been distracting the guests from the fact that there hadn't been a dance for nearly ten minutes, glanced at him inquiringly and segued from "Di tanti" into a Schubert lied; January nodded his thanks. The fiddler was sheet white in the gaslight and perspiration ran down the shivering muscles of his clenched jaw, but the music flowed gracefully, like angels dancing. January didn't know how he did it. Since an injury in April, January had been unable to play at any of the parties that made up his livelihood in America—he should not, he knew, be playing now; but finances were desperate, and it would be a long summer. He, at least, he thought, had the comfort of knowing that he would heal.

Voices around them, rough and nasal in the harsh English tongue January hated:

"Oh, hell, it's just a matter of time before the Texians have enough of Santa Anna. Just t'other day I heard there's been talk of them breakin' from Mexico. . . ."

"Paid seven hundred and thirty dollars for her at the downtown Exchange, and turns out not only was she not a cook, but she has scrofula into the bargain!"

Colonel Pritchard was an American, and a fair percentage of New Orleans's American business community had turned out to sample Aeneas's cold sugared ham and cream tarts. But here and there in the corners of the room could be heard the softer purr of Creole French.

"Any imbecile can tell you the currency must be made stable, but why this imbecile Jackson believes he can do so by handing the country's money to a parcel of criminals. . . ."

And, ominously, "*My* bank, sir, was one of those to receive the redistributed monies from the Bank of the United States. . . ."

"You all right?" Uncle Bichet leaned around his violoncello to whisper, and January nodded. A lie. He felt as if knives were being run into his back with every flourish of the piano keys. In the pause that followed the lied, while January, Hannibal, Uncle Bichet, and nephew Jacques changed their music to the "Lancers Quadrille," the drums could be clearly heard, knocking and tapping not so very far from the house.

You forget us? they asked, and behind them thunder grumbled over the lake. *You play Michie Mozart's little tunes, and forget all about us out here drumming in the* cipriere?

All those years in Paris, Michie Couleur Libre in your black wool coat, you forget about us?

About how it felt to know everything could be taken away? Father-mother-sisters all gone? Nobody to know or care if you cried? You forget what it was, to be a slave?

If you think a man has to be a slave to lose everything he loves at a whim, January said to the drums, *pray let me introduce you to Monsieur le Choléra and to her who in her life was my wife.* And with a flirt and a leap, the music sprang forward, like a team of bright-hooved horses, swirling the drums' dark beat away. Walls of shining gold, protecting within them the still center that the world's caprices could not touch.

In the strange white gaslight, alien and angular and so different from the candle glow in which most of the French Creoles still lived, January picked out half a dozen women present in the magpie prettiness of second mourning, calling cards left by Monsieur le Choléra and his local cousin Bronze John, as the yellow fever was called. Technically, Suzanne Marcillac Pritchard's birthday ball was a private party, not a public occasion, suitable even for widows in first mourning to attend—not that there weren't boxes at the Théâtre d'Orléans closed in with latticework so that the recently bereaved could respectably enjoy the opera.

And in any case, it would take more than the death of their immediate relatives to keep the ladies of New Orleans's prominent French and Spanish families from a party. Manon Desdunes—that very young widow gazing wistfully at the dancers—had lost a brother to the cholera last summer and a husband the summer before. Delicate, white-haired Madame Jumon, talking beside the buffet to Mrs. Pritchard, had only last summer lost her middle-aged son.

Always entertained by the vagaries of human conduct, January distracted himself from the pain in his arms and back by picking out exactly where in the ballroom the frontier between American and French ran, an invisible Rubicon curving from the second of the Corinthian pilasters on the north wall, to a point just south of the enormous, carven double doors opening to the upstairs hall. French territory centered around Mrs. Pritchard, plump and plain and sweet faced, and the brilliantly animated Madame Jumon, though now and then a Creole gentleman would pass that invisible line to discuss business with the Colonel's friends: bankers, sugar brokers, importers, and landlords, the planters having long since departed New Orleans for their acres. Every so often one of the younger Americans would solicit the favor of a dance with one of Mrs. Pritchard's younger Marcillac or Jumon cousins—and to do them justice, January had to admit that for Americans they were as well behaved as they probably knew how to be. For the most part, the damsel would be rescued by a brother or a cousin or a younger uncle twice-removed who would reply politely that Mademoiselle was desolate, but the dance was already promised to him. When Madame Jumon's surviving son, a craggily saturnine gentleman of forty-five, showed signs of leading Pritchard's middle-aged maiden sister out onto the floor, Madame quickly excused herself from conversation and intercepted the erring gallant; January was hard put to hide a smile.

"Don't see what they got to be stuck-up about," grumbled a short, badly pomaded gentleman with a paste ruby the size of an orange pip in his stickpin. "I don't care if their granddaddies were the King of Goddam France, they're citizens of the United States now, just like we are. I got a good mind to go back and take that gal's brother to account. . . ."

"Mr. Greenaway, please!" Emily Redfern, a stout little widow—who a moment ago had been bargaining like a Levantine trader with the burly Hubert Granville of the Bank of Louisiana—laid a simpering black-mitted hand on the pomaded gentleman's arm. "That was Désirée Lafrénnière! Of course her family. . . ." The Widow Redfern, January knew, had been trying for years to get on the good side of the old Creole families. Little did she know how impossible that task was.

Mr. Greenaway's pale blue eyes moved from the widow's square-jawed, cold-eyed countenance to her exceedingly expensive pearls. He smiled ingratiatingly. "Well, if it wouldn't intrude on your grief too much, M'am, perhaps you would favor me by sitting this one out with me. . . ."

"I'll lay you it'll be Greenaway and Jonchere, before midnight," said Hannibal Sefton, when an hour and a half later he and January slipped down the back stairs for a breath of air. "Greenaway's been drinking like a fish and he always starts up on the Bank of the United States when he does that. Jonchere's called out the last two men who supported Jackson. . . ."

"I'll put my money on the Colonel himself," said January, and gingerly moved his shoulder again. There had to be *some* position in which he didn't hurt.

"Call out one of his own guests?" Hannibal took his laudanum bottle from his pocket and took a swig; then offered it hospitably to January, who waved it away. He'd seen, and heard, Hannibal play like the harps of Heaven when he was so lubricated as to be barely coherent, but for himself music was a matter for the mind as well as for the soul. And the thought of being that defenseless terrified him. Being barely able to lift his own arms was fearful enough.

"A Frenchman? I think he'll call out either Bringier or Madame Jumon's son. . . ." For close to a year now January and Hannibal had entertained themselves at every engagement they played by laying wagers on who would challenge whom to an affair of honor before the evening was through. It was fortunate they played for pennies—or picayunes, at this low ebb of the season—for January could have won or lost a fortune at the game.

"Mathurin? With the Jumon money I'd think Pritchard would thank him for showing interest in that poor sister of his."

A sharp rustle sounded in the trees to the side of the house. January held up his hand, listening. The drums were silent.

Aeneas and the original waiter had been joined by a third man, young and barely five feet tall, hastily buttoning a white linen jacket and rinsing something off his hands with water dipped from the rain barrel. With him was a young woman in the first stages of pregnancy, retying the headscarf that all women of color, slave or free, were by law required to wear. They turned immediately to lay out the slices of beef and ham, the tarts and cakes and petits fours, on the yellow-flowered plates. "I'll be back," said January softly. He slipped down the gallery steps and around the corner of the house into the trees.

Given the trouble his curiosity had caused him in the past, January reflected that he should know better. In any case, he had a good idea of what he would find in the darkness where the trees got thick. *Though by this time,* he told himself, *if she'd been there—been part of it—she'd be gone.*

And what good would it do me to know?

He didn't want to admit it, but the drums had brought back memories.

Mats of leaves and pale shaggy curtains of moss quickly obscured the bright cool rectangles of the windows. Light glinted on puddles of standing water, and the ground gave squishily underfoot. Twenty feet from the house, January scented blood again and the heavy grit of quenched smoke still hanging in the air. He listened, but all was still.

Even so, he felt their eyes. Not those who'd risked a whipping to sneak out and follow the sound of the drums. Not those who'd sung the keening, eerie, driving rhythms of those songs in a half-forgotten tongue. The eyes he felt on his back were the eyes of those they'd come to see, to touch; to sing to and to give themselves to, flesh and hearts and souls.

January knew them well.

Papa Legba, guardian of all gates and doors, warden of the crossroad.

Beautiful Ezili, in all her many forms.

Zombi-Damballah, the Serpent King.

Ogu of the sword and the fire—January quickly pushed the thought of that burning-eyed warrior from his mind.

And the Baron Samedi, the Baron Cemetery, boneyard god grinning white through the darkness. . . .

A hundred feet from the house, trees had been felled. Here new construction would begin with the first frost of autumn. Embers still glowed where a pit had been dug, quenched now with dirt. From his pocket January took a box of lucifers, and scratched one on the paper. It showed him the rucked earth where the *vèvès* had been drawn, the dark spatters of spilt rum and the darker dribblings of blood. Near the pit a headless black chicken lay, feet still twitching, ringed by fragmented silver Spanish bits. Two plates also lay on the ground, each likewise surrounded by silver. One was heaped with rice and chickpeas. The other held a cigar and a glass of rum.

Those whose aid had been sought were known for liking tobacco, rum, and blood.

January lit another match and stepped closer, careful where he put his feet. The plates were white German porcelain, painted with yellow flowers. Around them, inside the ring of silver, dark against the paler dust of the ground, a line had been drawn in sprinkled earth.

If it had been salt, January knew, it would have been bad enough. Salt was the mark of curses and ill. But this wasn't salt.

It was graveyard dust, a cursing to the death.

There was nothing else, no sign to tell him who might have been here, who had done the rite. *She's probably home in bed. Nothing to do with this at all.*

January crossed himself and walked swiftly back to the house. Though the drums had ceased, he seemed to hear them, knocking in the growl of the thunder, in the darkness at his back.

Colonel Pritchard was waiting for him on the gallery. "When I pay four men for five hours I don't expect to get only four hours and a half." The American studied January with light tan eyes that seemed too small for his head. As far as January knew, the man had never been a colonel of anything—there was certainly nothing of the military in his bearing—but he knew better than to omit the title in speaking to him.

"No, Colonel," he said, in his best London English. "I am most sorry, sir. I heard a noise, as if of an intruder, around . . ."

"I have servants to deal with noises—if that's what you heard." The dust-colored eyes cut to Hannibal, who smiled sunnily under his gray-ing mustache; Pritchard's mouth writhed with disgust. "And when I pay for four men for five hours I don't expect to get only three men and a half. And you a white man, too." He plucked the flask from the pocket of Hannibal's shabby, long-tailed black coat. Pulling the cork, the Colo-nel made another face. "Opium! I reckon that's what happens when you spend your days playing music with Negroes." He hurled the flask away, and January heard it smash against the brick of the kitchen wall.

"I suppose that means an end to the champagne as well," Hannibal noted philosophically as they followed the master of the house back up the stairs. He coughed heavily, January reaching out to catch him by the arm as he half–doubled over with the violence of the spasm. Pritchard glanced over his shoulder at them from the top of the stairs, impatience and disdain on his heavy-featured face. "Just as well. I think we've seen the last of the chamber pot, too."

They remained in the ballroom, under the Colonel's sour eye, until two in the morning. Despite the open windows, the room only grew hotter, and the pain in January's back and shoulders increased until he thought he would prefer to die. *Your back carries the music,* he was always telling his pupils. *Strong back, light hands.* It surprised him that he was able to play at all.

At around eleven, after a particularly gay mazurka, Aeneas came to the dais with a tray of lemonade—"What's that?" Pritchard loomed at once from among the potted palms. "Who told you to give these men anything?"

"Mrs. Pritchard did, sir." The cook's English wasn't good, but he took great care with it, as if he feared the consequences of the smallest mistake.

"Mrs. Pritchard—" The Colonel turned to his wife, who, probably anticipating the objection, had positioned herself not far away. "I thought I made it abundantly clear that I'm paying these men in coin, after they have satisfactorily completed their duties, and not by permitting them to make themselves free with my substance."

"It's such a very hot night, Colonel," she said soothingly. Her English was just as awkward—and just as wary—as the cook's. "And, you understand, it is what is done. . . ."

"It is not 'done' in *this* house. . . ."

During their low-voiced altercation Aeneas stepped back beside the piano where January sat and whispered, "There's a boy back in the kitchen asking after you, Michie January. Says he's got to see you. Says he's your nephew."

"Gabriel?" January looked up, trying to cover the fact that his arms were too weak from the strain of playing to reach for the lemonade. It was far later than his sister Olympe would ever have permitted any child of hers to be on the streets.

Panic touched him at the recollection of the drums, the blood. . . .

"That's what he says his name is, yes, sir. He says he has a message for you, but he wouldn't tell me what."

January glanced at his employer. Pritchard was already looking over at him, clearly expecting the next dance to start up. "I don't think I'm going to be able to get over there until the end of this."

Equally impossible, of course, that the Colonel would consent to write out permission for any of his servants to escort the boy home.

"He's no trouble," Aeneas assured January. "I'll tell him he has to wait. He's already asked if he can help with the tarts and the negus."

That certainly sounded like Gabriel. But as he maneuvered his arms back to where the edge of the piano would take the weight of them and struck up the country dance "Mutual Promises," January felt his heart chill with dread. Something had happened.

He felt sick inside.

Let me introduce you to Monsieur le Choléra, he had said to the drums that had mocked him for the hard-won security of his freedom, for the complex beauties of the music that was his life.

January could still remember the first time he'd met St.-Denis Janvier, the sugar broker who had purchased his mother, himself, and his sister Olympe. Could still see in his mind the man's close-fitting coat of bottle-green satin and the fancy-knit patterns of his stockings, the eight gold fobs and seals that hung on his watch chain. Could still feel the rush of relief that went through him when that paunchy little man had told him, *I have purchased your beautiful mother in order to set her free, and you, too, and your sister.* Relief unspeakable.

I'll be safe now.

No more nightmares about his mother going away, as others on the plantation had gone so abruptly away. No more fear that someone would one day say to him, *You are going to go live someplace else now—* someplace where he knew no one.

All his life, it seemed to him, he had wanted a home, wanted a place where he knew he was safe.

He'd been eight. It had taken him a little time to learn to be a free man, to learn the ins and outs of a different station, what was and was not permitted. To learn to speak proper French and not say *tote* for "carry," or *aw* when he meant *"bien sûr."* But throughout the boyhood spent in the garçonnière behind the house on Rue Burgundy that St.-Denis Janvier gave his new mistress, throughout the years of schooling in one of the small private academies that catered to the children of white men and their colored plaçées, January had never lost that sense of being, in his heart of hearts, on firm footing. At least the worst wasn't going to happen. At least he wasn't going to be taken away from those he loved.

From "Mutual Promises" they whirled into "A Trip to Paris." The ladies laughed and skipped in their bell-shaped skirts, their enormous lace-draped sleeves that stood out ten inches from their arms; gentlemen flirted decorously as they held out white-gloved hands to white-gloved hands. Mr. Greenaway of the pomaded curls hovered protectively around the wealthy Widow Redfern, fetching her crêpes and tarts and lemonade and presumably soothing her not-very-evident grief while she talked business with Granville the banker. Granville himself showed surprising lightness of step in dancing with his drab little pear-shaped wife and with every pretty maid and matron on the American side of the room. From the sideline, Mrs. Pritchard watched with resigned envy.

The American ladies all seemed plainer than their French counterparts, duller, an effect January knew wasn't entirely owing to having less sense of dress. No American lady would be seen in public, even at a ball, in the rice powder and rouge that no Creole lady would be seen without. It seemed to him, too, that they laughed less.

He supposed if he were a woman married to an American he wouldn't laugh much, either.

St.-Denis Janvier had sent him to study with an Austrian music master, a martinet who had introduced to him the complex and disciplined joys of technique. Music had always been the safe place to which his soul had gone as a child: joining in the work-hollers, picking out harmonies, inventing songs about big storms or his aunt Jemma's red beans or the time Danro from the next plantation had fallen in love with Henriette up at the big house. All of this, Herr Kovald had said, was what savages did, who knew no better. Kovald had played for him that first time the *Canon* of Pachelbel—and January's soul had entered onto that magic road, that quest for beauty that had no end.

He had studied healing also, and in much the same fashion: first with old Mambo Jeanne at Bellefleur Plantation, who'd showed him and Olympe both where to gather slippery elm, mullein, lady's slipper, and sassafras in the woods. Later he'd been apprenticed to José Gómez, a free man of color who had a little surgery down on Rue Chartres. Reading the books Gómez had of the English surgeons John and William Hunter and watching dissections of sheep and pigs from the slaughterhouses, January had seen no difference between the music that was the life of his soul and the harmonies of blood and organs and bones. And when, finally, the long wars between France and England and the United States were done and it was safe to cross the seas, January had gone to Paris, to study surgery at the Hôtel-Dieu.

He'd been admitted to the College of Surgeons there and had continued to work at the clinic, unable to go into private practice either in
Paris or in New Orleans. To be sure, free surgeons of color practiced in
both cities, but they were invariably of a polite walnut snuff, or hue.
January had long accepted the fact that no American, and few Frenchmen, were ready to trust their lives to someone who so much resembled
a pantomime-show Sultan's Ethiopian door guard. "At least here in
Paris one is free," Ayasha had said to him, Ayasha who had fled her
father's harîm in Algiers rather than be wed against her will. "And no
one can take that from you." Ayasha had worked in Paris as a seamstress
since the age of fourteen. By the time January met her, she owned her
own shop.

No one can take that from you.

Except, of course, January had discovered, Monsieur le Choléra.

It would be two years in August since he had returned home and
found Ayasha dead.

Since then he had discovered that he had progressed not one step
farther than that terrified slave boy on Bellefleur Plantation, in terms of
what life could and could not take away.

It was June. A deadly time in New Orleans.

"That's absolute nonsense," blustered a railway speculator in a dark
gray coat. "Tom Jenkins says he's been down the river almost to the
Belize and there hasn't been a sign of yellow jack, much less the cholera,
anywhere in the countryside."

"Not in the countryside, no." Dr. Ker of the Charity Hospital took
a glass of champagne from the little waiter's tray with a polite nod of
thanks. "On the whole the cholera isn't a disease of the countryside.
We've had two cases of yellow fever here in the city."

"Two?" Granville snorted. "Well, *there's* a reason to turn tail and
run, by gosh! Are you sure they *were* yellow fever, Doctor? Dr. Con-
naud—he's my physician, and a splendid fellow with a knife, just
splendid!—says it isn't possible that there should be epidemics three
summers in a row."

"It's the newspapers," declared Colonel Pritchard. "Damned journalists'll print anything that'll sell their filthy rags. They don't care
about the local businesses, or what it does to a city's property values if
word gets around there's fever. All they think about is getting a few
more copies sold. As for you, Dr. Ker, I'm sure you'll find if you open

those two so-called fever victims up that there's some kind of reason for the same symptoms. . . ."

Was that what young Gabriel had walked from Rue Douane in the old French town to tell him? January wondered. What he wouldn't tell the servants of this stranger's house? That Olympe was sick? Or her husband, Paul? One of the other children?

Yellow fever? Cholera?

Not cholera, he prayed desperately. *Blessed Virgin, please, not that.*

And while his arms trembled with fatigue, and his heart squeezed with dread, and he felt as if someone were trying to pry his shoulder blades loose with crowbars, he skipped through moulinets, brisés, cross-passes, and olivettes, as lightly as a happy child running in a meadow of flowers. A wave of faintness passed over him; he concentrated on ballottes and glissades, on the glittering protection of the music's beauty that could almost carry his mind away from the pain. Hannibal swung into a lilting solo air, embroidering effortlessly as January lowered his throbbing arms to his thighs to rest. Like a bird answering a slightly drunk muse, Jacques took up the thread of music on his cornet. Uncle Bichet came in third on the cello, the round lenses of his spectacles flashing in the gaslight, an odd contrast to the tribal scarring on his thin old face. At intervals in his harangue against those who conspired to ruin the local real estate market with rumors of plague, Pritchard watched them dourly; watched, too, the unobtrusive door to the back stairs. January wished the Colonel buried alive in graveyard dust.

"Lemonade only, you understand?" January heard him say to Aeneas, when after a purgatorial eternity of heat and tobacco stench and aching muscles the clock at last sounded two. "Mrs. Pritchard will be over in the kitchen to weigh up the leftover chicken and pastries. I don't want the lot of you gorging on them or passing them out to those musicians. And I won't have them wasted. Mrs. Pritchard . . ."

His voice lifted in a preemptory yap. His wife—who might have been presumed to have earned a little privilege on the night of her own birthday ball—turned with a sigh from the farewell embraces of her friends. "He's quite right," said the Widow Redfern, who had wormed her way—Mr. Greenaway doglike in tow—into the Creole group of ladies. "I find one *always* has to count the champagne bottles after a party, and measure the sugar. It's really quite prudent of your husband . . ."

"Américaines," murmured Madame Jumon, flashing a humorous grimace as she kissed Mrs. Pritchard warmly on her unpowdered cheeks and took her departure on her son's black-banded arm. "What can one do?"

Gabriel was waiting in the kitchen. He was a tall boy, slim like his mother, January's sister Olympe, and handsome as his father, who was an upholsterer with a shop on Rue Douane. He had, too, his father Paul's sunny goodness of heart. As January crossed from the back gallery to the kitchen he could see his nephew, through the wide-flung windows, helping Aeneas and the kitchen maid clean up: endless regiments of crystal wineglasses, champagne glasses, water glasses; dessert forks, coffee spoons, teaspoons, dessert spoons; platters, salvers, pitchers, creamers, tureens; a hundred or more small plates of white German china painted with yellow roses, half again that many napkins of yellow linen.

Above the foulness of the privies on the hot night air, the dense stink of Camp Street's uncleaned gutters, from around the corner of the stables January could still catch the whiff of drying blood.

"Uncle Ben!"

"You look like you been pulled through the mangle and no mistake." Aeneas set aside the mixing bowl he was drying and unstoppered a pottery jar of ginger water. "Danny, bring Michie Janvier a cup." The little waiter fetched it; Gabriel discreetly supported January's elbow while January raised it to his lips. "You ever want to hire this boy out as a cook, you come speak to me about it, hear?"

"I'll do that." January returned the cook's grin, then studied the inside of the empty cup with mock gravity and measured with the fingers of his other hand the distance from the rim to the damp line the liquid had left. "Looks like a gill and a half I drank. You want to mark that down for the Colonel's records, in case he gets after you for where it went?"

Aeneas laughed. "Me, I'm just thanking God there's no way for him to measure the air in here, or he'd sure be after us about what your nephew breathed since eleven o'clock. Kitta, you got all the saucers in?"

They had to know, thought January, looking at the kitchen maid Kitta, the watchful-eyed little Dan bringing still more champagne glasses and yellow-flowered plates back from the house. He saw how they smiled at one another and how the little man relaxed when the woman touched his hand.

Which of them, he wondered, had sent for the voodoo-man?
Or woman.

January glanced down at Gabriel and saw the shaky relief in the boy's smile. Of course he wouldn't have told these people about sickness, if it was the cholera. That was a good way to get a thrashing from a man like the Colonel, freeborn or not. *How dare you go around scaring my servants with your lies?* Most Americans didn't understand the difference between free coloreds and black slaves.

"Thank you for looking after him," January said. "We'll be bidding you good night." He put a hand on Gabriel's shoulder and guided him from the kitchen and into the shadows of the yard.

Behind them Aeneas called out, "You mind how you go."

That'll be all we need, thought January. *Some officious member of the City Guard demanding to see our papers. "Are you aware that it's two in the morning? That the cannon in the Place d'Armes fired off at ten to warn people like you"*—meaning both blacks and colored—*"to be off the street?"*

He glanced back at the kitchen. The other musicians had already gone. By the grubby topaz glow of a dozen smoky tallow candles, the cook, the menservants, and the kitchen maid Kitta had recommenced the Augean task of washing every dish, fork, and sparkling bit of hollowware. Little Dan carried a yoke of pails to the cistern; firelight leapt over Aeneas's sweaty face as he fanned up the flames under the boiler to heat it. In the ballroom's four long windows the white beauty of the gaslight dimmed and disappeared. Carriage wheels creaked and slopped in the muddy street, and voices called a final good-bye: French. The Americans had left a full thirty minutes ago. A moment later Mrs. Pritchard emerged from the rear door of the house, carrying a candlestick; she murmured, " '*Soir*" to January and Gabriel as they passed from the kitchen's lights into the dark side yard that led around to the still-deeper darkness of the street.

There was no sound around them now save the gulping of the frogs, the incessant whine of mosquitoes, the drum of the cicadas in the trees. He asked softly, "What is it?"

Not the cholera. Please, Blessed Mary Ever-Virgin, not the cholera.

"It's Mama." Gabriel's bright smile, the cheerfulness he'd shown in the presence of the servants, dissolved, showing the fear in his eyes. "The City Guards came and got her. They say she done murder—killed a man."

TWO

January's first thought was, *She was out there after all.*

Blood and rum and graveyard dust.

And then, *Don't be silly. Even if curses had such power, that dust was laid down only three hours ago.*

Olympia Snakebones, the voodoos called her.

"This has to be a mistake." Paul Corbier poured coffee from the blue earthenware pot on the sideboard in the cottage's rear parlor, and carried cups to the table. Though it was near three in the morning the shutters stood wide to Rue Douane, and music from a ball still in progress—Creoles, without a doubt—down on Rue Bourbon mingled on the gluey darkness with the cicadas' eerie roar. "I know Olympe. She would not have done this."

January said nothing. Neither did the woman who sat opposite him, a tall woman whose serpent eyes accorded strangely with the skirt and blouse of blue calico, such as the market-women wore. Like all women of color she kept her hair covered, as the law required; but like all free women of color she turned the simple headscarf demanded by a white man's law into a fantasia of folds and pleats whose hue and complexity rivaled the flowers of the field. Alone among the women of color she had worked her tignon into seven points, like a halo of bright-colored flame points around her strong-boned Indian face. By this she was known, the crown of the city's reigning Voodoo Queen.

"I know it sounds foolish," Corbier went on. "She has the knowledge, and she has—had—the things in the house." He nodded through the archway that separated the dining room from the front half of the parlor. The candles on the table, and the squiggling fragments of reflected glare from the streetlamps hanging over the intersection of Rue Douane and Rue Burgundy, showed up dimly the shelves that filled the parlor's inner wall, planks and packing boxes neatly arranged, lined with intricately cut paper and aromatic leaves.

Bottles glinted, painted and decorated, between dark fat-bellied pots of cheap terra-cotta bought from Chickasaw and Choctaw on the Cathedral steps. Gimcrack gilding winked on small bright-colored tins such as candies and tea that were shipped in from England, and beads caught the light, woven in strings around calabashes stoppered with wax. A dish of beads, and another of animal bones; a third of brown glistening lump sugar set before a crooked stick in a sealed bottle. Strings of dried guinea peppers. Swags of lace. Clusters of feathers, tied with thread, hung from the shelves above, and clumps of drying herbs or bundles of hair. Strange-shaped sticks and roots; candles red, black, white, and green. The skin of a ground puppy that had been dried in the sun. Squares of red flannel. A ball of string. A snakeskin nailed to the wall, with a slip of paper rolled up in its mouth. A name written on that paper. Silver coins, and a few cigars. Salt, brick dust, graveyard dust.

Three spaces gapped in the confusion, like teeth knocked out in a fight.

"It's got to been some other voodoo," said Gabriel reasonably. "He poisoned this *oku* and made the Guards think Mama did it. That's all."

"*Has* to *have* been," corrected his father, with an uneasy glance at the woman, perhaps worried that his son had so casually spoken the word *voodoo* in the presence of Mamzelle Marie. "And we don't know that."

But the Voodoo Queen said only, "Olympe is a good woman." Marie Laveau's voice was deep, rich as fine coffee, and her French without the slurred patois of slaves and the poor. She was a woman who had only to sit in a room to be the focus of attention. Like a fire she seemed to radiate both heat and light. "Whatever she might do, she would not do a thing that she saw to be evil."

January noticed that Marie Laveau did not say, *That's impossible.*
Nor did Paul Corbier.

"They must have been watching the house, waiting for her to come
home," Corbier went on after a moment. "She hadn't even taken off
her coat when two men came across the street, white men. She saw
them and tried to run out the back door, but your friend Lieutenant
Shaw"—he glanced at January apologetically—"was in the yard already,
waiting for her."

"She bit him," said Gabriel.

That certainly sounded like Olympe.

"I hope it turns poison and he dies."

"What did they say?" January tried to put from him the memory of
the two times he himself had been in the Cabildo, but he saw the fear of
that prison in his brother-in-law's helpless eyes. "Who do they say she
killed? A white man?"

Olympe's big gray cat, Mistigris, flowed into the parlor from the
street and jumped into Mamzelle Marie's lap. In the silence January
heard Gabriel's older sister Zizi-Marie in the rear bedroom, whispering
to the younger children tales of Compair Lapin and Bouki the Hyena.
One of them began to cry, instantly hushed by the older girl's voice.

"They claim she killed a young man named Isaak Jumon," said
Mamzelle Marie, her long hand stroking the gray cat's head. There was
no emotion in her voice, as if the woman of whom she spoke were not
someone she would rise from her bed at two in the morning to help.
"He was the son of Laurence Jumon, that died this summer past of the
fever. His mother was Geneviève, that was Jumon's slave and then his
plaçée. Geneviève has a house on Rue des Ramparts these days, and a
hat shop there. Does well, I am told."

She scratched Mistigris's chin, and the big tom, evidently forgetting
his usual custom of biting anyone who touched him, closed ecstatic
eyes.

"Isaak was nineteen." Lightning flashed in the tar-black sky, then a
long slow grumble of thunder. "He worked with Basile Nogent the
marble carver, and had just married Célie Gérard, the coffee seller's
daughter, back at the end of May. They lived behind Nogent's shop.
Isaak hadn't had anything to do with his mother in many years."

"Did they say why she killed him?" asked January. "I assume
they're saying someone paid her to do it."

"No one paid her." Paul glanced swiftly at his son. "She wouldn't kill for pay, not a colored man, not a white man, nobody!"

There was silence.

Corbier turned to Mamzelle, his face working with concern and fear. "Can you help us?" he asked. "Do anything? Learn anything? Or you, Ben? You have friends in the Guards." Paul was a man of deep goodness, but without Olympe's brilliance. *Not a man,* thought January, *to know how to fight the law.*

"I know one man in the Guards," January corrected him quietly. "And if he was the one who came and arrested Olympe, it's because he thinks she's guilty. But I'll find out what I can."

"I also." Mamzelle Marie got to her feet, a movement both languid and filled with energy, like a cat's. Or a snake's. "But the ink bowl can only tell me so much. And I won't learn anything faster than morning, when you'll be able to go to the Cabildo and ask her things yourself."

Thunder sounded again, hard on the heels of the flash this time. January said, "If we're to get to our homes dry we'd best leave now. May I escort you to your door, Mamzelle?"

"There's nothing in the night that frightens me," she replied. "If you'll bear me company as far along as your mother's house it will serve."

From the packed-earth banquette of Rue Douane, January looked back and saw Paul close up the parlor shutters, then the doors behind them. The shutters were fast, but the doors still open, in the front bedroom on the other side of the house, and slits of muddy-gold candle glow shone through the jalousies. Zizi-Marie and the younger children would be huddled together still on their parents' bed. The light grew momentarily stronger, as Paul and Gabriel entered with another candle, then snuffed out in increments to darkness.

Paul Corbier would not sleep that night.

For a time January and the woman walked in silence, the fetid night clogged with the pungence of rotting garbage. The city contractors who cleaned the gutters were dilatory at best, even up on Rue Chartres and Rue Royale, where the rich had their dwellings. Here dead dogs floated, swollen, in water that whined with mosquitoes. Oily streetlamp glow shone yellow on the backs of the huge roaches that lumbered across their path, or on the frogs that hunted them. Once a City Guard in his blue coat passed on the other side of the street and glanced their way, but decided not to notice them. January wondered whether the man had simply counted the points of Mamzelle Marie's tignon and thought better of it.

As he walked he thought of a skinny little girl, like a coal-black spider, spitting on St.-Denis Janvier's polished calfskin shoes at that first meeting, then fleeing without a word. *Don't hurt her,* their mother's protector had said quickly. *She's just a child, and afraid.*

But Olympe, January knew, had never feared anything in her life.

It wasn't until they stopped at the throat of the passway that led back to the rear yard of his mother's pink stucco cottage on Rue Burgundy—the cottage St.-Denis Janvier had given her thirty-three years ago—that January asked softly, "Is there any reason you know of, that they'd think my sister poisoned this Jumon boy?"

It was not something he could have asked in the presence of the man who loved Olympe, or of her children.

Marie Laveau tilted her head, and regarded him with those mocking sibyl eyes. She knew everything, they said. She read your dreams. More to the point, January knew she listened to everything, watched everything; learned from the market-women who was buying what and meeting whom; from the rag pickers what they found in the garbage and the gutters outside the big town houses on Rue Chartres and behind the American mansions on Nyades Street; from the maids and laundresses of every wealthy family in town what stains they found on whose sheets. The slaves of bankers and brokers and planters from the Belize to Natchez sold her letters, or names whispered by night, or combings of their owners' hair; and as a hairdresser herself, to white and colored alike, she heard still more. She was queen of secrets, paid sometimes in money and sometimes in kind.

And this was not all she was.

But she only answered, "There's a thousand reasons men will think a woman poisoned a man. Don't you know that, Michie Ben?"

Thunder shivered the night again, lightning limning the roofs around them, and the sudden cold breath of storm made the seven points of her tignon nod and flicker.

She added, "Mostly men don't understand."

He saw the dark winds lift and ripple her dark skirts as she passed along the banquette in the direction of Rue St. Anne, and the swaying light of the next intersection splashed her briefly with color, blue and orange and red. Then she was gone.

There was a brickyard on Rue Dumaine, back in the days before the war with England, where the slaves of the town would meet at night. Sometimes it was only to talk or to sell things pilfered from their owners—a chicken, a shirt, a bundle of half-burned candles, a bottle of American whisky poured artfully off the tops of the master's supplies. But sometimes, after the whites were asleep, the drums would speak in the darkness.

As a young boy January had gone, although his teachers at the Académie St. Louis told him this was not a thing young *gens de couleur libre* did, and his mother vowed she'd wear him out with a broom if she ever heard of him acting like a slave brat. . . . But he'd been a slave brat only a few years before. And he missed the music and the dancing and the dark lusciousness of forbidden excitement that fired the air at the dances. Later, old Père Antoine had told him that what went on in the brickyard was the worship of devils. Though January never quite believed that, he came to understand that he could not be a child of God and a friend of the *loa* as well.

Olympe had taunted him with cowardice—Olympe who was then slipping out of the house regularly to dance with the voodoos and to learn from a woman named Marie Saloppe the secrets of herbcraft and poisons and the names of the African gods. From the first his sister had turned from her mother, and all her mother's efforts to make her a proper *fille de couleur. You think about how you're doing Ben and me a favor, every time you open your legs to that white man?* he remembered Olympe saying to their mother, bitter and mocking and wild—Olympe had spent a great deal of her girlhood locked in her bedroom.

But she would always slip out at night.

One night she had simply not come back.

Their mother had made no effort to inquire about where she might have gone. But three or four nights after that, when lying in the dark of the garçonnière January had heard the thick swift heartbeat of the drums, he had put on his clothes and made his way to Rue Dumaine, knowing that if she was in the city at all, that was where she would be.

The drumbeats drew him on. They'd built a fire behind the shelter of the brick kilns, but they kept the fire low. He saw only the yellow touch of it, outlining the square shouldering shapes of piles and pallets, of drays half-loaded, of sheds. The world was a stink of smoke and wet clay. But as he edged his way between those hard damp structures, like cemetery tombs in their close-crowded solidity, the blood stirred hot and unexpectedly behind his breastbone and in his loins at the tripping rattle of the hand drums, the tidal pull of the clapping hands.

He smelled blood.

They'd killed a chicken and a young pig and thrown them in the cauldron seething over the fire. Someone had brought tafia, the cheap liquor made from molasses squeezings; someone else had brought rum. Muted firelight mottled the *vèvès* scratched on the ground—circled crosses, spirals, and diamonds, like Mambo Jeanne had made on the plantation, and more complicated signs strung together, the secret signs of the gods. The dancing had begun.

The music tugged at January's heart.

Nothing here of the minuets and country dances that were the heart of the music lessons he had, at that time, been teaching for over a year. Nothing here of Mozart, or of Bach, of measure and beauty and passion contained. Like raw rum it hit him, and he felt his body move in time, unconscious as the movements of coupling. All around him men and women were moving, too, rocking, swaying, sometimes catching one another and turning under their arms, sometimes only standing, dancing with the body as the slaves did—hully-gully, they called it, the loosening into rhythm that makes work easier—and not tripping here and there like the restless whites.

Hands clapping, clapping. Voices wailing and dark, *"Eh, bomba, hen, hen, canga bafie te!"* Candles stuck among the bricks, darts of yellow light on naked muscles gleaming with sweat, on breasts bound only with a couple of kerchiefs, on ankle-clappers ringing bare hard feet. On whip scars and old brands and the tattoo-work of Ibo and Ewe and Senegal. January felt the wild desire to do as he'd done as a child, to tear off his clothes the better to dance. *Mbuki-mvuki,* the old men had called it at Bellefleur, a word for what *les blanquittes* had no word for.

Then he saw Olympe.

She was up near the end of the yard, half-glimpsed through the dancers; up where the Queen danced on top of a cage in whose darkness a snake's coils moved and shifted, up by the King, a squat scarred man wearing only a couple of red kerchiefs knotted around his groin and a belt of blue cord. Like many of the dancers Olympe had stripped, and wore only a thin shift, plastered to her body with sweat; her tignon cast away, her hair a black thick brush exploding around her face; her eyes shut in solitary communion with the music and the dance and the liberty to be utterly herself.

Men danced closer, touched the King's hands or the Queen's. They whirled to fill their mouths with rum and spit it across the blood-spattered signs on the ground, the smell of it a sweet sickish backtaste against smoke and sweat. "Zombi!" cried someone. "Zombi-Damballah!" and touched the serpent's cage. A gold eye like a sequin flashed within. The bodies swayed faster to the rattle of the drums. The music of darkness. Music like that which would pour from an open grave, from the door into the world beyond.

A man cried out and fell shaking to the ground a yard from January's feet. Two women propped him up, and he rolled his head and arched his back, gasped and babbled out words that made no sense. January had seen this before, too; but now it troubled him as it had not before he'd learned the ways of the Christian God. The man's eyes opened and his face changed: aged, shrank, fell in on itself, and when he got to his feet he staggered as if lame. "Legba!" cried someone, "Papa Legba, *hé*!" The man staggered and limped, reaching out to touch this person or that, crying out in a hoarse croaking voice, his eyes the eyes of something other than human.

Ridden, old Mambo Jeanne would have said. Ridden by Papa Legba, the god who guards the crossroads.

"Agassu, Agassu has her!" cried someone else as a woman fell moaning, and began to kiss the earth; another man roared like a bull, shook his head, tossing and charging at Papa Legba, who whirled haltingly away. "I am Ezili!" shrieked a man in a woman's thin voice, rolling and lolling his head and hips, "Ezili Dahomey! Ezili of a thousand lovers!" And among the crowding chaos, among the writhing dancers, the shadows and darkness, January saw Olympe's eyes snap open, her mouth gape wide with a sudden bellow of rage.

Saw her face change.

"Ogu am I!" The voice that rolled from her throat was nothing like Olympe's, nothing like the voice of any human he had ever heard. "Ogu am I, Ogu of the sword, Ogu of the fire!" Turning, Olympe snatched a stick from beside the snake cage, whirled it around her head.

People cried, "Ogu!" and tried to steady her, but she lashed at them with her weapon and, striding to the King, pulled the rum bottle from his hand.

"Give me that," she boomed, in that terrible alien voice, "my balls are cold."

Hands clapping, voices calling; heat and rhythm and darkness rolled over January in a wave. He watched in eerie horror as his sister swaggered around the brickyard, pushed through the crowd, called out in hoarse soldier slang to Papa Legba or Ezili, leaping and spinning around the fire. There was something in it of Italian comedy, January thought, those ridden by the gods improvising lines to one another, acting as the gods would act. . . . And something beyond that. Something Other, and frightening.

Olympe swayed, and a man caught her—the half-naked King, his manhood lifting under the thin guise of his red kerchiefs. The fire burned low, and the dancing redoubled in its speed and intensity; men and women caught at one another, clutching and moaning. Some disappeared behind the brick stacks, or into the dense pockets of shadow beyond the fire's glare; some fell as simply as animals to the ground. Olympe was panting, soaked with sweat, the King's arms dark bands across the stained wetness of her shift. Her head fell back; January saw the glint of the dying fire on the bones of her chest, the points where her ribs and pelvis and small shallow breasts stabbed out through the thin cloth. She was sixteen, thin and wiry, her face now not the face of a god but of a woman blind with ecstasy; and she twisted her head around, seizing the King's face between her hands, dragging his lips to hers.

At the sight of her a hot stab of lust went through January's flesh, disconcerting and urgent. A woman caught his arm, a young girl barely older than Olympe, panting, sweating, smiling, and pulling at him. "Dance with me," the girl gasped. "Dance. . . ."

January thrust her from him. He was eighteen, and unmarried; and if not precisely pure, he was as chaste as he could stand to be, knowing that he could afford to take no wife if he got a girl with child. *But it's all right,* something said in his mind—the *loa,* maybe, or the Devil, or his own lustful needing. *In the morning neither of you will know the other's name. It's all in our hands, not yours.*

He turned and walked away into the stacks of bricks, walked quickly, as if armed men sought him nearer the fire. Once he looked back, and saw Olympe naked in the dark King's arms.

The drums mocked him as he fled.

In the morning he had gone to Mass, confessed to the sin of idolatry, and burned before the Virgin's altar the first of a holocaust of candles, one by one over the next twenty-three years, for the pardon and salvation of his sister's soul.

THREE

"Why did you run away?"

Olympe, sitting in the rude chair Lieutenant Shaw had dragged over into the corner of the Cabildo's stone-flagged watch room for her, glanced up with a twist of scorn to her mouth, black eyes jeering. For an instant January was eighteen years old again, seeing her in the firelight of the brickyard. Her face hadn't changed much in the intervening years, except to lose what girlish roundness it had ever possessed. The wry quirk of her mouth was the same, over the slightly prominent front teeth; the sharp little chin had the same way of tucking sideways with the thrust of her jaw.

"Someday some white man's gonna sell you the whole city of Philadelphia, the Russian Crown Jewels thrown in for lagniappe," she said. "You are the most trusting man I ever did meet and worrying after you keeps me awake all night." And as she spoke she raised her arm from her lap and made the manacle chain jangle with a single mocking flick of her wrist.

"Where have you been?"

"Poisoning Isaak Jumon," she retorted, her eyes not leaving his. January looked away in shame. Her mouth softened a little—which it wouldn't have, back when she was sixteen—and she added, "Or maybe helping a friend. Which do you think?"

January grinned and replied, "Poisoning Isaak Jumon," and though the joke probably wasn't very funny Olympe burst out laughing, showing where childbirth had cost her two of her side teeth. Paul Corbier, standing behind her with his hands on her shoulders, looked shocked.

The sealed cold quiet, the iron stiffness that January remembered from Olympe's girlhood, broke and showed underneath the woman he'd met upon his return eighteen months ago: an angry woman gentled and softened by Paul Corbier's unquestioning love and the happiness she'd had with her children. When Lieutenant Shaw had brought her out of the cells she'd been like a wary animal, silent and cold and withdrawn—the girl he had known before his departure for France. Maybe that was why he'd spoken to her as he had.

"I'm sorry," he said now. "But they're going to want to know." He nodded to the watch room's main desk. Lieutenant Abishag Shaw, looking as usual like a scarecrow who'd dressed in a high wind and poor light, was engaged in quiet conversation with the sergeant, pausing every now and then to spit in the general direction of the sandbox in the big room's corner.

The oil lamps in their iron brackets along the walls had been put out; the smell of the burnt oil lingered. The wide doors stood open onto the arcade that fronted the Place d'Armes and from across that dusty square came the dim wakening clamor of the levees, stevedores loading crates of coffee and dry goods, books and cheeses, vinegar, corks, and pigs of lead, for transhipment up the river. They worked as swiftly as they could before the day turned hot, their voices a rough distant barking against the morning calm. Seagulls squawked and screamed at one another over the market garbage. The yammer of house slaves and market-women joined them, bargaining over tomatoes and peaches and bananas in the fruit stands that bordered the Place. In the courtyard behind the prison, whose doors were open also into the big square guardroom, a boy climbed the gallery stairs to dole breakfast to the prisoners, pressing himself against the rail as men in the blue uniforms of city lamplighters brought down from the cells the first of the slaves who'd been caught out without passes, to be whipped at the pillory.

Olympe's mouth hardened, and Paul Corbier reached out to take her hand. "I was helping a friend who had asked my help," she told them quietly. "As for Isaak Jumon, his wife, Célie, came to me Friday, a week ago today. She asked me to make a gris-gris against Isaak's mother, Geneviève. Isaak's father was a white man, and left Isaak property when he died last year; left it to Isaak, not to Geneviève or to Isaak's brother Antoine, who lives with Geneviève still. Geneviève claimed that the property was hers; that Isaak was her slave, and all he inherited came to her. . . ."

"Her *slave?*"

Olympe shrugged. January wondered if the contempt in her face was at Geneviève's greed or at his naïveté. "Don't ask me the why of it," she said. "But she got a judge to write out a warrant distraining Isaak as her property, and he fled, Célie says. So she came to me for a gris-gris, and I gave her one."

"What kind of gris-gris?"

The dark glance slid sidelong at him. "I didn't send her home with poison, if that's what you're thinking, brother."

"Yet there was poison in the house." Lieutenant Shaw ambled to them, hands in the pockets of his sorry green coat and greasy, light brown hair hanging down over his bony shoulders. He spoke French with a kind of clumsy fluency, ungrammatical as a fieldhand's and spattered with English misconstruction. "That was arsenic in one of them tins as we took off yore shelf, M'am Corbier, and monkshood in another, and the doctor I took them jars to says that was antimony in the third."

"Then why don't you arrest my brother as well?" asked Olympe in a reasonable voice. "He carries arsenic in his bag, when he works in the Hospital during the fever season. Salts of mercury, too, and foxglove, that can stop the heart. Arrest the doctor that told you the contents of those jars. I'll bet he has all that and more in his office."

"My friend is a healer, Lieutenant Shaw." Mamzelle Marie, who had entered quietly through the open doors of the arcade, made her way with leisurely grace to them and regarded the gawky Kentuckian with a mixture of amusement and insolence. "As a healer, Olympe, like her brother, has obligations to secrecy. Should a young girl give birth out of wedlock, she must trust that her midwife will not spread word of it. Must a slave who has slipped out of his master's thrall for an evening, and met with some injury, risk his life by letting the wound go untended for fear of a beating into the bargain?" She added, with the barest touch of mocking malice, "That might lose the owner money, were the slave to die. You wouldn't want that, sir."

"No, M'am." Shaw met the voodooienne's gaze calmly, arms folded over his chest. "And I do understand M'am Corbier's not wantin' to say where she was nor why she tried to run away the minute officers of the law showed up in her house. It's just that it looks bad, and it's gonna look worse when the state prosecutor asks her about it in open court." He scratched under the breast of his coat with fingers like stalks of cane. "That's all. M'am."

January glanced across at Olympe, wondering if indeed she had been outside Colonel Pritchard's house last night. *She would not do that which she saw to be evil.* But what was evil in her eyes?

"I am a voodoo." Olympe looked gravely up at Shaw. "Believe what you will, Lieutenant. I—and indeed almost any voodoo you speak to in this town—work more in herbs of healing than in poisonings. The whites who come creeping veiled to our doors to ask for love potions or tricken bags—or partners for their lusts sometimes—they have no idea who we are or what we are. In any case the girl Célie told me, *Not a death spell.* She's a good girl, confirmed and goes to church." In the past, January thought, Olympe would have given those last five words a derisive twist; now she simply stated them as a fact. Perhaps, he thought, because now she, too, had a daughter.

"I gave her a ball of saffron, salt, gunpowder, and dog filth, tied in black paper, to leave in Geneviève Jumon's house and another in her shop. Saturday night when the moon was full I took and split a beef tongue and witched it with silver and pins and guinea peppers, and buried it in the cemetery with a piece of paper bearing Geneviève's name. That was all that I did. And in truth I didn't need even to do that. The woman's evil and greed themselves will call down grief on her, with no doing of mine. About Isaak I know nothing. Are you so certain that he is dead?"

Shaw's pale brows raised, the gray eyes beneath them suddenly sharp and wary. "Why do you ask that, M'am?"

"Have you seen his body?"

"Where is she?" shouted a voice behind them. "What have you done with her? Pigs! Bastards! Murderers!" January turned in time to see a heavyset little man stumble through the Cabildo's outer doors, his well-cut gray coat awry and his eyes burning with rage and grief. "Have you no pity? No shame?" He flung himself at the nearest Guard, who happened to be Shaw, seizing him by the lapels and shaking him to and fro. Shaw, who January knew could have broken his assailant's neck with very little trouble, raised no hand to thrust him back, and a well-dressed tall gentleman dashed through the door in the next moment, followed by a small, plump lady whose dove-gray silk tignon matched her dress.

"Fortune," she cried, wringing her mitted hands, as the well-dressed gentleman seized Shaw's attacker and pulled him away. "Fortune, no!"

"Really, Monsieur Gérard, you must be more careful of how you step! You might have injured this gentleman, *falling into him* as you did. . . ."

"Gentleman?" The heavyset man twisted against the firm grip, face flushed dusky with rage. Though the peacemaker had spoken English—stressing the word *falling* as if that would alter what everyone in the room had just seen—Monsieur Gérard shouted in French, "These—these *Americans* dare to traduce my daughter and you say—"

"Of course it was an accident, sir." Still speaking English, the pacifier turned an apologetic smile upon Shaw, who was methodically straightening his coat. Not, thought January, that any amount of straightening would improve the appearance of that wretched garment. "Certainly Monsieur Gérard is most aware of the difference in your stations and also of the penalties attached to a man of color striking a white man such as yourself. Please accept my client's apologies, Captain. I am Clément Delachaise Vilhardouin, representing Monsieur Gérard and his daughter in this regrettable affair. I pray your indulgence for my client, who speaks no English."

The woman—clearly Madame Gérard—had caught up with the group now, and was holding her husband's other arm, sobbing "Fortune, Fortune, what could I do? They came at night, you would not return from Baton Rouge till the morning, they had a warrant for her arrest. . . ."

Gérard himself was silent, chest heaving and dark eyes smoldering. From the open doorway a woman's voice could be heard, shrieking crazily, "He's trying to kill me! My husband—my father—they killed all my children, smothered them one by one! Please, please, someone believe me! . . ."

A chorus from the other cells snarled out, like the cacophony of Hell: "I'll smother *you* if you don't shut up!" "Stuff her mouth, somebody!" "Can't a body get a drink in this stinkin' bug hole?" Beside him, January saw Olympe's jaw harden, her only change in expression. When he himself had been locked in the Cabildo, the shouting of the mad, sharing the cells with the thieves and murderers and common drunks, had added an edge of horror to the crawling fetor of the nights.

Vilhardouin, himself a highly dandified specimen of Shaw's own race—though probably neither of them would willingly admit such a thing—went on in quiet French, "You must understand, Monsieur Gérard, that this man was only doing his duty in apprehending your daughter. It is the Magistrate of the Court who wrote out the warrant for her arrest, at the complaint of a citizen."

"What citizen?" Fortune Gérard was trembling, tears of fury glistening as he raised his head. "Show me that citizen! I swear that I will—"

"The citizen what swore out that complaint," interrupted Shaw, and squirted a long stream of tobacco juice in the direction of the sandbox again, a target he couldn't possibly have achieved, "is the mother of the deceased, a M'am Geneviève Jumon; the woman this lady claims your daughter paid her to put a hex on." Perhaps, as January's mother had repeatedly asserted, tomcats spoke better French than Lieutenant Shaw, but January noticed that for an upriver backwoodsman he didn't do at all badly with a conditional subjunctive.

Gérard's face seemed to shrink on itself with venom. Had he not been a respectable man of color, well bred and conscious of his position in New Orleans society, he would have spit. As it was he replied, his voice like twisted wire, "My daughter would never have sought the company or assistance of a voodoo Negress poisoner"—his gaze traveled over Olympe in distaste—"for that purpose, or for any other, and I will personally sue the man who says differently. And as for the assertion that my daughter poisoned, or had anything to do with the poisoning of, her husband, a young man of whom I never approved . . ."

"Papa!" Iron clanked in the courtyard doors. The girl framed in its light took a hasty step toward the group in the corner, then hesitated, glancing for permission at the wiry little lamplighter who escorted her. Shaw beckoned, and the lamplighter, keeping a firm hold on the other end of the chain that manacled the girl's wrists, followed her over. "Papa, is it true?" Célie Jumon looked frantically from her father to Lieutenant Shaw to Olympe, huge brown eyes swollen in the fragile oval of her face. "They told me—last night they told me . . . Isaak . . ."

Shaw spit another line of tobacco juice, and said gently, "I'm afraid it is, M'am Jumon."

The girl pressed her hand to her mouth, but didn't make a sound. Her sprig-muslin dress was soiled and rumpled from spending the night in filthy straw, but she'd scrubbed her face and hands in the courtyard fountain and rearranged her tignon. In its simple green-and-white-striped frame the childish youthfulness of her face made a dreadful contrast to the horror in her eyes. Rising quickly, January guided the girl to his chair. Her mother fell on her knees beside her, stroking and kissing the shackle bruises on her wrists and weeping in stifled, soundless gasps.

The Lieutenant looked around him at the group that was rapidly outgrowing its corner of the watch room: Olympe, her husband, January, and Mamzelle Marie; Gérard, his wife, and Célie; and the two lamplighter Guards in charge of the prisoners. "Well, at least I won't have to go through this more'n oncet." He sighed philosophically, and scratched his hip. "M'am Jumon, I am sorry, because I know this's gonna be painful for you, but they're gonna want us all over to the Recorder's Court in a minute, and you'd all best know what we're goin' on.

"Last Monday night, which was the twenty-third, twenty-fourth June, Isaak Jumon's brother, Antoine, was brought by a servant he didn't recognize to a big house he'd never seed before, where his brother lay dyin'. Antoine says Isaak was far gone when Antoine got there, vomitin' an' clammy an' achin' all over an' pretty much actin' like someone that's been dosed real good with arsenic. Antoine did what he could for his brother—who he hadn't seen in a couple months owin' to a quarrel in the family—with the help of a old mulatto woman who was there, but it warn't no good. Isaak kept tryin' to tell him somethin' but was so sick Antoine couldn't make out what. Once he managed to say, *I have been poisoned.* Then a little later he said, *Célie,* an' died."

Célie looked away. Her mother, numbly stroking the ruin of her frock, tears flowing down her face, seemed barely to have heard.

"It's a long way," pointed out January quietly, "from *I have been poisoned* and *Célie,* to *I have been poisoned BY Célie.* If you don't mind my mentioning it, sir." He made a genuine effort to keep the anger from his voice, anger over the fear in his brother-in-law's face, over Madame Gérard's tears. He knew it wasn't the Kentuckian's fault.

"I don't mind you mentionin' the matter, Maestro," said the policeman evenly. "Fact remains the boy *is* dead, and M'am Jumon *did* go buy somethin' from your sister." Vilhardouin's hand shut restrainingly on Monsieur Gérard's sleeve. "And the fact remains your sister does so happen to have had a big pot of arsenic on a shelf in her parlor, not to speak of makin' a livin' sellin' strange things to people wrapped up in little bits of black paper. No offense meant, M'am. M'am." He nodded respectfully for good measure in Marie Laveau's direction.

The sergeants had begun whipping the errant slaves in the courtyard outside. Célie flinched at the crack of leather on flesh, hid her face when someone—a woman, by the sound of it—cried out, a strangled sound grimly silenced. Men came through the watch room, in the well-cut clothing and beaver hats of professionals, leading after them other men, or sometimes a woman or two, shabbily dressed in castoffs, usually barefoot, the women with their heads modestly covered in tignons. Twenty-five cents a stroke, January remembered—trying to force deafness and ignorance upon a rage that would otherwise have overwhelmed him—for a master to have his property whipped by the City Guards, if he didn't want to do it himself. The sergeant at the desk paused in talk with the Police Chief, to write out a receipt. In the courtyard beyond them two men in the blue uniforms of Guards emerged from a cell on the second gallery, bearing between them a shutter on which a body lay, covered with a blanket. The Guards hustled furtively along the gallery and down the stairs. As they turned a corner the shutter knocked against the newel post and an arm dropped out, limp, yellow as cheese.

Shaw was still explaining something to Monsieur Gérard—probably why a young man's word for a crime had to be accepted over the assertions of a respectable coffee merchant—as January made his way back to the courtyard doors. He intercepted the Guards and their burden as they reached the foot of the stair. "I beg your pardon, Messieurs, but would you mind telling me what this man died of?"

Knowing he'd be coming to the Cabildo that morning he had been careful to don his most respectable clothing: linen shirt, black wool coat, white gloves, gray trousers, and high-crowned beaver hat, the costume of a professional that he wore on those occasions when he volunteered his services to the Hospital and when he played at a ball. The men looked at him and then at one another. "Stabbed," said one in English at the same moment the other said, "Hung himself, poor bastard," in French. January looked down at the blanket, which was ancient and ragged and moving with lice. There was no sign of blood. The man who spoke English added, "We got to be gettin' on."

He watched them move around under the gallery to the little storeroom at the back of the court; watched them close and latch the door. His heart seemed to have turned to ice inside him. He knew, having seen the color of that arm, why they lied.

Glancing behind him, he saw that the Corbiers, Jumons, and officers of the law had left the watch room. Someone took back the chairs in which Olympe and Célie Jumon had sat; a lamplighter came in from the arcade with a couple of bottles, beer or ale, which he handed to the sergeant at the desk. In the courtyard, a man who was being triced to the pillory suddenly began to thrash and heave like a landed fish, screaming curses at his master, at the men who bound him, at whatever god had ordered the world to be so constituted that this could be done to him. While everyone in the yard—except the man's master—ran to help, January made his way under the galleries to the storeroom, unlatched the door, and stepped noiselessly inside.

Most of the time, January knew from past dealings with Lieutenant Shaw, the room was used as a storage place for records and for the shovels and buckets in use by those who cleaned up the gutters of the Place d'Armes. There was a cot in one corner where Guardsmen who sustained injuries in the line of duty could lie down—a situation not uncommon when a steamboat crew or a gang of keelboat ruffians were in town on a spree.

The form on the cot now was not a Guardsman. From beneath the tattered blanket the hand still projected, dangling to the floor, fingers purpling. Another body lay on the floor. Flies roared in every corner of the low ceiling, gathering already in the fluids that trickled slowly into the cracks of the brick floor.

The judas hole in the door let through just enough light to see. January pulled the blankets first from one man, then the other, and looked down into the bloated faces. An ugly orange flush mottled their skin and black vomit crusted their teeth and beards. One had clearly been a British sailor, with bare feet and a tarred pigtail; the other a trapper from the trackless mountains of northern Mexico, buckskin shirt stiff with sweat and filth. Both men already stank in the early summer heat. There was no question what had caused their deaths.

He laid the blankets back over their faces, and silently left the room.

January feared he would be too late to hear any of the proceedings of the arraignment—which in any case he knew would be short—but when he hurried into the Presbytère building and through the door of the Recorder's Court, the Clerk was still engaged in an angry convocation with Lieutenant Shaw: ". . . just a minute ago," Shaw was saying mildly.

"The case has been called . . ."

"It is an outrage!" Gérard put in, fists clenched furiously. "An outrage! There is no truth . . ."

"I reckon Mr. Vilhardouin"—Shaw pronounced the French name properly, something that always surprised January about the Kentuckian—"just sorta made a stop at the jakes, and he'll be along. . . . There he is."

At the same moment a voice behind January said coldly, "I beg Monsieur's pardon. . . ." An American voice added, "Get outa that door, boy."

January stepped quickly aside. Vilhardouin jostled brusquely past him, followed closely by a lithe, powerful man whose lower two shirt buttons strained over the slop of his belly beneath a food-stained yellow waistcoat's inadequate hem. As the two men proceeded up the aisle, the sloppy man paused here and there to nod greetings to this man or that: keelboat rousters in slouch hats and heavy boots, spitting tobacco on the floor; filibusters from the saloons along the levee; a gentleman sitting stiff and disapproving beside a shackled slave. The Clerk of the Court glared ferociously and demanded, "What brings you here, Blodgett?" and the man returned a stubbled and rather oily smile.

"It's an open court, Mr. Hardee." Blodgett's voice was gold and gravel, with a drunkard's slurry drawl. "Surely a man can come sit in an open court if he wants to."

As January slid onto the end of the bench beside Paul and Mamzelle Marie, Hardee knocked his gavel on the desk and said, "Are you Célie Jumon, née Gérard, wife of Isaak Jumon of this parish?"

She stood, small and pretty in her filthy dress. "I am."

"I object to these proceedings!" Monsieur Vilhardouin sprang to his feet. "Madame Jumon does not understand English and it is a violation of her rights to—"

"Monsieur Vilhardouin," protested the girl, "I understand—"

"Be silent!" ordered her father.

Vilhardouin turned back to the Clerk of the Court. "Madame Jumon does not sufficiently understand English to the degree that she can comprehend the charges brought against her."

Two louse-ridden and bewhiskered denizens of the Swamp and Girod Street applauded; a blowsy uncorseted woman hollered "You stand up for your rights, gal!" and Madame Gérard shrank against her husband in revulsion and terror.

A harried-looking notary was called in to translate, and asked in French if Célie Jumon was in fact Célie Jumon, then informed her that she was charged with feloniously conspiring to kill and slay Isaak Jumon, her husband, a free man of color of this city, on or about the night of the twenty-third to -fourth of June, and how did she plead?

"Not guilty," she said, forcing her voice steady.

"Hell, honey, no shame about it," yelled the blowsy woman, "I killed four myself!"

"Silence in the court." The Clerk spit tobacco into the sandbox beside him, a surprising display of fastidiousness given the wholesale expectoration going on all around him. "You are hereby remanded to custody until . . . Where'd that calendar go?" He shuffled the pages of the ledger handed to him. "Good Lord, who are all these folks? Damn Judge Gravier for leavin' town like this. Puts everybody back. Now Judge Danforth talkin' about goin', too. . . ."

"May it please the court." Vilhardouin stood again, somberly handsome in his exquisitely tailored black. "Given that the accused is below legal age, we request that she be released into the custody of her father."

The Clerk straightened up, and glared at him in annoyance.

"Her father, a householder and taxpayer of this city, stands ready and willing to put up whatever security is required," went on the lawyer. "To be denied this by a Clerk of the Recorder's Court—not even the Recorder himself, who is apparently elsewhere today—What did you say the Recorder's name is, Monsieur Blodgett?"

Blodgett looked up from the notebook in which he was busily scribbling. "Leblanc," he said, in English, and more loudly than was necessary if Vilhardouin was the only one intended to hear. "Clerk's name is Hardee." He made another note.

Vilhardouin turned back to the bench. "Should Mr.—er—Hardee

see fit to deny this mercy to both parent and child in Mr. Leblanc's absence, I fear that even the best efforts of Mr. Blodgett here will not suffice to make the story even remotely favorable when it appears tomorrow in the *New Orleans Abeille*. Mayor Prieur reads the *Abeille*—the *Bee*—does he not, Mr. Blodgett?"

Blodgett helped himself to his hip flask, and wiped his stubbled underlip. "So he does, Mr. Vilhardouin. So he does."

The Clerk's face blotched an ugly red. He tapped his gavel sharply: "Prisoner is released to the recognizance of her father, Fortune Gérard, a free man of color of this city, on a bail of a thousand dollars, in respect for her tender years. You want me to have that translated into Frenchy, Mr. Vilardwan?"

"Yes," said Vilhardouin, unruffled. "Please."

"Monsieur Gérard. . . ." January half-turned on the bench as Gérard, Vilhardouin, Blodgett, Madame Gérard, and the trembling Célie Jumon moved past them toward the court's outer doors. "If we could pool our information and resources . . ."

"Get your hands off me, M'sieu." The little man pulled his arm away, although January's fingers had not actually come in contact with his sleeve. His face was cold and set. "I wish nothing to do with you, or your sister; and I tell you that should she attempt to spread calumny against my daughter or imply that she would do so vile a thing as to consult with her on any matter whatsoever, it will go the worse for her and for you all."

"Papa . . ."

"Be silent, girl!"

"Are you Olympia Corbier," cut in the Clerk's angry voice, "also known as Olympia Snakebones? You are accused of conspiring to feloniously kill and slay one Isaak Jumon, a free man of color of this city, how the hell you plead?"

"Not guilty." When their mother beat her, January remembered, she had stood so.

"You're hereby remanded to custody . . ."

"Sir." January got to his feet. "Sir, my name is Benjamin January, a free man of color, brother to Madame Corbier." He was careful to speak his best and most educated English. "Sir, is there any possibility of releasing my sister into the custody of her husband? She is the mother of small children, and conditions in the Cabildo are such that to remain there would endanger her life. There were two deaths from yellow fever in the jail last night, goodness knows how many others are infected—"

"That's a lie!" One of the well-dressed gentlemen at the back of the court jerked to his feet. January recognized Jean Bouille, a member of the City Council, with a couple of chastened slaves in tow. "There is no yellow fever in New Orleans!"

"Who says there is?" The Clerk spit furiously. "There's been no such thing! That reporter gone? Good. Cuthbert—" He turned to address the Constable of the Court. "This nigger's saying there's people dyin' of yellow jack in the jail, and that isn't true." He turned back, not to January, but glaring out across the other men and women in the courtroom. "It isn't true," he repeated in a loud, harsh voice. "And I better not hear you nor nobody else goin' around sayin' such a lie or you're gonna be in some trouble yourself."

January felt them behind him, glancing at one another, looking at the Constable, thinking about the cells they would return to after leaving this room. The silence was crushing.

"If your sister thinks the jail's so goddam unfit she shouldn't have killed a man. Sit down."

January stood for a moment more, caught between his rage and that silence. He had been a slave and had lived in the quarters until he was eight, old enough to know what all slaves and prisoners know about keeping their mouths shut.

"I said sit down."

He lowered his eyes respectfully and sat.

"And you keep your opinions to yourself, boy, if you don't want to be took up for contempt."

He bowed his head, the flush of fury-heat rising through him almost depriving him of breath. "Yes, sir."

"Olympia Corbier, you are hereby remanded to custody of the city jail until the seventeenth of July of this year, when you will be tried by the Criminal Court of the State of Louisiana for your crime. Is there a Stefano DiSilva in this room? Stefano DiSilva, you're accused of willfully causin' a disturbance in Mr. Davis's gamblin' parlor on Bourbon Street. . . ."

January caught up with Shaw in the arcade outside. "That wasn't a real wise thing of you to say, Maestro," the Kentuckian remarked mildly. Whatever coolness had tempered the morning was now long gone, the sunlight molten in the Place d'Armes; the crowds around the covered market had thinned. Close by their feet a couple of Chickasaw Indians remained, still peddling powdered sassafras and clay pots from a blanket spread on the Cathedral steps.

"It was the truth."

Shaw spit, and actually got the tobacco juice into the gutter, for a miracle. "I'd be mighty careful who you said that to. What with the hoo-rah concernin' the Bank of the United States, and everybody in a panic about interest, and elections comin' on, and summer business bein' slow generally, there's a lot of folk in this town who wouldn't take kindly to talk of epizootic fevers scarin' away investors." He glanced sidelong as Councilman Bouille stalked out of the Presbytère doors and held his silence until he was some twenty feet farther down the arcade. His thin, rather light voice was gentle. "Truth may be a shinin' sword in the hand of the righteous, Maestro, but unless you got one whale of a shield that sword may not do you no good."

January drew in a deep breath, trying to let his rage dissolve. Bouille's slaves trailed at his heels, back across the Cathedral steps and into the Cabildo again. January wondered what the men had done and how many silver bits the Councilman was going to pay over to the city for their "correction." *The custom of the country,* he told himself, and wondered why he had come back here from Paris. Going insane from grief wouldn't have been as bad as this, surely?

"I take it," he said, "that Isaak Jumon's body was never found?"

The Kentuckian shook his head. "Though I sorta wonder how your sister knowed that, right off as she did. That boy Antoine says he was sent away from this strange house in a carriage and let off someplace he doesn't know where. He wandered around for hours in the pourin' rain, he says, till he got hisself home again. But he did see his brother die. He was real clear on that. And there's a lot of territory to cover, swamps and bayous and canals all around this city where a body coulda been dumped, and we'd never be the wiser. We didn't just light on your sister out of arbitrary malice, you know, Maestro. When I asked her last night where she'd been Monday she wouldn't give no good account of herself, nor could that gal Célie neither. . . . Yes, what is it?" A Guardsman came running from the Cabildo, calling Shaw's name.

"Trouble over to the Queen of the Orient Saloon, sir." The man saluted.

"It's nine o'clock in the mornin'," said Shaw wonderingly, and shoved his verminous hat back on his head. "Iff'n you'll excuse me, Maestro . . ."

He set off at a long-legged run.

January stood for a time in the sunlight of the Cathedral steps, watching him go. By this time, he thought, Olympe would have been returned to her cell, and he had had enough, for the time being, of Fortune Gérard's rage and Clément Vilhardouin's oil-smooth suaveness. He pushed open the Cathedral door, stepped through into the cool still gloom.

All that remained of the morning Mass was the smell of smoke and wax, and a market-woman telling her beads. A woman got quickly up from one of the benches usually reserved for the less prosperous of the free colored, a white woman in a pale blue gown, cornsilk hair braided unfashionably under a cottage bonnet. She was very American, prim and bare of a Creole lady's paint, and there was a hunted nervousness to her huge blue eyes as she retreated from him, drawing her child to her side.

More to it, thought January, than simply not seeing the person whom she clearly expected: a fear that was startled at shadows. He'd removed his hat already, so he dipped in a little bow and asked in his best English, "May I help you, Madame?"

Her gloved hand went quickly to her lips. "I—That is—No." She shook her head quickly, and looked around her at the shadowy dimness of the great church. "It is all right to sit here, is it not?"

"Of course it is," said January. He'd encountered Protestants who seemed to believe Catholics sacrificed children on the altars of the saints.

The child peeked around her mother's skirts, guinea-gold curls dressed severely up under a small brown hat, sensible—and suffocating—brown worsted buttoned and tailored over the hard lines of a small corset; tiny brown gloves on tiny hands. She at least showed no fear, either of him or of this echoing cavern of bright-hued images and flickering spots of light. "The nuns won't come and get me," she whispered conspiratorially, "will they?"

January smiled. "I promise you," he told the child. "Nuns don't come and get anyone."

The mother tugged quickly on her daughter's hand, to shush her or discourage conversation with a black man and a stranger. January bowed again, and went to the Virgin's altar, and though money was tight and would be tighter—Pritchard had indeed, as Aeneas had warned, docked his pay last night—he paid a penny for a candle, which he lit and placed among all those others that marked prayers for mercy rather than justice. *Holy Mother, forgive her,* he prayed, his big fingers counting off the cheap blue glass beads of the much-battered rosary that never left him. *Don't hold it against Olympe's soul, that she turned from you and your Son. Don't punish her for making little magics as she does. For serving false gods.*

The woman's soft voice drew his attention. Looking back, he saw the person she had come here to meet. A small man, wiry and thin; a ferret face whose features spoke of the Ibo or Congo blood. He wore a shirt of yellow calico, and a leather top hat with a bunch of heron-hackle in it. A blue scarf circled his waist—a voodoo doctor's mark, Olympe had said when she'd pointed the man out to January in the market one day, the same way the seven-pointed tignon was the sign of the reigning Queen.

January heard the woman say, "It has to work," and the man replied, "It'll work." He handed her something that she swiftly slipped into her bag.

Sugar and salt and Black Devil Oil to bring a straying lover home? Black wax and pins, to send an unwanted mother-in-law away?

It has to work.

The howl of a steamboat's whistle shrilled through the Cathedral as the woman opened the door. She disappeared with her beautiful golden-haired child into the square, the voodoo-man watching—Dr. Yellowjack, Olympe had said his name was—as she walked away. When time enough had elapsed that their departures would not be too close, he, too, took his leave. January stayed for a long time, praying for his sister's soul while the candle he had lighted flickered before the Queen of Heaven's feet.

FOUR

January's mother and the younger of his two sisters were in the parlor of his mother's pink stucco house on Rue Burgundy when he reached it again. The two women sat side by side on the sofa, a mountain of lettuce-green muslin cascading over their knees; the jalousies were closed against the full strength of the sunlight, which lay across them in jackstraws of blazing gold. Ten o'clock was just striking from the Cathedral, and the gutters outside steamed under the hammer of the morning heat. Entering through the back door, January shed his black wool coat—that agonizing badge of respectability—his gloves, and his high-crowned hat and bent to kiss first the slim straight elderly beauty, then the white man's daughter who had from her conception been the favored child.

"What do you know about Geneviève Jumon, Mama?" He brushed with the backs of his fingers the smooth green-and-pink cheek of her coffee cup where it sat on a table at her side. "May I warm this for you? Or yours, Minou?"

"Trashy cow," said his mother, and bit off the end of her thread.

His sister Dominique gave him a brilliant smile. "If you would, thank you, p'tit."

The coffee stood warming over a spirit lamp on the sideboard in the dining room. The French doors were open onto the yard, and he saw

Bella, his mother's servant, just coming out of the garçonnière above the kitchen, where January had slept since his return from Paris. On plantations, the garçonnières that traditionally housed the masters' sons were separate buildings—the custom of a country, January remembered from his childhood at Bellefleur, that preferred to pretend that those young men weren't making their first sexual experiments with the kitchen maids. Among the plaçées in the city the motivation was reversed: few white men wished to sleep under the same roof as a growing young man of color, even if that young man was that protector's own flesh and blood. Since January's return a year and a half ago, Bella had resumed her habit of sweeping the garçonnière and making his bed, in spite of the fact that January conscientiously kept his own floor swept and daily made his own bed.

His efforts in that direction, he understood, could never meet Bella's standards. Presumably, should St. Martha, holy patroness of floor sweepers and bed makers, descend from Heaven and perform these tasks, Bella would still detect dust kittens and wrinkled corners.

"I hope you're not going to mix yourself up in that scandal of your sister's," said his mother, when he returned with three cups of coffee balanced lightly in his enormous hand.

It was the first time in eighteen months that he'd heard his mother refer to the existence of any sister other than Dominique. The first time, in fact, since before Louisiana had been a state. She raised plum-dark eyes to meet his, bleakly daring him to say, *She's your daughter, too. Child, as I am a child, by that husband who was a slave on Bellefleur Plantation—the man whose name you've never spoken.*

It was astonishing, the pain his mother could still inflict on him, if he let her.

Instead he said, casually, "Olympe has asked my help, Mama, yes. And I knew you'd never forgive me if I didn't at least go down to the Cabildo this morning to try to find out why Geneviève Jumon's daughter-in-law would hate her enough to put a gris-gris on her."

His mother's eyes flared with avid curiosity, but she caught herself up stiffly and said, "Really, Benjamin, I'm surprised at you. Of all the vulgar trash. And Dominique, that isn't yarn you're sewing with, I can see that buttonhole across the room."

Livia Levesque was a widow nearing sixty and still beautiful, slim and straight as a corset-stay in her gown of white-and-rose foulard. She had worn mourning for exactly the prescribed year for the sake of St.-Denis Janvier, who had died while January was a student at the Hôtel-Dieu in Paris; later had worn it not a day longer for her husband Christophe Levesque, a cabinetmaker of color whom January recalled only as one of her many male acquaintances during her days of plaçage. Black, she had declared on several occasions, did not suit her complexion.

Her father had been white, though she had to January's recollection never even speculated as to who he might have been. Her daughter by St.-Denis Janvier had added to her mother's exotic beauty the lightness of skin and silky hair so admired by white men and by many of the free colored as well. Dominique glanced worriedly sidelong at her mother, apprehensive of a scene, and then said "Poor Paul! And the children—are they all right? Shall I send over Thérèse to help?"

"You'll do nothing of the kind," snapped her mother. "That girl of yours doesn't do her own work for you, let alone looking after some laborer's children, not that she'd have the faintest idea how to go about it. As for Geneviève Jumon, I'm not surprised her daughter-in-law wanted to do her ill—I'm astonished the girl didn't poison *her* instead of her son. A more grasping, mealymouthed harpy you'd never have the misfortune to meet. She's been above herself for years, for all that she started out as one of Antoine Allard's cane hands."

She shrugged, exactly as if she herself hadn't worked in the fields before St.-Denis Janvier bought her. "She's had nothing but ill to say about Fortune Gérard since he rented the shop floor of Jeanne-Françoise Langostine's house for his business—he sells coffee and tea, and charges two pennies the pound more than Belasco over on Rue Chartres—that she wanted, not that she's ever made a hat that didn't look as if a squadron of dragoons had been sacking a florist's."

She opened the top of a heavy-pleated sleeve and produced a white paper sack of what turned out to be goose down, which she carefully shook into the space between the outer sleeve and its thin gauze lining, so that the sleeve rapidly assumed the appearance of a gigantic pillow. After ten years of marriage to a dressmaker, January was familiar with the style, and he still marveled at the sheer ugliness of it.

"I daresay she was good-looking enough that Laurence Jumon bought her of Allard, back during the war, for four hundred and seventy-five dollars," his mother went on, "but that's nothing to give herself airs about. Allard's asking price was six hundred and fifty and Jumon bargained him down. Jumon always did drive a warm bargain." No thought seemed to enter her head that St.-Denis Janvier must have bargained with her former master in just such a fashion. All January could do was shake his head over the detail and comprehensiveness of her knowledge of everybody's business in town. He wondered if Marie Laveau bought information from her. *If not, she should.*

"Wasn't it Laurence Jumon who bought those matched white horses last fall?" Dominique fit a gold thimble onto the end of her middle finger. "With the black-and-yellow carriage?"

"They looked like fried eggs on a plate," replied her mother. "*And* they'd been bishopped. In any case grays are a stupid thing to get in a town that's hip deep in mud ten months of the year. That's all the good they did him; forty days after he laid out the money they were pulling his hearse." She began to set the sleeve into place with neat, tiny stitches, and January marveled again at the linguistic convention that termed white horses "grays." Typical, too, that his mother had adopted it: most slaves just called them white.

"So why did Célie Jumon buy a gris-gris from Olympe?" asked Dominique, eager as a child. "And why do they think the gris-gris ended up poisoning Isaak instead of Geneviève?"

"Olympe says the gris-gris had nothing to do with Isaak's death, that it wasn't poison at all," said January. "What I'm trying to learn now is, where was Isaak Jumon between Thursday, when Geneviève swore out a warrant distraining him as her slave—"

"Oh, shame!" cried Dominique.

"Sounds like her," remarked Livia Levesque.

"—and his death on Monday night. Not to mention such things as why Jumon didn't leave a sou to Geneviève, which he didn't."

"She'd have poisoned the boy herself, I wager, out of spite."

"Mama, surely not!"

"Could she have? Isaak would be staying as far away from Geneviève as he could. He didn't take refuge with Célie's parents. . . ."

"He wouldn't have anyway," said Minou, gathering a length of mist-fine point d'esprit over the head of the other sleeve. "Monsieur Gérard never liked Madame Jumon, even before the shop rental incident, because of her 'former way of life.' He was mortified nearly to death when his precious daughter Célie married her son. Although after

thirteen years you'd think Monsieur Gérard would forget about Geneviève being a placée. I mean, everyone else has, and he's always polite to
Iphégénie and Phlosine and me when we come into his shop. Although
just the other day he said to Phlosine—"

"Thirteen years?" January set down his cup. "Thirteen *years*? I
thought . . . I mean, I know Jumon never married, so there was no
reason for him to put his placée aside . . ."

"No reason? That hypocritical moneybox, no reason? And it wasn't
he that left *her*," Livia added, returning her attention to the sleeve. "*She*
left *him,* or rather bade him leave, for she kept the house *and* the
furniture and all he'd given her. And Jumon did marry, two years after
that, to get control of his mother's plantation I daresay, which she
wasn't going to turn loose to any man who hadn't done his duty by the
family and given her a grandson. Not that it did him the slightest bit of
good, or her, either. She went to Paris. The wife, I mean."

"Wait a minute—What?" It was unheard of for a placée to leave her
protector. "Geneviève left Jumon? Why?"

"Jealous," snapped his mother. "She heard there was marriage in
the wind."

"Oh, don't be silly, Mama, you don't know that!" protested Minou.
"And no one—I mean, we all know . . ." She hesitated, looking suddenly down at her sewing, and a dark flush rose under the matte fawn of
her skin.

"We all know men marry?" finished her mother.

Dominique drew a steadying breath, and when she raised her head
again, wore a cheerful smile. As if, thought January, it mattered little to
her that the fat bespectacled young planter who had bought her house
for her, and fathered the child who had died last year, would not one
day marry, too. "Well, if she's as grasping as you say, she wouldn't have
let him go for a little thing like that." She made her voice languid and
light.

"Hmph," said Livia, unable to have it both ways. "At any rate, that
whining *nigaude* Noëmie—his wife—went back to Paris, and Laurence's
maman sold up the plantations, and the brother's never had a regular
mistress at all, so far as anyone knows." She shrugged. "Laurence Jumon
never breathed a peep. When he was sick back in twenty-four he gave
Geneviève money to buy both their sons from him, in case he died, and
they'd still be part of his estate. That mother of his would have sold off

her white grandchildren, if she'd ever had any, never mind her colored ones. Jumon and Geneviève had parted company by that time, but he paid every penny to educate those boys, not that anything ever came of *that*. For all the airs Antoine and his mother give themselves Antoine's just a clerk at the Bank of Louisiana. And Isaak . . ."

Her gesture amply demonstrated what she thought of a boy of education becoming a marble sculptor. "He's as bad as you, Ben, wasting the gifts M'sieu Janvier gave you . . ."

"Not wasting them at all, Mama." January smiled at her. He'd long ago realized that being annoyed at his mother would be the occupation of a lifetime. "M'sieu Janvier paid for my piano lessons as well as for Dr. Gómez to teach me medicine. I think as long as I'm making money at one or the other . . ."

"Not much money."

But January refused to fight, though the wound hurt. "So Geneviève turned M'sieu Laurence out, because of this engagement—it would have given him control of more property, surely? A plantation?"

Livia looked as if she'd have liked to enlarge on her son's folly and ingratitude, but in the end she could no more resist slandering a rival than a child could resist a sweet. Besides, reasoned January, the conversation could *always* be brought back around to *his* shortcomings.

"Trianon," said Livia, with spiteful satisfaction. "And another one across the lake. Geneviève must have hoped to make free with some of the proceeds. But Madame Cordelia sold them up, and put the money in town lots. If she'd held on—"

"But you see," said Dominique, "Geneviève and Isaak have been estranged for just years. Isaak was the only one of the boys who was still friends with their father—and I always thought poor M'sieu Laurence seemed terribly lonely. He'd come to the Blue Ribbon Balls and chat with us girls, and be so gallant and sweet, not like a lot of the gentlemen who look at you so when they don't think you can see, even if the whole town knows you already have a friend. All he wanted to do was dance. . . ."

Livia's sniff was more expressive than many books January had read.

"No, truly, Mama, we can tell." Dominique gently discouraged Madame la Comtesse de Marzipan, the less obese of Livia's two butter-colored cats, from playing with the ribbons she was sewing on the sleeve. "At any rate, when he was taken sick last fall, both Isaak and

Célie visited him every day. At least that's what Thérèse tells me, and her cousin was one of M'sieu Laurence's maids. When M'sieu Laurence died he left Isaak—oh, I don't know how much money, and some property as well, I think."

"He left him a warehouse at the foot of Rue Bienville, half-interest in his cotton press, a lot on Rue Marais and Rue des Ursulines, which if you ask me isn't worth seven hundred dollars, fifteen hundred dollars' worth of railway shares in the Atlantic and Northeastern, and three thousand dollars cash."

January didn't even bother to inquire where his mother had obtained these figures. He merely whistled appreciatively. "Not bad for a marble carver living in the back of his employer's house. I presume they've only been waiting for the probate."

"Which would have gone through a lot more quickly had not four-fifths of the judges in this city turned tail and fled at the first rumor of fever."

"Well, yes," said Dominique. "But also, M'sieu Laurence's mother contested the will. You are going to do something about it, aren't you, Ben? Not about the will, I mean, but about Olympe being arrested? You can't let them—I mean, they won't really . . ." She let the words *hang her* trail off unsaid.

January was silent. Madame la Duchesse de Gâteaubeurre prowled idly into the room, levitated effortlessly up onto his knee, and settled her bulk, making bread with her broad soft paws.

"Olympe wouldn't have done such an awful thing!" insisted Dominique. "And as for Célie Gérard having had anything to do with it— stuff! Why would she have wanted to kill her husband?"

January remembered that sweet-faced child turning away from Shaw, her hand pressed to her mouth with the shock of having confirmed the doubts that had tormented her through the horror of the night. Mamzelle Marie's words rose to his mind: *a thousand reasons men will think a woman poisoned a man.*

Célie, Isaak Jumon had said. And died.

"I don't know," he said thoughtfully. "Maybe I ought to find that out."

"I knew about the will, yes." Basile Nogent rested his forehead for a moment on his knuckles, against the shoulder of an infant angel carved to look like a white boy. The sculptor was small and middle-aged and had the sad thinness to him that sometimes befalls men when their wives die. The empty silence of the other side of the little cottage, the stillness of the yard where the kitchen doors gaped dark and deserted, told its own story. January knew that thinness, that shadow in the eyes. It was what had driven him from Paris, what had driven him back to the strange land of his tangled birth roots and the only family he had.

It was clear to him, as if he had read it in a book, that Isaak and Célie had been this man's family. And now Isaak was gone.

"Isaak never spoke much about his family to me," Basile Nogent said, in the hoarse rough voice of a consumptive. "He told me once that he wanted to put them behind him and, another time, that he forgave them, both father and mother, for what they were, for what neither could help being."

He shook his head. "An old quarrel, he said. And I understood that it was a pain that he—that Isaak—knew he had to overcome. He saw his father many times, and his uncle Mathurin. He'd meet them near the coffee stands at the market, or in a café on the Place d'Armes; sometimes he'd go by the big house on Rue St. Louis and sit in the courtyard and talk. It is not good when families divide like that, for whatever reason. There." He pointed to the marble block of a half-carved tombstone, like a classical trophy-of-arms: sword, shield, wreath, and cloak. A graven ribbon looped the sword hilt, bearing the legend JUMON. "Mathurin Jumon commissioned that last September, at his brother's death."

A quirk of irony broke the grief of that wrinkled face, and he ran one thumb—a knob of muscle like a rock—over the curls of the cherub's temple. "There is a species of insanity that strikes when a will is read. I have wrought marble for forty years. . . ." His gesture expanded to touch the two rooms of his little shop, to the doors that opened into a yard filled with yet more images still: a dog sleeping on a panoply of arms; two putti struggling, laughing, over a bunch of grapes; Athene with her owl reading a book. "As three-quarters of what I do is to decorate graves, I see people every week who have just heard wills read." His breath whispered what might at another time in his life have been a laugh, and he coughed again. "I always told Isaak that when I die I'm going to be like the savage Indians and have everything piled up in a big pyre and burned with me."

The sculptor again briefly closed his eyes. Did he think he could hide the thought that went across them? wondered January. The grief that asked, *Who do I have to leave it to anyway?*

And the same, he thought, could be said of himself. And for an instant the memory came back to him, suddenly and agonizingly, as if he had found Ayasha's body yesterday; as if he had never seen that picture in his mind before this moment. As if he had not awakened every morning for twenty-two months in bed alone.

Ayasha dead.

He still couldn't imagine how that could be possible. Couldn't imagine what he would do with the remainder of his life.

"He was—a good boy." Nogent's voice broke into January's grief, like a physical touch on his arm. "A good young man." The rain that had been falling since early afternoon, while January had been on the streetcar to the American faubourg of St. Mary to teach his three little piano students there, finally lightened and ceased; a splash of westering sunlight spangled the puddles in the yard.

"Tell me about Thursday," said January. "About the day they came for him."

Nogent sighed again, as if calling all his strength from the core of his bones to do work that had to be done. "Thursday," he said. "Yes." He led January to the back of the shop, where the light struck a simple block of marble. At first glance the headstone seemed unadorned save for the name, LIVAUDAIS. But sculpted over the block was what appeared to be a veil of lace, the work so exquisitely fine that the very pattern of the lace was reproduced, draped half over the name, the name readable through it—a truly astonishing piece. "We were working on this for old Madame Livaudais. Two—two City Guards came with the warrant. Isaak put aside his chisel and looked at it, and said, 'This is ridiculous.' Very calmly, just like that. To the men he said, 'I see my mother has decided to waste everyone's time. Please excuse me for just a moment while I get my coat and let my wife know where I'll be.' Cool—cold as the marble itself. But the way he touched the block"— Nogent mimicked the gesture, resting his palm for a moment on the flowered delicacy of the counterfeit lace's edge, holding it there, bidding it farewell—"I knew."

The movement of his eyes pointed back to the kitchen building that lay athwart the end of the yard. A little flight of stairs ascended to the rooms above, a garçonnière and chambers that would have belonged to household servants, had there been any. "He went up to the rooms they had, over the kitchen there. I kept the Guards talking, led them away from the doors here so they would not see. He must have gone up the scaffolding of the cistern—you see it there in the corner?—and over the wall into the next courtyard, and so out onto Rue St. Philippe and gone. He didn't tell Célie; only that he was going with them. The Guards must have waited here for him twenty minutes before they went to look. I think he did that so Célie wouldn't be accused of helping a runaway to escape. Even then, he thought of her."

"May I see?"

Nogent followed him out into the yard and to the cistern, where, sure enough, January found the scuffing and scrape marks on the frame of the scaffolding that held up the enormous coopered barrel in a corner of the yard. Like most yards in the French town, Nogent's was hemmed by a high wall, brick faced with stucco that had fallen out in patches, affording handholds. The fringe of resurrection fern along the top seemed to be broken, as if by passage of a body going over, but with the new growth already flourishing it was impossible to tell. January made a move to scramble up himself and see, but the lancing pain in his arms as he lifted them brought him up short.

"And the night of the twenty-third?" he asked, turning back to the old sculptor. "The night he died? Was young Madame Jumon here then?"

"That animal Shaw asked the same." Nogent spoke without rancor—*animal* was in fact one of the more polite terms by which members of the French and free-colored communities referred to Americans. "And I tell you what I told him. Madame Célie and I had supper together, here in the house, just as dusk fell. Then I went to bed. I tire more easily than I used to, you understand." He coughed again, and January knew that what he said was true. He wondered if, like the fiddler Hannibal, Nogent welcomed Morpheus with a spoonful of laudanum for the pain.

"It was threatening rain all evening, M'sieu. I cannot imagine Madame Célie would have ventured forth. Then, too, she had the habit of remaining indoors at night, in the hopes that Isaak would come, or send word."

"So Célie was by herself in the garçonnière here?"

"Yes. But, of course, this animal would have a witness. And when she had none—and she a married lady whose husband was away!—he said, '*Ah, she is a murderess,*' and placed her under arrest."

January's eye traveled over the brick-paved yard, still puddled from the afternoon's downpour. The soft, pitted pavement would hold no track, of course, to show whether Célie Jumon had remained in place that night. And it had rained, not once but many times, as always in New Orleans in June.

"How long had Isaak Jumon been with you, M'sieu Nogent?" he asked.

"Two years," replied the sculptor. "Nearly three. He was truly a son to me."

"Do you know any who would want Isaak Jumon dead? Who would wish him ill?"

"Ah." Nogent was silent, his head bowed, his hand on the scaffolding of the cistern, the subliminal movements of his fingers defining and redefining its shape and grain. Then, "Who would want Isaak dead, M'sieu? I don't know. His father's mother, Madame Cordelia Jumon—I think she would have rejoiced in his death. She did what she could to take his inheritance away from him in the courts. His mother—Well, I never thought that her claim of him as her slave would hold up in court." Nogent shook his head. "But what mother would harm her son?"

What mother would try to have him declared her slave?

What mother would refuse to speak of, or to, her elder daughter who disobeyed, all those many years ago?

"He was a good boy, M'sieu. Not what people say, 'Oh, he was a good boy. . . .' But he had a great goodness in him, a goodness of soul. Did they speak of when he would be buried? Of who would carve the plaque on his tomb? That mother of his . . ."

"No," said January quietly. "No body has yet been found. That's another thing I'm trying to track down. If he was in trouble, was there anyone Isaak would have gone to? He was missing for four days before his death."

"It depends on the trouble," Nogent said at last. "His uncle Mathurin, I would think. Perhaps his father-in-law. But they both loved Célie. If either of them knew a single thing of this crime, they would not suffer her to be accused. She is . . . a girl of great sweetness, M'sieu. And great forbearance. She is a girl who does not get angry; but that night, when she'd heard all that his mother had done with the warrant, and the Guards out looking for him, and an advertisement in the paper calling him a runaway slave . . . she came into the kitchen where I was sitting, and she kicked the side of the hearth, kicked it and kicked it and kicked it, not saying a word, because she was well-taught and well-bred, but with tears of anger running down her face. Whoever has said that she had anything, *anything* to do with his death is a fool."

January was silent, thinking about the young man dying in the big house alone, the young man who whispered, *I have been poisoned.* And then, *Célie.* And died.

There's a thousand reasons men will think a woman poisoned a man.

But which woman? January walked along Rue Dumaine in the wet, gathering dusk. Who else could give "no good account of themselves" on the night of Isaak Jumon's death?

In the Place d'Armes, gulls squabbled with pelicans over the garbage of the fruit stands while the women closed up their shops. The brick arcades of the market were dark save for lanterns around the coffee stand, and the world smelled of wet sewage, coffee, and the slow black rivers of soot disgorged by the steamboats into the sullen sky. A snatch of song touched him, where a late-working gang heaved cords of wood aboard the *Missourian:*

> *Kimbebo, nayro, dilldo, kiro,*
> *Stimstam, formididdle, all-a-board-la rake . . .*

African words, the wailing rhythm a thing of the bones and the heart rather than the mind.

Rose Vitrac was in her room above and behind a grocery on Rue de la Victoire, a slim gawky woman dressed neatly in contrast to the assortment of slatterns and market-women occupying the rest of the building. As January's shadow darkened the doorway, she raised her head from the pile of Latin examinations that had overflowed her small desk onto bed, spare chair, and floor. "Ignorant little toads," she remarked dispassionately and propped her gold-rimmed spectacles more firmly onto the bridge of her nose. Half a dozen candles burned in a cheap brass branch on the desk, different lengths and colors, bought half-consumed from the servants of the rich. "Why don't Creoles bother to educate their children? Or make certain they're actually studying what their tutors are paid to teach? Here's one who seems to think Cicero was merely something that was served at Roman banquets."

"I'm sure if Mark Antony could have arranged it he would have been."

"You have a point. I hope you've come to seduce me into dinner at a gumbo stand somewhere along the levee. I think if I read many more of these I shall go out into the street and start killing young boys at random, and such things give one a terrible reputation, even in this part of town."

Rose Vitrac had owned and taught at her own school for young ladies of color, before a combination of financial ill luck, yellow fever, and the determined enmity of one of her investors over her assistance to a runaway slave had conspired to ruin her. She now eked a kind of living from translating Latin and Greek for a small bookshop on Rue d'Esplanade, and correcting examination papers for two of the boys' schools in town. "Not much of a living," she admitted ruefully, as she and January descended the gallery stairs, "but decidedly superior to prostitution or sewing."

Or marriage, she didn't add—and she would have, once, January reflected, walking beside her along Rue Marigny. She was a woman who had been hurt badly by men, once upon a time, and deep in her heart still mistrusted them, sometimes in spite of herself.

There is time. January moved his aching shoulders. *And given my own possibility of earning anything like a living in the near future, maybe it's just as well.* Next month it would be two years since Ayasha's death. Seeing that shadow in Basile Nogent's tired eyes, the darkness of that empty house, had uncorked inside him once again that blood-colored river of pain, and he felt obscurely guilty, walking along the levee in contentment with Rose.

Ayasha, I haven't forgotten.

The time would come for them, he knew. Fate and God and Monsieur le Choléra permitting. But when he woke in the night with the memory of a woman beside him, it was Ayasha's body he sought; it was Ayasha's hair he sometimes imagined he could smell in the moonlight. His love for Rose had not made the pain grow less.

Over seven cents' worth of jambalaya from a market stand, Rose listened to January's account of the past eighteen hours: what he'd learned from his mother and sister, what he'd seen at the jail, and all Nogent had said. "Here's the advertisement Geneviève Jumon put in the *Courier* Friday," he said, spreading it out where the lantern glare fell on the tabletop. "Considering my mother's attitude about money maybe it's just as well I was in Paris when St.-Denis Janvier died, and that he didn't have much to leave me. Is there a chance you can get close to Célie Jumon? Talk to her? My sister says her father won't let someone of Dominique's stamp near her."

"And I have a more respectable appearance?" Rose peered at him over the tops of her spectacles, amused. "Well, I'll certainly try. But the one I think we need to talk to at once is Monsieur Antoine Jumon. That little scene in 'a house where he'd never been before' and mysterious servants smacks a little too much of penny dreadfuls for my taste."

"Shaw seems to have accepted it," said January thoughtfully. "Or at least his superiors did."

"Once the complaint was brought I can't see how they can have done otherwise. The boy *is* gone—and there's a good deal of money involved. And a witness."

"How very providential for Geneviève."

"Would you climb into a coach-and-four with masked bravos, or however it was he went there? Antoine seems a singularly trusting boy."

"Maybe he's too young to remember being a slave." January sipped his coffee and watched the line of municipal gutter cleaners being escorted back along Rue du Levee toward the Cabildo for the night. "Witness or no witness, I want to know what happened to Isaak's body. Obviously it wasn't chucked out into the road. Even the gutter cleaners would have noticed that."

"Well . . ." Rose looked doubtfully after the retreating coffle. "If you say so."

"Unless they find it, the state's case is practically nonexistent. There's no proof he was poisoned, so they'll have to set Olympe and Madame Célie free."

Behind the small thick ovals of glass, the gray-green eyes flicked to his, then away. Eloquent silence as she stirred her coffee, laid down the spoon with a tiny clink.

"You don't think so?"

The eyes touched his again, then again dodged away.

"Your sister is a voodoo," said Rose, after a long silence.

January opened his mouth to say, *What does that have to do with anything?* And closed it again.

He knew exactly what that had to do with it.

"Who's going to be on that jury, Ben?" she went on. "Slaves, who don't automatically cry *Devil-worshipers* when they walk past Congo Square on a Sunday afternoon? Freedmen, who've been to the voodoo dances themselves and—and presumably have seen enough of what goes on there not to be blinded by just the name and the rumor? I assume there are good voodoos and bad voodoos, the same way there are good Christians and bad Christians. But do you think any white jury is going to think of that?"

January was silent, remembering the candle he'd lit that morning, the prayer he'd prayed for his sister's soul.

Framed in her spotless white tignon, Rose's long, oval face had a bitter weariness to it, a kind of tired anger. "Maybe I'm wrong," she said. "Maybe whites—and colored, too—don't automatically believe calumny. But I was driven out of my business by rumors and lies, Ben. I'm a—a pauper now, at least in part because people don't ask questions about what they hear.

"Down in the Barataria country where I grew up, there are miles of what we call the trembling lands: miles of sawgrass and alligator grass and cattails, miles where plants have matted together like blankets spread upon the waters—but it's still water underneath. Sometimes you can get out of it just filthy and embarrassed and looking for a dry place to scrape yourself clean. Sometimes you don't get out of it at all."

She stood. "Forgive me, Ben. Maybe those giants I see all around me are really only windmills after all. But be careful." She clasped his hand, and walked away into the dwindling crowds of the market arcade, as nine o'clock struck from the Cathedral.

Candles glowed in his mother's parlor, shutters and French doors open onto the street to reveal a small cluster of her cronies drinking coffee. The musical babble of their voices reached him on the banquette: "Of course, Prosper Livaudais was paying her husband's valet to let him know the minute the husband was out of town . . ." "They say the baby's a miniature of the Marçand boy . . ." "And where she got the money for that new tilbury is anybody's guess . . ."

January made his way down the passway between her house and the next, ducking through the narrow gate at the end and into the little yard. The kitchen, too, had all its shutters thrown wide, illuminated from within like a stage to display Bella washing up the supper pans. "Could you leave the stove hot long enough for me to boil some water for a bath?" he asked, and Bella pursed her wrinkled lips and nodded.

"If you hurry," she said. "I'm heatin' water already for M'am Livia's bath, but you know how she gets about extra wood burned."

January knew how his mother got. "I'll be down to haul the water in two shakes of a lamb's tail."

He climbed the steps at a lope, working his way gingerly out of the black woolen coat; for weeks after his injury he hadn't even been able to put it on without assistance, or to get himself into a shirt. He still needed help sometimes if he had to dress in a hurry. A fencing master he knew had given him exercises, to be performed faithfully every evening, to strengthen the weakened muscles, and although the thought of lifting and rotating two ten-pound scale weights made him flinch he knew he'd better do it while the water heated. It would, he reflected, make the bath afterward more than ever a joy.

The garçonnière was dark, doors and shutters left open to the cool of the night. As he crossed the threshold something gritted underfoot, as if gravel or sand had spilled there.

What on earth? Bella kept the place so clean the threshold cursed your foot.

In his small desk he found lucifers and scratched one by touch in the dark. As he put flame to candlewick he saw that Bella had been in to remake the bed to her own satisfaction after he'd made it up that morning.

In the middle of the blanket lay a severed chicken foot, claws curled like a withered demon hand.

He looked back at the threshold. His foot had scuffed it out of shape, but he saw that a cross had been drawn there, in salt mixed with crumbling dark earth that he knew instinctively was graveyard dust.

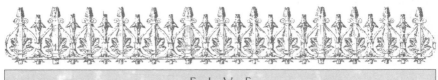

FIVE

If asked, Benjamin January would have denied all and any belief in magic. To his childhood catechism had been added the writings of Pascal, Newton, Leibniz, and Descartes, and the severed foot of a chicken was to his rational mind nothing more than so much leathery skin and bone.

He slept in the storeroom over the kitchen that night, and told himself this was because he did not want to disturb any sign in the room that, by daylight, might have told him who had entered to lay the fix. He did not, however, sleep particularly well. In the morning, before the day grew hot, he made his way to Rue St. Anne, to the house of Marie Laveau.

The voodooienne was making breakfast for her children in the tiny kitchen behind the pink stucco cottage: copper-colored dragonflies floated weightless and sinister above the puddles in the overgrown yard. "I wouldn't have disturbed you this early, except that I know it has to have something to do with Olympe."

Amusement flickered like marsh light in her eyes, mocking the drums that had whispered in his dreams. "You're that free of enemies, Michie Janvier?" It was early enough that she had not put up her hair; it lay over her shoulders like the pelt of a bear, Indian-black, springy and astonishing. "No other piano player in this town wishes to take your place in all the best halls? No rival for the hand of Mademoiselle Vitrac?"

"Were it as simple a thing as a rival keeping her from me," replied January, "I'd welcome him and give him tea." He didn't ask how Mamzelle Marie knew about Rose Vitrac. In some ways it was a relief to talk to someone who knew everything anyway. "Show me a dragon and I'll slay it. But the rival I have to overcome is Mademoiselle Vitrac herself. Herself, and the ghosts of her past."

"I'll tell you a secret, Michie Janvier." She set aside the sticky balls of rice she was molding with her hands, glanced into the pot of oil that hung over the great clay hearth, gauging the bubbles around its edge, then turned back to him with her ironic half-smile. "With all women worth the winning it is so."

She poured out coffee for him and gave instructions to her eldest daughter, a lithe tall damsel of seventeen with her same silent witch-dark eyes, about how long to leave the callas to fry in the oil, then went into the house. She emerged a few minutes later with her seven-pointed tignon tied and stout, sensible boots on her feet. Slaves went barefoot, January had been taught as a child, and poor freedmen working in the cotton presses and on the levee, and market-women and girls who took in laundry. He wondered whether Mamzelle Marie's mother had thrashed her as his own had thrashed him and Olympe.

He couldn't imagine anyone with that much nerve.

"Mambo Oba did this," she said, kneeling before his threshold to regard the scuffed cross. She snapped her fingers twice, crossed herself and touched the string of dried guinea peppers she wore about her neck, and stepped around the cross to enter his room. She put a red flannel over her hand, to pick up the chicken foot from the bed, and used another—she carried three or four of them stuck through her belt—when she squatted by the little plank desk to retrieve from behind it a ball of black wax stuck through with pins. On the gallery at January's side, Bella crossed herself several times and made a sign against Evil.

"It's bad, Michie Ben," the old servant murmured. "You'd have slept in this room, that Mambo Oba would have come in the night and rode you to death. My brother, he had a fix put on him so, and snakes grew under his skin so he died."

"Who's Mambo Oba?"

"She lives over on Rue Morales, near the paper mill." Mamzelle Marie reemerged from the room with the two flannels held gathered by their corners, carefully, as if they contained filth. "I'll go there to her myself and find out who paid her to fix you and what else she might have done. Bella, would you scrub the floor of the room and the steps here with brick dust and put brick dust on the soles of Michie Ben's shoes?"

"I put the brick dust on his shoes last night," said the servant, with a quick shy grin. "I knew he'd go out this morning."

Mamzelle Marie gave her a wink, her sudden sweet smile like a doorway into a room unsuspected. "You're a wise woman, Bella."

"Bella!"

All turned, to see Livia Levesque standing in the back door of the house. January had brought Marie Laveau down the passway at the side of the house to the yard, rather than risk an encounter between the voodooienne and his mother: he had heard his mother speak often enough about superstition and those who preyed on the ignorance of blacks. He saw recognition widen his mother's eyes and the way her lips folded tight, but she called out only, "Bella, you bring my coffee in here now."

" 'Scuse me, M'am." Bella curtsied quickly to Mamzelle Marie. "I'll do as you say, M'am, first chance I get." She nodded toward the house, into which her mistress had vanished in a rustle of mull-muslin skirts. "Don't hold it against her, M'am, please."

"I don't hold grudges, Bella." Mamzelle smiled. "There's no greater waste of time in this world."

She and January watched the old woman hasten down the steps and across the little yard; and January reflected that Bella, whom Livia had bought when first St.-Denis Janvier had given her her own freedom, was exactly what Livia herself might have been: exactly of the same extraction of white and black, no more educated or better reared. Under other circumstances, might his mother and this woman have been friends?

"Michie Janvier."

Mamzelle Marie held out to him a little bag of red silk, hung on a cord of braided string, smelling vaguely of dried whisky and ashes.

"Will you wear this?" she asked. "Give it a name, but don't tell anyone what that name is; wear it next to your skin, under your right armpit, and take it out every now and then and give it a drink of whisky. It'll keep you safe."

January was silent. In those sibyl eyes he saw again the reflection of last night's dreams. Dreams of being lost in the *cipriere*, with mist rising from the low ground and night coming on. Dreams of seeing something whitish that scuttered among the trees, a slick sickly gleam of rotting flesh. Dreams of the smell of blood.

He had been a child in the dreams, with no strength to meet a capricious world. In those days the only thing you could do with an overseer who hated you was make a ball of red pepper and salt and the man's hair and throw it in a stream, so he would go away, or mix blood and graveyard dust and the burned-up ash of a whippoorwill's wing in a bottle, and bury the bottle where the man would walk over it, so that he would die. God and the Virgin Mary had brought him out of slavery, Père Antoine had told him. God would keep him safe. In times past he'd worn a gris-gris Olympe had made for him and had prayed, half in jest, to Papa Legba as he'd now and then addressed the classical gods, like Athene or Apollo. But lately he'd put the gris-gris away, unsure what it meant to wear such a thing. To seek the help of the *loa* was, at best, an act of mistrust in the goodness and the power of God.

Satan has no power, the old priest had said, over a good man whose heart is pure.

Of course, Père Antoine had never been any man's slave, either.

The full bronze lips quirked down at one corner when he did not put forth his hand to take the little red silk bag. "You think God didn't make jack honeysuckle and verbena, with the power to uncross any that's crossed?" she asked. But in her tone he heard no anger. Only exasperation, like a mother whose child refuses to wear a coat on a cold morning.

He shook his head. "I'm sorry, Mamzelle, and I thank you. But I can't."

Paul Corbier and Gabriel were at the Cabildo when January got there. A grudging Guardsman led them all from the watch room through the yard and up the two flights of rickety steps to the gallery where the women's cells were. The madwoman whose children were dead still sobbed and muttered somewhere, pleading for someone to stop her father and her husband from entering the cell at night and sitting on her chest. More loudly, a drunken voice interminably sang "The Bastard King of England." The day had already turned hot.

"Mambo Oba?" Olympe shook her head, leaning against the barred window in the cell door to look out at her brother, husband, and child. "She's no enemy of mine. When I was with Marie Saloppe, Mambo Oba set herself up against us, and we put fixes on one another; I think she sent a gator to live under the floor of Saloppe's house. But that was years ago. We see each other at the Square, now and then, or in the market." She shrugged. "That's all in the past."

"Hmn," said January. The conflicts among the voodoos in town— breaking into one another's houses to steal bottles or idols or calabash rattles supposedly imbued with Power, placing crosses and fixes on one another's houses or followers—had given January a mistrust and a disgust for them, even before the final dance at the brickyard. It had seemed as childish and petty as the tales they told of the *loa*, how the goddess Ezili had had an affair with this god or that god, creating scandal; how the god Zaka would run away in fear from the Guédé, the dark lords of the Baron Cemetery's family; less like gods than like children, and ill-mannered ones at that. It had seemed to him greedy, too, for it was clear to him that money lay at the bottom of it, fear and influence over the minds of potential customers. He knew perfectly well that when white ladies, or colored, paid Olympe to tell their fortunes, Mamzelle Marie took her cut.

"Mamzelle Marie says somebody likely paid Mambo Oba," said January, and his sister nodded.

"Likely. She always was the kind who'd put a fix on her next-door neighbor so the neighbor would pay her to come take it off."

"I thought you all did that."

"Only when the rent's due, brother." The fine lines around her eyes deepened with a malicious smile.

January glanced at the Guard who stood nearby, gauging the broad Germanic cheekbones, the fair hair, and the heavy chin. Leaning close to the window he asked, in the fieldhand African-French of their childhood, "Where were you on the night Isaak Jumon died?"

And he saw her eyes change. Wondering if he'd pass that information along.

"Olympe, your life is at stake here. They arrested you because you wouldn't say."

"They arrested me because I'm a servant of the *loa*," she replied. "That journalist Blodgett, he's been here twice. Asking about pagan gods, and hoodoo, and demons, writing notes in his little book to make white folks gasp and whisper over their tea. What does it matter where I was, if I sold poison that could be used anytime?"

"Olympe . . ." said Paul desperately, and Gabriel bit his lip.

And January understood. "The twenty-third," he said. "St. John's Eve. Were you at a dance?"

Behind her in the cell a free colored woman got into a shoving-match with a slave over who would next use the communal latrine bucket, and Olympe glanced quickly back over her shoulder like a cat when another cat enters the room. There was a bruise on her face, and the lower edge of her tignon bore a line of crusted blood.

A bitter smile creased the corner of his sister's mouth. "If I were," she said, "you think I'd say? If a hundred men and women saw me there, do you think any of them would be able to testify in court? Do you think any of them *could* testify without getting a beating for it, for being out past curfew, for slipping away from their masters, to be with one another and the *loa*?"

"There must have been freedmen there," said January. "Or free colored."

"Oh, I'll buy a ticket to that," Olympe returned sardonically. "Let's see: a man gets up and says to that churchgoing jury, *Oh yes yes, that voodoo witch who lays spells of ill luck on those who cross her, oh yes I saw her there I saw her there clear?* You are a fool."

Rose was right, thought January. The woman in the Cathedral came to mind, making her furtive purchase—if it was a purchase—from Dr. Yellowjack while looking around as if she expected the Protestant God to strike the building for idolatry. It would take more than absence of proof to free Olympe.

More quietly still, and still in the half-African patois of the cane fields, he asked her, "How did you know they hadn't found a body?"

Her brows pulled together, as she turned the matter over in her mind. "When the men came to get me I kept my shell with me," she said at last. "The shell that calls the *loa*. I kept it in my mouth. Later I asked the shell, and I asked the spider that spins a web in the corner of the cell, and I asked the rats in the walls: who it was that had killed

Isaak Jumon. And they all three told me the same: that Isaak Jumon isn't dead."

"His brother saw him die," said January. "Why would his brother lie?"

Olympe shook her head. "I don't know, brother. I only know what they said, those voices out of the dark."

"You pig-faced whore!" screamed a voice in the cell.

"Who you callin' whore, bitch?" screeched another.

A chorus of screams ensued, and the Guard thrust January and Paul aside to come up to the bars. This proved an ill-judged interference, for someone hurled the contents of the communal latrine in question over him, and the women continued to tear at one another's hair and shriek.

Cursing, the Guard shoved January and Paul back along the gallery, "You two get out of here, now! Damn stinking wenches. . . ."

"He's the one stinking," giggled Gabriel, and his father shook him hard by the shoulder as they descended to the courtyard.

"Damn them," Paul whispered desperately. "Damn them for keeping her there." They crossed swiftly through the watch room, quieter than it had been yesterday without the Guardsmen and clerks and prisoners on the way to the Recorder's Court, though even on Saturdays, masters brought in their slaves to be whipped. The heat in the room was terrific, and flies swarmed and circled in the blue shadows of the ceiling.

"Are you well?" asked January, as they came out onto the arcade. "Are you managing, with the children?"

His brother-in-law nodded, and gave Gabriel a quick hug. "With my boy here to help me, yes. And Zizi-Marie is the best assistant in the shop a man could ask for. But Ben, listen. I've got an offer of work, a big order, from Drialhet at St. Michael Plantation. It's nearly fifty miles up the river. Olympe says I should go, that you'll—you'll look after her here. I shouldn't ask it of you, but . . ."

"No," said January immediately, "go." He knew that in the slow summer season, it was Olympe's earnings, from reading the cards and making gris-gris, that put food on the Corbier table. "Should I stay with the children? I'm supposed to be looking after my mother's house when she leaves for the lake, but . . ."

"I'll be back every few days," said Paul. "And Zizi-Marie is old enough to look after things. But—do what you can for Olympe. Please. Gabriel and Zizi-Marie will come to see her, bring her food and clean clothes. And she'll need an attorney, a lawyer to plead her case . . ."

"I'll see what I can do." January wondered if such a person could be induced to plead on credit, like a grocer, until Drialhet paid up or the winter season of balls brought money again.

What am I thinking? he wondered then, as he watched his brother-in-law and his nephew make their way up Rue St. Pierre away from him. From above, dimly, he could still hear the madwoman screaming in her cell, the windows of which pierced the high wall three stories over his head. Could hear voices raised, cursing, weeping, quarreling.

He remembered the dead man, bundled away in the storeroom under the stairs, like dust swept under a rug.

Olympe would need all the luck she could get, he thought, to even make it to her trial.

When Paul and his son had gone their way January drew from his pocket the copy of last Friday's *Courier* that Basile Nogent had given him. The advertisement said:

> FIFTY DOLLARS REWARD will be given to any person apprehending and lodging in jail a quadroon boy called Isaak. He is very white and has a fine complexion and will try to pass himself as free. He is 19 years old, 5 feet, 6 inches tall, slenderly built but with great strength of chest and arms, has a narrow face and fine teeth, black hair curly rather than woolly, and a small mustache. He reads and writes, and speaks French, and English only brokenly. Apply to Mr. Hubert Granville of 1005 Prytane Street.

Hubert Granville. January folded the paper up again thoughtfully. Perhaps it was only a coincidence, but Hubert Granville was the vice-president of the Bank of Louisiana, at which, if he remembered rightly, fine education or no fine education, Antoine Jumon was employed as a clerk.

Nine o'clock was striking from the Cathedral. From the streets that led into the Place d'Armes, dilatory servants still made their way, baskets of split willow on their arms, bound for the markets along the levee downstream. To his right Rue Chartres stirred with activity, shopkeepers or their servants scrubbing the thresholds, the slaves of the wealthy washing down the flagged carriageways that led back into the secret courtyards that lay behind those shops. A pralinnère strolled past him with her sugared wares, brown and white, nearly brushing elbows with the journalist Blodgett, bustling half-drunk on some errand on the levee with his notebook in his hand.

January smiled. Saturday was a half-holiday, and the day was early yet. The banks wouldn't close until one.

A singularly trusting boy, Rose had said of Antoine.

Well, we'll just see how trusting.

Anyone unfamiliar with the crowds, the din, the frenzied hauling of cotton bales and hogsheads of sugar and rum from point to point along the levee during the winter months would have compared the long riverfront today with a hive of bees at swarming time. But to January's eye the activity today was slow: too few crates, too many men standing idle. Eight steamboats loosed their columns of grimy smoke from tall stacks trimmed in crowns of gold, where in the winter there'd be three times that many lined up two deep along the wharves. Mates and super-cargoes yelled directions at their gangs, while slaves unloaded trunks and portmanteaux from their masters' carriages; captains strolled among the crowds with manifests in their hands; pilots in the dusky shade of the market arcades drank coffee and traded minutiae about the height of the water the other side of Red Church and whether the bar off some nameless island below Natchez had crumbled away yet or not. A respectable-looking little gentleman in a gray coat was showing a gold watch to an obvious Yankee businessman and talking up what was clearly an auction scam; a couple of men dressed as stevedores out of work—and there were enough of those around the docks these days— lolled suspiciously close to a pile of crates of English saws and chisels left on the dock beside the *Philadelphia.* January picked his way through the knots of men, unobtrusive in his rough clothes and blue calico shirt, and searched the faces for the one he knew.

In time he saw the man he sought, in the midst of a gang of workmen unloading crates marked PORCELAINES FINES DE LIMOGES from a dray in whirlwinds of straw and packing. He waited until the fore-man—distinguishable from the men he worked with only by the shaggy beaver hat he wore—was called to the deck of the *Bonnets O'Blue* by the mate, then ambled over.

"Ti Jon."

Most of the men had slacked off the moment the foreman's back was turned, wiping their brows or whistling for the young boys who sold ginger beer along the levee. January gestured to one of these, and offered Ti Jon a drink.

"Ben." Ti Jon brought up the kerchief he wore around his neck— the only thing he had on above the waist—and wiped his face.

"World treating you well?"

The stevedore shrugged. "My railway shares are down." A few inches under January's great height, Ti Jon was lean-bodied and, like January, African dark. He belonged to a man who lived on Rue Bourbon, to whom he paid seven dollars a week for the privilege of finding his own food, lodging, and work. Monsieur Dessalines didn't care where Ti Jon acquired any of these things so long as he made his appearance Saturday nights with his week's money, a situation that suited Ti Jon just fine. "This business with the Bank of the United States has caused me to put off running for Congress until the next election, not this one."

"I think that's wise," said January gravely.

"Yourself?"

"Oh, I'll run," said January. "I have faith in President Jackson. And, I just got back from playing for the crowned heads of Europe, so I have a little time on my hands."

"I read about that. The *Paris Daily Democrat* said you were a veritable genius."

January pulled a modest face. "Well, I was. But I strained a muscle in my back lifting all the gold they threw on the stage."

"Well, my mama always said there's no such thing as an unmixed blessing." Ti Jon sipped his ginger beer and grinned at the make-believe. "What can I do for you?"

"I'm looking for someone. Boy name of Isaak Jumon."

He saw Ti Jon's eyes change. Wary.

"I thought he might have gone to the Swamp."

"His mother send you?"

January shook his head. "I've never met his mother. From all I've heard of her I don't think I want to."

"You don't." The dark Congo eyes glanced at him sidelong, tallying information that he didn't want to reveal. Asking himself how much he could or wanted to say.

"The police say my sister poisoned him. That she was paid to do it by his wife."

"Now that's a lie." Ti Jon glanced at the foreman, still deep in conference with the mate over where the crates of PORCELAINES FINES should be stowed. "Whoever's saying it. Isaak spoke of nothing but that girl. How he loved her, how he felt bad for running away like he did, leaving her no place to go but back to her father. He kept saying he'd go back to her, he'd find a way to go back." He was silent then, a muscle standing out for a moment in his jaw. Then, "He's dead?"

January nodded.

"What a damn shame. He was a good boy, steady. It right, that the girl's gone back to her daddy?"

"For now. But she'll go to trial for it next month, and hang, along with my sister, unless we find the truth of what happened."

"Filz putain." Ti Jon was silent for a time, arms folded, gazing unseeing into the confusion of the levee. Then he sighed. "A week ago Thursday, he came into Widow Puy's grocery asking after a place to stay."

January had spent a night in the attic over the Widow Puy's, on the occasion of having had a white man tear up the papers that proved him free. It had cost him fifty cents for sleeping room with a dozen other men, men who'd mostly reached the same arrangement with their masters that Ti Jon had, though a couple of them, January guessed, had been runaways. He'd had to leave his boots as collateral while he got the fifty cents from his sister Dominique. It was the last time he'd ventured out of the French town with fewer than three copies of his papers hidden on his person.

"I figured him for a runaway and found him a job sweeping up at the Turkey-Buzzard. Later on he told me—That true, what he said about his mother claiming him as her slave? Damn." He shook his head in wondering anger. "Some people shouldn't be let to have children or should have 'em taken away and given to those who'll treat 'em well. When did he die?"

"When did you see him last?"

Ti Jon's glance flicked aside. "Saturday," he replied. "Saturday morning. A week ago. This advertisement came out in the papers Friday, and Isaak said when he read it Friday afternoon he couldn't hardly work at the saloon, feeling every man who came in was looking at him and would be waiting for him in the alley out back when he came out. You know what it's like down the Swamp."

January knew what it was like down the Swamp. "You know where he went?"

Ti Jon shook his head. "Just he was leaving town. I got to go."

The foreman was still deep in colloquy with the mate. In any case it was inconceivable that Ti Jon wouldn't know everything that went on among the runaways and sleepers-out of the slaves in New Orleans. January's eyes met Ti Jon's for a moment, seeing the lie in them. Seeing also the opaque look that said, *I know you know, but what you know isn't going to do you any good.*

Why?

A man passing close by the dray cried out in anger, his hand going to his pocket; a boy went darting away into the crowd. Foreman, mate, and half the loading-gang turned to watch as others joined the hue and cry, turning the Place d'Armes almost instantly into a shoving seethe, but January guessed what was actually going on, and turned his head in time to see the three loiterers by the *Philadelphia* casually shove three boxes of the carpentry tools off the edge of the wharf. Then they walked away quickly, in different directions, hands in pockets, without looking back. There'd be men in a rowboat under the dock, to hook the crates aboard.

But all that was none of his lookout. He'd seen such things before. The foreman yelled from the deck of the *Bonnets O'Blue,* "You men! We ain't got all day!" and Ti Jon nodded to January.

"Thanks for the drink."

"Thank you," said January. "If you hear anything else of where Jumon might have been, please let me know. There's lives at stake."

Ti Jon hesitated. "I'll let you know."

Since the Widow Puy would in all probability not appreciate being waked to answer questions about a boarder whom she barely remembered, January repaired for an hour to number 8 Allée d'Échange. There under the ruthless tutelage of Augustus Mayerling he worked his injured arms and back against scale weights and beams of various sizes until he felt the limbs in question were about to fall off and he'd have to carry them home in a basket in his teeth. "Good." The Prussian fencing master handed him a towel to wipe his face. The long upstairs room, despite its row of windows thrown open to the narrow gallery, was stiflingly hot. "It means the muscles are healing satisfactorily."

Trembling with fatigue, January reflected that it was good to know someone was satisfied with the progress of the day so far.

The Widow Puy told him little that Ti Jon had not already related. Yes, a young man of Isaak Jumon's description had stayed there last week. She didn't remember when he'd first arrived. It could have been Thursday. January had the impression that it could also have been Monday or Saturday or last Easter for all she knew or cared.

She shrugged, a heavyset woman in a sweat-stained green calico dress and a tignon to match. She sat behind the plank counter of her grocery like a snapping turtle in a hole in a bank; on the shelf behind her, jammed in between bottles of opium and papers of pins, he saw a green glass bottle stoppered with red wax, which contained a root or bundle of some kind, surrounded by a few silver and copper bits, cigars, and fancy-cut paper. "Long as they pays me my money I don't care who they are or where they from."

Past bins of flour and rice, barrels of onions, kegs of molasses, and stacks of yellowing newspaper on every level surface in the big dim room, doors opened into the yard, harsh squares of light. Men's voices came beyond, dimly, the rhythm of those with nothing much to do.

"You remember anyone coming to see him here?" January asked her. "Or him getting any messages from anyone?"

She shook her head. She probably didn't recall that many details about her last four husbands—anyway the man measuring out half a penny's worth of crowder peas for a little girl with a market basket certainly wasn't the man who'd been here eighteen months ago.

"You remember when he left?"

"Saturday."

"You sure?"

Her eyes went flat. "No," she said, in the voice of one who has all her life used contrariness to punish those who questioned her veracity.

"Thank you, M'am," said January, telling himself never again to antagonize a potential source of later information. "You've been very helpful." He bought three linen handkerchiefs for more than they were worth and took his departure, circling the building to join the group in the back.

It was late enough in the morning that the men who hadn't found work had returned, to while the remainder of the day away in talk of women or of work yet to be found. One man had the deep, wet cough of the later stages of consumption; another, big and young with a slave's tin badge on his faded shirt, moved and breathed like a man who has strained his heart. January shivered, rubbed his own aching shoulders, and wondered how long it would be before the owners of these men sold them off for what they could get. There were worse things, he realized, than torn and dislocated muscles that would eventually heal.

The men remembered Isaak, but he had told none of them more than he had told Ti Jon, and most of them less. They'd guessed him for a runaway, but it was none of their business. Several of them were, January guessed, runaways themselves, making a fair living at casual labor and having no intention of leaving New Orleans. All said Isaak'd left Saturday morning. All referred him to Ti Jon.

"He had this note when he came back here Friday night," said the man with the bad heart. "I saw it, but I can't read. I wisht I could, or figure."

"Do you know who it was from?"

The man shook his head. "Maybe his wife. Or his sweetheart. He said he had a wife."

"He didn't touch it like it was from his wife," said a man with the sores of scrofula on his face. "A man with a paper from his wife, he'll hold it between his hands like this, even when he's not reading it, or lay it up by his face, or keep it in his breast pocket near his heart. This he read, two, three times, by the moonlight sittin' out on the steps"—he nodded up at the shallow platform outside the door that let into the attic where the men slept, at the top of a rickety flight of steps—"but he just shove it in his pants pocket and sat lookin' up at the moon."

It was after ten in the morning when January left Puy's, and clouding up, the dense heat smelling of rain. If the banks closed at one, ten was the proper time to see if Hannibal was awake. It might take an hour or so to sober him up. But at this hour, thought January, wading through the weeds that grew thick along the sides of the undrained muck-hole streets, Hannibal wasn't the only one who'd be awake in the Swamp.

When first January had come to New Orleans as a child, the old town walls had still stood, and pastures had stretched beyond them toward the swamp and the lake. Upstream a few Americans had begun to build their houses and shops along Canal Street—named for a waterway that had never been dug—but for the most part everything beyond the walls was a wilderness of cypresses and cattails, silt and saltgrass, and ferns.

He had had no fear to walk there or anywhere else outside the walls.

The walls were gone now. But in his heart and his imagination they remained, a bastion against the upriver Americans, human garbage of the flatboat and keelboat trade, river rats, and filibusters whose numbers had doubled and tripled and then waxed ten- and twenty- and fifty-fold with the passing years. Foul-mouthed dirty men whose cold eyes saw no difference between slave blacks who could be bought and sold and the free colored man or woman whose ancestors had founded the town. Slick scheming men who would buy anything or sell anything or do anything to anyone as long as it could turn a profit, and the coarse whorish women who followed them for gain.

The Swamp had streets, but that was about all that could be said of the place. No one had bothered to pave them, or run the gutters essential to keeping the marshy town drained. The slots between the crude plank buildings, the tents and shanties that housed brothels and barrel houses and cheap lodging places, were themselves gutters, ankle-deep in reeking ooze that steamed faintly under the morning's pounding heat. Untended privies competed with the stench of dead dogs, rotting garbage, expectorated tobacco, and fermenting alcohol in a putrid miasma that veiled the whole district; even at this hour of the morning January could see into the open sheds to games of poker and faro still in progress from the previous night or the previous week. Outside the Turkey-Buzzard a man lay in the muck. Flies swarmed around a gaping wound in his chest. Even from across the street January could see he wasn't breathing.

He walked swiftly, his eyes on the ground, keeping to the sloppy runnel in the middle of the way lest he encounter any who considered it their right as white men to have the drier ground along the walls. There were a lot of runaway slaves living in the Swamp; slaves, too, like Ti Jon, who "slept out," finding lodging in its back rooms, attics, and sheds. These, January knew, could be insulted, shoved in the mud, beaten, or killed with impunity. The City Guards did not come here. When whores called out to him from shanties barely wider than the beds they contained, he did not raise his eyes.

Hannibal lived above Kentucky Williams's saloon in Perdido Street these days. He had only to make it that far. . . .

"Michie January?"

He halted, surprised. A child stood at his side, panting as from a run; one of those hundreds of ragged urchins who darted around the Swamp and Girod Street and the Basin District like flies above a gutter on a hot June day. The boy held out a folded sheet of paper. "Are you Michie Ben January?"

"I'm Ben January."

"This for you, then."

Puzzled, he handed the child a picayune, and the boy pelted away, trying to outrun the crowd of larger boys who emerged from nowhere to try to take the coin.

January unfolded the paper, his mind going back to the chicken foot on his bed.

The paper was blank.

He turned it over.

Blank.

The hair prickled on the nape of his neck as he realized what the paper was.

He looked around him, fast, but the man who'd paid the child to get him to identify himself in the open street had already stepped from under the awning of a run-down saloon, a knife in his hand. January had an impression of a sun-bleached mouse-brown beard and long braids wrapped in buckskin and red rags, a shirt sewn from the blue wool goods traded by the British posts to Indians in the Oregon Territories. A fur trapper, a mountain man, calm and businesslike as if he were going after a lamed deer.

January ran. Even if the law would permit him to raise a hand against a white man in his own defense—which it didn't—he knew that every Kaintuck river rat and keelboat ruffian in the district would be on him like wolves if he did so. In any case he knew his arms, his back, his body were not up to a fight. He was taller than the trapper and probably fifty pounds heavier, and he ran like a jackrabbit: down Jackson Street, through empty ground rank with waist-high weeds and splashing with oozy water, around the side of a coarse-built barrel-house-cum-bordello where the whores shrieked "He's gettin' away from you, Ned!" and someone yelled "Two dollars on the nigger!" as he and his pursuer pounded past.

Behind him he heard the man yell "Stop him!" in English. "You, boy, stop!" And he raised the knife, flashing in the clouded sunlight.

Men poured, whooping, out of the Ripsnorter Saloon—it was a slack hot morning in the slow season, and the fight promised diversion—and formed a barrier between the buildings, heading January off in a weed-ridden soggy field. There were two pistols and a rifle among them, and January tried to veer away. The mountain man swerved at his heels, lunged, and struck; January's feet skidded in the muck beneath the weeds. He tried to catch the knife hand and twist it aside: it was like a child trying to avert the blow of a man. His arm crumpled like soaked pasteboard in a wash of breathless pain, and he ducked out of the way as the blade scored his flesh.

They fell, hard, the white man on top, January's arm collapsing under him as he tried to catch himself. He rolled from under the knife and mud splashed on him with the force of it stabbing into the ground. Rolled again, trying to bring up his arm through a red haze of agony, sobbing with shock and despair and sheer terror, and then someone grabbed the trapper from behind and hauled him back like a housewife uprooting a carrot.

It was a black man, huge—January's own formidable height and as heavily built, head shaved, scarred eyes, and a mouth like an ax cut in an ugly face. He whirled the trapper with astonishing neatness and head-butted him, hard: January saw his rescuer had only one arm, his right, the left a stub not quite down to the elbow. The trapper staggered and the cut-armed man let him go, and in a single move elbowed him across the face, then back-fisted him with a blow like a hammer's.

The trapper staggered, lunged again with his knife, and a man from the crowd leapt out and tried to pull him back. January glimpsed Hannibal's frayed black coat and long hair as the trapper whirled and walloped the fiddler aside with the back of his hand, with force sufficient to knock him down. The cut-armed man dragged January to his feet, the crowd churning into a melee, grabbing at January, grabbing at the cut-armed man. The trapper flung Hannibal off him a second time but never got a chance to make another lunge at January, for out of the confusion barreled three women, harpies, a six-foot Amazon named Kentucky Williams and her equally fearsome partners, Railspike and Kate the Gouger—all of whom, January knew, had a soft spot for Hannibal in what passed in them for hearts.

"Three dollars on Kentucky!" somebody yelled as the cut-armed man shoved January by main strength through the mob, and the sky split with a roar of thunder and rain sluiced down.

The downpour was short, but it effectively discouraged pursuit. When January and Cut-Arm ducked into a ramshackle shed behind a store on St. John Street—a store that seemed to sell nothing much besides liquor and some of the most slatternly women January had ever seen—most of their pursuit had already fallen aside. The few who ran on past seemed more interested in finding shelter themselves than picking up the trail. "You know him?" panted Cut-Arm, and January shook his head.

"He had a boy come out and give me a note, blank, so he could see me say I was Ben January. So he didn't know who I was, either."

Cut-Arm sniffed, and his dark eyes gleamed in the shadows as he listened for the sound of further pursuit. "You got someplace to go?"

January nodded, and touched the shirt-pocket where he kept one copy of his papers. "I'm free," he said. His mother—and many others among the free colored—would have been careful to specify that they were free colored, dreading lest they be taken for freedmen, freed blacks, emancipated by a white master out of generosity or in payment for faithful service. Though of course, he reflected, that was exactly what he was, and what his mother was, deny it though she certainly would. "I came over here to find my friend Hannibal the fiddler, the one who tried to help you in the fight."

He felt a small pang of shame at having abandoned Hannibal to his own devices—the fiddler could never have survived an all-out attempt on his life—but knew Hannibal would be the first person to say "For God's sake run for it!" At least Hannibal wouldn't be clubbed to death merely for striking a white man. And with Kentucky Williams and her girls on the scene, Hannibal's chances of getting clean away were good.

"No white man had to help me," said Cut-Arm softly, his voice deep, the growl of a bear. "And you'd be best if you stop calling any white man friend. Not the one who freed you, not the one who mixed himself in the fight. None of 'em. When it comes to a choice they'll all betray you. Where's this white man of yours live?"

Cut-Arm went with him as far as the foot of the rattletrap ladder that ascended the back of Kentucky Williams's house. The two men moved quietly in the slanting rain through the weedy lots, the stands of cypress, and loblolly pine. In two of the saloons they passed, other fights had already started up, women shrieking and men cursing, furniture smashing against rickety plank walls. Few came out in the rain who might have seen them go by, but once, near the corner of an alley, January saw a dark shape signal Cut-Arm that all was clear.

Hannibal had already returned, and sat in the gray light of the doorway of his attic room, reading *Topography of Thebes,* when January climbed the ladder through the thinning drizzle. "So what was your quarrel with Mr. Nash?" the fiddler inquired, and coughed heavily. His long dark hair was soaked and he'd shed his wet coat in favor of a blanket around his thin shoulders. "Don't tell me you dared imply that the college he attended has a second-rate rowing-team?"

"That was it." January glanced back down into the flooded yard. No trace of Cut-Arm was to be seen. "I should have known better than to say a thing like that to a Harvard man. Thank you." Hannibal had a small cut over one eye, but other than that he seemed little the worse for leaping into the fray, save for the drawn exhaustion of his face and the way he slumped against the doorframe.

Behind him the roof leaked noisily. Peering through into the attic's sepia gloom, January saw a mattress and a drapery of frayed mosquito-bar. A dozen stacks of books were all arranged on planks laid down between the rafters above the thin ceiling of the room below, placed so that the leaks dripped between them.

"You know the man?"

Hannibal coughed again and withdrew a bottle of opium from under the blanket's folds. "Edward Nash, hight Killdevil among the mountain men for his affection for that particular tipple: *If I had a thousand sons, the first human principle I should teach them would be, to forswear thin potations.* Damn," he added, taking a swig, and held the bottle up to the light. "Speaking of thin potations . . . They swear to me they don't steal it, but they do. They think I don't notice when they water it." He coughed again, the deep racking shudder of tuberculosis, and leaned against the frame of the door, jaw tight with sudden pain.

"God knows what those girls want with opium," he went on after a moment in his hoarse, light voice, "considering the poison they peddle by the gallon downstairs. I don't know what I'd have done if they hadn't shown up. I left the lovely Kentucky in charge of the situation. Ungallant, but I thought it best." His eyes slipped closed; in the rainy light, his face looked deathly.

"Still . . ." And the dark eyes flicked open again. " 'ξ ὦμεν γὰρ οὐχ ὡς θέλομεν ἀλλ᾽ ὡς δυνάμεθα,' as the maggot said to the King of France. Our Mr. Nash came to town in May with four years' worth of fox and beaver pelts, his own and those of his partners back in Mexico. He sold the lot for close to three thousand dollars and started drinking. And gambling. He did some of both here, but mostly over at the Flesh and Blood on Tchoupitoulas Street. I've never seen one man get so drunk so quickly and stay sitting up so long after he should charitably have been put to bed. Charitably at least for the local Paphians, who would have access to the inner pockets that the gamblers missed. *Keep thy foot out of brothels, thy hand out of plackets, thy pen from lenders' books. . . .* In any case he's been hanging around town ever since, trying to raise sufficient funds to get back to Santa Fe and face his associates with some semblance of honor."

January was silent. He saw again the chicken foot, the graveyard dust. The child holding out to him the folded note in the street. "I gather," he said at last in a mild voice, "that someone suggested to Mr. Nash a means by which he could redeem himself." And he related the incident of the boy and the blank note. "Olympe's husband is leaving town today—he has to feed his family and go when work is offered. Anyone would have known that. And seen me stand up in the court yesterday morning."

"That's crazy." Hannibal took another sip of opium and worked the cork back into the bottle. "Who'd want to have your sister hanged? I mean, if you're going to go after a voodooienne, why not tackle Mamzelle Marie? Who'd want to see the death of what appears to be a perfectly innocent sixteen-year-old girl?"

"I don't know," said January grimly. "But somebody does. Do you suppose the lovely Miss Williams and her equally lovely friends might be able to ascertain more details of Mr. Nash's current employment?"

"I don't see why not. I doubt he'll be in much of a mood to talk to the Fair Maid of Lexington herself—when last I saw them together Kentucky had bitten a sizable chunk from his left ear and was hammering him over the head with a slungshot—but the thing about the Swamp is, that everyone knows someone who knows someone. Rather like Oxford University in that sense. . . . But that can't have been the reason you came here, surely?"

"No." January rubbed his short-cropped hair to shake some of the rainwater out of it. "Though I was on my way to see you. Which brings me to the favor," he went on, "that I wanted to ask of you."

The Bank of Louisiana stood on Rue Royale, a massive structure of Doric pillars and imposing facade set back from the street, within a few steps of the Merchants' Bank, the United States Bank, and the Louisiana

State Bank. Grouchet's, a small eating house that catered to the better-off among the free colored, stood next to the Merchants' Bank across the street. Slightly more expensive than could be afforded by junior clerks at any of the banks, at a quarter to one on a Saturday afternoon it was not crowded. From its front windows, January had a splendid view of the front doors of the Bank of Louisiana and of Hannibal Sefton, loitering before the windows of The Sign of the Magnolia pretending to admire boots.

Hubert Granville emerged from the bank's bronze doors. His corpulent bulk was surprisingly natty in a coat of snuff brown superfine, his red-blond hair carefully pomaded and combed. He extended a thick hand from beneath the shelter of the porch and, finding that the rain had ceased, stepped out, but did not don his hat, for a woman followed immediately behind him. She would have been tall even without the pattens that protected her shoes from the mud, and though January couldn't see her face clearly at the distance, she carried herself like a woman of beauty. Her gown of black mourning crêpe showed off a ripe, matronly figure; her tignon matched the dress in hue and trimmings and even at that distance seemed to him one of the most elaborately decorated he'd ever seen on a woman of color.

No veil. Full crêpe, no veil usually meant a child or a parent recently deceased, not a husband—no widow in her senses would swelter in the crêpe of first mourning past the moment when she could dispense with veils. . . .

The woman glanced back at the bank, asking a question. Whatever Granville replied, it was reassuring. The banker held out his arm, the woman took it, and together they proceeded down Rue Royale in the direction of the Magasin de Commerce.

Shortly thereafter, as the Cathedral clock sounded one, the clerks of the bank emerged. Young men with flourishing side-whiskers and elderly gentlemen in steel-rimmed spectacles, dressed—as January had taken care to dress upon his return from the Swamp—in the tailed coats, embroidered waistcoats, and high-crowned chimney-pot hats that were as wildly inappropriate for New Orleans in the summertime as crêpe mourning. January counted them off with his eye: several white men of assorted ages, a free colored far too dark to share parents with the fair-skinned Isaak Jumon, a much-lighter-skinned man of thirty at least. . . .

And there he was. The youngest clerk, looking every day of seventeen and every Caucasian atom of a quadroon, arrayed in a nip-waisted black frock coat of the boldest cut and three black silk waistcoats, one over the other, jet buttons gleaming at a hundred feet away. . . .

And there was Hannibal, strolling over to him, casual and polite, coat brushed, long hair braided in an old-fashioned queue, and new gloves of black kid on his hands. January could see when the fiddler handed Antoine the card of one Quentin Rafferty—Hannibal had a collection of cards, neatly separated into those that specified an occupation and those that did not—and the most recent copy of the *New York Herald* he'd had in his attic, pointing out two or three articles he claimed to have written under various pseudonyms. And he could see, by the boy's tilted head and the angle of his shoulders, that Antoine Jumon was buying every ounce of that particular load of goods.

Hannibal could be astonishingly convincing when he tried.

". . . wouldn't be printed in New Orleans, so there's no worry about that," the fiddler was saying a few moments later, as he and Antoine Jumon entered Grouchet's. "In fact it's standard policy for our paper to change all the names of a story of this kind. It's the story itself that's the thing, my friend, the . . . the piquancy, the *bizarrerie* that characterizes the streets of any city, that particularly Gothic strangeness that makes true human experience so much more curious than the borrowed effusions of mere art. Don't you agree?"

"It's true," said Antoine earnestly. January had moved his seat from the window to a table farther in and so had to admire the adroit way in which Hannibal steered the boy to a chair from which January could watch his face while he spoke. "You know, I've often thought that true experience, seen through a mind attuned and sensitized, is far more satisfying than anything one could read or see. But I never thought"— he turned his face away a little, his brow suddenly twisting in grief— "my brother . . ."

"Tell me about it," urged Hannibal, and nudged the boy's crêpe-scarved top hat—which Antoine had set on the table, where it blocked the view of his restless hands—out of January's line of sight.

Antoine had been reading in his own room—a garçonnière above the household offices—at his mother's house on Rue des Ramparts, on the night of Monday, the twenty-third of June. It was very late, and raining heavily, when he heard knocking on his door. "There was a woman there, sir, a woman of color, masked and wearing a hooded cloak. She asked me if my name was Antoine Jumon, and I said yes; she asked if I had a brother named Isaak, and I said yes. She asked, where was my mother? I said I didn't know. I thought she must be in the house asleep. The woman said, 'If you love your brother, come with me. Hurry, there is no time to lose.' "

"Did she speak French or English?" asked Hannibal, and the boy looked up, surprised.

"French, of course." It didn't seem to occur to him to wonder why the purported Mr. Rafferty, of a New York newspaper, would have been carrying on the entire conversation in French.

Antoine had gone into the main house, but his mother was not in her bed. His guide would not be stayed, however, and urged him into a fiacre waiting in the street. "I did not see the coachman's face, M'sieu, because of the rain. We drove—hours it seemed—in the darkness, before she ordered the coach to halt and led me out. I had only confused impressions of a great, dark house looming over us with a single candle burning in one upper window, watching us like some malignant eye. She took me through a dark antechamber, to a small, bare room where my brother lay dying on a rude mattress laid on the floor beside the fire."

"Did you know he was dying?" asked Hannibal gently, looking up from the notebook in which he was jotting. The boy's mouth trembled with distress.

"His face—ah, God! He was in terrible pain, white and ghastly; he vomited and . . . and could not contain his bowels, though the servant woman there had cleaned him, and there was not much more in him to void. He—he said, *I have been poisoned, Antoine,* in a terrible voice, as if his throat were scraped and raw."

His eyes squeezed shut, and his black-gloved hands began to shake in earnest.

"Please excuse me," muttered Antoine after a moment. "I—I am not well. My constitution is weak. . . ."

"Perhaps this will help a little?" Hannibal held out to him the square black bottle from his pocket. "I am myself not of strong constitution."

Antoine's eye fell on the bottle, and January could see that the boy recognized the shape of it at once: Kendal Black Drop, triple-strength tincture of the best Turkish opium, brewed by a Quaker family named Braithwaite at eleven shillings the bottle. And he could see the grateful, gentle light in Antoine Jumon's eyes. "Thank you," said the boy. "Thank you very much, sir."

And took a slug that would have felled a horse.

"There isn't that much more to tell," said Antoine, after a moment. "I was—I was much affected, so much so that I could barely speak. I clung to my brother's hand and wept. He tried to speak to me, tried to tell me something, over and over, I don't know how long I was there. Time seemed to stand still, to stretch and to shrink. There was a fire in the grate; sometimes all that I could hear was the rain, and the hissing of the coals, and all I could do was stare at the goldwork patterns in the red velvet of the pillow beneath my brother's head, and the way the firelight made jewels of the sweat on his brow. The woman servant there brought me water in a pitcher of fantastic make, like a—like a lettuce, with serpents and insects peering and slipping among the dark leaves. Evil! Horrible! I poured the water out when she turned away. My brother whispered again, *I have been poisoned.* Then he said, *Mother,* and *Tell her,* and *Célie. . . .* Célie was my brother's wife, M'sieu, married only a month. And then—and then he died."

He looked aside again, covering his mouth with his hand. Hannibal signaled the young woman in the kitchen door to bring them coffee, and waited while Antoine took a sip.

"I'm sorry," said Antoine after a moment, and drew a deep breath. "Isaak fell limp in my arms, M'sieu. After a little time the woman servant helped me to my feet, led me from the room. I—I was led out, led by the hand into a—a waiting fiacre. . . . It was still pouring rain, M'sieu, and the carriage—the carriage stopped, I knew not where, and the coachman bade me get down. After that I wandered long, long through the rain, hours it seemed; turning corners here and there among dark houses and still darker stands of trees. At long last I saw lights before me, and made my way to them. They were the riding lights on the masts of ships in the river, and so at length I was able to find my way home. It was dawn, and my mother was awake and waiting for me. And I told her that my brother was dead."

To which Geneviève doubtless responded, thought January dourly, with a discreetly stifled whoop of joy.

"But this is shocking." Hannibal added a dollop of opium to the boy's coffee. "Astonishing! Do you—forgive me for asking—do you have any idea who might have poisoned him? Had he enemies?"

Antoine's voice sank to a whisper. "He was surrounded by them." January had to strain to hear. "Our grandmother—you understand, M'sieu," he added self-consciously, "that my brother and I are—I am, he was, M'sieu—men of color, but our father was a wealthy white man of this city. He left my brother considerable property, but owing to . . . owing to a *division* in the family, nothing was left to my mother or me. But *his* mother, M'sieu, our father's mother—she is a terrible woman! She tried to have my brother's inheritance taken away from him before he got it. Yes, and also tried to take that which my father left to his estranged wife, Noëmie, who lives in Paris—Noëmie who hated this country, hated my brother and my mother and me! And the father of the woman that my brother married, he, too, hated my brother. He would have liked to see his daughter a widow, and himself in control of the property she would inherit. And my uncle, my father's brother . . ."

Sudden, ugly rage flashed across the boy's gentle eyes.

Very softly, Antoine said, "My uncle Mathurin is a consummately evil man, M'sieu. My brother—would not see it. Isaak was—very good, my brother. He forgave, even those who had no business being forgiven. Because Mathurin showed him kindness, he thought that he was kind, and I assure you, M'sieu, that this is not the case. My uncle is a powerful man in this city, M'sieu. He has powerful friends. If my brother died, eventually the property would have gone to him. Had I to name one who would have harmed my brother, M'sieu, I would say that it was he."

"Antoine."

The boy whirled, face flooding with guilt. Framed in the doorway of Grouchet's stood the mourning woman January had seen leaving the bank with Hubert Granville. At closer range he saw that she had, indeed, been a beauty once. *Even if*—his mind leapt to the realization as Antoine rose to his feet and stammered, "Mama"—*even if she'd started out life as one of Antoine Allard's cane hands.*

January had seen the look in her eyes a thousand times before, at the Hôtel-Dieu, at the Charity Hospital—the look as she turned her son's face to the light of the windows, and warily studied his eyes. She did not even try, as the wives of drunks and addicts so frequently do, to pretend she was doing something else. January wondered if Kentucky Williams and the Perdido Street harpies had watered Hannibal's Black Drop to a degree that it wouldn't contract the pupils of Antoine's eyes.

"I was concerned when you didn't come home," said Geneviève Jumon, with false and steady cheerfulness. "You know that I don't like you wandering about the town without letting me know where you'll be." She glanced past her son at Hannibal, who had tucked pad, pencil, and opium bottle out of sight.

"Mama, this is M'sieu Rafferty, of New York," said Antoine quickly, and just as quickly, Hannibal very slightly shook his head. "He is the—the owner of an art gallery in that city. I sent him some of my sketches and paintings, and he was kind enough to look for me when he came to New Orleans."

"And very beautiful they are, M'am." Hannibal rose to his feet and bowed gracefully over Madame Jumon's hand. "Your son has a great deal of talent. Unformed, of course, and undirected, but technique is easy to acquire when the heart, the fire, is there. . . ."

January folded up his newspaper and casually strolled from the café.

"What did you think?" he asked ten minutes later, when Hannibal joined him at the coffee stand in the market arcade where he'd supped with Rose last night.

"You mean other than the fact that our boy is obviously an addict and was just as obviously taking advantage of Mama's absence on the night in question by dosing himself to the verge of insensibility with Smyrna nepenthe? St. John's Eve is just about the shortest night of the year. If he'd driven 'hours' to this mysterious house and wandered around for 'hours' afterward—not to speak of the 'hours' spent staring at snakes in the water pitcher—it would have been noon by the time he got home."

"There is that," agreed January, who signaled one of the pralinnères with a gesture of his finger. Hannibal paid for both pralines—a brown and a white—and handed the remainder of the money back to January. Coffee and soup at Grouchet's, though not overwhelmingly costly, had cut deeply into January's slender resources, and there was still his mother to pay for room and board. "Did you notice that it was a woman servant who brought him there, and a woman who attended

Isaak—the same woman, maybe? Even at that hour of the night it wouldn't be impossible to hire a hack."

"A pity Mama put in an appearance before we could get a description out of him." Hannibal checked his notes. "I observe that in addition to Célie's name Isaak also mentioned their mother's—interesting, given the reason he was in hiding in the first place. And Mama, of course, was absent from home that night."

"And evidently hadn't told Antoine where she was going, or when she'd be back," mused January. "Curious. Though if she was behind it and didn't want to be placed on the scene of the death itself, I don't imagine she'll be difficult to trace. In fact, she'll be cudgeling her brain for some way to mention casually the thirty-seven people who saw her in the hours before her son's death."

"Did they?"

"I don't know," said January. "I can only assume she did to Shaw, since he made no attempt to arrest her as well. But I'm certainly going to find out."

Saturday, 28 June

M. Mathurin Jumon
Rue St. Louis
New Orleans

Dear M. Jumon:

In my investigation of the horrible accusation that has been leveled against Madame Célie Jumon, your name was mentioned as a possible source of information about your nephew Isaak Jumon, of whom, I have been told, you were quite fond. I understand that you have probably already spoken to Madame Jumon's attorney, a M. Vilhardouin, but it is my understanding that M. Vilhardouin is carrying on his investigation only insofar as concerns Madame Jumon and not the woman who is accused along with her, a Madame Corbier. By investigating on behalf of both, I hope to gain a clearer insight into the circumstances of your nephew's death.

Might I trouble you for an hour of your time, at your convenience, in order that I may learn further particulars about your nephew that might point out some direction for further investigation? Please let me know a time and venue most convenient for a meeting. Many thanks for your help and consideration in this matter.

Your obedient servant,
Benjamin January, fmc.

SEVEN

At the subscription ball for the St. Margaret Society, held that night in the Théâtre d'Orléans, January took the opportunity to more closely observe Mathurin Jumon, that *consummately evil man.* He saw, as he had seen Thursday night at the Pritchards' party, only a tall, powerfully built man of an age only a few years greater than his own, whose dark-browed handsomeness blended with the black of his well-cut mourning attire, assiduous in attendance on his brilliant mother. Madame Cordelia Jumon appeared to have come to the ball sheerly in order to be congratulated by all her acquaintances for garnering the strength to do so: she spent most of it seated in one of the Théâtre's stage boxes, sipping the negus and punch her son brought to her and dissecting a piece of plum cake into smaller and smaller pieces without ever actually eating any. Since the musicians' dais stood on the stage, ensconced in imitation archways from last spring's performance of *Barbarossa,* January was able to hear a good deal of what was said by the assorted ladies who ascended to participate in Madame Cordelia's little court, at least between dances when his concentration wasn't divided between the beauty of the music and the pain in his shoulders.

"Dearest, are you sure you're well enough?" That was Elaine Destrehan, one of the most prominent of the Creole matrons.

"Nonsense, child, of course I am." A martyred smile and a discreet cough. "I'm as strong as a horse." A beautifully calculated gesture that implied imminent collapse, the Théâtre's gaslights glimmering on the two-inch band of diamonds and pearls worn over the glove of sable kid. Most women came out of mourning for their children in three months, but Madame Jumon had merely exchanged crêpe and bombazine for black silk, which formed an admirable backdrop to the diamonds she wore. "My dear Mathurin looks after me so well."

Her dear Mathurin, January noticed, did not, as so many of the men present did, disappear into the lobby and thence through the discreetly curtained passage that led to the Salle d'Orléans next door, where a Blue Ribbon Ball was in full swing. The wives of January's fellow musicians in Paris, or of the artists who'd lived in the same building on the Rue de l'Aube—scarcely missish women—had not been able to credit it when he'd told them of the Blue Ribbon Balls: not that the free colored demimonde would have such entertainments, but that they were so frequently held within a hundred feet of the respectable subscription balls. "And they countenance that?" his own wife, Ayasha, had asked incredulously. "That the mistresses of their husbands and brothers—and fathers, ya-Allah!—will be dancing in . . . What? Another room?"

"It's actually the building next door," said January, a little apologetically. "But the same man owns both buildings, and they're connected by a passageway. It's the custom of the country."

"It is my belief that the men in your country all need a good lesson," Ayasha had replied. At the memory of that hook-nosed brown face, that sable ocean of hair braided and pinned in halfhearted imitation of a white woman's weaker tresses, January's heart still constricted in his breast. She had added, with a malicious glance sidelong, "And the women, too."

He brought his mind back from the memory, as he had perforce learned to do. The music helped, the bittersweet solace of a Mozart waltz: yearning, parting, sentimental regret, layered like a *soupe anglaise*. His back and shoulders ached like fire, and his heart hurt, cut to ribbons by the knife of time. But the music lifted to its next quick movement, as if it sighed, shrugged, picked up its beribboned petticoats, and said, *Life goes on.*

And life did go on.

"Such a shame," said Mrs. Pritchard, when Mr. Greenaway brought her punch, "that poor Emily Redfern couldn't attend, after all the work she's done for the society. . . ."

"And the fortune she handed over," added her husband grudgingly. "Hard cash, too. She must be the only person in town these days with cash money at hand, and she has to hand it over to some charity. . . ." He was already in retreat toward the lobby doors.

"She feels it very much," sympathized little Mrs. Granville, pretending not to see the men's departure. "Hubert and I dined with her this evening, and with that nice Mr. Vilhardouin"—she got the pronunciation more or less right, and Greenaway stalled in his tracks like Balaam's ass—"such a kind gentleman, and so careful of Emily's comfort, only he is a Catholic, of course. I wonder what can be keeping him?"

Greenaway resisted Pritchard's impatient gesture, shook his head—after that January saw him look around every time a newcomer entered the planked-over parterre of the theater. When Clément Vilhardouin finally did make an appearance ("*So* sweet of you to have stayed to keep poor Emily company!" effused Mrs. Pritchard. "I know it must have bored you *terribly* to miss the ball!"), Greenaway stalked over to the attorney with the obvious intention of learning exactly what had passed.

January hid a grin and wondered if he could get a note to Hannibal, playing for the Blue Ribbon Ball at the other end of the notorious passageway, laying odds on a Vilhardouin–Greenaway duel before the end of the night.

Most of the women in the room, however, were left *bredouillées* by their escorts, making a tapestry along the walls while the men appeared and disappeared into lobby, passageway, and Salle. Hubert Granville was especially prone to this sort of intermittence, though when present he was attentive to the point of uxoriousness to his stout little wife. "No, I'm steering clear of investments in banks for now," January overheard him say to Colonel Pritchard, while they waited for their respective ladies to return from Madame Jumon's box. "At least till after next month's elections." The music intervened, a lively mazurka, and January caught only the tail end of his account, ". . . thought I'd be able to put in a lot more, but it may not work out that way."

"Stick with niggers," advised Pritchard, and spit tobacco in the sandbox concealed behind the potted palms. "I sold that boy Dan of mine, the runty one. Stole every damn thing that wasn't nailed down—

Well, I couldn't prove it, of course, but it threw a scare into the others, you bet! Fetched nine hundred dollars from a feller taking a coffle up to the Territories. . . ."

"Do you imply, sir, that the climate of this city is unhealthy?" roared a voice from the parterre. Granville, Pritchard, and Judge Canonge—one of the few justices in the city who had not already decamped for the summer—sprang down to separate Councilman Bouille from Dr. Ker. "There is no yellow fever in this city and there never has been! I will have my friends call on you, sir!"

January shook his head. Had it been only that morning that he and Paul had spoken to Olympe? That afternoon he had received a note from Ker, asking if he would be able to volunteer his time at the hospital to assist with the fever cases that had already begun to come in. Many of the wealthier inhabitants of the town had either already left for summer cottages along the lake, in Milneburgh or Mandeville or Spanish Fort, or for the North; those who remained spoke of nothing but their plans to depart in the near future. The faces of the two men, dead in the back room of the jail, had haunted his dreams last night, and he thought of Olympe tonight in her sweltering cell, the voices of the whores and the madwomen dinning in her ears.

He could tell when the Blue Ribbon Ball ended, around two-thirty: there was a sudden flood of men back into the ballroom, and Monsieur Davis, owner of both the Salle and the Théâtre, emerged from between the Gothic stage flats to ask if extra dances could be added to the program when the agreed-upon twenty-one were finished. The violinist Cochon Gardinier, overflowing his tiny gilt chair, glanced at January, at the Valada brothers on flute and cornet, at Alcibiade Gargotier on the viol. January shifted his shoulders, which felt as if red-hot wedges had been hammered under them, and thought about the penniless months ahead. "Sounds fair to me."

It was only when the dancing was done, and the musicians paid—only when he descended the narrow rear stair in the wake of Cochon and the others—that it came home to January how absolutely deserted now the streets of the French town would be. It had rained again during the dancing, and the streetlamps over the intersections threw glistening patches of yellow on mingled water and mud. The coaches of the last guests were departing, and the little bands of torch-bearing slaves. It was three streets up to Rue Burgundy and several streets over to his mother's house, and somewhere out there in the darkness, thought January, almost certainly, lurked Killdevil Nash.

Heart thumping hard, he reascended the stairs, crossed through the Théâtre, where the last of the establishment's slaves were stripping the tablecloths from the refreshment tables, passed into the empty lobby and through the curtained passageway, where no colored men went save those hired to clean the place. The Salle d'Orléans itself was deserted and silent, the ladies who danced there long since departed to their highly expensive beds.

Logically, thought January, an assassin would be waiting where he could watch the service door of the Théâtre, on Rue St. Anne, and from there follow him up Rue St. Anne to Rue Burgundy. While this was going through his mind he was descending the service stairs of the Salle d'Orléans, following a narrow hallway among the offices to the Salle's downstairs lobby, from which doors opened into the gambling rooms that fronted onto Rue d'Orléans. At this time of the morning—it was nearly four—they were still surprisingly active, though the men there, steamboat pilots and sugar buyers and one or two of the more nearly situated planters, had for the most part taken off their coats and settled into hard play. Little stacks of gold double-eagles, of silver cartwheels, of English and German and Spanish coins, glittered on the baize cloths under the gaslight: deeds to plantation land, papers for credit and slaves. Dealers laid the spreads of cards, red and black and gold—poker, faro, *vingt-et-un,* long and short whist. The air stank of tobacco, the blue haze of its smoke and the faint sweet squishiness where it smeared the floor underfoot stank of liquor, of hair oil, of men's sweat.

On the way through the lobby he took a waiter's towel from the back of a chair and laid it over his arm, removed his hat, and shifted his grip on his music satchel, carrying it reverently in one hand and his hat in his other. Then he entered the gambling rooms, looking inquiringly to the right and the left as if seeking someone: "Are you Michie Preobazhensky, sir?" he asked one man, and then another. "Michie Preobazhensky?" Still with the air of one dutifully seeking the owner of the bag and the hat he stepped out onto the Rue d'Orléans banquette, and in this persona walked along it for a little distance.

He looked around him. The street was deserted, though farther down Rue Bourbon he could see lamplight and gaslight from at least two other gambling establishments and hear music from one of them.

He felt a pang of pity for whoever of his colleagues that was, playing still at this hour. *I hope they're getting paid decent.*

He put his hat back on, took his satchel by the handle again, and like the Three Wise Kings of the Bible, went home by another way. No one molested him en route. The sheets of his bed had been changed and by the light of his candle he saw that the pillow had been opened, probably searched by Bella for ouanga balls, and sewed back.

It still made him uneasy to lie in the bed, remembering the cross on the threshold last night—it seemed years ago—and the severed chicken foot, not to mention Killdevil Nash's cold eyes. He did not sleep well, and when he did, his dreams were dreams of fear.

It had been a long and exhausting day.

Mist still drifted on the sunless river when January emerged next morning into the Place d'Armes and made his way along the stuccoed colonnade of the Cabildo to the Cathedral's doors. His head buzzed and his eyes ached from little sleep, but the scent of incense was calming. A few Ursuline nuns knelt in vigil close to the altar; otherwise, the occupants of the church consisted mostly of shopkeepers' wives, of servants in their soberest headscarves. The wealthier of the town—white, black, and colored, including January's mother—would attend the more fashionable Masses later. January wondered where the blond woman with the golden-haired child was now, and what it was she'd had from the voodoo-man.

He slipped his rosary from his pocket, rested his forearms on the back of the pew ahead of him to take the weight from his aching shoulders, and fingered the blue glass beads. In his dreams last night he had found the chicken foot on his bed again, but when he'd tried to pick it up it had turned to a rotted thing, like decomposed meat, in his hand. On the wall over the head of his bed, where in the waking world a crucifix hung, he'd seen nailed the dried snake that was tacked to the wall in Olympe's parlor, a rolled-up slip of paper in its mouth; he had known that that paper bore his name. At the shutters he'd heard the dead white thing from the *cipriere* pat and rattle the hinges and the latch, whispering to be let in.

"Do you remember the First Commandment?" asked the priest softly, when January confessed to the sin of doubt. By his voice January knew it was Père Eugenius, a young Spaniard new to the parish, to whom he always confessed if he could. "*Thou shalt have no other gods before me.* You felt fear, you said. . . . Of course you felt fear, for you were taught to fear these things as a child. God understands what fear is. When a gun goes off near your head, you duck—of course, you duck. But a soldier then gets back up and goes on doing his duty.

"Satan will use your fear, my son. He'll use it to get you to do things that look harmless—and they may be harmless. But then he'll ask you to do similar things, things that look the same, that are evil, and against the will of God. When you put your faith in something other than God, you damage your faith. Light a candle for yourself and pray to have your faith made stronger, that you may trust in the armor of God."

After hearing Mass and taking Communion, January lit a candle, not only for himself but for Olympe as well. Coming out of the Cathedral he thought he saw Mamzelle Marie, kneeling before the statue of the Virgin, telling over the beads of her rosary, the halo of votive lights outlining the seven points of her tignon with gold.

When January reached home his mother looked up from her *pain perdu* and coffee and said, "Remember that your month's money is due Tuesday, Benjamin. These came for you." She held out to him two folded sheets of paper, the grimier of them simply creased into quarters, the other sealed the old way with three neat chunks of crimson wax and addressed to "Benjamin January, fmc."

Unfolding it, he read,

Mr. Janvier,

It cheers me considerably to realize there are still men in the world who understand that more information widens the possibility of arriving at a correct conclusion, despite whatever distaste they may feel for some of that information, or some of the people who may impart it. Please consider my time at your disposal this afternoon between luncheon and dinner. I very much look forward to the opportunity to do whatever I can to assist my poor nephew's widow, and your unfortunate sister, in clearing their characters and freeing themselves from this appalling difficulty.

Most sincerely,
Mathurin Jumon

The other was scrawled in Shaw's erratic hand.

~~Myst~~
~~Maistr~~
Mr. January——
We found a body.

"Nasty varmints, crawdads." Abishag Shaw spit tobacco onto the floor of the smaller of Charity Hospital's two surgical theaters, and produced a brass knuckle-duster from the pocket of his coat to prop open a copy of Orfila's *Treatise on Poisons* on a lectern dragged in from a classroom next door. "Had one for supper t'other night musta been five inches long."

"Do you think Madame Geneviève will be *able* to identify him?" January tied a vinegar-soaked rag around his mouth and nose, and blinked a little in the fumes of it as he considered the bloated, ghastly thing that Shaw's men had fished up out of Bayou Sauvage early that morning.

"I ain't got the smallest doubt she will, and give us a good three-hanky weep for our trouble. Iff'n she don't bury someone she won't have no claim on the money, now, will she?" Shaw blew his entire chew into the sandbox and pulled up the rag that had been around his own neck—the corpse had been in the water five or six days. "You familiar with this German feller's test for arsenic?"

"I've heard of it." January checked off with his eye the apparatus spread over the theater's smaller table: carboys of acid and distilled water, a small alembic, and assorted other paraphernalia essential to the production of sulfuretted hydrogen gas. A brazier of coals contributed its heat to the already suffocating ambience of the room. Rose, he reflected, would be fascinated, as she was by anything chemical. "It sounds perfectly straightforward."

He picked up a scalpel and advanced on the corpse, already deeply regretting Bella's *pain perdu*.

"You know this isn't going to tell us much," he gasped, as he and Shaw retreated to the window from the rolling surge of gases when the gut was punctured. *Shall I compare thee to a summer's day in the cemetery during the cholera?* . . . "There are vegetable poisons that could have produced almost the same symptoms as arsenic but won't show up on a test. Indian tobacco, or Christmas rose—Mamzelle Marie or any root doctor in town could tell you a dozen."

"Includin' your sister." Above the edge of the dripping rag, Shaw's gray eyes had a lazy sharpness, not surprised, but interested in how much he knew. "And they could tell *you*, Maestro. All I or any of the Guards would get is just *I don't know nuthin' about no poisons*. And I did think of that. But if we do find arsenic in this poor jasper's tripes it might tell us somethin', too. That it?"

"That's it." January laid the detached stomach on the table, and began to slice it into sections, trying hard not to breathe.

"What do we do now?"

January nodded at the vessel of distilled water. "Make soup."

"Frankly," Shaw went on, as they began the tedious process of boiling and filtering, "I don't think our little friend here is any more Isaak Jumon than you are. He seems to been in the bayou the right amount of time—five, six days—but his arms and hands is chewed so bad it's hard to tell iff'n he was a sculptor; hell, it's only his hair tells us for sure he was even a man of color. All he had on was them britches and they could be a wheelwright's or a sculptor's or a fieldhand's. And even allowing for the way a body's muscles stretch when they been soaked that long, I'd say he's too tall. But we'll see what Miz Jumon says."

What Geneviève Jumon said, dropping her reticule and fan and clasping her free hand to her face to join the one already holding a vinegar-soaked rag, was, "Oh, Isaak! Oh, my son!" She stood in the theater's doorway, separated from the table by easily twenty feet of student benches. "Dear God, what has that vile woman done!" Then she swayed, and staggered back into the arms of Hubert Granville.

Shaw, who was in the midst of adjusting a retort to pipe the sulfuretted hydrogen gas through the filtered solution, wiped a hand on his shirt and inquired mildly, "Do you identify this man as your son, Isaak Jumon?"

Antoine, almost concealed behind Granville's green-coated bulk, gulped and retreated into the corridor.

"Yes!" Madame Jumon pressed a hand—carefully, as her black kid glove was now soaked with vinegar—to her forehead, leaving a long nigrous smear. "Oh, God, my son!"

"You're sure?" Shaw left the solution to bubble odoriferously and picked his way toward them. "You might want to come a little closer for a better squint. . . ."

"You leave her alone!" gasped Granville, as Madame Jumon shrank from the policeman's sticky grasp.

"I would know my son anywhere, M'sieu," she retorted in a strangled voice. "There is no need to go closer."

January, who had been measuring every limb and surface of the corpse and making notes, slipped past them into the corridor; with his face covered, in his rough trousers and calico shirt, they gave him barely a glance. Assuming him, probably, to be one of the hospital servants.

Granville, he thought. Granville offering Madame Jumon his arm, to escort her up Rue Royale. Granville's address on the advertisement . . .

Granville saying something at the St. Margaret Society Ball about trying to raise money . . .

Antoine was seated, trembling, on a bench in the hall. On a Sunday morning this part of the building was relatively deserted, save for a couple of orderlies ominously making up one of the classrooms into an emergency ward. Light through an open doorway, and from the window at the end of the hall, twinkled on the boy's cut-jet coat buttons and shone dimly through the long scarf of mourning crêpe hanging from the back of his high-crowned hat.

He was weeping.

January sat beside him, very quietly, kneading some of the tension from those thin shoulders. "It's all right, son," he said. "It's all right. No, keep your head down a spell, till you feel better." He spoke in the roughest bastard Creole that he could, the language of the slaves, and didn't lower the rag mask from his face. In any case Antoine didn't look up.

Behind them in the operating theater he could dimly hear the run of Shaw's voice, and Geneviève Jumon's—"Yes, of course, he had a signet ring, gold, given him by his father when he turned seventeen. . . ."

And worthless as an identifying mark, reflected January. If the ring hadn't slipped off after prolonged immersion it could be said to have been taken off before the body went into the water.

"It sure good of Michie Granville to look after your mama that way," he said to Antoine after a time. "Must be a terrible shock for her."

Antoine sighed, and January saw again the look in Madame Geneviève's scornful, suspicious eyes. "I'm sorry," whispered the boy wretchedly. "Yes, I'm glad he's there for her. I wish I could . . ." His voice trailed off, and the small black-gloved hands trembled.

"He a family friend I guess?"

"He looks after Mama's investments." There was a wistful note in Antoine's voice. "He's clever with investments."

And at seventeen, thought January, Antoine Jumon knew already that he would never be anything but what he was: clerk, failed artist, addict. Forever a disappointment to the mother who regarded him with such contempt. He wondered suddenly if that was what had set Hannibal's feet on the road that had brought him up penniless in New Orleans, alone and ill, an Oxford-educated opium addict with a hundred-guinea violin: the desire not to have those who expected better of him see him as he knew he was.

"Antoine." Madame Geneviève was standing in the theater door.

Antoine got quickly to his feet and staggered. January caught his elbow without rising—the stab of pain through his back as he raised his arm above shoulder level was like being knifed, but he didn't dare let her notice his height. The mask still covered his face and the hall was dim; he said, "He still a li'l woozy, M'am. I'd a gone put cold water on the back of his neck but I di'n't want to leave him."

"Thank you." She made her face smile like a woman operating a puppet made from a folded napkin, and at once turned her attention to trying to see, in the gloom, if the pupils of her son's eyes looked as they should.

"Antoine, I expect you to be of support to your mother through the funeral." Hubert Granville emerged from the theater behind her, and January remained seated as the three of them walked away along the corridor, silhouetted against the wan glare from the doorways along the route: the man's heavy square solidity, the rich curves of the woman, and the boy trailing behind, weedy and defeated in his tight-waisted coat and extravagant, veiled hat.

Redolent of old blood, tobacco, vinegar, rotten eggs, and sweat, Lieutenant Shaw stepped into the hall to watch them go.

"You didn't happen to ask," inquired January softly, "where Madame Geneviève was the night her son died, did you?"

"Matter of fact, Maestro, I did." Shaw pulled down his rag mask and began to fish through his pockets for his twist of tobacco. His brownish hair dripped with sweat. "And I wrote the Sûreté in Paris askin' if this Noëmie Jumon was still where she was when she wrote tryin' to get her share of her husband's will, not that *that* did her a lick of good. And I been checkin' the passenger lists of ships from France, on the just-in-case. But M'am Geneviève was at a tea squall with her pal that night: a woman name of Bernadette Metoyer, who runs a chocolate shop in the Place d'Armes."

And who at one time—January knew from his mother—had been Hubert Granville's mistress.

EIGHT

"I was horrified to learn of Isaak's death." Mathurin Jumon's harsh, handsome face bore the marks of dissipation; puffiness under the eyes that spoke of late nights and bad sleep; the fine-broken veins that char- acterized a drinker's nose; and a pallid, unhealthy complexion. The blue-gray eyes were bright and intelligent in their discolored and wrin- kled lids, and the late-afternoon light made January slightly embarrassed by his too-ready subscription to Antoine's suspicion of his uncle.

Just as well, he thought, folding his hands before him and lowering his eyes respectfully to the woven straw mats of the office floor, *that Creoles as a rule didn't offer visitors of color any kind of refreshment. Hesitation about taking it would look bad. A polite request to test the hypothetical lemonade on the nearest stray dog would look worse.*

The Rose and Metzger tests on the stomach of Shaw's victim had yielded no sign of arsenic. Not enough, January knew, to clear Olympe of administering poison of some kind—*I have been poisoned,* Isaak had said, dying. Not, *I have been dosed with arsenic.* And it could, of course, always be argued that the body wasn't even Isaak's, though January looked forward with morbid amusement to Geneviève Jumon's efforts to have it both ways in court.

But it was something. A first-rate lawyer could possibly use it to confuse the jury enough to get both women off. If, thought January, Olympe were not a voodoo. If the jury were educated enough to understand the distinction—which at this time of the year was a dangerous assumption to trust. And January shuddered at the thought of having no better weapon than obfuscation to defend his sister's life.

Isaak Jumon was dead. Célie Jumon had bought something from Olympe, poisoner and voodooienne.

That might be all the jury would hear.

"When they told me he had been poisoned, and that Célie of all people was accused . . ."

"Who told you this?" asked January.

"The police, initially." Jumon settled himself behind his desk in the office that opened off the courtyard of the family town house. It was a large room, flagged with granite that had come over as ballast from France, the whitewashed walls undecorated save for a portrait of a fair-haired girl clothed in the extravagancies of French court dress some fifty-five years ago.

When the butler had shown January in, Mathurin had been counting money. It ranged in neat stacks along the edge of his desk. Mexican silver, mostly, piled tidily; half a dozen Dutch rix-dollars; four gold sovereigns and six gold half-sovereigns, plus an assortment of American eagles, half-eagles, and notes. Creole families, January knew, held property in the name of the family; it was only when Cordelia Jumon saw clearly that neither Laurence nor Mathurin would produce an heir that she had sold off the lands and divided some of the money between her sons to invest. January wondered whether this was Mathurin's money, or his mother's.

"A vile species of Kentucky buffoon who looked like he came down the river in a load of turnips, but he seemed to know his business. Please sit down, Monsieur Janvier, please sit down." Jumon gestured to the divan that stood at right angles to the desk of plain-wrought dark cypress wood, facing two long windows into a spacious courtyard thick with banana shrubs and roses. Beyond a screen of greenery, the kitchen could be glimpsed, and the tall, slant-roofed quarters of the slaves. The air was laden with scent, butter and onions and roasting squabs mingling with roses and sweet olive on the heat-clotted afternoon air.

"This Kaintuck officer came to me Wednesday and asked if I had a nephew Isaak," continued Jumon. "When had I last seen him, were our relations such that Isaak would have come to me in trouble? Then he said that he had received a report—which later turned out to be from Isaak's mother, who as you probably know is a common hatmaker—that Isaak was dead. I suppose the police have told you the contents of this report?"

"Only that Isaak's brother was brought to a house he did not recognize, to be with his brother when he died."

"That's what they told me, yes." Jumon hesitated, trying to pick his words with care. "Now, Antoine was always . . always a very *fanciful* little boy. Not always truthful, I'm afraid, and inclined to exaggerate when he thought he could win either admiration or sympathy, especially sympathy. At least he was so as a child. I haven't spoken to him in close to thirteen years. He may have changed." He sat looking down at his hands: big, muscular hands, despite their smoothness, square and coarse and heavy. "But then, people rarely do change, do they? Fundamental change is . . . can be much more difficult than one thinks."

He fell silent.

"Do you think he lied?"

Jumon startled. For an instant January had the impression the man was going to snap, *Of course he lied. . . .* And what he was thinking of was not Isaak's death.

Instead he sighed. "I don't know." As he passed his hand over his face January smelled the cognac on his breath. He was dressed neatly, in the tailored wool coat and high stock of a gentleman that January considered such a horrifying absurdity in a tropical climate, in spite of the fact that he was clad so himself at the moment: he'd taken great care, on his return from the hospital, to bathe and dress in a fashion that said, *I am a free man of color. I have nothing to do with those people who clean out your lamp chimneys and chamber pots, those people whom you can buy and sell.* "In a way it hardly matters. What matters is that the police believe him—and his mother—and are prepared to hang two women on the strength of it."

A servant woman appeared in the courtyard doors, middle-aged, once pretty, with the figure of a slightly overweight Juno and a kindly face. "Michie Mathurin, sir . . . Oh, I'm terribly sorry, I didn't see you've a visitor."

She started to back away and Jumon said, "No, Zoë my dear, it's quite all right." He raised his eyebrows at January as he spoke, wordlessly asking if it was in fact all right, something an American wouldn't even have bothered to ask, and January gestured his permission.

"Excuse me, sir." The woman Zoë curtsied to January, then turned back to her master. "And I'm sorry to disturb you, sir, but your mother sent me to ask you, when will you be ready with the carriage to ride out to Milneburgh, to dine with M'am Picard?"

January saw the surprised look that crossed Jumon's face and, a moment later, the glance the white man traded with the servant: mutual understanding, exasperation, resignation to the foibles of one they both knew too well. Zoë shook her head, it's not MY doing, sir, and Jumon made a wry face.

"Thank you for the warning, my dear." He sighed. "And I suppose the answer is, within half an hour."

Zoë tucked away a quick smile, but couldn't keep it out of her eyes. "That's what it most generally is, sir," she said, and curtsied again. "I'll go let Benedict know, and tell Zeus to put up the mirlitons and see what he can save of the squabs." She stepped forward and picked up an old-fashioned drinking-goblet from among the papers on Jumon's desk, brilliant in the office's rather shadowy confines.

January said, in some surprise, "That isn't a Palissy goblet, is it, sir?"

Jumon beamed. "You're familiar with rustic ware?" Taking it from Zoë's hands, he turned the brightly enameled terra-cotta lovingly, cherishing it. "A childish weakness of mine, sir. My mother's always chiding me about dishes that should look like dishes and not like toads and leaves and dead fish. One doesn't see much of it on these shores."

"I don't think I've ever seen any on this side of the Atlantic, sir." Taking the man's undisguised pride for permission, January stepped forward, hands clasped politely behind his back, to study the vessel. It was a beautiful example of outré baroque style, the cup wrought as if of writhing kelp through which seashells and fish emerged. Within, pebbles, shells, crabs, and a little purple sea urchin seemed embedded in sand on the inner surface of the bowl, and at the bottom, through the dregs of the dark amber liquor, a perfectly wrought crawfish raised delicate claws, like St. George's Laidly Worm emerging from its well. Every detail was exquisitely executed, every bladder on the kelp, every scale on the fish and spine on the urchin, even the bubbles clinging to the leaves; sea snail distinct from barnacle, sand dab distinct from sardine.

The black bright eyes of the crawfish seemed to be boring into

January's. He thought of the man at the Charity Hospital, and looked rather quickly away.

"I can't prove it's a Palissy, of course." Jumon sighed. "My business agent tells me it's probably less than a century old, and Italian rather than French. But if it's a fake it's a good one. I shouldn't be drinking from it, of course." He shook his head. "I forget that these things can break. Only the other morning poor Zoë had to bring me the news that she'd found my best serpent pitcher—a genuine Palissy, that was—in pieces on the floor here." He nodded toward the fireplace. "I can only assume it was one of the cats. I'd like to think any of the servants would have let me know if they'd broken it accidentally."

He smiled after Zoë as she bore the goblet away through the jasmine and orange trees. "I suspect she shares my mother's opinion of platters that have half the food on them turn out to be part of the plate, but she's too kind to express it to me." He turned back, shaking his head a little. There was a hard tuck in the corner of his mouth, exasperation or calculation, thought January, or maybe only a momentary wondering about how much of a half-cooked dinner could be salvaged and put to later use, in this heat.

"To return to last week. A few days after the policeman's visit I received a note from Monsieur Gérard, the coffee merchant, whose daughter my nephew had married. A perfectly lovely girl, sweet and sheltered . . ." His smile changed and lightened the whole of his saturnine face.

"I should tell you that in spite of his mother, Isaak was on excellent terms with my brother and myself. That fact brought my brother a great deal of joy over the past five years. I know Laurence planned to attend their wedding, and in spite of my mother's rather—rather unfortunate attitude about his will, Isaak and Célie were of great comfort to me after—after Laurence died."

From the wall, the portrait of the smiling girl gazed down with brilliant gray-blue eyes, and January recognized the bracelets of diamonds and pearls on her wrists as those Madame Cordelia Jumon had worn to the St. Margaret's ball last night. A rapid mental calculation confirmed his thought, that that young lady in pink hoops and a fantasia of blond lace, with tiny models of water mill, miller, miller's donkey, wife, and cuckolding lover embedded in her high-piled fair hair . . . That was Madame Cordelia, Célie's age, at the Court of France.

Jumon sighed again. "I think that, except for the priest, I was the only white man present when Isaak and Célie were married." Though his movements were perfectly steady, and his speech clear, something in the droop of his left eyelid triggered the thought in January's mind that the man had been drinking, and drinking rather a lot. "And do you know, I felt honored to have been invited? In spite of being obliged to come up with a succession of the most ridiculous subterfuges to attend. My mother had a soiree of some sort that afternoon, and she would never have let me hear the end of it if she knew I'd gone to the wedding. The mere thought that Célie would have done such an abominable thing is—is altogether beyond the belief of anyone who knows her. Anyone who has seen them together . . ."

"According to young Master Antoine," said January carefully, "his brother died in 'a wealthy house,' a big house to which he—that is Antoine—had never been. Might Isaak have been trying to make his way here when he was taken ill?"

As if, he thought, there were two houses in New Orleans—or in Louisiana or the rest of the continent for that matter—that boasted Palissy water pitchers. Disingenuity on Jumon's part? The desk might have been moved, and the small chair in the corner had upholstery of crimson and gold and the look of a piece that needed a cushion, but even befuddled on opium Antoine couldn't have missed the portrait that dominated the room.

"I have thought of that." Jumon's heavy brow darkened with distress. "I will never forgive myself for being away that week. I was only across the lake in Mandeville, seeing to opening our house there—the weather here doesn't suit my mother in the summertime. Doesn't suit anyone, for that matter," he added with a swift, cynical grin. "Isaak must have tried to send me word that he was in trouble. I've made inquiries, but the Duplessises next door have already left town for the summer, and the Viellards on the other side are on their plantation now, of course. And Isaak had a key to the gate. He would have come here, to Zoë. If indeed," he added, "Antoine's testimony is accurate." He shook his head. "Antoine is, as I've said, a fanciful boy."

He looked up quickly as something dark moved in the brightness of the courtyard, and again his whole face transformed with his smile. "Mama!" He got to his feet; January also. "How are you this afternoon? Are you rested from Mass?"

Her voice was cool and flat as February ice in the Paris streets. "I'll manage." From behind a veil of the finest black lace January felt himself touched by the briefest of cold gazes and dismissed. Cordelia Jumon brought a black-bordered white handkerchief to her lips, and coughed.

"Mama, forgive me for my delay here." Uncertainty flawed Jumon's attempt at a good-humored chuckle as he bent over her hand. It was strange, thought January, to see so physically formidable a man with a look in his eye like a jack hare listening for the distant belling of the pack. "Benedict is just now getting the carriage."

"Tell him not to trouble himself." That flat alto held nothing: no warmth, no caring, not even reproach; but the woman's slim erect body was a silent sable curse. "By the time we reach Milneburgh it will scarcely have been worth the journey, and I see that you have other matters to attend to this afternoon."

She coughed again, more heavily, and turned to leave. Jumon caught her arm: she flinched as though he'd struck her. "Oh, Mama, forgive me, I'm so sorry. . . ."

"It's nothing." She massaged the joint, fingers trembling, while her son stood with his big hands hovering uncertainly. She waited for a moment, as if to give him time to explain himself—there was in her stance, and the way she held her head, the echo of Geneviève and Antoine. Reproach at his inebriation, and the unspoken welcome of the weapon his weakness gave her. Then she turned like a dead queen's ghost and moved back toward the stairway that led up to the gallery.

"Mama, please." Jumon strode after her without a backward glance. Well, thought January, one didn't ask pardon or leave of a colored guest, after all. He watched them as Madame Jumon mounted the stair, Jumon's voice drifting back in flat snippets of echo: "Please don't be angry."

"I'm not angry, son."

"You are. I can see you are."

"I only thought—and perhaps this is no longer true, but I can only go on what you have told me—that when you requested me to accompany you to Milneburgh for dinner we should have time enough to enjoy ourselves along the lakeshore."

"Mama, it was you who wanted to dine with the Picards."

January felt a twinge of pity as the voices died away into the loggia, knowing perfectly well that with a woman like Madame Jumon—or his own mother—pointing out that something was her idea and not your own was merely an invitation to frozen silence, followed by an equally glacial agreement and an unspoken, *You know that this is only lip service and so do I. Are you satisfied, my son?*

The only way to win was to walk away.

This, obviously, Jumon didn't do, for he did not return to the office. Somewhere in the house, January thought, the scene was being played out: exhausting, hashed-over, filled with unspoken feelings and unsaid words, like the quarrel of lovers whose love has soured to poison but not yet died. But to leave would be impolite and might well alienate a man whose help he'd need if he was to free Olympe—if the man wasn't the one who'd put her in prison in the first place. The one who'd paid Mambo Oba, and Killdevil Ned. So he remained, standing, for he had not been given permission to sit down again. . . . Appalling, what habit could do.

Only it wasn't habit. There were men who'd thrash a black man for "making himself at home in my office" unbidden.

"Michie Janvier."

The woman Zoë appeared in the doorway, her smile friendly but neutral, carefully distancing herself from anything that had transpired between master and mistress. "Something's come up that calls Michie Mathurin away. He's sorry he won't be able to come back to you for maybe some hours. Can you come again, another day? He'll send you round a note, saying when will be best."

The woman had come from the direction of the kitchen, not the house. January guessed she'd seen Jumon and his mother from the kitchen and had deduced from long experience what was taking place. Her smile, and the easy way she spoke, told of long practice in covering for the man.

Still, there was nothing to say but "Thank you, Mamzelle Zoë," as he donned his high beaver hat. "What do you think of this story about Michie Isaak, Mamzelle?" he asked, as she walked him across the fancy brickwork of the fountained court and through the carriageway, where grooms hitched a pair of matched grays (*Bishopped,* he'd heard his mother say derisively, and indeed the off-wheeler did look considerably older than its partner) to a carriage lacquered cobalt and black. "About his being brought to a big house to die? I know Michie Jumon heard nothing from his neighbors, but sometimes folks hear things that their masters don't."

Her glance ducked away from his. "Oh, no, sir. That is—Michie Isaak came here many a time, with Mamzelle Célie. Not to the house, of course, because of Madame. But Madame was here that night, and all the other servants. Someone would have heard, if he'd tried to come in."

She curtsied deeply, as they stepped through the archway and onto the brick banquette of Rue St. Louis. "I gives you good day, sir." Her smile was friendly and completely unreadable. Then she turned and disappeared into the shadows behind Laurence Jumon's expensive carriage-team, glimpsed once more as a swift flash of red-and-purple tignon in the sunlight of the courtyard beyond, then gone.

NINE

January looked around him at the quiet street. As Jumon had said, half the town houses were shuttered, and the knockers taken down from the doors, the planters long since gone back to their acres, the bankers and brokers fled to cottages and cooler breezes by the lake. Dragonflies darted and whirred above the sparkle of the gutters.

Isaak had a key, thought January. He might not have been strong enough to use it, though. And if he went to the quarters above the kitchen, every servant in the place would hear.

But Isaak had been there. Somehow, somewhere . . .

He took a step or two down the brick banquette and scanned the street again.

Even the shops in the ground floors had a deserted look, as if this were Boston, where they kept the Sabbath like good Protestants thought it should be kept. The only activity, indeed, was on the shop floor of the Jumon house itself. The shop there was old-fashioned, with small square panes of glass in the window like the dark little boutiques he'd seen in Paris, fitted up before the Revolution and before one could obtain large panes of glass. These panes had been painted with letters of red and gold, which a young workman was now patiently scraping away: ——LIOTTE, FINE WINES AND BRANDIES.

January strolled to the shop door, looked past the young man into the large, empty salon. Even the counters had been removed, leaving only bits of sawdust and straw on the floors. A few stray chairs, a table, and a couple of wheelbarrows; old-fashioned chandeliers and sconces; a smell of varnish and soap. Of course, there would be no gas laid on in a building this old. Through a door at the back, a smaller chamber could be glimpsed, and the edge of a brick fireplace. "Excuse me." January addressed the workman in his most Parisian French. "Monsieur Jumon told me that I might have a look at the shop floor."

Virgin Mary don't let him come out right about now.

Given what January knew of his own quarrels with his mother he knew he was probably safe.

"Go right on ahead," said the young man with a grin, pausing in his work. "You with Michie Braeden? Dentist what's movin' in?"

"He's commissioned me, yes. I won't be but a moment."

"She led me through a dark hall, to a smaller chamber, lit with a fireplace. . . ."

The flue would communicate, January guessed, with that in the rear parlor above. Straw mats had been laid down to protect the floors. More were piled in a corner. Easy to obtain a sheet from the laundry, a cushion, and a pitcher from Mathurin's office—too much risk of being heard by the other slaves, to slip into the kitchen. . . . A large cabinet of dark walnut, its baroque multiplicity of tiny drawers and compartments speaking of dentistry rather than wine, had already been moved in. It filled one wall.

The town-house bedrooms would be two floors above. There wasn't even a window looking back into the court. This close to Rue Bourbon it would be easy to find a hack, even at midnight. . . .

January smiled and bestowed a half-reale he couldn't spare on the sign painter, then made his leisurely way across the street to Au Cheval de la Lune, a tiny shop that sold laces, fans, perfumes, and books. "Pardon me," he said, bowing, "but you wouldn't happen to know where"—he fished hastily in his mind for what the wine merchant's sign had said on the hundreds of occasions he'd passed it over the last eighteen months—"M'sieu Guliotte has moved to, would you? I was told he had a small stock of vintage St.-Macaire for sale."

The woman behind the counter replied at once, "M'sieu Guliotte's opening again on Rue Condé, between St. Philippe and Ursulines. But that won't be for another two weeks."

"Good heavens," said January, in a tone of surprise, "when did he move out?"

"Just not even two weeks ago," she answered. "They had the place cleared out within two days, getting it ready for new tenants to move in on the first. A dentist, a nice German gentleman."

January remained a few minutes more, chatting leisurely with the shopkeeper, who like everyone else had little custom this time of year. He saw the blue carriage with its dazzling white team emerge from the gate and trot smartly away up the street, saw servants come out and close the gate behind. Stepping out onto the banquette once more, he studied the tall, pale blue town house, uncommunicative in the flat smoky glare of afternoon. Remembering another respected scion of a Creole family who had kept slaves chained in the attic. The torn and twisted muscles of his shoulders throbbed as he rubbed them, and his gaze followed the thin colonnettes, the dark latticework of the galleries, up to the dormers in the roof, barred windows like half-shut eyes.

Madame Cordelia Jumon was over seventy, consumptive, and frail, for all her lively brilliance. Almost certainly a woman to take to her bed as soon as the dinner candles were snuffed, and to stay there.

And Mathurin Jumon had been in Mandeville the night Isaak Jumon had died.

Thoughtfully, January donned his hat again and walked slowly up Rue St. Louis, toward the growing tap and rattle of the drums that had begun to beat in Congo Square.

A man's voice called out high and free, *"Dansez calinda!"* and the pulse of drums responded, drawing at the marrow of January's bones.

"Higha!" sang out a voice.

"Malagalujassay!"

"Higha!"

"Lajassaychumbo!"

"Higha. . . ."

Men and women clustered the paling fence that surrounded Congo Square, the dusty open space ringed with plane trees, separated from the turning basin by a couple of seedy-looking shacks and from the cemetery wall by only a few muddy streets. Artisans and shopkeepers in their best black or blue coats, new-come from evening Mass at the Chapel of St. Antoine, brushed elbows with Irish shopgirls and chaca laundresses in calico dresses, idlers angling for a look at the dark, half-naked figures swaying and leaping in the Square itself. A few stalls remained of the market that the place had once been, back among the trees: someone was making gumbo at a few pistareens per bowl; a woman sold pralines from a tray, and another, gingerbread, soft and sweet: *estomac mulâtres,* they were called. Gritty smoke caught January across the eyes as he edged his way toward the gate.

> *Oh, yes yes, Mamzelle Marie,*
> *She knows well li Grand Zombi.*
> *Oh, yes yes, Mamzelle Marie,*
> *He come here to make gris-gris. . . .*

And there she was. Head rolling as she danced, body sending off waves of electricity, like the madness in the summer air before the coming of a storm. Dominating them, drawing them, focusing upon herself the crazy leap of the music—*Power.*

And January, watching her, knew it was true. Whatever *Power* was, Marie Laveau had something beyond her web of secrets, something beyond loyalties, love, or fear. *Charisma,* the old Greeks had called it; the god, Plato had said. Whites would have termed it insolence.

Power.

A seven-foot king snake coiled her body, writhed with the writhing of the dance. Smoke from the gumbo pot veiled her in the dapple glare of sun and plane-tree leaves; and she smiled, drinking something from the air of the Square, from the somber joy of the dancers, as they drank in the Power from her.

Close by him January heard someone say, "See there? That's her. Marie Laveau. That's the Voodoo Queen."

The hammer-and-lift of the drumming, the wailing, the dance filled the Square: bone-deep, groin-deep, soul-deep. Pain and memory, loss and hope, weariness and exultation at having survived another day.

"What are they doing, Mama?" asked a child.

"They're dancing, dear. That's how Negroes dance."

Men stripped to bandanna loincloths, bells jangling around their ankles, turning the women under their arms. Graceful movements, serpentine as those of the woman on the boxes, absolutely alien to the waltz or the Lancers or the bright beauty of contredanse. Others danced alone, feet planted, bodies swaying, or stepped gaily, highly, in patterns half-remembered, half-invented, faces intent with relief or release, or beaming with joy. Eerie, wailing, the voices rose and fell like storm wind over the Atlantic, like the far-off jangling of chains.

"Why do they dance like that, Mama?" The little boy was probably thinking about his own experiences with stern-voiced teachers and white gloves and pumps that pinched.

They dance that way to forget that they have to step off the banquette to let YOU pass, Young Massa.

They dance that way to forget that they, or those they love, can be sold off like two-year-old colts and taken someplace to be worked to death if their new owner chooses, for no better reason than that their owner wants a new buggy.

They dance that way so they don't kill themselves from despair. Sir.

It was not, of course, a real voodoo dance. Only a get-together, with food pitched in to be shared around, and catching-up on the week. Information—Mamzelle Marie's wealth—was in a lesser way the currency of them all. When you're powerless, chained, and naked, you pay a great deal of attention to the doings of those whose whims can take from you what little security you might have. Around the edges under the trees, men threw dice in the shade or chatted up women; here and there sat the voodoo doctors, the root men, the wangateurs. January recognized Dr. Yellowjack among them, with his glazed leather hat and aigrette of heron-hackle, and with him others Olympe had pointed out in the street: Dr. Brimstone and Dr. Chickasaw; and the scar-faced, terrifying John Bayou. People came up to them to speak, or sought out the women in many-pointed tignons or snakebone necklaces, to have their fortunes read. He wondered which of those was Mambo Oba, and what Mamzelle Marie would have to tell him of her. What had looked, at the time, like a simple matter of voodoo rivalry had become a hundred times more dangerous—whoever had paid Mambo Oba had almost certainly also paid Killdevil Ned.

My reputation will never recover if I go in. January glanced around him. Any of the people in the mostly white crowd outside the fence could be a prospective employer, if not a giver of parties then a parent of children whom they might not want to take piano lessons from a man who'd been seen at the dancing in Congo Square. But Mamzelle Marie would have seen him—at six feet three, with his high beaver hat, he was unmissable in any crowd—and would know if he sought her out in private later, that he had drawn a line for himself at speaking to her here. So he worked his way to the gate, where a blue-uniformed City Guard idled with his cudgel and cutlass, and passed through. Two young women lounged, panting and shiny, in little more than a few kerchiefs covering their breasts and wrought into skirts. But their faces held none of the blind ecstasy that had filled Olympe's that night at the brickyard; they chatted through the palings with two young white men in the long-tailed coats and bright waistcoats of clerks. As January edged through the gate, one of the clerks gave the girls some money, and they slithered out past him as he went in.

Laundresses? Seamstresses? he wondered. *Slaves making a few reales they needn't show their masters?* His old distaste for the voodoo dances returned.

Still, he worked his way through the dancers to the crowd around Mamzelle Marie. Men would dance up to her, touch her hand, sometimes kiss her extended wrist, or the shining scales of the snake she held. Women would clasp her hand, or sometimes her ankle, as she swayed on her platform of boxes. A woman selling pralines in the crowd put two of them on the edge of the platform, like an offering. There were other offerings, on the platform and on the ground near the serpent's cage—dishes of congris or rice, cigars, copper, and silver coins. A piece of pound cake on a plate. The ground around the boxes was wet with rum.

He waited for Mamzelle Marie to finish her dance, to step down and touch the hands of this woman and that, disciples as Olympe was a disciple, or friends as Olympe was a friend.

And that, too, he thought, was Power.

Her eyes glinted and she smiled, lazy and impudent and dangerous, like sunlight on the edge of a knife. "Michie Ben."

He removed his hat. "Mamzelle."

"I went to the house of Mambo Oba." A woman handed her a horn cup of lemonade, and Marie Laveau drank thirstily. Sweat streaked her face, wet the edge of her seven-pointed tignon, and made dark blotches on the calico of her blouse. "She's gone. The house is closed up. Even her cats are gone; her clothing, her money, her calabash rattle and the shell she uses to speak to the *loa,* gone. The neighbors say she left Friday night."

January was silent, chilled. Mamzelle Marie watched him, and with its flat spade-shaped head against her dark neck muscle the Damballah serpent watched him, too.

"What can I do?"

Her mouth tucked a little as she thought, maybe wondering what it was that he would be willing to hear. "Pray," she said at length. "Ask the Virgin Mary, or St. Antoine, or St. Peter to help you, to deliver you from harm. You go to the Chapel of St. Antoine, to the old statue of St. Peter that stands in the back. Put brick dust on your shoes, and carry in your mouth a split guinea pepper, with a paper in it on which you write your wish: Deliver me from Harm. Leave it there at his feet."

St. Peter? wondered January. *Or that other old man who guarded all doors who carried keys?*

"Then when all is over, and for the best," Mamzelle went on, "go back and thank him. Leave a piece of pound cake, or a couple of cigars, or a little rice, or silver, at his feet. It's good to give good things to those who help you," she added, a dark smile flickering across her face. "And it's good to tell others still in fear that prayers do get heard."

"Well, look at you, pilgrim!" Cut-Arm came up out of the crowd, naked but for a loincloth of bandannas, and jingling bells on his feet. He held a laughing woman on his good arm and another had her hand closed around the loincloth at his other hip. "Didn't know I was coming to the aid of a toff. Doesn't a toff like you know better than to go hunt adventure in the Swamp?" January's rescuer leaned down from his great height to kiss Mamzelle Marie's cheek.

"Sometimes you go hunting other things." January had seen the judgment in the big man's glance, a scorn opposite to his mother's scorn: scorn for the clothing he wore, for the culture that was his hard-earned guarantee of advancement in a world where the money that bought safety and peace was all in the hands of the whites.

"In the Swamp you're going to find only one thing," said Cut-Arm. "Same thing you find in all of this whole town. Boys . . . Ladies . . ." He addressed the half-dozen men and women who came up around him. The men were near-naked, as he was, slipping now into rough smocks and trousers, the clothing of the poorest of the poor slaves—January saw, a little to his surprise, Colonel Pritchard's diminutive waiter Dan among them, and with him was the young woman Kitta who'd been with him in the kitchen that night, the woman who'd gone to the voodoos, the woman who was with child. Both touched Mamzelle Marie's hands, the ceremonial transmission of Power or blessing:

"Will we see you when the moon comes full?" Cut-Arm asked of Mamzelle Marie, and she returned him her enigmatic smile.

"It might so be."

"Until then." He kissed her hand. To January he said, "And you, pilgrim, you beware of how you go. The white man's like a dog, once he gets on the hunting trail. He doesn't give up."

"But why?" asked January, baffled. "That's what I don't understand."

"That's what the deer doesn't understand, minding its own business in the woods." Cut-Arm laughed curtly. "But the deer ends up in the stewpot, all the same."

Walking away from the Square down Rue d'Orléans through the dove-gray evening, January heard the voices behind him, the dark uneasy music pulling at his heart.

> St. Peter, St. Peter, open the door,
> I'm callin' you, come to me!
> St. Peter, St. Peter, open the door. . . .

Livia Levesque's house was deserted when January returned to it at last. At a guess, his mother had gone to dinner at the home of one of her cronies, for a comfortable evening of cards, coffee, and the bloody slaughter of every reputation they could lay tongue to—January would have given a good deal to be privy to what his mother had to say to her friends on the subject of Geneviève Jumon. The kitchen doors stood wide, the waxed-oak table scrubbed, and every bowl and pot and cup secure in its place in the cupboard. In the laundry, also open to the dense hot stillness of the evening, a huge tub of clothing soaked, the water faintly yellowed by dissolving slivers of soap. Washboards, irons, a box of starch were laid out ready for the following day. Bella, presumably, was with cronies of her own, sitting under the gallery of some other house in the French town—Bella didn't hold with going above Canal Street "where all the Kaintuck riffraff lives"—where the family had gone out for Sunday dinner elsewhere.

In the kitchen a red pottery bowl held jambalaya, protected from flies by a plate laid over the top. Coffee warmed on the back of the stove. January filled a cup, carried both vessels with him up the steps to the garçonnière, his mind already savoring the joy of an evening all to himself in the parlor with the shutters thrown wide to the street, playing on the piano all those pieces that brought him the greatest joy: Bach and Mozart, the overture from *The Italian Girl in Algiers* and strange old jigs and planxties Hannibal had taught him. His room was dark and the door was shut and he had no idea why he stopped on the threshold, his hair prickling on his head, knowing there was something wrong.

He set down bowl and cup beside the door, and pushed the shutter wider. The evening was settling down fast, as it did in Louisiana, but enough blue light lingered that he could see all around the little room. It was barely eight feet by ten and contained nothing but the narrow bed he'd slept in as a boy, mosquito-bar tied neatly back; a small desk with its chair; a stand bearing slop jar, basin, and ewer in white German ware. The bed was as Bella had left it earlier in the day, smooth and flat as a tidal beach. The rag rug made a dark oval, exactly in the center of the pale floor.

January took a lucifer-match from his pocket and lit the candle, then knelt and began to look in every corner and shadow of the room.

In time he found what he sought, worked in between the sheet and the coverlet—even in the hottest days of summer Bella would not tolerate any bed dressed in sheets alone—at the foot of the mattress. Black flannel. Sniffing it cautiously, January identified at least red pepper and iron, and the rotting flesh of something that felt, through the flannel, like a snake or lizard head. An ouanga. He made a move to untie the stringy root that bound the bag shut, but didn't. Couldn't. He only stood with the thing in his hand for some time, not sure why he was trembling. Anger, he thought. Anger that his room had been thus casually violated again.

Far-off voices still drifted to him from Congo Square. It wouldn't be long before the cannon in the Place d'Armes sounded curfew. A faint breeze from the door made the candle flicker, the shadows curtsy and loom. His eyes were drawn to the crucifix above the head of his bed. For a moment he thought he saw a dried snake there instead, with his own name written on the slip of paper in its jaws.

He wondered if his confessor had ever come back to his cloistered room and found a chicken foot on his bed.

He carried the ouanga downstairs to the kitchen and pitched the black flannel bag deep into the back of the hearth, poking it into the banked embers with a stick of kindling. It caught with a great blazing leap of blue fire—alcohol, or possibly gunpowder—and the stench of burnt feathers and hair.

When it was consumed he climbed the stairs again, picked up bowl and cup and spoon. But a thought came to him as he was about to reenter his room, and he carried all three down to the yard again, and dumped the jambalaya into the privy. He went into the kitchen and poured the rest of the pot of coffee after it, and set the dishes next to the sink, for Bella to wash after breakfast. Then he let himself out the gate of the yard, and walked down Rue Toulouse to the levee, where women sold gumbo and jambalaya from stands among the brick arcades of the market. Though he could ill afford it, he bought himself something to eat there.

That night he dreamed that there was another little flannel juju somewhere in his room, and that every time he sought for it, it moved someplace else, rustling like a mouse in the dark.

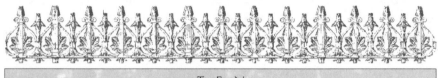

TEN

"Ben, darling, I know you and Olympe were right and I was wrong about Madame Lalaurie last spring, but don't you think you're letting what happened affect your judgment just a little?" Dominique judiciously spread two gowns on her bed and studied them: pale yellow mull-muslin frothed with layer upon layer of white lace and a clear lettuce-green tulle trimmed with plum-colored bows. "Do you think the waist on the green is a bit high, Ben? They're wearing them lower this year."

Having come to manhood at a time when women wore clinging high-waisted gauze gowns with virtually nothing under them, January thought all women dressed like idiots these days, his dear friend Rose Vitrac not excepted. He knew better, however, than to say so. "The lower waist is more becoming."

"I think so, too. And I never did like those silly aprons." His sister cast aside the green tulle and with it apparently all recollection of her ecstasies last year on the subject of the dress's ornamental, lace-trimmed apron. There was more in her of her mother than Dominique would care to admit. "I mean, why would Mathurin Jumon keep his nephew locked up in his attic for five days? Why not just poison him the night he got him into his evil clutches? Wouldn't Grand-mère Jumon have something to say about it? Or the servants?"

"Grand-mère Jumon isn't well," said January. "And she's seventy years old—I doubt she's been up in those attics for years." He seated himself on the rocking chair of red cypress that stood near the open window. Beyond, in the cottage's yard, his sister's cook, Becky, emerged from the kitchen with a stack of white porcelain dishes balanced in her hands; set them down on the bench under the gallery; and commenced to wrap each in newspaper, laying them in a wooden crate at her side. Straw littered the flagstones all around her. Knowing what the kitchen at his mother's house was like on Mondays, with the washtub boiling all day and a cauldron of red beans set for good measure over the back of the long-burning fire, January completely understood the decision to risk getting rained on by doing the packing outside.

Back at his mother's, Bella was doing her packing outdoors, too.

Most of the wealthy brokers, landlords, and bankers who could afford to do so rented cottages on the lakefront during the summer season, in Milneburgh or Mandeville or Spanish Fort. Many, as Mathurin Jumon had said, were already gone. Though it was only a short train ride from Milneburgh to the city, many also rented cottages—or at least rooms or suites of rooms—for their colored plaçées, especially if there were children involved. With the steadily advancing summer heat, the stink rising from the gutters and the summer infestations of every insect from fleas to mosquitoes to roaches and palmetto bugs, to say nothing of the risk of fever, people had been leaving New Orleans since early June.

Soon, January reflected, there would be "no one at all left in town," as the wealthy Parisians had lamented at the balls where he'd played. No one a wealthy person would know, anyway.

Only the poor.

No wonder the property owners of the town were having, as Shaw would call them, conniption fits.

"And then again, Madame Cordelia may very well have been in on it," January went on, as Dominique began the endless process of selecting pelerines, stockings, tignons, reticules, fans, gloves, petticoats, and shoes to go with the yellow ensemble. "That would let Mathurin establish an alibi by going to Mandeville. And it would be easy to bring Isaak to the house in the first place: the men at the Widow Puy's all agree that Isaak received a note of some kind on Friday afternoon."

"And so he arrived at the house and the woman who has just

finished trying to wrest his inheritance from him in the courts hands him a cup of opium-laced coffee and says, *Oh, cher, drink this.*" Dominique turned with her arms full of lace. "Which reminds me, have you tried the coffee they serve at the Café Venise on Rue du Levee? They put cocoa in it, I think, and hazelnut liqueur—really excellent, although Mama says they only do that because they buy inferior beans. Still, I'm going to get some hazelnut liqueur and experiment with it, for Henri. I'm told they sell a really excellent hazelnut liqueur at . . . Oh, thank you, Thérèse," she added, as her maid entered and set on the marble top of the bureau a tray bearing two glasses of lemonade. Thérèse looked at January, looked at the chamber's dishabille—Dominique had pulled two more frocks from the chifforobe and laid them out in a fluffy meringue of petticoats—and met her mistress's eye with a patient and disapproving sigh. Men, even brothers, had no place in a woman's bedroom, particularly not men of color.

When the woman left, his sister Minou turned back to him. "Or maybe she struck him over the head with a slungshot?" She returned, rather disconcertingly, from her excursion into coffee and romance to the subject at hand. "And then what? Carried him up to the attic herself? Isn't that a little—a little Sir Walter Scott?"

January breathed half a chuckle at the mental image. "Maybe," he replied. "But the fact remains that Isaak was under that roof on the night of the twenty-third and that he died there of poisoning with his wife's name on his lips. And I'm rather curious as to how he came there, and when."

Dominique arched her eyebrows.

"You said Thérèse was related to one of Laurence Jumon's maids?" he asked.

"Oh!" Her face broke into a sunny smile at the thought of an intrigue. "Of course! Cousine Aveline! The one who was having an affair with that awful groom of Monsieur Bouligny's. Do you know, that groom was stealing oats from Bouligny and selling them by the peck to—"

"Could Thérèse be persuaded to talk to her?"

"P'tit, Thérèse will talk to *anyone* about *anything*! I absolutely can't get a word in! Do these topazes go with the primrose silk, p'tit? There's going to be a ball at the Hôtel Pontchartrain on Friday night—Henri's mother is holding one opposite that awful Mrs. Soames—but Henri

promised to take me to supper, masked, at the Café d'Auberge in Spanish Fort that night, and sometimes candlelight isn't kind to a yellow this
bright."

After another hour of Minou's nonstop chatter, and a substantial
breakfast of poached eggs, scallops, and grits ("Oh, Becky doesn't mind
making it up, p'tit—and I'm absolutely *enslaved* to her cream sauces"),
January made his way to the prison, where under the eye of a City
Guard he was escorted once again up to the third-level gallery, to the
narrow barred window of Olympe's cell. Behind her in the dim chamber he could hear women's voices arguing—harsh and foul-tongued
English—and the sound of stifled weeping. The smell that breathed
from that close hot twilight was unspeakable.

"Gone?" Olympe frowned, reaching her hands through the bars to
take January's. Her fingers felt thin, callused, and knotted; her face
appeared more gaunt even than it had on Saturday under a tignon that,
though clean, was already damp with sweat.

"Cleared out and gone, Mamzelle Marie says. Calabash, seashell,
cats, money. . . . But I found a tricken bag in my room last night
when I came home."

"Hidden?" asked Olympe. "Or out where you could see it?"

"Hidden in the bed."

Her eyes narrowed, dark with uneasiness. "Voodoos sometimes have
more than one house," she said after a time. "Especially if they've been
around awhile. And a man may hire more than one voodoo to warn
you away, or to put the death fix on. Have you checked under the
steps? Or in the yard, for places where something may have been
buried?"

January shook his head.

"There's fever here." She lowered her voice, leaning close to the
bars. "Not in this cell, but in the one on the end of the gallery. The
Guards will beat us, if word of it gets out. It's just jail fever, they say,
not yellow jack. But last night I saw him: I saw the fever walking along
the gallery, like a ghost made of smoke and sulfur. He's here, Bronze
John. Mamzelle Marie, she's burning green candles for me every day,
and bringing me fever herbs."

January remembered the candle he had lit in the Cathedral only
that morning, for Olympe's forgiveness in the eyes of God. "We'll get
you out," he promised, squeezing her fingers again. "Did Célie Jumon

tell you anything about where Isaak might have gone in trouble? Or anything about his uncle Mathurin? Brother Antoine seems to think Uncle Mathurin might have been the one to do Isaak harm." Considering the neat columns of money ranged along the edge of the desk, Mathurin had certainly been able to afford to hire Killdevil Ned.

"I know nothing of him." She removed her fingers from his, to scratch her arm. Though Gabriel brought her clean clothes every day, January could see the fleas on her bright tignon and the white sleeve of her blouse. "He has dealings with the voodoo doctors sometimes, I know, but then many white men have."

January supposed that if a respectable young matron could hide herself in the Cathedral to meet Dr. Yellowjack, it was nothing for a Creole gentleman to make arrangements with him for the secrets of his business rivals, or for girls like those who'd passed him in the gate at Congo Square. From another cell on the gallery he heard the hoarse voice of Mad Solie panting, "M'sieu! M'sieu! Tell them! When you leave this place tell them that I didn't kill those children! It was my father and my husband that killed them! They tried to force me to do it but I wouldn't listen, I wouldn't do it!"

And another woman's weary voice, "Will somebody shut her up before she starts Screamin' Peg off again?"

"They're trying to murder me in here! They come into the cell every night, and stand at my feet, and whisper to me, whisper to me, holding my children's little heads in their hands!"

"What about you?" he asked Olympe. "Are you all right here?"

She sighed, and shook her head. "I'm as well as I can be. You know me. I can sleep through anything, and some of the girls here let me have one of the beds. When Gabriel brings me food, I share it around. I tell their fortunes, too, though I don't always tell the truth." She glanced back over her shoulder at the shapeless indistinct shadows of the cell. "Gabriel brought me a letter from Paul; said it came with a little money that Michie Drialhet advanced him. He says he'll be back . . ."

"Monsieur Janvier?"

January had heard the creak of footfalls approaching on the gallery stairs, but hadn't thought much of it. The recollection of Killdevil Ned, however, had lurked in the hazy interstices between last night's waking and sleep—the knife descending, the memory of his own physical weakness, helpless against the mountain man's strength. As a result he nearly fell over the gallery rail, leaping back. The graying little man who had spoken to him recoiled, equally startled, from this extreme reaction, and someone in the next-door cell hooted with laughter and yelled, "Got a guilty conscience, Sambo?"

"Please excuse me," begged the little man, removing his rather aged beaver and holding it over his heart. "I'm terribly sorry if I startled you. It is Monsieur Benjamin Janvier, isn't it?"

January felt as if there were a dozen north Mexico trappers concealed in every cell along the Cabildo's upper gallery, taking a bead on him with their rifles. . . .

But he couldn't say so to the man who stood in front of him, thin-shouldered and diffident, in a rather bright green long-tailed coat and pantaloons of an unlikely buttercup hue. "I'm he, yes."

The visitor produced a card. "The Widow Pâris said I might find you here, when I came to speak with Madame Corbier," he said. "Please pardon my presenting myself with no better introduction than this."

Vachel Corcet, fmc.
Attorney at Law
350 Rue Plauche

"I'm afraid if you're here to speak to Madame Corbier you've been misinformed," said January. "We have no way of paying you."

But Olympe, resting her elbows on the sill of the narrow window, only studied the sagging face in its frame of carefully pomaded curls and for the first time a slow smile touched her eyes. "P'tit," she said to January, "there's something you don't understand about Mamzelle Marie." She extended her hand to Corcet. "I thank you, M'sieu Corcet. Mamzelle—the Widow Pâris—told you my brother's started making inquiries already about this?"

"She did, yes." Corcet's eyes shifted and he wet his lips with a mouselike pink tongue. Working for Marie Laveau was clearly not something that overwhelmed him with delight. January wondered what the Voodoo Queen had said to the attorney to cause him to offer his services gratis. "And that someone is evidently determined not to let him pursue the investigation. If you have a few minutes to bring me up to date on what you might have learned? . . ."

Together, January and Olympe told him all they knew, while the

Guard spit tobacco over the gallery railing and a voice in the courtyard below intoned, "Theseus Roualt, you are hereby sentenced to five lashes with a whip, to be paid for by your master William Roualt. . . ."

"It's clear to me that, whatever feelings of affection he professes— and whether or not he actually had anything to do with the murder— Mathurin Jumon has a stake in his nephew's death," said January at last. "And he has an equal financial stake in seeing that Isaak's bride doesn't inherit, either. A wife's claims on a dead man's property are clear. But in the absence of that wife, if it comes down to a court battle over close to five thousand dollars between a dead man's dead father's white brother and that same dead father's colored former mistress, I suspect I know which way that verdict is going to go."

"And Mathurin can't get rid of Célie," remarked Olympe bitterly, "without he gets rid of me as well."

"Conversely," remarked Corcet, turning his hat brim in soft, nervous hands gloved with yellow kid, "if you are cleared, Madame Corbier, Madame Célie will be cleared as well—hence the attempts against your brother. I wonder if Clément Vilhardouin has experienced similar difficulties?"

"Not likely we're going to find out," said January. "Though it would tell us something if he has."

"Does Monsieur Jumon strike you as the kind of man who would murder his nephew—and cause his nephew's bride to be hanged—for money?" asked Corcet. "He appears to have plenty of it already, if his mother's jewelry, carriage, clothing, and house in Mandeville are any indication. He does a great deal of charity work, you know, in a quiet way: settling annuities on deserving invalids, for instance. He has provided for the education of a number of young people who might not otherwise be able to afford it. Mathurin Jumon does not appear to be an evil-intentioned man. Or a man who would kill for gain."

Olympe snorted with derision. "Charity work. There's half a dozen of the most charitable men and women in this town send their slaves down to be whipped if they pass the time of day with a milk seller in the kitchen door. Two of 'em I know of wash the cuts out with salt brine afterward. And worse things," she added, with a glance at her brother, who had nearly lost the use of his arms through an encounter with a white woman renowned for her charity.

"Hmm." January watched the sunlight on the plastered wall fade, and tried not to hear the crack of the rawhide in the court below him, and the whipped man's stifled cries. He thought again about those neat stacks of coin. Anonymous. Congealed power, able to act for good or for ill. "And it may be," he said, "that a white man wouldn't consider a colored one to have the same rights of inheritance, even in the face of the law. But no, he did not impress me as a killer. But I'm almost certain Isaak died in his house. Now, by his account Antoine isn't to be entirely trusted, but I doubt Antoine could have made up a description of a seventeenth-century rustic-ware pitcher. We'll know more, of course, after our sister's maid has talked with one of the Jumon servants."

Leaving the Cabildo with the clouds gathering overhead, January started to turn along Rue Chartres, and so to his mother's house again. But as he stepped out from beneath the arcade, the bright-painted sign above a chocolate shop drew his attention. Tables had been set out before it on the Place d'Armes and for a moment he stood watching the proprietress, a lively, pretty woman in her thirties, boldly flirting with a man in a steamboat captain's gold-trimmed cap. Turning, January crossed before the Cathedral, hands in the pockets of the rather worse-for-wear corduroy jacket he'd bought many years ago in Paris, and made his way in a leisurely fashion—his mother's house would still be a wilderness of trunks, packing materials, and laundry—to a stationery store in the Rue Condé. From there he sought out a table near the coffee stand by the vegetable market, where he composed a note.

My dearest Madame Metoyer—

Please forgive the presumption of this communication, but I understand that you are acquainted with a young lady by the name of Babette Figes, whom I have seen, in your company, at the Blue Ribbon Balls at the Salle d'Orléans. I have attempted, unsuccessfully, to attain an introduction to Mademoiselle Babette through her sister Marie-Eulalie; would it be possible to come to an understanding with you on the subject? If you will so kindly permit me, I will look for you at the next Ball to be given.

                              Until then,
                              Your obedient servant,
                              Baron Herzog von Metzger

After a moment's consideration he applied a lucifer to the sealing wax he'd purchased along with the sheet of cold-pressed paper, and pressed one of his jacket's elaborate buttons into the resulting crimson blot.

The maidservant at Bernadette Metoyer's cottage on Rue St. Philippe was duly impressed with January's tale of the besotted Baron—"I can't imagine what Marie-Eulalie was thinking of, to snub a man like that!" From there, it being midafternoon and laundry day, an offer to assist in the wringing of sheets and petticoats, and the maneuvering of tubs and buckets of hot water from the sweltering kitchen was gratefully accepted. January shed his trimly cut, albeit shabby, jacket, glad that he'd worn one of his old and threadbare linen shirts to Dominique's that morning instead of a rougher-looking calico, gritted his teeth against the agony in his back and spoke his best Parisian French, with a slight German accent as befit an European nobleman's house servant. It was an easy transition from commonplaces to conversation to confidences.

"Lord, no, Michie Athanase, that was keeping company with Mamzelle Bernadette, he gave her this house and five hundred dollars when he married Mamzelle Cournaud. I remember the day he signed over the deed, and Mamzelle Bernadette crying her eyes out saying how she's going to kill herself, praying God for strength to carry on, just till he walked out the door. Then she stands up with this big old grin on her face and throws her arms around me. . . ."

"A strong-hearted woman, Mademoiselle Lucy. My master's mother, you know, she saved the family plate from Napoleon's armies. . . ." January had been a musician in Paris for ten years. Every tale and anecdote and bit of gossip he'd ever heard there—not to mention substantial blocks of Stendhal and Balzac—flowed easily to his tongue.

" 'Course, M'am Cournaud I hear is melancholy. . . ."

"My master's wife, the Baroness, is the same. In fact she suffers a periodic delusion that she is pregnant with half a dozen rabbits. . . ."

"Maybe she's witched!" Lucy's dark eyes widened, and January felt, as he had when a young man illegally shooting in the *cipriere*, that satisfied moment of wholeness: a deer stepping exactly into a clearing, unaware of his presence.

"I understand that there are such sorcerers here?"

She flung up her hands, her round face beaming. "Lord, aren't there!"

"In fact I heard that there was such a gathering only a few weeks ago. Have you ever been to such?"

Lucy crossed herself quickly, but there was a flicker in her eyes. "Lord, no, Mamzelle Bernadette wouldn't let me go. She had her sisters over that night, playing cards, and even playing for pennies and bits she lost close to fifty dollars!"

"I didn't think respectable ladies of this town—I mean honest shopkeepers, like your mistress—had so much money to game with."

"My, when you've been in town a bit longer, Michie Gustave, you'll learn! Mamzelle Bernadette's sister Blanche couldn't play much, being like Mamzelle a woman in business—she has a hat shop over by Rue des Ursulines—but her other sister Virginie, that's plaçée with young Michie Guichard, and Marie-Toussainte and Marie-Eulalie, they could just gamble with the money their protectors give them. . . ."

"I think I've seen your mistress's sister's hat shop," said January. "Aux Fleurs Jolies, with the pink sign? . . ."

"Oh, no, that's M'am Geneviève's, on Rue des Ramparts. But she was here, too." And Lucy giggled. "For a few minutes, anyway."

January leaned his elbow on the doorway—his arms felt as if they were about to drop off at the shoulder—and gave her his most interested and (he hoped) most charming grin.

"She didn't even take off her hat." The maid chuckled. "And my, what a hat! Good thing M'am Geneviève didn't meet no Guards, or she'd 'a been arrested sure, for wearing such a hat! With a crown this high, and roses, and lace off the back of it. . . . She hadn't hardly come through the door when a carriage comes up in the street, and she gives everybody a kiss and says, *Now, remember I was here all night!* And off she goes with Michie Granville that runs the Bank of Louisiana!"

"Monsieur Granville!" January managed to look both startled and hugely entertained. "Why, M'sieu le Baron took dinner with him and his wife the other day. He said a more united couple would be difficult to find."

"Oh, he's quite the man." Lucy twinkled in a way that made January wonder exactly how far afield the banker's fancies had taken him. "He kept company with Mamzelle Bernadette, back when he was President of the Union Bank, and with her sister Blanche after Blanche parted company with Michie Lisle. He has a little house out on that new canal, on Constitution Place, that his wife doesn't know about. That's where I think they went, M'am Geneviève and Michie Granville." And she simpered, pleased with herself.

Walking back to his mother's house through the slanting rain, January mentally calculated where the new development had gone in along Florida Walk last year. Constitution Place, if he remembered correctly, lay just over a mile from the Jumon town house on Rue St. Louis.

The rain grew heavier. Thunder growled over the river. As he dodged along the banquette from one gallery overhang to the next, January found himself glancing back over his shoulder or around him at the passways and carriageways between the houses on Rue Burgundy, wondering which of them concealed a man with a rifle. Which of those empty houses, shuttered tight now while their owners were at the lake, could be used for an ambush? The trappers who hunted in the Mexican Territories could shoot the head off a squirrel at a hundred yards: his aching shoulders cringed under the wet corduroy and he found himself stopping and starting, hurrying and slowing, as if that would somehow save him.

Times were slow. Tomorrow would be the Culver girls' last lesson for the summer, before the family went back to their native Philadelphia to avoid the fever. In a way he was glad—he felt safer within the French town—but he knew already his mother was not going to abate one dime of the rent she charged him to live in the room he'd occupied as a boy. If she wasn't demanding an extra dollar a week toward household provisions while she herself was enjoying lakefront breezes in Milneburgh, he knew it would cost him nearly that to feed himself. His remaining savings were slender. That morning's breakfast at Dominique's had been uncomfortably close to a cadge, and his skin crawled with embarrassment at the thought.

In ordinary circumstances, after the last engagement of the social season—Councilman Soames's Fourth of July Ball in his lakefront summer house—January would have sought what meager employment was offered by the gambling halls, or played an occasional danceable out at the Milneburgh hotels.

But playing in a gambling hall he would be, for all intents and purposes, alone, without backup or defense. And obliged to remain where anyone could see him and come at him, through gruelingly long evening shifts.

And it was a long way back from the lake, once the steam-train ceased running at midnight.

"Honestly, Ben, I knew there would be trouble if you took up the cause of that voodooienne," his mother greeted him as he came through the passway at the side of the house and emerged into the yard. That, too, was the result of long childhood training—neither he nor Olympe had ever been permitted to enter the house from the street. "The whole affair has got Bella in such a state she burned the coffee and scorched the back of one of my petticoats."

January stepped through the French doors into the dining room, shed his coat and slapped the water out of his cap. Three crates stood along the wall, among neat piles of old newspapers. His mother, who loudly deplored Dominique's habit of taking everything that might possibly add to her comfort or beautiful appearance when she traveled, would not dream of spending three months without her own coffee set, veilleuse, writing equipment, tea service, wineglasses, sewing box, and music box; her favorite trinkets and backgammon set; not to speak of the crimping-irons, gauffering irons, and other equipment Bella had to bring to care for her mistress's extensive wardrobe. Though Livia owned a cottage on the lakefront, she rented it out every year to a white sugar broker and his family and stayed in two lovely rooms of the small boarding hotel in which she owned a half-interest: she was currently, January knew, negotiating to buy another cottage.

January sighed and made a mental note to confine Les Mesdames— dozing on top of the crates—to the spare room that evening lest the cats disappear when it came time to fetch out their wicker travel boxes. He opened his mouth to say, "*That voodooienne* is your daughter," but didn't; "I'm sorry, Maman. Bella will get over it when you get out to the lake, you know, and by the time you return, this will all be taken care of."

Livia Levesque glanced sidelong at him, as if to ask how he could remain so cavalier in the face of burnt coffee, and for a moment her eyes were exactly like Olympe's. Then she sniffed and turned away. "Remember to air out all the rooms every day," she said. "The front steps will need to be cleaned as well. You know how filthy the air is, with the steamboats making all their soot and the rain turning it to mud. I truly don't know what this city is coming to. And make sure the gutter in front of the house stays cleared out. Those people the city hires haven't done their job in months. Send me your month's money care of the Hôtel Villefranche, as usual. I'll take July's tomorrow morning before I leave."

It would leave him without a picayune—and he knew already she'd let the stores of food run down because she was leaving—but there was a tone in her voice that would not even hear, Can't you let it go for a week?

"I'll give it to you now."

"No, tomorrow will do."

Returning to the garçonnière, he checked the room carefully for further signs of interference; and though he found none, he could not rid himself of the thought that there was some evil there somewhere: the feathers of his pillow twisted into the shape of a rooster or a dog, or a ball of black wax and turpentine secreted under the floor. A white man would hire a killer, he thought. Maybe even hire a voodoo for that first warning. But the second tricken bag—and the sense that there were others, secret words of death—pointed to color.

Mosquitoes whined in the corners of the ceiling, but such was the curdled heat that he couldn't bear to close up the shutters. He spread out the mosquito-bar around the bed, took his candle and checked the inside thoroughly for chance invaders. Bringing several candles in under the bar—though it was still twilight outside, in the room it was now quite dark—he settled down with Wolf's *Prolegomena in Homerum*. A decent antidote, he thought, to the eerie shadows of secrets and half-guessed-at fears.

When he crossed through the rain to the house again for supper he found a letter by his plate, folded in the old-fashioned way and sealed. "That came for you this morning," said his mother, without glancing up from her perusal of the *Louisiana Gazette*. The seal was broken. It crossed January's mind for he knew not what reason to wonder if Madame Cordelia Jumon read her son's letters.

He unfolded the paper, though he recognized the Italianate beauty of the handwriting on the address.

Benjamin,
    I have made contact with Madame Célie Jumon. She and I will meet you at Monsieur Nogent's on Wednesday at noon.

Rose

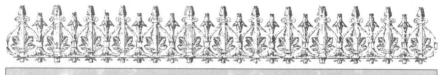

ELEVEN

"I hope you don't think I'll be of any use to you if your mother's place is stormed by armed bravos." Hannibal looked vaguely around the attic, coughed, and picked up the nearest bottle—they dotted every horizontal surface, in various stages of depletion. *"Persuasion is the resource of the feeble; and the feeble can seldom persuade."* He coughed again, and sat down on the bed, while January found the fiddle case, wrapped the time-stained and ancient instrument in its usual swaddling of half a dozen frayed silk scarves, and began to assemble from the various corners of the long, mildew-smelling space some books, shaving tackle, and a couple of threadbare linen shirts. "Still, *what stronger breastplate than a heart untainted?*"

"At the moment you're in better fighting shape than I am," January replied. Through the open door drifted men's shouts, cursing and laying wagers, and beneath them the savage snarling of dogs. "And it's mostly your presence I need, so there'll be less chance of me being taken unawares."

Hannibal drained the bottle and set it with great care back on the rafter from which he'd taken it. *"The watchdog's voice that bayed the whisp'ring wind,"* he quoted, *"And the loud laugh that spoke the vacant mind*—and you'll be getting both together for the same price." There was tired bitterness in his voice, to which January had no reply. With his mother's departure for Milneburgh that morning he had betaken himself immediately and by the most circuitous possible route to Perdido Street, to inquire of Hannibal if he'd like to spend the summer in Bella's room instead of in the attic of Kentucky Williams's saloon. The fiddler's breathing was labored, and two or three plates of congris and grits, uneaten but carefully covered to thwart the local rodent population, attested to a resurgence of his illness.

"You'll be all right," said January finally, and Hannibal turned, drug-bright eyes glittering.

"It's kind of you to lie to me," he said, "but in point of fact I am not going to be all right. I am going to die. If not of this bout, of the next, or the next. That's why I left Dublin, and that's why I came here. I'll try not to be a burden to you but I undoubtedly will be; you could more profitably purchase a watchdog for fifty cents." He was trembling, his face ghost-white, like a skull in the dark straggling frame of his hair, and there was anger and a savage contempt in every tone and word. He must have heard it, for he looked away, biting his lip. January saw the cuffs of his sleeve were spattered with blood.

"I know I could." He walked over and laid a hand on the fiddler's shoulder. "But at the moment I don't have fifty cents." And he felt the stabbing bones under the patched linen shake suddenly with a breath of wry laughter.

"Don't look at me to loan it to you." Hannibal stood, steadying himself on his friend's arm, and checked the books January had boxed up. "That should do—Athéné has more of them over at her place." Athéné was his name, in jest, for Rose Vitrac. "You might consider finding Mr. Nash's employer and offering to murder yourself for two hundred dollars—I gather that was the fee agreed upon. Can you carry those? Not that I'll be able to help you in that, either. . . ."

"Two hundred?" remarked January, as they descended the outside stair. Coming into the open made him flinch, and brought his breath quick with panic, a situation not improved by the presence of some fifty men in the muddy yard behind the saloon, watching a dogfight. "I'm flattered."

The smaller of the two dogs, a lean yellow wolfish animal, had been wounded badly, bleeding and snarling as it tried to defend itself against a heavy-boned brindle mastiff with the torn ears and scarred face of a longtime champion. The stink of blood mixed with that of churned mud, spit tobacco, and piss: slouch-hatted gambling men, keelboat ruffians in greasy plaid shirts, filibusters with knives at their belts and in their boots. January glimpsed the blue boiled wool of a trade-goods shirt and shuddered, but the man wearing it, although a trapper, was short and dark in buckskin leggins; kneeling on the edge of the crowd screaming "Tear him! Tear him, Duff!"

"Surprising what a little cocaine hydrochloride will do for a dog's spirits," remarked Hannibal, leading the way down the steps with a certain amount of care. Though his speech wasn't slurred January knew that he had to be very drunk, or very drugged, to speak of Dublin, or of anything touching on his life before coming to New Orleans; he paused at the bottom of the steps, his own shoulders screaming at even the weight of a dozen books, for the fiddler to get his breath. "Billy must have killed four of the poor brutes before he got the dosage right. This one's lasted better than most."

He skirted the outside of the crowd, where pickpockets skirmished discreetly, like wolves around the fringes of a herd. Kentucky Williams slouched in the rear door of the saloon, angling her head as if by doing so she could see what was going on in the ring of jostling backs. She wore a soiled Mother Hubbard, and quite clearly nothing under it except a pair of men's boots.

"Kentuckilla my pearl." Hannibal bowed deeply, and kissed her grimy hand. "What is it that you were telling me about the gentleman who hired Mr. Nash to assassinate my friend?"

Williams took the cigar out of her mouth and blew a cloud of smoke. "This's just what I heard from Kraut Nan down to the Salt River Saloon. Say, wasn't you the nigger got his back hurt? Set them books down," she ordered January. "You boys want a drink?" It wasn't ten in the morning but she'd clearly had two or eight herself. January shook his head. Even Hannibal avoided the potations dished from the barrel behind Williams's plank bar. "All I heard was it was a white man," she informed January. "A toff. Slick tailed coat, plug hat—big bastard, Kraut Nan says. Walked in, handed the man the money, walked out. No word said. Didn't even buy a drink, but Ned came straight over and bought one, so she knew it was money he give him."

"Did Mamzelle Nan say whether he was dark-haired or fair?" January remembered Mathurin Jumon's powerful height, Hubert Granville's broad shoulders and heavy neck.

The saloonkeeper thought about it a moment. Then she shook her head, and scratched under one massive breast for fleas. "Just he was big."

"Big is all Kraut Nan sees in a man anyways," remarked Railspike, sauntering back from the crowd. She added a physically impossible speculation concerning Kraut Nan's amorous capacity and added, "You the nigger askin' about that boy Isaak over to the Turkey-Buzzard? Gimme a drink, fiddler."

Hannibal produced a bottle from his pocket and handed it to her; she didn't even bother to check whether it contained laudanum or whisky, just drained it, and threw it against the side of the rude plank shack. Unlike Williams she was a handsome woman, if one found a square chin and a strong cast of feature handsome. Her eyes were pale, cruel in a face lined with dissipation and smeared heavily with rice powder and rouge.

"Great big feller come in, black as the ace of spades," she said, in her coarse upriver English. "I forget what day this was. Ace of Spades asks if they had a boy name of Isaak workin' there. Well, I'd already figured Isaak for a runaway. He was a sweet kid, told me all about his wife and wouldn't have nuthin' to do with the girls that worked the back room there. But Ace of Spades didn't look like a slave-catcher, so I said we did, though he wasn't in. Then Ace of Spades give me this note for him—a map, it looked like, drawn on a square piece of paper about so big." Her large, coarse hands sketched the shape of a quarto book page.

"Was it anywhere you know?"

She made a wry little mouth with her scarred lips, and shook her head. "Hell, I don't get out of town much—who wants to go tromping around the mud? There was kind of a square with crosses down at the bottom, and a couple of lines that might have been canals or bayous. I remember there was a tree on it, with a twisty limb, like that"—she scrunched and maneuvered her arm momentarily into a sideways V—"I give this to Isaak when he came in, and he looked at it and stuck it away in his pocket, but I seen him take it out and look at it two, three more times during the day. So he musta knew where it was."

January nodded—he knew where it was, too. "Do you remember anything else about the man who came with the note, M'am?"

Railspike shook her head, lank curls swinging. Behind her the noise redoubled. Men howled, shrieking, as a single yowl of pain ripped the air. Then the crowd seethed, reconformed itself, men paying off and demanding money, while the little trapper and a friend dragged Duff back, bloody foam dribbling from his jaws, and a big fair man in a plaid shirt savagely kicked the defeated yellow hound, dying already in a great soak of gore.

"You stupid cur! Rotten whoreson shit-eater!" Near the fence two men were shoving each other and shouting already about whether the defeat did or did not constitute a fair loss; January wondered if one of them had been dosed with cocaine, to turn him into a fighter, or whether the doglike ferocity was just the result of booze.

"Oh, yeah," remembered Railspike, "he had just one arm. 'Cause he reached acrost himself like this"—she demonstrated—"to get the note out of his pocket. Big ugly bastard."

"Thank you, M'am," said January softly. "You've both been most helpful."

"Here, now!" Williams gestured with her cigar as he bent to pick up Hannibal's books. "Don't you go hurtin' your back again with those! I'll get somebody to haul 'em over to the French town for you. You just give us the direction. . . ."

January started to decline—the fight by the fence had blossomed into full-scale hostilities and men were arriving by the score; it would be only a matter of time until Killdevil Nash appeared. But rather to his surprise Hannibal said, "Thank you," and gave her the number of Livia Levesque's house.

"Are you insane?" demanded January as they left the yard. "You think any of those boys is going to actually deliver books instead of selling them?"

"You obviously haven't tried to sell books in this town." Hannibal cradled his violin and his remaining bottle of opium. "They're as safe as if they were common dirt. Now let's find a grocer—with your mother out of the way we can ask Rose to lunch and learn how she breached Forteresse Gérard and got in touch with Madame Célie."

"You're going to ruin my reputation yet." Rose Vitrac competently brushed aside the pile of onion pieces from the chopping board and went to work on a pepper.

"I thought Madame Lalaurie did that last year."

"So she did." The former schoolmistress nudged her spectacles more firmly up onto her nose with the back of her wrist, blinking with the vapors of the onion. "But I have dreadful premonitions of being forced to go to Hannibal every six or seven months for a new set of papers, to establish a new identity. . . ."

"You don't think there's people in this town who do just that?" Hannibal emerged from the kitchen, wiping his hands on one of Bella's linen towels. "How do you think I get opium money, when I'm too under the weather to play?" He turned his face aside, and coughed again. "Admittedly I'm not one of the best, but still . . . I always knew those years of penmanship exercises at Eton would come to something."

"I'm sure your masters are very proud of you." Rose turned back to January. "Which reminds me—Monsieur Landreaux, who has a book-shop on Canal Street, has asked me if I'd translate four plays for him: *Helen in Egypt, The Heracleidae, Plutus,* and *The Knights.* He's preparing a special edition for boys—he's arranged a printer in New York—but he needs the translations by the end of July. I was wondering if you'd like to do two? It isn't much—ten dollars apiece—but I know it's hard to find work in the summers. Are you interested?"

"Mademoiselle Vitrac," said January, inclining his head, "that sound you hear is me sharpening my pens. Thank you."

"*The Knights* is a little racy." She swept the peppers into a bowl. "So you'll have to edit as well."

"To the pure all things are pure." January collected up the various little dishes of spices and vegetables, and carried them into the roaring heat of the kitchen. "And I think that as an older, wiser, and more experienced man I should be the one to translate the Aristophanes. . . ."

"You mean Aristophanes is more fun to translate than Euripides."

"That, too," agreed January. "Now tell me about Madame Célie and the ruin of your reputation."

A very small quantity of sausage grilled in a pan set on a spider over the hearth coals, with the crawfish and redfish that had been all the three friends' pooled resources could obtain from the market. While January made a roux and Hannibal checked on the rice bubbling slowly in its cauldron, Rose related how she'd observed the coffee mer-chant's house for most of Sunday morning and the pretext by which she'd spoken to his daughter after she'd discreetly trailed them to Mass.

"As I'm about the same complexion as Monsieur Nogent, it wasn't difficult to pass myself off as his sister," said Rose. "I slipped a note to Madame Célie as we spoke, so that she could assure her father later that yes, she did recall Monsieur Nogent speaking of a sister in Mandeville. When I went to the shop this morning and left a note for her—perfectly aboveboard and saying only that Monsieur Nogent is ill and misses her terribly—her father seemed to find no difficulty in my chaperoning her to Nogent's house tomorrow. What he'll think if the truth is revealed I daren't speculate."

"*Cannot a plain man live and do no harm, | But that his simple truth must be abused | By silken, sly, insinuating Jacks?*" Hannibal inquired. He perched on the edge of the table where there was at least a stirring of air from the open doors. The thick smell of sausage and garlic was insufficient to cover that of red pepper and turpentine, painted along the base of the walls to discourage ants. Outside in the little yard, the sun beat mercilessly on the open ground, and cicadas had begun to drum in the palmetto and banana shrubs that grew to the sides of the garçonnière.

"By the way, has anyone considered that Madame Célie's father has just as much to gain by Isaak's death as either Mathurin or Granville, provided he can keep his daughter out of quod? She's underage, after all, and five thousand dollars can turn a lot of interest in five years. He'd have to get rid of Olympe, and a note from him would have fetched Isaak just as smartly as one from Mathurin."

"It was a white man who hired Nash," pointed out January.

"You're saying a black man couldn't use a white one as a cat's-paw?"

"And Monsieur Gérard could not have kept Madame Célie from knowing Isaak was in the house," added Rose. She scraped onions, peppers, celery, and garlic into the roux and, while January stirred, added water from the jar beside the stove. "The shop on Rue Royale has only a tiny storeroom, and their house is like this one. . . ." She nodded across the yard at the pink stucco cottage: four small rooms, comfortable but not elegant and certainly impossible to conceal a prisoner in even had Monsieur Gérard been capable of bringing Isaak there unnoticed.

"Have it your way." Hannibal poured himself out another cup of chicory-laced coffee. "Just don't assume that because Gérard loves his daughter that he wouldn't try to rid himself of her husband—or of your sister, Ben. When's the funeral, by the way?"

"This afternoon," said January. "Though I had to find that out from Shaw; it isn't posted anywhere. Shall we go buy an immortelle and pretend to lay it on a fictional uncle's grave?"

The funeral of Isaak Jumon was an extremely small affair. Sitting on the low slab of a tomb in the New Cemetery, already three-quarters sunken into the earth, January watched the black-clothed forms as they came through the gate from Rue Bienville: pallbearers maneuvering a rather plain pine coffin down the narrow aisle, a priest—January's confessor Père Eugenius, in fact—Antoine Jumon in an even more dandified absurdity of mourning with plumes as well as a scarf on his hat and a candle the size of a child's leg in a cut-paper holder. Madame Geneviève followed, a crêpe-black specter veiled to her knees, leaning on the arm of Hubert Granville. There was a sizable space between the mourners and the catafalque: from where he and his friends sat, January could smell the corpse.

"Give me an ounce of civet, good apothecary, to sweeten my imagination," murmured Hannibal, pressing a handkerchief to his nose. "Are you sure you want to go in for a closer look?" But he stood when January stood, and followed him and Rose quietly as they moved from tomb to tomb, working their way closer to the churchyard wall. Because of the height and closeness of the sepulchers, some barely a yard apart along the weed-grown brick paths, it was possible to come quite near to the cortege—

"—fortunate he belonged to a burial society," Bernadette Metoyer was saying, holding a musk-scented handkerchief to her nose and taking advantage of her distance behind the reeking coffin to chat with her sisters—January recognized them from the Blue Ribbon Balls—and their friends. She nodded toward their destination, a tall square tomb with TRAVAILLEURS DE ST. JACQUES carved on its pediment. Marble slabs, simply inscribed, blocked the mouths of nine of its ten compartments. "At fifty cents a month it's more than she ever laid out."

"Not that I wish to be morbid," said Marie-Eulalie Figes, plump and pretty in a frock of tobacco-colored mousseline de laine, "but that's the kind of improvidence that's going to get poor Geneviève buried in potter's field. That dreary little wheelbarrow of a hearse—pish! And he her eldest son and the only one worth the powder to blow him to hell, in my opinion. And these gloves!" She held up her hand. "Cotton. *Cotton!* And only a little rag of crêpe for an armband, and a penny dip candle. . . ."

"It was Mathurin Jumon we have to thank that there are gloves and crêpe and candles at all," said Agnes Pellicot, a formidable plaçée who had invested her money wisely and was Livia Levesque's closest friend. "Had he not given Geneviève money I don't think she'd even have paid for a hearse. Antoine isn't best pleased."

"By the smell of him," commented Virginie Metoyer, resplendent against all city laws in a mourning bonnet that reminded January forcibly of Plutarch's accounts of Alexander the Great's funeral car, "Antoine will be fortunate to get to and from the tomb without falling down."

January left on the nearest tomb the wreath of zinc ivy he'd brought, and edged from behind a square brick edifice to watch them walk away among the carven trophies of mortality. He'd glimpsed Basile Nogent as one of those who bore the casket, and wondered how many of the elderly sculptor's works surrounded them, each whispering, *You, too, someday.*

Yet there were other words, darker words, whispered by those crowding houses for the dead of stucco, marble, and brick. On a low benchlike grave, barely large enough to shelter a coffin, he saw a cheap plate bearing a slice of pound cake and the glint of silver dimes and reales thrust into the cracks of the bricks. Someone there who had had Power in life. Someone—root doctor or voodooienne—who like the *loa* might be able to come back and help those still struggling in the mortal world. Other tombs were marked, white chalk or red brick dust, or dribbled with wax where candles had been burned. Plates of rice or congris. Scraps of lace. Cigarettes.

Thank him, Mamzelle Marie had said. *Tell others still in fear that prayers do get heard.*

What kind of prayers? January wondered. Colonel Pritchard dead of yellow fever, maybe? A master who changed his mind about selling a slave? A woman who changed hers about whom she would lie with? Someone coming to Paul Corbier's door with work to support him and his family through the slow drag of the summer heat?

(*A bookseller needing four Greek plays translated quick?* whispered a voice in the back of January's mind, and he pushed that thought aside.)

"Ego sum resurrectio et vita," Père Eugenius's voice drifted down the gloomy alleyway. *"Qui credit in me, etiam si mortuus fuerit, vivet: et omnis qui vivit et credit in me, non morietur in aeternum. . . ."*

January crossed himself. Beside him, Hannibal whispered, "Not bad, if your poor sap from the bayou gets a snug grave and a proper burial out of it, whoever he is. Better than the potter's field." He stood, arms folded, looking down toward the little group, and it occurred to January that the potter's field was undoubtedly where Hannibal would one day lie. Then the fiddler grinned, all somberness vanishing from his face, and added, "Think what an embarrassment on Judgment Day." He coughed, the violence of it doubling him up, and he caught for support the empty iron flower-sconce on a tomb marked GRILLOT. From its peaked roof a marble angel regarded him with disdainful eyes.

And as if in response, outside the cemetery wall January heard a horse snort, and the restless jingle of harness. Quietly he stepped back between the tombs and made his way to the gate, Rose and Hannibal at his heels. He could still hear Père Eugenius's voice, *"Benedictus Dominus, Deus Israel, quia visitavit et fecit redemptionem plebus suae. . . ."*

And behind it, Madame Geneviève's hysterical wails.

Just beyond the graveyard gate, the hearse awaited return to town from among the weedy fastnesses of the surrounding Commons. As Bernadette Metoyer had said, it was a plain two-wheeled cart, drawn by a single horse. No plumes, no finery, no crêpe for Isaak Jumon. Beside it a barefoot child held the reins of a very handsome bay gelding, hitched to a green-and-yellow chaise.

"It's at this point," remarked Hannibal, slouching against the gatepost, "that you signal a conveniently passing fiacre, spring into it and cry, 'Follow that chaise. . . .'"

"Which is why the heroes of novels are always noblemen," murmured January. "They're the only ones with cab fare in their pockets at all times. Do me a service, would you?" He checked his watch, and then Hannibal's—which for a wonder was out of pawn—to make sure they read approximately the same time. "Stay here and see what time Granville and Madame Geneviève leave, if they leave together."

"And if they don't leave together?"

"Then I'll have had a long walk for nothing." January stripped off his black coat, and turned up his sleeves against the afternoon's deadly heat. "It's half an hour's walk to Constitution Place. The Metoyer sisters should be enough to delay Madame Geneviève's departure until I can get there. I'm going to find out at least which house there is Granville's, and if it looks like they could have kept Isaak there."

As he stepped through the cemetery gate he looked back. He saw Rose and Hannibal among the tombs, the tall slim woman in her green-gray frock and spectacles, the shabby dark-coated skeleton. Beyond them, his back to a crumbling sepulcher, a man watched the funeral, black-coated, black-hatted, black-gloved, an enigmatic shadow in the hot daylight. Though he was at too great a distance to be sure, January would have sworn that it was Mathurin Jumon.

TWELVE

Thanks to the chattiness of the Metoyer sisters, January had at least ten minutes after his arrival at the head of Florida Walk to loiter and catch his breath.

The whole suburb of Franklin, laid out on what had formerly been Marigny lands, was, like the neighborhood around Colonel Pritchard's house, thinly inhabited. But streets had been laid out—mucky cuttings through the trees—and houses built. Here and there stood handsome residences of two stories, with new gardens brave against the older, sullen growth of cypress and loblolly; more frequently, cottages like his mother's, neat, foursquare dwellings of stucco and brick. *Good if you were a young couple just wed,* reflected January, loafing along with hands in pockets and coat thrown casually over one arm. Good if you sought a quiet neighborhood in which to raise up your children, away from the noise of the old town and the swarming filth of the levees. Good if you wanted the hush of the swamps, the chirp and twitter of egrets and mockingbirds, the thrum of the cicadas in the hot thick summer mid-afternoon. . . .

Good if you were a well-off gentleman seeking a quiet place, not to establish a permanent plaçée in the Creole fashion but to tup a parade of lady friends away from the prying American eyes of your business associates and people who took tea with your wife.

Not so good if you were looking for a place where a young man might have been held against his will for several days.

On the other hand, thought January, looking down the prospect of Florida Walk toward Constitution Place—evidently the "canal and basin" advertised by the sellers of these prime properties was the half-dug ditch down the middle of the street—this part of Franklin was far out enough from the river to be very quiet and very isolated. Sellers of fresh vegetables, of lamp chimneys, of milk strolled the weedy verges of the streets, calling their wares in wailing, singsong African-French: "Miiiilk sweet-fresh-miiiilk just come up from the market miiiilk. . . ." A gang of children fleeted past, white and colored together, voices like the thin jangling of chimes. Someone was chopping wood—or kindling, by the sharp thin clinking sound. The green smell of the swamps weighted the air.

It would be easy, thought January, for someone to take aim with a rifle from any one of those unbuilt lots, those raw straggling stands of magnolia and oak. . . .

He shivered, and kept moving.

In time Hubert Granville's green-and-yellow chaise appeared from the green shade of Elysian Fields Street, and January quickened his loafing pace. Even after the vehicle overtook and passed him it wasn't difficult to keep it in sight. Yesterday's rain had transformed the street to an ocean of muck, and the smart bay gelding had to lean heavily into the collar and drag. Hubert Granville was a good driver, though. He didn't use the whip but kept up a series of encouraging clucks and flips of the reins, letting the beast have its head. As they passed him January made sure to stoop and pick up some imagined coin from the weeds around his feet, so they wouldn't begin to wonder why every black man they saw was nearly six and a half feet tall. . . .

But standing and looking as they moved away, he saw that Granville wasn't alone in the chaise. And the woman beside the banker, veiled to her knees and crowned with a thoroughly illegal bonnet that did indeed look as if a regiment of dragoons had been sacking a flower shop, was unmistakably Geneviève Jumon.

They drew up before a cottage on the swamp side of Constitution Place. Granville was still nose-bagging the horse as January idled closer, then turned down one of the muddy, unnamed streets and disappeared into the trees of a still-virgin lot to observe.

There were four cottages in a row on that side of the square, identical to one another and to his mother's: four rooms, kitchen, and quarters in the rear. The windows were American-style sashes, not old-fashioned French windows: the yards a little bigger and not quite so close together. Close enough, he thought, that any kind of jiggery-pokery would not go unnoticed by neighbors.

A young woman in a calico dress emerged from one of the cottages, bid Granville a saucy "Grüss Gott, Herr Vilmers," as she proceeded down the street. The shutters of both of the other cottages stood open, the windows wide. A black kitten balanced on a sill, watching a dragonfly with lunatic golden eyes.

Granville helped Madame Geneviève from the chaise, and escorted her solicitously into the house. As he opened the door to let her in she flipped back her veils, with the gesture of one relieved unspeakably to be freed of uncomfortable nuisance, and yanked off bonnet, veils, and the tignon underneath. She shook out her dense black uncoiling hair as Granville placed a hand on the small of her back, guiding her inside.

"They didn't even tell me he was being buried." Célie Jumon pressed her small hands together, fist inside fist, and her mouth trembled with shock and grief and rage. "They didn't ask me. Not Papa. Not—not that woman who I suppose I have to call my mother-in-law. Not Mama. . . ."

"Madame Jumon may not have told your parents," said Rose kindly, and glanced from January to Monsieur Nogent and the lawyer Corcet, sitting on the other side of the plain cypress-wood table in the Nogent garçonnière.

"And if it helps any," said January, "and I don't know if it will, I truly don't think the man they buried was your husband. Your mother-in-law wanted to identify some body as her son's as quickly as possible, so that legal matters could be put in train without the complication of a missing body."

Célie glanced up swiftly, wide brown eyes flaming with hope. "You don't think—there isn't a chance that? . . ."

January shook his head. "Antoine saw him die—though Antoine was almost certainly under the influence of opium at the time. In fact Antoine might have been fetched specifically so that there would be a witness to the death." In the back of his mind he heard Olympe's voice, *They said he was alive. All three said he was alive.*

Loa. A spider. Dark voices in a dream.

He would have given his blood, his freedom, his right hand, to have had someone come up to him as he stumbled blindly through the markets of Paris and say, *I'm so sorry, it was all a mistake, Ayasha is alive after all.* . . .

Dreams of agony, of coming up the stairs, opening the door, to see her sitting in her chair by the window with a lapful of some rich woman's frock, stitching calmly in the paling winter light. Open the door and she smiles—Open the door and she's dead on the bed with her hair hanging down, her hand reaching for the water pitcher. . . .

"Madame Jumon." Corcet's soft tenor broke through the bleak and terrible reverie. "Forgive me for asking this, but the matter has been spoken of—mentioned—not by anyone here, you understand. . . . It was brought up at one point that in the event of your husband's death, your father would control such monies as would come to you. . . ."

If he expected the young woman to cry out, or bury her face in her kid-gloved hands, or spring to her feet and smite him across the face, the lawyer was disappointed. Madame Célie sighed, her soft mouth tightening, and she looked down at her folded fingers for a moment. "Did *she* say that?" she asked at length. "Madame Geneviève?"

Corcet hesitated, but January knew there was no point in inflaming enmities and said, "No. It was just a suggestion by a third party who has nothing to do with anyone."

She made a little sound that could have been mirth, and a tear crept from under her lashes, quickly caught. Mourning did not become her. The dress she wore, high waisted and worked high at the neck, had clearly been recut from a stouter woman's gown, probably her mother's. She'd turned back the veils she'd worn over her tignon, but the dark clouds of them surrounded her face and turned her delicate café-crème complexion gray.

"It's the kind of thing that she'd be likely to say, that's all." She drew a deep breath. "And anyone who didn't know Papa well—and he isn't an easy man to know—would probably believe it. But it isn't true."

She touched the handle of the coffee cup before her, white china, simple like the rest of the room. When old Nogent had shown them up the garçonnière steps, Madame Célie had gone ahead, smiling, touching the doorframe and the table, the chairs of cypress and bent willow, like old and beloved friends. It was a plain room, barely better than a servant's, but January thought of what it would be, to live with Père Gérard and his anxious wife.

Madame Célie had made coffee for them, a hostess in exile.

Now she said, "At the jail, you said—or maybe it was your brother-in-law, M'sieu Janvier—that you knew your sister would not do such a thing. Even though she is a voodoo and even though there was poison in her house. Just so I know that Papa wouldn't have harmed Isaak for money.

"Papa . . . is very fond of money." She made again that swift single breath of a chuckle, and glanced up ruefully under long lashes. "Well, I don't think that's any secret from you. And he didn't want me to marry Geneviève Jumon's son. He didn't want to be connected with her in marriage, and quite frankly I have to say I agree with him.

"Grand-père and Grand-mère were very poor when Papa was born, you see, and they all—Papa and his parents and all his brothers and sisters—had to put up with not only inconveniences, and hunger, but . . . but indignities. The way people treat you. There was not enough money for all of them to leave St. Domingue together, when the trouble started, so Papa came here first, to work and send money so that the others could come away before Christophe's men came out of the jungles and took Port-au-Prince. . . . And the others did not get the money in time. They never came. Papa doesn't know to this day what happened to them. Papa says that money is the only thing that keeps us safe, the only thing that protects us, now against the Americans as well."

She was silent, tracing the rim of the cup with her fingers, looking down at the black reflection within. Then she said, "But Papa would never have harmed anyone for money. Not for five thousand dollars or five hundred thousand dollars."

Still she did not look up. January thought about that plump little man, furious over his daughter's reputation, furious over his family's standing, hiring the •best white French lawyer, blackmailing the Recorder's Clerk by bringing a reporter into the room. . . . Thought about Olympe, that morning when he had gone to see her at the Cabildo. The stench of the cells and the creeping, endless trails of ants. The drone of the flies.

"Would his mother have done it? Geneviève Jumon?"

Célie shook her head. "She is—a wicked woman, M'sieu. But I don't see how any woman could . . . could do that to her own son."

Even if she were under the influence of a man who wanted more money for his own investments?

"What about Uncle Mathurin?" he asked. "If it comes down to a renewal of the lawsuit, the money may very well come to him, and Antoine seems to think he's the devil in shoe leather."

She laughed softly. "Antoine." And there was very real affection in her smile. "Antoine called me the Fata Morgana, and Messalina, and compared me to Jezebel sitting in her window—and later of course when we came to know one another he pretended he'd never said any such things. Antoine has never liked Uncle Mathurin, and he hated his father. In that, he's like his mother."

Her face clouded. There was a darkness in the back of her eyes, the memory of scenes that had passed between herself and her husband's mother.

"Why is that?" asked January.

She shook her head. "I never knew what the original quarrel was," she answered. "It must have been serious, for a woman like that—a plaçée, I mean—with two small children to abandon her protector. She has a—a foul temper, but she's also a woman who keeps an eye on the main chance, as they say. It wasn't M'sieu Laurence's marriage, at any rate. That came later.

"Isaak wouldn't speak of it," she added after a moment. "Only that he had a choice between taking on his mother's bitterness—poisoning himself and our children, he said—or putting aside the past in order to regain the father he had lost." She pressed her hand very suddenly to her mouth. Rose put an arm around her shoulders, and after a moment Madame Célie drew breath again, and seemed to relax.

"It's true Uncle Mathurin is a cynic and deist and doesn't attend church. But he has done a great deal of good. Secretly, the way Jesus said one should, with not even the left hand knowing that the right one is slipping money to those in need. Sometimes we'd meet them, Isaak and I, when we went to the house—we'd wait for him in the garden outside the garçonnière, and we'd see them coming out. I remember there was a young Russian man, Dobrov I think his name was, a sailor who'd jumped ship: Uncle Mathurin gave him money to live on while he learned French, and went to school to learn accounting so he could find a job. There was a young woman he supported after her husband passed away in the cholera—perfectly aboveboard, as I think they say. . . . Isaak carved a horse for her little daughter, with tiny roses on its saddle and bridle. He loved children. . . ."

Her voice thinned again, and this time she sat longer, perfectly still, as if fearing that movement would set off unbearable inner pain. Only her hand closed around Rose's, tight, a grip upon a lifeline.

Then, quite steadily, she said, "I can't believe he's gone. I can't believe he's gone."

January closed his eyes, the scent of his dead wife's hair clear as a nightmare in his nostrils again.

A very fanciful little boy, Mathurin Jumon had said.

My uncle Mathurin is a consummately evil man.

The tall house standing aloof on Rue St. Louis, empty save for one old woman sleeping alone. A Palissy-ware teapot and a mattress of straw in an empty room.

He visited Olympe at the Cabildo the following morning, taking Gabriel and the two younger children with him. January wasn't easy in his mind about bringing Chouchou and Ti Paul to the jail; and at the sight of the four-year-old, Mad Solie began to shriek that the child must be taken away, taken away quickly or her father would come and murder him.

"Shut her up," growled a hoarse voice from the same cell, "she's scarin' the little bastard."

The shrieks abruptly stopped.

"It'll be all right." Olympe pressed her face to her smallest son's plump hands through the bars. "It'll be all right." Another woman might have been in tears; Olympe's face was like wood.

Behind her in the cell a voice asked in English, "Kin I kiss 'em, too? I sure do miss my little boy."

"I still think we oughta get a real big gris-gris and lay it on that M'am Geneviève," opined Gabriel, as January descended the gallery stairs afterward with Chouchou, silent as ever, by the hand. Gabriel carried Ti Paul, and January felt a weary anger all over again that he could not lift his niece and nephew in his arms, as he had been used to do. "We could take and split an ox tongue and write her name in it, with some silver money and peppers, and sew it up and leave it on a tomb in the graveyard, and call the spirit Onzoncaire—Onzoncaire'll do anything, if you remember to pay him off with a sheep's head and a bottle of whisky."

As they reached the bottom of the stairs the sergeant at arms in charge of such things cracked his rawhide whip over the back of a slave triced to the post in the center of the yard. Gabriel flinched, but tried to look casual, as if it didn't have anything to do with him. "Onzoncaire's this hoodoo spirit with red eyes, and dog's teeth, and . . ."

"We've had enough gris-gris around here," January told his nephew grimly. "And if I hear you doing *any* calling of *any* hoodoo spirits, I'll get your papa to wear you out."

"Mama does," pointed out Chouchou.

"Your mama knows good from evil," said January, though he knew Père Eugenius would have a quarrel with this statement. "I bet your mama never called on any hoodoo spirit with dog's teeth." He wasn't at all sure this was the truth, but Gabriel, he noticed, looked thoughtful.

In the big watch room he inquired after Lieutenant Shaw, and was told—as he expected—that the Lieutenant was out on his rounds. He handed Sergeant deMezieres at the desk a note detailing all he had observed after the funeral, and what he had learned from the Metoyer maid about Geneviève Jumon's actual or probable whereabouts on the evening of her son's death, and what Railspike and Kentucky Williams had had to say about Isaak's departure and Mr. Nash's employer.

Not, he thought uneasily, as he stepped out into the liquid warmth of the arcade's shadows, that it would do him a particle of good if Mr. Nash were waiting for him somewhere in the crowds of the Place d'Armes. On the way to the Cabildo that morning he had instructed Gabriel to run *immediately* in the event of trouble, taking the younger children with him. . . . He hoped the boy would actually do so.

"Would Onzoncaire take care of Uncle Ben," asked Chouchou gravely, "if we paid him off?"

"Sure," said Gabriel, then cast a worried glance up at his uncle. "I mean—well, I guess God could, too."

"Thank you," said January, wondering why he tried. "And I'm sure God thanks you, too."

For the rest of the day he worked at his translation of *The Knights*. But the absurdly involved efforts of Demosthenes and Nicias to find a tyrant for Athens were insufficient to distract him from the thought of that tall silent half-empty house, and the baroque gleam of sunlight on a Palissy-ware cup. Both Dominique and his mother had departed for Milneburgh Tuesday, and it would take Minou a day to settle in, before she could reasonably expect Thérèse to take a half-day off to make inquiries of the Jumon servants. And on Friday, the Fourth of July, he knew Henri would be coming in from the family plantation, and Minou would be picnicking with him along the shores of the lake, no doubt with her handmaiden in attendance. But a note, at least, he thought, as he brushed his black coat and pressed his good linen shirt preparatory to the long walk to the Soames's residence in Spanish Fort, would be appreciated.

The long walk—over an hour along the shell road that rimmed Bayou St. John—was the result of lacking the twenty-five-cent fare for the steam-train. He and Hannibal made it together in the gluey heat of twilight, accompanied by those other musicians of the town likewise affected by the slow season: Philippe deCoudreau, Ramesses Ramilles, Casimir and Florimond Valada, Jacques Bichet, and others, all comparing notes about the contenders for French and American social prominence who had, as they frequently did, scheduled their entertainments for the same evening, as a way of forcing their acquaintances to publicly proclaim who they thought more critical to their social success.

"I hear there's a fix been put on you," remarked deCoudreau. "We better watch out, or poor M'am Soames's piano strings gonna bust in the middle of the grand march, and we all get rained on like hell on the way home."

"Where'd you hear that?" asked January, and from the corner of his eye saw the Valada brothers exchange a quick, worried look between them, and fall back a pace or two.

DeCoudreau shrugged. "Where does anybody hear anything, Ben? It's just around."

"Around like that story last year that you were getting married?" inquired Hannibal, stopping, as he had stopped a dozen times, to rest. "And to Liliane Verret, of all people?"

The matter passed off in a laugh, but in fact Mrs. Soames's piano went massively out of tune halfway through the dancing later that evening and a total of ten gentlemen had to be forcibly restrained, at one time or another in the evening, from challenging one another to duels or entering combat outright. Two of these challenges were issued by Madame Redfern's jealous cicisbeo Greenaway, and only forcible restraint kept him from issuing a third to Clément Vilhardouin—one of the few Frenchmen in attendance—when the lawyer mentioned he had dined with the lady again that evening.

This was a high percentage even for an American entertainment— "Two's the average," remarked Hannibal, surreptitiously dumping an ounce of opium tincture into the watered beer, which was all the hostess considered appropriate to offer musicians. "It must be the election coming up, or else somebody sneaked actual alcohol into her liquor."

In addition to the gubernatorial supporters of Mr. White speaking ill of his rival General Dawson, Colonel Pritchard attempted unsuccessfully to call out the Reverend Micajah Dunk for implying that the female slave Kitta who had escaped from Pritchard's household had done so because Pritchard had sold her husband Dan—"I am not implying such a thing, sir, I am stating it outright," responded Dunk— and two entrepreneurs who were attempting to raise capital in Philadelphia each separately challenged Burton Blodgett, once it was realized that the journalist had entered the party, clad in sloppy evening dress, unnoticed by a back door. Evangeline Soames said her majordomo had undoubtedly been bribed and would be whipped.

It rained like hell on the way home, long after the final steam-train had departed. After Philippe deCoudreau's seventh jest on the subject of hexes and fixes, January had to pinch his own hand very hard between thumb and forefinger to remind himself not to throw the jolly clarionetist into the bayou.

So it was not until the following day—Saturday—that January made the five-mile walk again to Milneburgh, to speak to his sister's maid on the subject of what the Jumon servants had seen on the night of June twenty-third.

"But they're all packed up and gone, M'sieu Janvier." Thérèse regarded him with some surprise, as if he should have known this and saved himself the walk. "The Jumons have a house in Mandeville."

"Henri and I took the ferry across yesterday—to Mandeville, I mean," put in Dominique, stirring the lemonade the maid had brought to them with a long silver spoon. The rear of the little white cottage Henri had bought for his plaçée stood on stilts over the water. Wavelets clucked and whispered among the pilings and the gray knobbled pillars of the cypress knees that studded the shallows in the shade. "It's ever so much nicer than Milneburgh. More exclusive, if you understand. Quieter. Sometimes I'm sorry they put the steam-train in between here and town; one gets all those—well, those uptown chaca girls and their beaux, and all the clerks and shopgirls on Sunday outings, bowling and shooting at the shooting galleries and eating ices in the taverns and making such a ruckus."

She sighed, and fanned herself with a circle of stiffened china silk, for even on the narrow terrace above the water, the day was warm. Beside her in a white wicker cage, a half-dozen ornamental finches provided riveting entertainment for her plump white cat.

"Is it possible," asked January patiently, wondering why no one had ever strangled his youngest sister, "for Thérèse to go out there and speak to her cousin—Aveline, is it?—sometime soon?"

"Oh, but p'tit, we just have weeks and weeks of time." Dominique regarded him with widened eyes and reached to put a hand on his knee. "And they're not going to let poor Olympe out of prison any the sooner because of what you'll find out from Cousine Aveline."

"No," said January. "But Cousine Aveline's information may be only an indication of something else we need to find out. And we have, in fact, eleven days to find out everything we need, whatever that might be."

"P'tit, I'm so sorry!" Minou reached behind her and took Thérèse's hand. The maid, clothed in a sober but extremely stylish frock of green muslin in contrast to her mistress's fantasia of honeycomb smocking, lappets, and lace, looked rather put out that her efforts in the direction of locating evidence had not been properly appreciated. "Thérèse, dearest, you won't mind going out to Mandeville tomorrow—oh, no, the day after tomorrow, Iphégénie and Marie-Anne are coming for tea—oh, no, Tuesday, because Becky needs the help Monday with the laundry. . . . Tuesday definitely, p'tit. . . . You won't mind going to Mandeville Tuesday to speak with your cousin, will you, dear? Only you'll have to be back to serve at dinner, because Henri will be here. Would you believe it, p'tit?"

She reached out again and grasped January's hand. "Would you believe that dreadful Redfern cow has issued invitations to a Bastille Day party? Doesn't she know *anything* about France having a King again, even if it is only that awful Louis-Philippe? Even *Henri* knows that!"

As it happened, January knew all about Mrs. Redfern's Bastille Day gala because he'd been contracted to play at it. A thought had come to his mind concerning the absence of the Jumon household in Mandeville and the vacancy of the houses on Rue St. Louis. He accepted his sister's invitation to lunch—trying not to appear too grateful—and turned the thought over again in his mind while walking back along the shell road to town: walking quickly and staying as close as he could to the other strollers and riders and passengers in carriages, out taking the half-holiday air.

Hannibal was still asleep when January reached home—he'd been coughing blood the last hour of the ball, keeping himself to the back of the group and concealing his illness with the skill of practice. Bella's room stank of opium, but January couldn't find it in his heart to be angry. In the kitchen January found half a pot of coffee warming at the back of the hearth. Though there was no evidence that anything in the kitchen—or in the garçonnière, where January had scattered thin dust on the floor that would take any scuff or track—had been disturbed, he poured the coffee down the outhouse: with some regret, coffee being ten cents a pound. He drew water from the cistern to bathe, and afterward lay on his bed to get what sleep he could, and dreamed of his father.

"They help you out, but you got to pay them off," his father said, touching the sheep skull nailed to an oak tree in the *cipriere,* the offering to whatever spirit it was who had granted someone a wish. The bark of the tree was blotched with brick dust and candle wax, and among the roots of the tree little handfuls of rice and chickpeas were carefully laid out on leaves. "Bosou, he guards those folk that run off into the *cipriere.* They live there in a village as we lived in Africa, away from the whites. But they don't just forget him, any more than they'd forget a man who helped them. They show respect, as you must show respect, and Bosou guards the way behind them. Maybe one day he'll guard the way behind you."

In his dream it was as he remembered it, the trail of ants creeping up the bark of the tree, the hum of the flies and the wriggling of maggots in what was left of the sheep's flesh, the stink of blood and rum.

"You got to thank them," his father said. "You got to thank them."

Then he stood on one foot with his back to the skull and snapped his fingers, and watched while January—a tiny boy-child as he'd been then—did the same, and spoke words January didn't remember. In his dream he heard instead a quote from Lucretius: *Augescunt alie gentes, alie minuuntur / Inque brevi spatio mutantur saecla animantum / Et quasi cursores vitae lampada tradunt.*

Some races grow, others diminish, and in a short span of time the living are changed; like runners they relay the torch of life.

Which he knew could not be right.

But as he and his father walked away he felt eyes in those empty sockets, watching them, and distantly he heard the tapping of African drums.

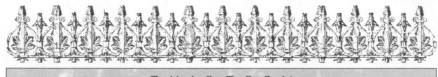

THIRTEEN

"I never thought I'd thank God the rich all leave town by the end of June." January put his head out of the narrow passway between houses, scanned the still silence of Rue St. Louis. By the dim reflection of the oil lamp at the next intersection all was still; a heavy stillness rank of heat and stench and mosquito whine. A cat darted from an alley, bolted across the street, vanished.

Stillness again.

"If we can't get a witness about what happened here, at least there's no one to keep us from seeing what there is to be seen."

"There is nothing either good or bad but thinking makes it so." Hannibal coughed, one hand holding himself upright against the crumbling stucco and the other pressed to his side. "If you ever find out how to make consumption good by thinking, please let me know. I've been trying for years. Did you ever track down the map your cut-armed friend brought to Isaak, by the way? Find where the meeting place was, if it was a meeting place?"

"I'm sure it was." January waited, listening, watching the alley from which the cat had fled. A hundred feet away, on Rue Bourbon, music jangled and men quarreled over their cards in the gambling halls that still ran full-open, but here the stillness was weirdly complete. Only the croaking of the frogs in the gutters sounded—*ouaouarons,* the slaves called them, not proper French *grenouilles*—and the roar of the cicadas around the streetlamps. "But with whom, and for what purpose—that's another matter."

In time, satisfied with the hush, he stepped from shelter and led the way across the street, holding close under his arm the dark leather bundle of his medical bag. The Jumon town house rose above them, somehow more isolated than a plantation would have been, perhaps because even when the family was absent, a plantation was never empty. There were always the hands in the quarters, children's voices, the clack of axes, and the smell of animals. Here there was nothing but the lingering stench of gunpowder and hooves burning somewhere, and the gutters' unending stink. January walked calmly, unhurried. Though curfew had long ago sounded, only some twenty Guards held night watch in the French town. By the sound of it, the taverns of Rue Bourbon would be occupying most of their attention.

"I went out there this morning," he continued, as they concealed themselves again in the dense arch of shadow that was the carriageway. "It was pretty clear from Railspike's description that that map showed the waste ground out past the Protestant cemetery and the end of Gravier's canal. There's a little bayou there, and an oak with a twisted-back limb. Old Michie Crippletree, we used to call it. All the slaves used it for a meeting place, because everyone knew it. I expect whites who grew up around here knew it, too."

Hannibal drew a pair of thin-nosed pliers and a length of bent wire from his pocket and set to work on the carriage-gate lock. "And did you find the teacup Mathurin Jumon served Isaak the arsenic in?"

"I found *a* teacup with arsenic stains in it," replied January gravely, his eyes moving ceaselessly up and down the dark streets. "I didn't attach much importance to it because the teacup was Sèvres *pâte dur* instead of Palissy ware. Oh, and there was a copy of Laurence Jumon's will impaled on the tree trunk with an Arabian dagger, and one of Isaak's visiting cards. Why do you ask?"

"Just curious. And up she comes." He pushed the wrought-iron gate inward a little, then closed it to behind them, pulling out the black ribbon that tied his hair to bind the gate loosely shut again. "Was the visiting card also impaled on the tree trunk with a dagger?"

"On the other side of the tree," extemporized January, scratching a lucifer and shielding the candle he took from his bag. "Separate dagger."

"Also Arabian?"

"Venetian." Their whispers echoed in the arch of the flagged carriageway. "Quattrocento. Cellini, I think."

"Cellini made good daggers." Hannibal nodded wisely. "An excellent choice. Tasteful."

"Which would argue that it had to have been Mathurin. I mean, I can't see Hubert Granville having the refinement to buy a Cellini dagger." They emerged into the dark courtyard, the closed and shuttered bulk of the slave quarters looming before them against the sooty sky. The fountain muttered softly; the candlelight showed up a cat's eyes, hunting frogs among the banana plants.

"A point, my friend. A most distinct point."

"All daggers," said January, in a tone of deep solemnity, "have a point," and Hannibal went into a fit of coughing from trying to stifle a laugh.

From the courtyard there was no way to break into the shop, but whatever had been there, January guessed, had been cleared out for the new tenant: JOSEF BRAEDEN, he had seen the legend inscribed on the door. DENTIST. For a few minutes he held his breath, as he and Hannibal moved into the center of the brick-paved space; it was always possible that one or two of the slaves had been left behind to watch the house. But Madame Cordelia, it appeared, would not lessen her comfort in the Mandeville house—or else she was unwilling to let any of her servants remain unsupervised in the city for two months. No light flared in any of the rooms that opened from the galleries that rose above the kitchen. No voice called out, demanding who was there, and when January and Hannibal climbed to check them, the rooms were vacant and stripped of their simple goods.

A brief visit to the local livery stable had already informed January that the six Jumon horses were gone. On the other side of the courtyard, the inevitable garçonnière lay above the office where January had spoken to Mathurin Jumon, reached by a narrow stair. "A Chubb," whispered Hannibal, fingering the lock as January handed him the long-bladed scalpels, the forceps, and the bullet-probe he'd brought, along with his mother's kitchen candles, in his bag. "I figured Grand-mère Jumon for a locker-upper."

"With the jewels she wears?" breathed January back. "We'll be lucky if we can get into the main house."

"We should have gotten Dago Crimms to help us. He'd have kept his mouth shut, and he wouldn't have taken much." The fiddler's hands were shaking as he worked with the picks, and he stopped twice, once to press his hand to his side to still his coughing, and again to take a cautious sip of opium. In the narrow yellow glow of the candle his face was set and lined with pain.

"It would only take one item traced back to us," said January grimly, "for all of us to be in a lot more trouble than we are."

"Oh, Dr. Yellowjack's generally pretty careful where he fences his plunder. Yellowjack's Dago's receiver," Hannibal added. "Savvy old bastard. Works it all up through Natchez. Never lets himself come into view at all—always uses a cat's-paw of some kind, tells one person one thing, another another. . . . Which is the way not to get caught. And here we are." The latch gave under his hand. "Like ladies and moneyed relatives, it's all in how you ask."

There was a library on the floor immediately above the office, and above it, two small bedrooms. Holding the candle aloft, January had an impression of a beautiful desk of Syrian work, inlaid shell and colored woods in ebony, of gold-stamped books on the shelves instead of the workaday ledgers downstairs, of chairs under Holland covers. On desk and mantel, and locked behind the glass fronts of cabinet shelves, platters, ewers, tureens gleamed in the tiny flame: exquisite glazes, fantastic and intricately accurate shapes. Snailshells, salamanders, fish so meticulously rendered, January could tell a drum from a bass; strawberry leaves, clover, lettuces, worms. *Nothing that anyone these days would remotely describe as good taste,* thought January, studying a bowl sculpted in the likeness of a forest floor—ferns, mosses, pebbles, tiny flowers, small snakes, and pillbugs all exact. *But a garden of bizarre delight all the same.*

Another portrait of Madame Cordelia Jumon smiled from behind a protective draping of gauze, and drawing this aside, January gazed up for a moment into the long, delicate face, the haughty nose, and the dark eyes beneath a snowy extravaganza of high-piled, rose-swagged hair. Lapdogs peeped from beneath the flounces of a green Court gown wider than its wearer was tall. He tried to picture this girl—for she seemed no more than sixteen—operating a plantation such as the one on which he'd been born.

He'd heard someone—his mother? Dominique?—mention in passing Hercule Jumon's decease when the two boys were small. That would have put it somewhere in the nineties. After the fall of the King, anyway. This lovely, Court-raised girl, left a widow in her teens, would have had no home to return to. In his mind he heard Célie Jumon's voice: *Papa never knew what happened to them. . . .*

"Well, it answers one question anyway," remarked Hannibal, as they made cursory investigations of each garçonnière bedroom, then passed along the gallery to the rear of the main house. "Why Laurence's wife left. That bedroom of his doesn't look like it's ever been cleared out. Not that any woman in her senses would share quarters with Grand-mère Jumon, but I'm sure living in the garçonnière wasn't what she had in mind, either."

"I don't see how she could have kept her son from taking up residence in the main house once he'd married." January held the candle close as Hannibal knelt to study the lock on the shutters that covered the central door. Another Chubb, bright against the yellow paint. By the marks in the woodwork, the house had had half a dozen different locks in its some fifty years of existence.

"Allow me to introduce you to my aunt Boadicaea one day. I'll bet she kept him out in the garçonnière at Trianon, too, wife or no wife. My guess—just watching her with Mathurin at the balls—is that she was jealous."

January remembered Mathurin's voice, calling out desperately for his mother to wait. *Mama, please. . . .*

Did Laurence's voice have that tone as well? Had he always turned first to his mother, to see what she said? Did he leave his wife standing, as Mathurin had left January, to hurry after Maman when she was in a taking?

Certainly he had left Madame Cordelia in charge of the household, the keys, the stores, the servants. The money, though in marrying he had automatically gained a share of the family affairs. Maybe he'd thought things would change, after he was wed.

"It isn't as if there isn't plenty of room in the house," he said, as Hannibal pulled open the shutters and set to work on the lock that defended the door within.

"Did you see the portraits in the boys' bedrooms?"

January nodded. The one in Mathurin's room portrayed Cordelia as Diana at some long-forgotten palace fête, complete with bow and dogs.

The one in Laurence's room had been done later, to judge by the high-waisted gown and the two slaves kneeling allegorically at her feet. He thought about it a moment, then said, "There could be a hundred reasons for him not to have a portrait of his wife in his bedroom."

"There could." Hannibal straightened up, and pocketed his pick-locks. Darkness seemed to flow out through the open doors: straw matting, patchouli, frowsty heat. "But I'll bet the same one is at the top of both of our lists."

Four more portraits of Cordelia Jumon adorned the main house. The one in the drawing room was done in golds, to complement the soft apricot walls; the one in the dining room in lighter, brighter hues, befitting the flowered summer chintz of the draperies and the exquisite neo-Gothic furniture of the room. There were two in Madame's bed-room, one of them painted in the past five years, showing enormous Marie sleeves and the bell-shaped skirts still in fashion. But all the painters had rendered her face as the face of youth, pink-cheeked, smil-ing, not much more than seventeen.

It wasn't hard to see where Mathurin got his love of collecting. Dresden figurines, Chinese vases, Venetian glass cluttered the marble-topped tables, draped in gauze to protect them from summer flies. Cabinets housed trinkets, statuettes, dried flowers, each item a gem of exquisite taste. Madame's bed, shrouded in Holland, would not have disgraced German royalty, and even through layers of gauze the lusters of the chandeliers winked and twinkled in the invading sliver of light.

"Selling the land must have realized a bundle," remarked Hannibal softly. "I imagine Cordelia did it when Laurence's wife left and it was clear there would be no children. All this furniture is only about seven years old. I remember the Gothic craze; look at that table. The dishes in the dining room are new, too."

Beyond a final twist of upstairs corridor a stair no wider than a ladder ascended, and dust powdered down around them as January pushed up the attic trapdoor, glimmering in the light.

It was above the level of habitation that the house's age showed. Waist-thick cypress beams supported the slates of the roof, pegged to-gether without nails, the numbers still visible where the Senegalese house carpenters had assembled them. Dust and time and darkness congealed in three stifling slant-roofed chambers, chambers crammed to bursting, it seemed, with everything the two Jumon boys and their

mother had ever owned. Trunks, crates, boxes, barrels held every garment they had ever worn, every gimcrack and knickknack that had ever
caught their fancy, down to expensive French toys—including one of
those toy guillotines that had been so popular in Paris in the nineties—
and tin after empty, bright-colored tin that had once contained sweets.
Newspapers and old books stacked the corners; armoires in outmoded
styles bulged with dresses equally unfashionable; bolts and rolls of dam-
ask, brocade, taffeta silk still lay in the paper they'd been sold in, colors
that had once been the high kick of fashion, out of style even before
they could be made up. Sets of dishes, at least six of them, Limoges and
Crown Derby and Sèvres edged in gold; a Chippendale dining room
table and chairs and another carved with the crocodile feet and sphinxes
popular during Napoleon's reign. Boys' shoes, dozens of pairs, in a box,
graded in sizes, worn and outgrown; wineglasses packed in straw. In
another box, rusted chains. January nearly dropped them, repelled:
spiked collars, such as some masters still put on disobedient slaves.
Manacles and irons kinked and clotted together in a lump with dirt and
oxidation.

"That isn't surprising." Hannibal led the way into the central and
largest of the attic's three chambers. "A young girl like that, left a widow
on a plantation, might feel she had to enforce discipline however she
could." He coughed in the dust, and took another swig of opium.
"We've both seen worse."

A wedding veil and dried bouquet, done up in tissue. An intricately
wrought wreath of someone's hair.

The third attic was the smallest, crammed like the others. January
shone the light carefully over the secret shut trunk lids, the tight-nailed
cases, the piles of books and newspapers thick with dust. "You couldn't
have kept anyone up here," remarked Hannibal, scraping the unsullied
dust on the floor with the toe of his boot. "Not without leaving a sign."
January knelt, squinting and peering at the dust on the floor, on the
trunks: years' worth of it, decades. Under the layer of grime the floor
was scratched. The attic seemed the smallest because its three sides,
where the hip of the roof ran down to the floor, had at some time in the
past been boarded across, forming smaller storage areas too low to enter
without kneeling. Two of these were simply latched. The third, the
smallest, across the downstream end of the house, was locked, with an
old-fashioned sash-ward lock, the only lock in the house that hadn't
been replaced or renewed.

"You can't say she kept him in the cupboard," protested Hannibal. "Anyway, it would have disturbed the dust if it had been opened, and you can see it hasn't."

"Open it anyway," said January. "I want to broaden my outlook."

He wasn't sure what he expected to find there. Bottles of arsenic, perhaps, or Isaak Jumon's clothes. He knelt, and crawled a little way in on all fours, holding the candle before him, and the smell rose up around him and made his flesh shrink on his bones.

An old faint stink ground into the wood of the floorboards, attenuated by time: piss, and waste, which even cleaned up cannot ever be completely eradicated. All the attics had stunk of mice and rats. This was different.

Someone had been kept up here, long ago.

He angled the candle's light into the black awful space's farthest corners, and spiders edged away, indignant at the interruption of their affairs. The dead husks of withered palmetto bugs made long black streaks of shadow.

The floor was scratched a little, old scratches. All around the lock, the wood of the door was scraped, as if someone had ground at it patiently, hopelessly, with a chip of metal or a bit of stone, or maybe the edge of a ring, in an effort to get free. Drips and spatters and little squiggles stained the floor, black with age, amid a paler brown mottling, puddle after puddle after puddle, cleaned up but never cleaned up enough. Something lay in the farthest corner, where the roof met the floor, and January stretched on his belly to pull it out, mouse-chewed and dropping a clatter of rodent pellets as he brought it to him. It was only a rag, knotted hard in a circle and then later cut with what looked like scissors, so that the knot remained. Opposite the knot, the tough, damasked linen was stained black. January touched the cut ends together. The circle they made wasn't quite fourteen inches around. Too small to have gagged an adult.

"There's more of them back here," said Hannibal quietly.

January backed out of the cupboard, to see his friend sitting on the floor near the high-piled trunks and boxes, hands filled to overflowing with chunks and scraps and bights of sheet, cut and knotted, wrinkled, stained with mouse-piss and blood.

"There's a whole cache of them behind the trunks. As if she just cut them off, and shoved them out of sight."

January turned them over in his fingers, disgust and loathing rising like physical nausea in him as he identified which bonds had to have been tied around wrists not more than an inch in diameter, which had bound ankles, or been gags. No chicken foot, no beef tongue sewed up around silver and guinea peppers, no black wax and graveyard dust, had ever touched him with what he felt now: the sense of evil in its purest and most gruesome form.

He said, "Let's get out of here. I've seen enough."

From halfway up Rue St. Louis he looked back at the house, tall and impenetrable, shrouded in its galleries between tall impenetrable neighbors. For some reason it reminded him of the square brick tombs in the cemetery, names scriven on the marble of those who slept there forever: rotting bones, for the most part, shoved back into corners until time would compound them forever with the earth. At a horse trough outside a grocery on Rue Dauphine he stooped to wash from his hands the filth of the attic's floor, black streaks like graveyard dust in the starlight.

It was five days before January heard from Thérèse.

Having made the journey to Milneburgh once to jog his sister's memory on the subject, he didn't feel able to do so again. In any case he could ill spare either the train fare or the time. For two days he worked at his translation of *The Knights,* attempting to deal tactfully with jokes about wrestling coaches and such lines as: *Lying, stealing, and having a receptive arse are all absolute necessities for a political career. . . .*

Had that bookseller ever *read* this play?

And every day, working at his desk, January would smell it, the bitter stench of hair and hooves and gunpowder burning, where someone had made smolder pots in a courtyard to disperse fever from the air. Walking back from Rose's rooms in the evening, he passed Dufillio's apothecary on Rue Chartres and saw that the show globes on display—enormous alembics and bulbous jars of colored liquid, blue and green and crimson in equal proportion most of the year—were now uniformly filled with red, a glowing warning to those travelers who came off the steamboats and walked about the city in the mosquito-whining dusk. There were fewer women in the markets, fewer stevedores even among the diminished numbers along the levee; fewer children played in the packed earth of the Place d'Armes. The Guards, when he went to the Cabildo in the mornings to see Olympe, hovered near to watch and listen, and hustled him and Gabriel quickly out. It seemed to him that the prisoners were very quiet.

On Wednesday a note reached him from Dr. Ker, asking his help at Charity Hospital with fever cases.

In two days, nearly a hundred had been brought in, mostly impoverished Germans and Irish from the shacks where Girod and Perdido Streets petered out into the marshes behind the town. For two days January worked late into the nights, wiping down bodies flushed with jaundice, making saline draughts, watching in helpless frustration as the various volunteer physicians of the town administered whatever remedies they considered appropriate for a disease as mysterious as death itself: bleeding, emetics, "heroic" doses of calomel and mercury ("If their gums don't bleed, it ain't enough to work"), plasters that raised blisters on the emaciated flesh. Sometimes their patients recovered, damaged kidneys releasing blood-black urine in a flood. Sometimes they died.

And with every new case brought in, with every wrung and wasted corpse January helped carry down to the courtyard for the dead-carts, he thought, *Not the cholera. We can deal with the yellow jack if the cholera doesn't return.*

The *Louisiana Gazette* ran an editorial furiously denouncing the white-livered cowards who fled the city—*the healthiest spot in the nation!*—at the rumor of a little summer fever. Père Eugenius, meeting January late one evening in the brick corridor of the hospital, remarked dryly that members of the City Council had requested that the Cathedral not toll the passing bells, "Lest folks coming through on the steamboats get the wrong impression." Twice Burton Blodgett was ejected from the hospital's courtyard at the request of Councilman Bouille, when the journalist showed signs of trying to get up conversations with the volunteers who worked the wards.

On the second occasion, Bouille—who had been in and out of the hospital all day in an effort to accommodate Ker's requests for help and to assure the staff that there was, in fact, no epidemic—all but wrested the journalist away from a plump German gentleman named Weber, who had been a physician in Bavaria but was insufficiently versed in French or English to have much of a practice in New Orleans. "There is no cholera, understand?" He almost shouted the words at the German. "*Verstehen? Der ist nein.* . . . You make him understand," the Councilman ordered January, who happened to be nearby. "And you!" Bouille added, turning in fury to the loitering reporter and snatching the notebook from his hand. "Sniffing about where you have no business, seeking scandal and panic, like a muckraker hoping to stir up treasure from the bottom of a pool by fouling it for all who rely upon it for sustenance! All you care about is your miserable rag—no, not even that, but your wretched name, your delight in seeing 'Our Correspondent' in print!"

"I care, sir," retorted Blodgett, drawing himself up to his full height in the glare of the gallery lamps, "about the First Amendment of the Constitution—and also the laws of this city which guard a citizen against theft of his property." He held out his hand for the notebook.

Bouille ripped the pages from it and threw them to the wet bricks of the courtyard. "Citizen? Citizen?"

"He is a citizen and a taxpayer." Dr. Ker descended the gallery stair and crossed the courtyard quickly to the growing knot of volunteers, medical students, and surgeons. "The notebook is his property—and in fact, Charity Hospital is public property—"

"Easy for you to say," snapped the Councilman, a wiry little French Creole who had been in three duels that January knew about. "*You* are not a native. *You* have no stake, *you* do not care what businessmen and investors in the rest of the world think of our city. You, an enemy of this nation! But I assure you, I will report your attitude to the Council, and you"—he turned on Blodgett again—"The editors of every paper in this city will hear, not only from me but from other members of the Council, members whose assistance and advertising they may require in future—"

"City Councilman Bouille says that there has been no cholera," translated January quietly, to the thoroughly alarmed German. "And he would appreciate it if you do not speak on the subject to anyone. This is how panic and rumor start, which can ruin businesses."

"People in the rest of the world, even in the rest of the United States, they do not understand our city," Bouille stormed, cheeks mottled with rage. "They have only to see words like *fever* and *cholera* and they panic, like fools, like women, like children!" He stepped aside to avoid two volunteers carrying a dead man to the gate. "They think, 'New Orleans is a dangerous place!' And it is not. It is the most healthful spot in the world. As its *true* inhabitants know! You shall hear from the Council," he ranted at Dr. Ker, "your editors shall hear from the Council," he continued, whirling again on Blodgett, who had stood this whole time like a man who perceives himself about to be martyred for Justice's sake, "and you, sir, shall hear from my—"

"I think it would be best if I had a few words with Mr. Blodgett outside," said Ker firmly, and took the reporter's arm in his hand, nearly dragging him toward the hospital gates. Bouille looked as if he would follow and complete his challenge, but it began to rain again, a driving black downpour that cleared the court in moments.

Encountering January later in the fever ward, Ker muttered, "I don't hold with dueling as a rule, but there are people for whose sake one is almost willing to sacrifice one's principles."

January laughed. "Don't lower your standards, sir. Bouille isn't worth it."

The doctor laughed in turn, and went upstairs, to the small ward where two women had just been brought in, vomiting and with a number of other symptoms that bore a fearful resemblance to the scourge that had swept the city two summers before.

Returning home late, January found a note from Dominique, delivered at some time the previous day by being pushed under the garçonnière door. It said simply—or as simply as any communication from Dominique ever said anything—that due to social exigencies of the most pressing kind, Thérèse had not been at liberty to make the journey to Mandeville to inquire after her cousin Aveline until Wednesday. Upon arrival in that charming resort (its advantages over Milneburgh cataloged in full, with speculation appended concerning the cost of Mandeville real estate and Henri Viellard's abilities and inclination to purchase a cottage there), Thérèse had discovered that Aveline had been sold. Thérèse, who during her last visit with Aveline had been severely twitted on the subject of serving "a woman who ain't no better than she should be," considered that this served Aveline right.

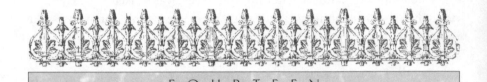

FOURTEEN

A VIOLENT ALTERCATION IN DEFENSE
OF THE CONSTITUTION
AN AMERICAN REPORTER RISKS DEATH

In 1776, the founders of this great Republic fought David-like against the Goliath of tyrannical Foreign Monarchs for the rights enumerated in the Constitution, chief among which was the right to Freedom of the Press against any form of censorship, coercion, or hindrance. Yesterday afternoon, a representative of the American Press in this City likewise bravely laid his life in the balance in defense of those selfsame rights against just such a foreign would-be tyrant, a pettifogging bloodsucker named Bouille who, with the backing of the foreigners whose grip upon the throat of this beautiful City the recent elections attempted to loosen . . .

"*Ya-allah,*" muttered January. He shoved the *Abeille* into his pocket as his brother-in-law sprang from the deck of the steamboat *Boonslick* and threaded toward him amid the morning confusion of the wharves. Gabriel, who'd accompanied January to the levee, ran to meet his father, full of news and questions; "It's going well," said Paul Corbier, clasping January's hand. "I go back in the morning, but Michie Drialhet says no matter how much or how little work gets done, we'll make up the time somehow, for me to be here the seventeenth. Is she well?"

"She's well."

Fever was in the air. Or more literally fever's fear. Even to the uninitiated, the market and the levee had a slack air, and those who sold, or loaded, or unloaded, or bargained in the long morning shadows of the market arcades were few, grim, and silent. One would think, looking about, that there were no wealthy people in the city, or that the well-off men had neither wives nor offspring. Only servants and the poor.

"The crisis seems to be over for the moment," January replied to his brother-in-law's question about the past three days. "Ker paid me off this morning—out of his own pocket, I suspect—and slipped me and Weber and the other volunteers some food from the hospital stores, since there's no funds to cover us. But even without new cases of fever coming in, half the ones still in hospital have developed pneumonia."

"I'm not sure but that isn't worse." Paul added a couple of oranges from a market stand to the bread Gabriel had brought from home in a willow basket. "At least the yellow jack is over quickly. Pneumonia . . ." He shook his head. January remembered his own bout with pneumonia—lung-fever it had been called then—as a young man, weeks of lying exhausted in bed even after the fever and delirium had cleared. And at that, he had been carefully nursed by Bella. The patients who crowded the hospital wards, yellow with jaundice and wheezing as they tried to breathe, muttering in broken Gaelic or the dialects of upcountry Lombardy and Bavaria, stood as little chance of recovery as had the slaves on Bellefleur, once the sickness had them.

You needed to be well fed, and you needed to be strong. And more than anything else, you needed to have someone willing to look after you.

January sighed and ran a weary hand over his face. He had had no sleep last night and barely any the night before. His whole body ached, and he could only silently bless Augustus Mayerling, the fencing master, for giving him what healing his arms had had, that he'd been able to make it through the past three days. The exercise with weights was something else he'd have to start up again, now that he had a little time.

"The fabric's finally arrived for Drialhet's carriage seats." Basket on his arm, Paul hurried along the cool shadow of the arcade. "His factor's meeting me this afternoon. . . ."

In the Cabildo's great doorway they almost brushed shoulders with Burton Blodgett, in a traveling reek of rum—glancing back at him, January saw the journalist was making notes. *Damn the man. . . .*

"I'm sorry, M'am," a Guard was saying to a woman who stood near the courtyard doors. "Nobody's permitted to see the prisoners."

"But he's ill!" protested the woman, a stout blond girl in a cotton frock and sunbonnet. "He has the palsy, and sometimes he doesn't know where he is."

"I'm very sorry, M'am." The man kept his face stony and his voice without expression. "No one's permitted in."

"What's this?" January walked quickly over to the pair. "Excuse me, sir," he added, remembering that the Guard was white and as such entitled to deference, "but my brother-in-law and I are here to see my sister . . ."

"I'm sorry. No one's permitted . . ."

"Is there trouble, sir?"

"There was." Sergeant deMezieres came out from around his big desk and glanced in the direction of the doors, to be sure that Blodgett had truly gone. "Night before last there was a rumor of an attempt at escape and threats of violence." He brought the words out as if he'd learned them by heart and did not even attempt to look at January as he spoke. "Chief Tremouille thought it best no one be admitted for a time."

January opened his mouth to snap, *Rumor, hell,* and closed it again. In his best French—and thankful he was still dressed as a professional in his black coat and top hat—he said, "Surely a woman might be permitted a visit from her husband and child."

"And I have to see my husband," added the blond woman, crowding up to January's side. "If he can see his sister, I can see my husband." January wanted to slap her.

"I'm sorry. I had this from Chief Tremouille and it's final. Now, everything will be well in a few days."

The hell it will. But January knew that to speak of the fever now would not help Olympe or open a way to see her. And with Blodgett nosing around, it might very well result in his, and Paul's, being detained on some petty charge to keep them quiet.

"Thank you," he said, keeping his eyes down. One always started out by saying *Thank you* to a white man in authority. "Might you be able to do us the favor of letting us know how she is?" He was aware of Gabriel, standing half-hidden behind Paul with his hand thrust deep in his pocket, eyes shut, whispering something under his breath. "Madame Corbier? She's in the women's cells . . ."

"She's well," said the sergeant immediately. "All of them are well. There's no"—he stopped himself from saying *yellow fever* and changed it to—"no reason for concern about the . . . the incident a day or two ago. Everyone up there is well and healthy."

January had to bite his lower lip not to say, *It's good to know you have such an exact knowledge, right off the top of your head, of the condition of every prisoner in a pest hole that crowded.*

It'll only come back on us, Olympe had said.

"Thank you. You've relieved our minds."

"Putain," spat Gabriel, as they emerged from the building into the arcade again. January saw the young blond woman standing a few feet away, her face to the stuccoed brick of one of the arches, hands pressed to her mouth as she wept. "You were right, Uncle Ben. That voodoo doesn't work for sour apples." The boy pulled a little wad of red wax from his pocket and tossed it away into the gutter. "I paid that Queen Régine fifteen cents and I did everything she said exactly, turned around and walked backward and jumped on one leg and snapped my fingers three times—"

"And now you've lost your fifteen cents," said January. "And had the Devil in Hell laugh at you besides."

"You'd have spent the money better burning a candle for your mother's safety," interjected Paul quietly. He dug in his pocket, and carefully brought out a silver dime and a couple of cut bits.

"You'd have spent the money better on rice and beans." January put a staying hand on Paul's wrist. "Which is what your father has been working all summer to keep on the table."

Paul gently shook off his grip, and held out the coins to Gabriel. "So now go do that." He nodded toward the Cathedral. "Make your confession first."

"No, Papa, that's food money." The boy looked genuinely distressed. "I got that fifteen cents I gave Queen Régine holding horses outside Monsieur Davis's gambling parlor. You know we can't—"

Paul pressed the coins into his son's palm. "We need to show God we're sorry. And to ask His help. Go make your confession, and burn the candle."

Wretched, the boy ran off toward the arched doorways of the church. Paul sighed, then turned back to January. "It isn't wrong, you know, what she does. She thinks very carefully, and I do not believe I have ever seen her do anything that would offend God. But children . . . they don't understand sometimes. To them it all looks the same."

Maybe to God it all looks the same, thought January. The stench of the gutters, the reek of burning horns and hooves, darkened the air as with a vapor; from the corner of his eye he saw Blodgett step delicately to the edge of the arcade, ignoring the weeping woman, and pick the ball of crimson wax from the gutter, turning it speculatively in his hands. *Or maybe we're only frightening ourselves with games, and God neither knows nor cares. Maybe the Devil in Hell is laughing at us all.*

"Maestro."

January turned. Lieutenant Abishag Shaw slouched over to the archway where he and Paul stood, and spit a line of dark tobacco juice at the bloated corpse of a rat floating in the gutter's reek.

"Your sister's well. She been helping out with the other ladies that was—affected—by this 'incident' you hear tell of."

January's eyes met the cool gray ones for a moment, then lowered again, as he knew they must before a white man's. "Were many women 'hurt' in this 'incident'?"

"Two so far," said Shaw. "And three of the men." He was silent for a time. Then, "Speakin' of it around the town won't help no one, you know. Nor would me losin' my job with the Guards, nor you gettin' on the bad side of Chief Tremouille and the City Council and all them."

January drew a deep breath. "I know that," he said. "Thank you for telling us."

"I got a thing or two else to tell you besides," Shaw continued, "if'n you got the time to walk a little with me on the levee."

The puddles left by last night's rain steamed faintly in the soot-grimed light. Stevedores sweated in grim silence or sang the eerie wailing hollers in half-forgotten tongues: Gaelic, African, fisherman-Greek.

"I made a few inquiries concernin' Hubert Granville and Miz Geneviève's money." Shaw pushed his disreputable hat back on his head, and ran a bony hand through his lank hair. "Antoine's right, insofar as he knows, in that Granville's been investin' her money for her for years. He's got a little syndic of women he does that for."

"Bernadette Metoyer and her sisters," guessed January.

"They's in it," agreed Shaw, unsurprised. "Our friend Granville takes a little percentage—that's what he tells Miz Granville, anyways. My guess is that ain't all he takes, but that's neither here nor there. But it seems—lookin' at the records anyway—that his bookkeepin' is of the permeable order, and he'll sort of scootch the money back and forth with his own investments, which works passably well if nuthin' else goes wrong. Now, with money tight an' business slow an' Mr. Jackson up in Washington unravelin' the Bank of the United States an' sendin' that money every which way, it appears that a man who has the money to set up a bank stands a good chance of gettin' more from the government in the near future, and it looks like that's what Mr. Granville been tryin' to do. Only he ain't quite there yet."

"Would five thousand dollars do it?"

Shaw scratched, and spit at an enormous palmetto bug making its unoffending way across the bricks of the market arcade. "Might so be."

The palmetto bug scurried off, offended but unsullied.

"What about the night of the twenty-third?"

"Granville was in Constitution Place all right. With Miz Geneviève, or at least with a widow in black and veils, accordin' to Hallie Birnbaum, what has the cottage next door. The cook girl for the Careys acrost the square says Granville's carriage was there round about seven when she was finishin' up supper, an' didn't leave till close to mornin'—she was up lookin' after her little girl who's sick. But the way them folk know about each other's business I purely doubt Granville or Miz Geneviève could have kept Isaak prisoner either in the house itself or in the coach house without somebody sniffin' wise. And besides, what would be the point?"

"To force him to sign something, maybe?" January shook his head. "Whoever gave him the poison, he was *somewhere* from Saturday to Monday." For a moment it crossed his mind to speak of what he had found, or had not found, on Rue St. Louis, but he wasn't at all sure what he could say. The stink of old blood, like a stain of graveyard dust on his mind, but nothing, he thought, that had to do with Isaak. Instead he asked, "Should I see what I can find from the woman Zoë? I could probably get across to Mandeville and back by Monday night when I'm supposed to play at Madame Redfern's."

"And of all the damn stupid things I've ever heard of in this town." Shaw sighed. "A ball celebratin' Bastille Day—with every royalist an' Orléaniste an' seven kinds of Revolutionary radicals an' leftover Jacobins an' who knows what-all else rufflin' an' spittin' at each other—has got to be the stupidest." He shook his head. "We'll be cleanin' up corpses for weeks. Duelin' *is* illegal in this state, you know. You can go to Mandeville, Maestro, but I doubt it'll do you much good. Yeah, I'd like to know a whole hell of a lot more about what went on at that house than I do now, but askin' that Zoë woman ain't the way to learn it. You seen how she looks at Mathurin, an' he at her. They's right good friends, not to put too fine a point on it . . . an' anyway no testimony of her'n is gonna stand in court anyway."

Because she is a slave, thought January bitterly. Not that Zoë would testify against Mathurin Jumon in any case. He remembered the smile in her eyes as she'd looked at Jumon in the shadowy study, the smooth way she'd stepped in to cover the argument with his mother. The way Jumon had half-grinned after her, *I have a feeling Zoë does not approve . . .*

Cold panic zinged him, half-guessed, half-perceived—a glimpse of buckskin and trade-goods blue from the corner of his eye.

He swung around, his breath jagging in his throat.

But whoever it was, if it was indeed anyone, had faded into the shadowy mill under the market arcades. Only a few fishermen, bargaining in Greek with a woman in a bright tignon over a netful of snapper and oysters; a lean-jawed steamboat pilot with a goatish Yankee beard joking with Ti Jon; Dr. Yellowjack, sitting by himself at a small table with coffee, watching the sun glare in the Place d'Armes with cold, narrow eyes.

"You know he fences stolen goods?" January nodded toward the small, wiry wangateur as he and Shaw walked on. He lowered his voice, unable to rid himself of the feeling that whatever he might say, the voodoo doctor would hear.

"I know." They turned down an aisle between stalls of greens and tomatoes and aubergines, edging past those slothful housewives and late-sleeping servants who would have to pay for their laziness with wilted lunches. Shaw glanced back at the taut little figure in its bright calico shirt, its leather top hat and hackle feathers stuck in the brim. "Provin' it on him's another matter. Nor could we prove he's the one who brokers half the faked papers in this town—everythin' from turnin' slaves to free men down to bringin' in Congos from Havana to sell with papers claimin' they's Creole niggers born up-country here. He smuggles girls in, too, Congos or brights that don't speak no English nor French, for a whippin' parlor he's supposed to have someplace outside town. We searched that house of his on the bayou two, three times. . . ." He shook his head. "He's a bad customer, Yellowjack Joe."

His gray glance slid sidelong to January again. "You all right yourself, Maestro? Keepin' safe?"

"Getting a little tired of looking over my shoulder." Tired, too, though he would not say it, of searching his room every time he came home, and of keeping food locked up.

"Well, I have my men keepin' an eye out for Mr. Nash," said Shaw. "But with two of 'em down with what Councilman Bouille insists is indigestion"—and an angry glint flared in his eyes—"we can only do what we can. Constable LaBranche went down the Swamp t' other day—on another matter, not lookin' for Nash—an' ended up stabbed, an' damn lucky he wasn't killed. But we'll get him."

"I'm sure you will, sir," said January. "I'd just rather it was before he got me."

In the summer of 1789, goaded beyond endurance by an incompetent King, a spendthrift court, and a government that would not tax anyone who actually had money, a mob of out-of-work laborers, uneducated riffraff, and starving women attacked and razed the fourteenth-century fortress of the French King on the outskirts of Paris. Urged on by journalists and pamphleteers, they slaughtered its tiny garrison, paraded the severed head of its commander through the streets (January had always wondered what happened to the head), and freed "in the name of Liberty" exactly seven men, one of whom had begged not to be let out of his cell because he was insane and knew himself unable to survive in the outside world.

The uprising triggered by this event had swept the House of Bourbon from the throne of France.

And this, apparently, was all anyone in America remembered about the chain of events that had opened the way for Napoleon Bonaparte's dictatorship and twenty-five years of the bloodiest and most violent endemic warfare Europe had ever known. In Paris, January had talked to the survivors of those days—his landlady among them—and knew that the various garbled and politicized accounts in circulation in the New World were very far from the truth. He knew, too, that every party involved in the chaos of old-style Revolutionaries versus moderates versus Jacobins versus Bonaparte versus Louis XVIII versus the House of Orléans—the dead King's self-serving cousins who had subsequently grabbed the throne—had at one time or another taken refuge in New Orleans, that pocket-sized version of *la France d'outre-mer*.

So only a woman who had been paying attention to nothing for the past thirty-five years but the size of her bank balance and the social status of those who greeted her on the street would have even considered issuing several hundred invitations to a "private party" in celebration of Bastille Day.

Benjamin January duly presented himself at the back door of the Redfern summer mansion on Rome Square in Milneburgh as the sun was setting on the fourteenth, in company with nearly every other first-rate musician in town: Mrs. Redfern did nothing that she did not overdo. The marble-topped buffet tables in the dining room groaned with joints and saddles of ham and beef on expensive platters of pink-and-gold Meissen, rémoulades of mushrooms, peach flan and wine ices, crêpes, vol-au-vents, artichoke hearts, and pâtés à l'Italienne. Red, white, and blue bunting transformed the ballroom into something that more closely resembled a rally for the recent election. Cornucopias of flowers vied with the scents of floor wax, tobacco, and the stink of the gas lamps overhead.

"I'll be very curious," remarked Hannibal, sipping the watered lemonade that was the only refreshment permitted the musicians in their penitential sweatbox of a parlor off the main ballroom, "to see who actually shows up for this affair." He produced a flask of Black Drop from his pocket and doctored first his lemonade and then himself. It was the first time in two days, January knew, that he'd been on his feet.

"Not a Frenchman in the city, I'll wager." Cochon Gardinier picked a wafer-thin slice of bread from the platter on the table and examined it with pained indignation, as if he had been offered a fragment of napkin on which to sustain himself.

"Thy son asked thee for bread, and thou gavest him a stone," provided Hannibal helpfully. "I've seen larger visiting cards, myself."

"And tastier ones."

"Well, you're both wrong about the Frenchmen, anyway." Jacques Bichet slipped in from an exploratory ramble and a chat with La Redfern's servants. "The guests are starting to arrive, and you know who the first one was through the door? Mathurin Jumon."

"Mathurin Jumon?" The others stared at him.

"But his mother was one of the Queen's ladies in waiting," January said. "Her family's fortune was destroyed by the Revolution."

"His mother's not with him, is she?" asked Uncle Bichet, looking up from tuning his violoncello. "It's only once in a month of Sundays he's out without her somewhere around, but I've seen her make him cross over the street so as not to talk to a Bonapartiste. Hell, she won't give but two fingers to the most virtuous Orléaniste on earth."

"So what's he doing here?"

"He isn't wearing a mask, by any chance?" inquired Hannibal facetiously. "I mean, every Bonapartiste and Revolutionary in town is going to see him, not to speak of the Americans."

"Interesting," remarked January thoughtfully, "that he took the trouble to be the first to arrive." He walked out into the narrow hall, and opened the little door into the ballroom just a crack. Past a screen of potted ferns, Mrs. Redfern stood in the columned triple arch of the main doorway to the vestibule, and in the absence of any other guest— it was a good twenty minutes short of the time on the invitations—was chatting with Jumon. January had seen an almost exact replica of her dress last month in Dominique's latest edition of *Le Petit Courier des Dames.* The winglike projections over the enormous gauze sleeves were the very newest mode. She must have had it made up, in lace-trimmed sable bombazine, in the past three weeks.

"Yes," murmured Hannibal. "He's one of the prizes, as far as she's concerned. He must want very much to impress her, and coming this early is the only way he can get credit on her books for being here without meeting anyone who'll peach to Mama."

The two men regarded one another for a moment, baffled. *"Madame Redfern?* I knew about Vilhardouin courting her, but . . ."

"He wasn't interested in her as of the Pritchard party," pointed out January. "And why would he need to hang out for a rich widow? His mother's expenses aside, he's a wealthy man. There he goes."

With almost preternatural timing, Jumon wandered from the ball-room as Madame Redfern turned to greet the next guests in the door-way: Hubert Granville and his wife, followed almost at once by the lovestruck Orell Greenaway, who immediately took charge of Mrs. Red-fern's fan, presented his dance card to her for inscription ("To sit them out with you, Madame, and bear you company") and empurpled the surrounding air with compliments. It was unlikely that she noticed Jumon was no longer in the room.

"Business?" speculated Hannibal, as they returned to the parlor to collect their music. "La Redfern is one of the wealthiest women in the city these days."

"He sold at least one of his brother's slaves at the beginning of the month, maybe more. With the price of slaves these days he can't possibly be hard up."

Nearly a dozen new guests were in the ballroom when the musicians took their places and began to play, light airs from last season's operas, ballads and études, a soft fill behind the chatter of voices in the big, overly decorated room. Mathurin Jumon did not reappear.

There was talk among the men of business and the election, of the Bank and of tight money and slow times, while the women discussed the cut of gowns and how to keep servants from stealing and, worse, spying; and as before, as always in New Orleans, the ballroom split along a distinct linguistic frontier.

Familiar after nineteen months with the politics of French New Orleans, January easily identified the Creoles who turned up as either the old-time radicals like Hilaire Morel, the owner of the Café Venise, or Bonapartistes like the Widow Langostine and Judge Laverge, who immediately got into arguments with the radicals over whose fault it was that the Revolution failed and those execrable Orléaniste swine ended up on the throne. The only Orléaniste in sight was Clément Vilhardouin. The lawyer complimented Madame Redfern on her efforts to reconcile the Creole community and unobtrusively found reasons to sit closer to her than Orell Greenaway did.

"You know Michie Jumon, that was the first one here tonight?" January asked Madame Redfern's housemaid, in the kitchen during the brief break after the fifth dance. The housemaid, whose name was Claire, nodded—January had a chatting acquaintance with her from meetings both here and at the market, and liked the woman.

"Big man with the pearl in his neckerchief?" Claire's hands moved quickly as she spoke, arranging on an enormous tray ring after ring of peach *tartelettes*. A Protestant from Virginia, she'd been slow to make connections among the largely Catholic slaves in town, and though she was less lonely now than she had been, she still counted January as one of her first friends. "He's sitting in the library. Gaspar just took him coffee there, not five minutes ago."

Obviously a man who didn't intend to let Jeanne-Françoise Lango-stine—one of the worst gossips in the Creole community—carry tales back to Madame Cordelia. "Could you do me a favor, Miss Claire?" said January quietly. "Now and then and *only* if you have the time, could you check on what he's doing there and who he sees? My sister's housemaid heard this Michie Jumon was going to sell off her cousin. It's got her nearly crazy thinking it would be to some broker or dealer. Don't put yourself out—I understand you're gonna be run off your legs tonight—but if you've got a moment and can find out without causing yourself trouble, I'd appreciate it."

Claire smiled warmly. "I'll do what I can, Mr. January."

"Thank you, Miss Claire. It's all any of us can do."

He returned to the ballroom, trying vainly to work the ache out of his shoulders and arms, and swung into a light *valse brillante,* perhaps the only thing that kept the banker Linus Rowling from calling out the stoutly Jacksonian slave dealer Jim Pratt—the two men were already visibly squaring off with their friends, who at the first bars of the music were hauled from the field of combat by their wives and fiancées, leaving the principals feeling rather silly. At the same time, however, the attorney Vilhardouin stepped between Mr. Greenaway and Madame Redfern, upon whom Greenaway was advancing with hand outstretched for the third time that evening. Over the music—and through his own concentration on timing and lilt—January couldn't hear what was said, but he could guess from Vilhardouin's gestures that it concerned scoundrels and fortune-hunters who showed up early to force their attentions on a woman in mourning. Granville and the Reverend Dunk separated the two men, but Hannibal said in an undervoice, "Twenty-five cents says Vilhardouin calls Greenaway out before supper."

"And this twenty-five cents is going to come from which wealthy aunt's legacy?" inquired January, and the fiddler laughed.

"A jitney, then."

"Done."

"It does my heart good to see the French community extending the hand of friendship to the Americans," intoned Reverend Dunk, clapping Vilhardouin on the back. "It truly goes to prove, does it not, that we are all brothers in liberty?"

Vilhardouin, whose family vineyards in Bordeaux had been wiped out by Napoleon's wars, cast an eye at Madame Redfern and managed the sour rictus of a smile.

By the time Claire Brunet managed to relay a message to January, the news was old. January watched the men as they came and went, and none was gone for a longer period of time than was required to relieve themselves, or else they departed in groups and came back smelling of cigars. But Orell Greenaway came close to causing a jealous scene when Madame Redfern vanished for close to half an hour; only Vilhardouin's return in company with Colonel Pritchard during that period kept him from sallying forth to trap the supposed lovers: "Don't be an ass, man," growled Granville. "She probably just tore her petticoat. My wife does that all the time."

But Madame Redfern came back, not in company with a woman friend and flounce repairer, but with her business manager, an anthropomorphized weasel named Fraikes, rubbing his hands and looking pleased with himself. "Six seventy-five is a good price, Madame, a very good price indeed."

"I didn't hear who they was talkin' of selling, Mr. January," said Claire, coming to the door of the wretched little musicians' parlor during the next period of rest. "But Mr. Fraikes, he paid over money to Mr. Jumon right away, in cash, hard money, that I guess Mrs. Redfern's about the only person in town who has it these days. But Gaspar tells me they talked about selling 'him' and sending 'him' over in the morning, so it couldn't have been your cousin, could it?"

"No," said January, infusing voice and expression with all the gratitude he could counterfeit. "No, it isn't. Thank you, Miss Claire. Thank you so much."

"It isn't as if the money were all tied up in a family plantation still," mused Hannibal, after she'd gone. By common consent the other musicians had arranged the room's three chairs in a line for the fiddler to lie down on, and Jacques had fetched a wet cloth from the kitchen to lay over his eyes. Hannibal had grown paler throughout the evening, fight-

ing the racking cough; the first thing he'd done when out of the ballroom was cough until he could barely stand.

He took a swig of opium, made as if to take another and then
changed his mind, and replaced the bottle. "When they sold up the
land I imagine both Laurence and Mathurin got a share of cash, to
invest in town property, which is what Laurence left to Isaak. Granted,
most of the slaves probably still belong to Cordelia, but Jumon can't
need money so desperately that he curries favor with a social climber
like La Redfern for the sake of six hundred and seventy-five dollars.
Can he?"

"I don't know," said January, and slipped back into his coat and
gloves. "Once more into the breach, dear friends— It's certainly something," he added, helping Hannibal to his feet, "that I plan to find
out."

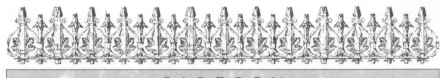

FIFTEEN

"Jumon is selling up, all right." Augustus Mayerling extended a long-fingered hand out sideways to the length of his arm, rather like a very well dressed scarecrow in a vest of gold Florentine silk, the sleeves of his white linen shirt rolled halfway up forearms of sinew and rope. "*And* turn . . . touch my hand. Touch my hand. Smooth, smooth. . . . No, without moving your hips touch my—so!"

January straightened his body again, sweating and panting but triumphant. Three weeks ago he had barely been able to lift the weighted beam to his shoulders; a few weeks before that, unable to raise so much as a filled cup. Now, although the movement left him aching, he could swing and maneuver the seven-foot rod at most of the targets the fencing master set him.

Early sunlight just clearing the roofs of Maspero's Exchange and the Destrehan town house slanted through the long windows of the Salle d'Armes, thrown open to catch whatever cool remained of the dawn. Even at this hour the air smelled of burnt gunpowder and sewage; a woman down in Exchange Alley sang drearily of the virtues of soap. Farther off, a steamboat whistle hooted.

Another day. The last before Olympe's trial began.

"Madame Redfern, as you heard, bought not only Mathurin

Jumon's personal valet Claude, but a matched carriage-team of white horses, very expensive, for cash money I am told." Mayerling extended his other hand, cold pale sherry-colored eyes watching with scientific exactness the play of January's bare shoulder muscles as he turned to touch the target now here, now there. "The matter was discussed last night at the Café Venise—Hilaire Morel, you understand, gossips like a schoolgirl and says that Americans know nothing of true Revolution— and Athanase de Soto, a pupil of mine, said that Monday afternoon he met Jumon in Milneburgh before the Redfern fête and purchased ten head of Jumon's cattle, apparently for something less than they were worth."

"But why?" January straightened again and stood with the beam across his shoulders, regarding the Prussian in bafflement.

Of medium stature and slender build, the fencing master was one of the most demanding in the city, no more so on his pupils than on himself. Most mornings when January arrived—long before any of the aristocratic Creole pupils who would have been appalled to know that a man of color was allowed into the Salle—it was to find Mayerling already lifting iron scale weights or the weighted beam to further develop strength and flexibility, or engaging and disengaging the salon's door handle with neat, small circles of his *colichemarde*.

"There are any number of reasons." Mayerling shrugged, and came to help January lift the beam down. "It is the slow season, and his mother is a monstrously expensive woman; he may have had investments in the Bank of the United States that now are in danger."

The fencing master threw January a linen towel, to wipe the sweat from his face and hair, and used another himself. The morning sunlight, just moving down the wall, tipped the ivory brush of his military-cut hair and made tiny, crinkling shadows in the saber scars that laced the beaky face. "I observe he is not selling anything to which his mother might hold claim. In fact to sell to La Redfern, for cash—and to feel the need to sweeten her by attending her party—says to me at least that he is doing this without Madame Cordelia's knowledge. In any case, before returning to Mandeville yesterday, he sold two women servants, Zoë and Irene, to the American dealer Bill Palmer."

"Zoë?" January paused in the midst of putting on his shirt, shocked. "Are you sure?"

"This was the name, yes." In some surprise at his reaction,

Mayerling regarded him for a moment. "I took note because they were Byzantine Empresses, Zoë and Irene—I kept wondering if there were a third named Theodosia somewhere. This is important?"

January nodded. The look of amused complicity in Jumon's eyes; Zoë's smile. *I don't think she approves. . . .* The affection unmistakable in his voice.

Then fury for the woman's sake and sickened disappointment, as if he himself had been sold. Maybe only the old fear he'd had as a child, waiting for his mother to be sold away from him, for his friends or aunts or others whom he loved, to disappear. The pain of that betrayal must have been worse than anything in her life. He tried to hear Mathurin's deep voice: *I'm terribly fond of you, Zoë, but . . .*

But what?

"I don't think he'd have done that if he weren't desperate."

And his personal valet. Longtime friends, with him for years. . . . *How could he? How* COULD *he?*

Even as he thought the words January felt contempt for himself, for his own naïveté. He could almost hear Olympe's sneer. *Write a note and send it by a boy down to the dealers on Baronne Street, is how, brother. That's how they mostly all do it.*

Like a man regretfully deciding to have an old dog shot because it's become flatulent or incontinent in the house, and sullies his carpets or disturbs his guests.

The jewels on Madame Cordelia's wrists. The fabrics purchased on whims and never even cut. The pink-and-gold dishes, the mantillas— seven, eight, ten of them—in their boxes.

And like a devil's voice whispering in his heart, the sentence formed itself: *If he betrayed her, if he sold her, does she love him still? Or will she be willing to talk?*

Mayerling came over to him, a kind of chilly concern in the strange hazel eyes. "You knew this woman?"

"I'd met her. I saw them together."

"Ah." The Prussian considered, head tilted to one side like a bird. "Palmer does not give top prices, but he pays in cash. I understand he's leaving today, for the Mississippi Territories, to sell where the prices are high." There was a flex of irony in that light alto voice, nothing so definite as disapproval, but the kind of deliberate neutrality Mayerling cultivated in dealing with his pupils, all of whom were the sons of wealthy slave owners, and slave owners themselves. A member of the Junker nobility, he had come to this country, January knew, with secrets of his own, and he kept a great deal to himself. Still, when January's breath caught in pain as he tried to shrug into his coat, the sword master helped him on with it with the matter-of-fact skill of a valet.

"Thank you," said January, and glanced at the sun on the wall. Early yet. There was a chance he could still find Palmer—and his chattels—at his offices on Baronne Street, though his skin crept at the thought. Automatically he checked his coat pocket for the papers that proved him a free man and breathed a sigh of gratitude that he had intended to make another attempt to see Olympe at the Cabildo that morning, and so had dressed like a man of some substance. With any luck Palmer would pay more attention to the quality of his clothing and the excellence of his English than to the color of his face and hands.

"Myself, I am on a handshaking basis only with Mathurin Jumon," said Mayerling, as he walked with January down the narrow stairs. "But my wife"—and there was unalloyed delight as he spoke of the woman who in her childhood had been one of January's piano pupils—"my wife belongs to several of the same charitable societies as Madame Cordelia Jumon. They are related, for all I know: all these Creole families seem to be. Shall I ask her to go to Mandeville and speak with this redoubtable lady? According to Madame Mayerling"—he spoke his wife's formal title, as men must even in the presence of their friends— "Madame Jumon is a woman who has suffered greatly in her life and continues to suffer at voluble length. It should not be difficult to learn details."

> *Oh General, don't you never catch me.*
> *Oh General, don't you never catch me.*
> *Oh General, don't you never catch me,*
> *I'm on a ship, I'm gone out to the sea.*

The words floated, rose, faded like the pull of the tide, the voices of women riding up over the deep bass of men. January stopped, listening, on the rough wood banquette, and the rattle of a dray hauling bricks down Baronne Street at a reckless hand gallop drowned out the song. When the vehicle was past there was nothing, as if it had somehow drawn the song after it and away into the general clamor of the street.

"Sir, you buy me, I'll work for you good."

January turned to see an elderly man in the rough calico shirt and osnaburg britches of a fieldhand sitting on a bench outside a dark little shop front. HARRAHAN AND CLAINE, said the green-and-yellow sign next to the door. The man smiled engagingly; he, a younger man, and two teenaged girls were chained to the bench by light ankle shackles.

"I can do 'most anything with horses: drive 'em, feed 'em, train 'em . . ." He coughed, the rattling, wet cough of pulmonary consumption, and forced himself to smile.

"I'm a fine cook, sir," said a woman a few doors down, as January passed. "Make bread, cook you up the finest chicken and dumplings you'll ever see. . . ." She smiled, showing where teeth had been lost to childbearing. Her hands were the rough hands of a fieldworker. January wondered if she'd ever been in a kitchen in her life. "You just try me out, sir, you'll never be sorry."

And as he walked on, past a cavernous brick exchange where not only slaves, but mules, wagonloads of hay, boxes of bean coffee, lots of rosewood furniture, and fine pressed letter paper were being dickered over by dark-coated brokers, he heard the older woman who sat on the banquette with the would-be cook say, "You want to be careful, honey. I had me six different masters and the colored was always the roughest."

He was aware of men looking after him, once caught a fragment of conversation about ". . . big buck nigger . . ." but didn't stay to hear anything further. Mostly the men here, the dealers and brokers, the owners of ironworks or cotton presses, were Americans, and the voices he heard were all in English. His flesh crept with the sensation of being in enemy territory, naked and disarmed before enemy guns. All he could do was stand straight, walk easily, as if he had no fear—as if all things were as they had been when he was a youth, and the city largely French. As if a black man, particularly one as African-looking as he, were not automatically assumed to be someone's slave.

In a way it was the same as being in the Swamp.

In a way it was worse.

> Master bought a horse, he bed it in the stall,
> Master bought a dog, he bed it by the fire,
> Master bought a cow, he bed her in the barn,
> Here I sleep out on the ground. . . .

The singing from the yard behind a dealer's faded. It was drowned in the whine and yarp of a mouth organ, the slap of a boy's bare feet on the boards as he danced to show a pair of prospective buyers how lively he was, smiling gaily. Smiling—no one wants to pay for a sullen slave. January edged past and went on, feeling men's eyes on his back.

I should have looked for Shaw, he thought. *I should have got Corcet to do this.*

Corcet at least was fairer of skin. He was an attorney. . . .

January shook his head at himself inwardly. *And I'm a surgeon, and what good has that ever done me, going among Americans?* He only wanted, he understood, not to be the one to have to come to this place, not to have to deal with slave traders. As if Corcet would not find it as hateful and as frightening.

The sign that bore the name William Palmer, Esq., was mounted on a square building of yellow bricks, much like a dozen others up and down the street. Coming into the hot, shadowy vault of the room, January could see through the open door at the rear to a small yard with benches around three sides. The yard was empty. A chinless youth with the sores of scrofula on his neck and ears looked up from a ledger. "Mr. Palmer?" asked January politely.

"Just missed him," said the clerk, and spit on the sanded floor. He glanced past January at the door, waiting.

For January's master, January realized.

"Have you any idea when he might be back, sir?"

The boy was still waiting for a white man to come in. He glanced at January a little impatiently and shrugged. "A week Sattiday maybe. He's gone up to Baton Rouge with a load of niggers. Left this mornin' on the *Philly.* You got a message for him?"

"No, sir," replied January, trying to will his mind away from this jumped-up child, without a whisker on his face, holding out his hand to him now in the complete expectation that January was only the winged Mercury charged by some white man with a note to another white man. "No message."

He walked down to the levee, trying not to hate the boy for the unconscious arrogant glint in his eye, for the assumption that he, a man of forty-one, had no life, no past, no future, except insofar as it concerned running errands for another man.

No wife, no sisters, no mother who had been a slave and wanted to remember none of it. No fears, no music, no dreams.

Only: *Here, Ben, take this down to Bill Palmer on Baronne Street—You ask around, one of the white gentlemen'll tell you where it is. And don't you linger round the market on the way back, boy. . . .*

And he couldn't even say, I'm no man's boy, because this pipsqueak with brown stains on his lips didn't even ask if he was—simply assumed that no man of color would have business of his own.

Let it go, Ben, he told himself. *Let it go. It's the custom of the country, and you knew that when you came back.* But he could not let it go. As he made his careful way down Canal Street, where there were enough people, enough businessmen—Creoles, shopkeepers, and more-or-less-honest workers—where there were people who would come to his aid should he be attacked, his mind returned to the blood-smelling darkness behind Colonel Pritchard's house, to the hot gleam of firelight in a brickyard years ago, to the drums. To a woman dancing with the rainbow serpent Damballah.

It was a place for hate to go, he thought. A place to pretend you were free. A place to forget. Like the frail golden palaces of music, the safe glowing heart of Mozart and Bach and Boccherini, it was a place to hide your mind in, when the pain got too bad.

There were half a dozen coffles of slaves being loaded on the steamboats, down at the wharves that fringed the levee for over a mile above the Place d'Armes. Even in the slow season, demand for slaves was high. Men moving into the new cotton lands of Mississippi and the new states of Missouri and Alabama, could make a fortune in two years: clearing a plantation, getting a crop in the ground, selling the whole concern with the cotton standing that same year and buying another plantation. . . . If they had slaves.

On the wharves January moved more carefully. Twice, along Baronne Street, he thought he'd glimpsed Killdevil Ned. Loafing idly, staring into shopwindows or watching with avid interest while a prospective buyer stripped a light-skinned woman to the waist in front of a dealer's office. . . . But always there, when January turned around. Waiting his chance. Insolent, in his way, as the clerk at Palmer's: *I'm watching you, nigger, and there's nuthin' you can do about it.*

And there wasn't.

The boats were loading, all along the quays, a dozen of them, large and small. In the winter and spring there'd be scores. Tall strange boxy confabulations, like boardinghouses mounted on rafts, white paint glaring in the smoky morning light, black stacks oozing grime, gilding glinting, while men off-loaded the produce of the upriver plantations and towns, and loaded on German tools and French wines, paint, starch, barrels of gloves, rolls of fabric for someone's carriage upholstery, a Patent Washing Machine. . . .

The chained slaves waiting for shipment on the wharf were silent, mostly. January looked at their faces as he passed them, and saw their eyes.

He had felt anger and pity for Zoë, betrayed by a master she loved. But every one of these people had been betrayed.

The *Philadelphia* had left for Baton Rouge early, as soon as it grew light enough to see the river. For a time January stood by the empty wharf, amid a knot of Irish stevedores and American and Creole merchants who waited while the *Grand Turk* backed and filled and angled to take the *Philadelphia*'s place, only watching the opaque green-brown waters, the pelicans and gulls squabbling for scraps. When the wind shifted, the smell of the town came over him, gunpowder and burning, pestilence and decay.

The trial was tomorrow. He thought he glimpsed Killdevil Ned again as he made his way back along the levee, but lost sight of him by the time he reached the Place d'Armes. He didn't know if the trapper followed him home.

SIXTEEN

At no time was the cast of characters assembled at the request of the Bailiff of the Criminal Court of the State of Louisiana particularly inspiring of trust in the jury system. Watching them take their seats on the benches of the courtroom on the upper floor of the old Presbytère building, January felt a certain longing for the intendants and *juges d'instruction* of France.

In the summer the situation was worse, for the men of property and responsibility had already largely abandoned the town. What was left to make up the bulk of the jury pool was a disproportionate number of laborers, stevedores, saloonkeepers and café owners, small merchants such as January had rubbed elbows with on the wharves, and pettifogging businessmen like those along Baronne Street; frequently men of small education and intense prejudices. On the whole this batch didn't look too bad, thought January, taking his seat beside Vachel Corcet at one of the long tables near the empty jury box. But he would have felt more sanguine about the whole thing if there'd been more of them who looked like they had the intelligence to read and write.

"State your name," said the Clerk of the Court, and spit.

These were the twelve men, January reflected, they'd have to convince that just because Olympe worshiped African gods, it did not mean she was a poisoner.

"Henry Shotwell."

"I object to these proceedings, sir!" Monsieur Vilhardouin was on his feet. "It is prejudicial to the defense of my client, and indeed a slight upon the entire community of New Orleans, to assume that English is the language to be spoken in this Court!"

Henry Shotwell, a heavyset man in an over-gaudy tie and stickpin, removed his cigar from his mouth and said, "Oh, for Chrissake," and the Clerk of the Court turned red.

The State Prosecutor set down the bundle of papers he'd been perusing and rose, and January, seeing him for the first time, groaned inwardly. It was Orell Greenaway.

"Let me remind Mr. Vilhardouin," said Greenaway, glaring venomously up at Vilhardouin's tall elegant form, "that the State of Louisiana is now part of the United States, and that the official language of the United States is English."

"We true citizens of the City of New Orleans," retorted Vilhardouin, in French, "were sold to the United States against our will and without being consulted in the matter—"

"Welcome to our ranks," muttered January dourly.

"—and we were assured that our rights would be respected as citizens on an equal standing with those who invaded us."

"I very much fear," retorted Greenaway, in English, "that I have never had the opportunity to study a foreign tongue."

"It was not foreign upon these shores!"

The Judge banged his gavel. It was, January was relieved to see, J. F. Canonge in charge of the Court, the gray-haired and formidable pillar of Creole society who had been conspicuously absent from Madame Redfern's Bastille Day celebrations: During the Revolution his father had been a soldier of the Loyalist cause. "Monsieur Vilhardouin begs Mr. Greenaway to take into consideration," translated the Judge, "that the rights of the French citizens of this territory were guaranteed when they were ceded, without their knowledge, to the United States. Monsieur Shaw," he went on, turning his leonine head to address the Lieutenant, who was lounging in the back of the court cracking his knuckles, "please request that an interpreter be sent in."

Greenaway directed a glare at Vilhardouin that would have taken paint off a fence. Henry Shotwell flipped aside his coat skirts and seated himself again, took a flask from his pocket, imbibed a stiff jolt, and relit his cigar. The man next to him, who looked like a minor clerk or an apothecary's assistant, wrinkled his nose and fanned at the smoke, as if the whole room weren't choking with the fumes of the fever smudges in the courtyard behind the building. Had Hannibal been with him and not flat on his back in an opium stupor after hemorrhàging half the night, January would have offered handsome odds on at least one challenge before the end of the day.

He wondered if Corcet was a betting man.

The interpreter was the same harried-looking notary who'd been press-ganged at the Recorder's Court. While this gentleman was inquiring of the Judge when he was expected to get his own work done, January saw Hubert Granville rise from the bench, where he sat beside Madame Geneviève and Antoine, and go up to speak to Greenaway, his forefinger jabbing instructively. At the same time Mathurin Jumon went up and spoke to Vilhardouin. There appeared to be genuine distress in his face, and it crossed January's mind, absurdly, to wonder if the money Mathurin sought so desperately to raise was in some way destined to save Célie.

Antoine, plumaged in mourning nearly as elaborate as his mother's, turned in his seat, his eyes following the big man. He hastily straightened when Mathurin turned his head. His black-gloved hand made a feint at a pocket, but he caught his mother's warning glance, and resettled it in his lap. Mathurin, for one moment, stood looking at him. Then he, too, averted his face.

Granville returned to his seat and said something in an undervoice to Madame Geneviève.

"State your name. *Donnez votre nom, s'il vous plaît.*"

"Aristide Valcour."

"State your occupation. *Donnez votr' occupation.*"

"I am a mechanic at the municipal waterworks."

"*Je suis méchanique au—*"

"I object, Your Honor." Greenaway stood. "How can I be certain that this interpreter is giving a true and impartial translation of the prospective juryman's statements? I request that a man better versed in the *true* language of this country be called in—"

"The true language of this country is French!"

"*La langue vrai du cette pays c'est—*"

"It was the last time you paid any attention to what was going on around you!"

"How dare you—"

Vachel Corcet bolted to his feet one second behind Vilhardouin, reached out half-instinctively to stop him and at once pulled back. Granville, Shaw, and Mr. Shotwell all sprang forward and interposed themselves between the two lawyers: "Don't be a fool, man!" yelled the banker. In a rear corner of the courtroom, Burton Blodgett, a sweaty wad of rum-soaked wool and rumpled linen, scribbled gleefully in his notebook.

"Monsieur Vilhardouin," said Judge Canonge, "as you may have observed, it is a hot day. Due to Judge Gravier's illness, and Judge Danville's departure, there are one hundred and thirty-two cases on the docket to be heard, and more coming in every day. It is now nine-thirty in the morning. If we could settle this matter, grave though it is, with expedition as well as justice, it would be an act of mercy not only to all in this room but to those poor souls locked up in the Cabildo, awaiting their turn on Justice's scales."

Face flushed under the dark glory of side-whiskers, Vilhardouin straightened his somber tailcoat and resumed his seat.

"Mr. Greenaway." Canonge switched effortlessly to English as perfect as his French. "As a notary of this city Mr. Doussan is completely versed in both languages native to the population and I take it as a mark of disrespect to the judgment of this Court that you express doubt as to his ability or inclination to translate words as they are spoken."

Greenaway drew himself up to his full five-foot-four-inch height. "I accept the Court's decision." He spit, quite accurately, into the brass cuspidor.

The jury selection continued. Vilhardouin challenged Colby, Shotwell, Quigley, Horn, Lupoff, and Haldeman; Greenaway challenged prospective jurors Pargoud, Seignoret, Bringier, Valcour, Lanoue, Rouzau, and Villiere, all challenges taking place at length and through the medium of the harassed Monsieur Doussan, who gamely and vainly tried to work at his own papers in between quarrels. At the back of the courtroom Lieutenant Shaw continued to chew and spit like a placid locust, watching everything with narrowed gray eyes. During the proceedings Monsieur Vilhardouin rose from his seat two or three times to go to the doors of the courtroom and question the Bailiff outside: Blodgett, seated beside Shaw, leaned and craned unashamedly to hear.

"Monsieur Gérard and Madame Célie Jumon have not yet arrived," murmured Corcet to January. In the front row beside Granville, Madame Geneviève Jumon, and Antoine, Paul Corbier sat rigid in his go-to-church black corduroy coatee. His hands were folded around the brim of his shallow-crowned beaver hat on his knees and his eyes were straight to the front. He'd come in last night on the *Bonnets O'Blue,* harried and visibly thinner; January had supped with the family, and even Gabriel's cooking hadn't been sufficient to make the meal anything but an ordeal of silent anxiety.

By eleven the jury had been chosen: four Americans, five Frenchmen, a German, a Greek, and a Jew, comprising a saloonkeeper—though January was well aware that the Blackleg Saloon on Canal Street was as much a house of prostitution as it was a tavern—a paperhanger; a furniture dealer; the boss of a stevedore gang from the levee; three fishermen, one of whom spoke neither English nor French; a tailor; the man who mucked out stalls at Postl's Livery Stable on Baronne Street; a printer's devil; a shoemaker; and the husband of a woman who sold mantillas. They sat strictly segregated, Americans and French, and glared at one another while the Bailiff brought in Olympe.

She walked straight, cold, and self-contained. Her dark-blue calico dress and yellow tignon were faded but clean, for although no one was allowed to visit prisoners, Paul had handed the clothes over to Shaw earlier in the morning. "How bad is it?" whispered January as Olympe took her seat on the other side of Corcet.

Her dark eyes flickered to the Bailiff, who was watching her closely, and she said in a breath, "Two in our cell. Another last night."

"Shapannan?" He named the smallpox god, the god who must not be named, knowing Olympe would know he spoke of cholera, and she moved her head slightly, *No.*

"Our friend John."

Bronze John.

Thank God for small favors. Women as dark as Olympe, men as dark as January, seldom came down very sick of it. Cholera would take anyone.

Audience was filing into the courtroom. Mamzelle Marie. Olympe's friends among the market-women and laundresses in the poor neighborhoods around the city pasture, Alys Roque and Lizette Génois and Nan LaFarge. Basile Nogent. Four young women who appeared to be shopgirls or laundresses took their places near the table where Greenaway sat;

the State Attorney went immediately to speak to them. Soothing their fears, January decided, watching him—over the noise of the crowd he caught the words *silly superstition* and *you don't really believe that.* Leaving them, Greenaway went to exchange a further word with Granville; and Antoine looked around again at Mathurin Jumon, glowering as if he would draw a dagger and fall upon him shouting, *Thus is evil punished!* It had been Rose's intention to attempt another meeting with Madame Célie, so Gabriel had been asked to stay with Hannibal, but scan the crowd as he would, January could see no sign of the schoolmistress's neat tignon or round-lensed spectacles.

January wondered where Killdevil Ned was. Watching the building, perhaps? Waiting for him to come out?

Clément Vilhardouin got to his feet again and went to the doors: "Really, Mr. Villardang," remarked Greenaway, strolling over behind him and lighting a cigar, "looks like putting up bail for the wench wasn't such a good idea after all."

Vilhardouin rounded on him. "Only a cowardly poltroon whose natural recourse in times of danger is behind a woman's petticoats would dare to imply—"

At that moment Monsieur Gérard entered, face clotted with anger. Célie Jumon followed in her father's wake, her swollen, fear-haunted eyes and trembling mouth a shocking contrast both to her frock of simple mourning crêpe and to Olympe's threadbare calm.

"The Criminal Court of the State of Louisiana is now in session," intoned the Bailiff, first in English and then in laborious French. "All rise for the Judge."

Geneviève Jumon, resplendent in a fantasia of bombazine and silveret, with veils draping a tignon of quite startling elaborateness, testified as to her "friendship" with Laurence Jumon: that he had freed her, educated her two sons, Isaak and Antoine, given her property, promised to look after her. Yes, Isaak had been on extremely good terms with his father. Yes, there was every expectation that Monsieur Laurence Jumon would provide handsomely for his son. She spoke good, slightly accented English—elegantly gesturing aside the offer of assistance from Monsieur Doussan—while the stableboy and one of the fishermen helped themselves to their hip flasks and the shoemaker frankly dozed. While she repeated herself in French, Mr. Shotwell handed cigars to Mr. Quigley and Herr Flügel and offered one over the rail of the jury box to

Hubert Granville, at the same time trading a quiet-voiced joke with the banker, who chuckled and made a suggestive gesture with his hands.

"And did you speak to your son against his courtship of Miss Gérard?"

"I did." Geneviève straightened the diaphanous folds of her veils. "I warned him about that girl from the start. Behind that innocent convent-bred facade I detected a hard-eyed and grasping little hussy—"

"I object!" Vilhardouin shot to his feet at the same moment Monsieur Gérard slammed his fist down on the table before them, and in the audience Mathurin Jumon shouted, "Shame!" "This is a judgment extremely prejudicial to the welfare of my client!"

"And how else would you describe a girl—Oh, all right." Greenaway lit another cigar and waited while Monsieur Doussan repeated the entire interchange in French for the benefit of jurors Valcour, Huguet, Seignoret, Roux, and Fragonard. "How else would you describe a girl who attaches herself to a young man who expects to inherit several thousand dollars from his mother's lover?"

"My daughter expected nothing!" cried Gérard. "She was foolish, yes, in throwing herself away upon the son of a common whore—"

"Silence!" roared Canonge, whacking away with his gavel.

"A whore, is it?" snapped Geneviève, whirling in a storm of sable point d'esprit. "It's your daughter, rather, who—"

"Be silent or I'll have the room cleared! Madame Jumon, please confine your remarks to observed facts and not to your opinion of your daughter-in-law and her family." Célie's eyes were blazing, and Mathurin Jumon was half-risen from his seat, face crimson with rage.

"The observed fact," retorted Madame Geneviève, "is that I mistrusted the girl from the start, and for very good reasons!"

"You thought in fact that Célie Gérard was attempting to ensnare your son for what he might inherit?" asked Greenaway smoothly. Granville frowned in grave agreement, evidently seeing his dreams of his own banking establishment ripening satisfactorily: Blodgett flipped up another page of his notebook and bent over it like a starving man devouring a cream pastry.

"Yes," said Madame Geneviève. "That is what I thought and what I still think."

"Thank you," said Greenaway. "Your witness, Mr. Villardang."

"Madame Jumon," said Vilhardouin. "Did you not, on the nineteenth of June of this year, the day after a probate jury awarded your son

Isaak approximately five thousand dollars' worth of property and in-come from his late father's will, swear out a warrant distraining your own son Isaak on the grounds that he was your slave, in order that the property would then pass to you?"

"And in what other fashion," returned Madame Geneviève, "—oh, all right!" She folded her hands with a martyred air as the translator interrupted to repeat Vilhardouin's question in English for the benefit of jurors Shotwell, Quigley, Templeton, and Barnes. "In what other fashion could a mother protect a young man bent upon a foolish course that would only end in his ruin?"

"And did you, Madame," continued Vilhardouin, "inherit so much as a sou from the man who left you fifteen years previously?"

"I object!" Greenaway sprang to his feet. "I object to this blatant attempt to destroy Madame Jumon's credibility!"

"You mean you object to showing up this woman's harassment and greed for what it is?"

"It is not she who is on trial."

"Gentlemen!" shouted Canonge.

"It is she whose lies will blacken and perhaps condemn to death an innocent girl!"

"That girl's 'innocence' is precisely the issue here!"

"The crassness of your credulity, sir, cannot surely extend to belief that this girl would have—"

"I should say that *your* stupidity in considering every pretty cocotte an innocent astounds *me,* sir, but in fact it does not!"

"Gentlemen, sit down, both of you!"

The lawyers turned, panting, to meet the Judge's glare.

"Objection sustained," declared Canonge. "What Madame Jumon inherited or didn't inherit from her protector is irrelevant."

Greenaway sat down. Vilhardouin turned back to Geneviève Jumon in time to catch her smug little satisfied smirk. While Vilhardouin continued his questioning ("My son was, as anyone can tell you, fool-ishly in love. Isaak would have handed over everything he owned not only to his—*wife*—but to the management of her father . . .") Janu-ary saw the doors at the back of the court open, and Rose Vitrac step through. Célie Jumon turned her head, throwing Rose a look of plead-ing desperation. Rose made her way politely to Basile Nogent's side, in keeping, January realized, with her persona as the sculptor's sister.

Célie glanced at her father, glanced at Rose—". . . legally a man in years, but he was at heart very young for his age, and easily swayed . . ." Geneviève continued—and Gérard, who had been watching Geneviève on the stand with poisoned eyes, laid a hand over his daughter's arm and closed it with such brutal tightness that Célie bit her lip in pain. "I acted wholly for my son's benefit in this," Geneviève Jumon was saying, clasping her kid-gloved hands before her well-corseted heart. "The chance circumstance of my having purchased my son, at the orders of his father, showed me the easiest way to save him from himself. Would that I had thought of it earlier."

"Have you seen this?" Rose slipped up to January's side and passed a folded newspaper to him.

TRIAL OF A VOODOO QUEEN, announced the lead line on the second page. January closed his eyes and groaned. Every member of the jury would have read it—those who *could* read. He wondered if Mamzelle Marie or Dr. Yellowjack could be convinced to bury bottles of red pepper and pins in Burton Blodgett's dooryard.

Looking like an undertaker's mute, Antoine Jumon was called to the stand and entered into his recital of the events of the night of the twenty-third. He was interrupted promptly by Fragonard, the foreman, evidently, of the French side of the jury: "If it please Your Honor," said the shoemaker, "it is, as Your Honor said, extremely warm in here, and this pigeon looks to be singing for a while. Might those of us who do not speak the language step out for some cold punch in the arcade and come back when it's time to hear all this again in French?"

"Do!" said the stevedore cheerfully—thereby destroying his own earlier assertion that he neither spoke nor understood French. "That way we can take a bit of a stretch whilst you're listening."

"You'll do nothing of the kind," snapped Canonge. "And I don't care what other justices of this Court have done in the past. That's why Mr. Doussan is here: to translate as we go."

"That ain't hardly fair."

"If you make one more remark out of turn, Mr. Barnes," said the Judge, "you shall be expelled from the jury, and we'll start selection once again."

"Shut up, you idiot," hissed Shotwell, as his compatriot opened his mouth to protest again. "You want us all stuck here another golblasted day?"

"Monsieur Jumon." Vilhardouin stepped up to the box. "On the night this—mysterious woman—came to fetch you at your mother's home, had you been imbibing anything?"

Antoine's eyes shifted. "Imbibing? No."

"No alcohol?"

"No, nothing."

"No opium?"

"Really, sir!"

"I object!" protested Greenaway. "This is a blatant attempt to damage the credibility of yet another witness, and, by implication, to damage the credibility of the Bank of Louisiana, at which he is employed. If a man has had a drink or two, that would in no way impinge upon his ability to observe and understand what goes on around him."

"I'm sure *you* would prefer to think so, runt."

"Gentlemen—"

"Runt?" Greenaway screamed the word as he lunged to his feet, face mottling. "You Gallic hypocrite! You who do nothing but guzzle and fornicate and attempt to seduce innocent widows dare to imply an American cannot hold his liquor?"

"Imply? I have seen you facedown in a gutter on Tchoupitoulas Street too jug-bitten to do up your fly buttons!"

"Whoreson puppy!" Greenaway had by this time reached his opposing counsel before the witness stand, in which Antoine still sat, wide-eyed with alarm. "I wouldn't take words like that from a real man, let alone a wine-sodden monarchist pansy frog!" Seizing his rival by the lapels, he backhanded Vilhardouin across the face with a violence that rocked the Frenchman on his feet. "Name your friends!"

"Gentlemen!" roared Canonge, and Monsieur Gérard, pale, lurched to his feet and raised a protesting hand, though he dared not remonstrate against a white man.

Both attorneys whirled on the Judge. "That is precisely the point, Monsieur," said Vilhardouin in a tight, deadly voice. Greenaway's blow had left a pink welt across his cheek, just above the neatly shaven dark line of his side-whiskers. "As a gentleman—the *only* gentleman involved in this altercation," he glared from his six-foot elegance down at the panting Greenaway, "—I have received provocation which cannot be ignored. Your Honor will appreciate that I cannot be seen to take unchallenged a blow from any man, particularly not one such as he, and have any hope for advancement in this city. And perhaps this," he

added viciously—speaking in English, January noticed, though Canonge's native language was French—"is precisely what my opponent
intends, having no more evidence to argue his case than he has inches."
He stepped gracefully back as Greenaway lunged at his throat. "I request a continuance of this trial until such time as I have had satisfaction from this bastard pipsqueak." He turned to the crimson-faced
prosecutor. "Tomorrow, then."

"Where and how you please, you fornicating French liar!"

Canonge rolled his eyes and banged the gavel. "This trial is continued over until Monday morning. And I hope the two of you come back
in a better frame of mind."

Paul was on his feet, struggling to reach Olympe as the bailiffs led
her from the room. Through the tumult in the chamber as messengers
were dispatched to locate the various candidates for seconds, January
saw his brother-in-law's lips form his wife's name. Gérard pulled Célie
to her feet, thrust her before him toward the door, cursing as he did so
at Blodgett, who interposed his slovenly form before them, pad in hand.
Rose, too, was making her unobtrusive way toward father and daughter,
but Gérard caught sight of her, glared furiously and, seizing Célie by
both shoulders, dragged her through the door.

"The imbeciles!" Vachel Corcet's hands shook as he gathered up his
notes. "Fools, both of them. . . ."

"But gentlemen." Abishag Shaw slouched over to January and the
lawyer, putting on his wretched hat. "Maybe just as well. Gives me
more time to ride on up to Baton Rouge and see iff'n I can find our gal
Zoë. This ways I should be back, easy, by Monday morning."

"Thank you." January clasped his hand. "Thank you."

The chill gray eyes studied his face. "I tried just now to get in a
word with Mathurin Jumon. He skinned out of here like he had a
creditor in the room. Maybe he had, though damned if I could find
a word about it from any of the bankers I talked to. I must admit I'm
right curious about what this Miss Zoë'll have to tell. You don't get
yourself shot 'fore I get back, Maestro."

"I won't."

January watched the policeman's grimy hat disappear over the
crowd.

"Ben. . . ."

He looked around, and saw Rose standing at his side. "Did you get
a chance to speak to Madame Célie?"

"Not now, no." She drew him aside, into the corner of the jury box where Mr. Stefanopoulis was still dozing, abandoned by all his colleagues. "But I had a note from her early this morning, dropped from her window in a perfume bottle. Her father's been keeping her pretty closely locked up." From her reticule she drew the bottle—attar of roses, sold by a woman named Loge in Rue Dumaine, one of the hundreds of self-proclaimed former aristocrats of the ancien régime who kept shops in New Orleans. Dominique wouldn't wear Madame Loge's perfumes (*"They're very nice of course, p'tit, but so . . . obvious"*), but gave them to her maid Thérèse.

The paper rolled up inside was small, a slip half the length of his finger.

It said, *I have heard from Isaak.*

SEVENTEEN

"I've thought it prudent, on the occasions of my past two visits to Madame Célie, to lend her books." Rose Vitrac pretended not to see the arm January offered her as they skirted the muck of puddles that constituted the Place d'Armes, using her hand instead to hold up her flowered foulard skirts. "Not novels, of course, though Célie loves them—she and Isaak used to read to one another in the evenings. Evidently *Notre-Dame de Paris* was the first fiction she'd ever read. Papa Gérard is rather strict about that. I lent her St.-Lambert's *Catéchisme Universel* yesterday. In an hour or so, after Papa Gérard has had time to cool down, I'll go by the shop and ask its return."

They spent the hour in Hannibal's room, filling him in on the events of the trial. "Let's just hope our friend Vilhardouin made good notes for his defense," remarked Hannibal, his thin, husky voice fairly steady and his words only barely slurred. Propped on every pillow and folded blanket in the house, he actually looked a little better than he had the previous night. His violin lay on the bed close to his knees, and the room was redolent of the black coffee January had made for them all, and of herbed steam. "Papa Gérard must be just this side of apoplexy."

Paul had invited January to the Corbier house for supper again that night, an invitation January had turned down; when he walked Rose to the gate he met Gabriel, bearing a crock of beans and rice. "We got too much," argued the boy, when January tried to tell him to take it back for his family. "Papa figured this would take care of you and Hannibal both for a couple days."

It would, and in the absence of other income—*The Knights* would not be finished until Monday at least—it was all that was likely to sustain them. January felt like a parasite but didn't argue very hard. He and Hannibal dealt with classical Greek syntax and the absurdities of Aristophanic logic until the creak of the yard gate alerted January to Rose's return. He stepped out on the gallery, only for the pleasure of watching her cross the yard: an absurd joy, he knew, more suited to some fair-haired Ivanhoe than to a respectable musician of forty-one. She moved like an egret in her strangely awkward grace, and paused in the middle of the yard to hold up a thick blue book.

"I'm surprised Papa let her learn to read at all," remarked January dourly, as Rose halted at the top of the garçonnière steps to kick off the mud-crusted pattens that protected her shoes.

"You wrong him." Rose steadied herself on the gallery railing. "Easy to do, I admit. Monsieur Gérard may be hot-tempered and opinionated, but he's very concerned that his daughter have every advantage— every advantage a woman of color in this country is allowed, at any rate. So many white men assume that any woman of color is a courtesan, or would become one immediately if offered money—an assumption they'd kill another man for, if he made it of their sisters. Papa Gérard wanted Célie to make a respectable marriage. No girl is able to do that if there's the slightest question about her reputation. And he wanted her to be able to manage her household, and her husband's financial affairs, to the best advantage. And he isn't a fool. He knows that if a woman is widowed she must be able to support herself. For that it does help if one is able to read."

She followed January into Hannibal's room and took the chair he brought up for her, clearing some of the mess of foolscap and Greek lexicons from a corner of the fiddler's bed to take his own seat.

January was silent, remembering for the first time his own mother asking St.-Denis Janvier to send her a tutor, so that she could learn to read. Livia had carried it with a high hand and turned it into a demand, as if it were a polite accomplishment and not a necessity, but he realized now that had her protector died in the first year or two of her plaçage, she might have had no recourse but prostitution for herself, and hard labor for the children she would have been unable to educate.

Rose propped her spectacles more firmly onto her nose, opened the back cover of the *Catéchisme Universel,* and took out a folded note.

Celie,

I am alive and wel but I canot come back to town just yet. Stil I love you and I must see you. Come to were the 3 cypreses stand at the end of Bayoo Profit tonite at midnite, or Thursday nite at midnite. I wil wait for you there. Do not for any reason tell your father or the lawer. You may bring somone with you that you can trust, but only one.

Yore loving husbund,
Isaac

"So much for the fortune Laurence Jumon spent on his son's education," remarked Hannibal, leaning around to look over January's shoulder. "If Antoine spells that badly I wonder Granville hired him."

"It's a page torn out of the back of a book." January held the heavy, soft-textured paper up to the light slanting in through the door. "Octavo size—one of the blanks at the front or back to make up the signatures. Look where it's yellowed around three sides? But my main question is, Why would Isaak write to Célie in English?"

"He wouldn't." Rose gestured with the *Catéchisme,* and January now saw that one of the blank pages at the end, and the marbled inner cover paper, were lined with neat, small handwriting. "Here's what Célie writes."

Dear Madamoiselle Vitrac, thank you, thank you so very much for helping me. I do not know what to do. I found this note last night, lying on my window sill, with Isaak's gold signet ring. I do not know how it came there, but whoever sent it must know that Papa does not allow me to receive letters. I do not think that this is Isaak's hand, though if he had been sick or injured he might write differently. He speaks some English but cannot write it easily; I cannot think of any reason that he would write in it, rather than in French. But if it is Isaak I must go to him.

Please, I beg you, help me to get out of the house tonight and speak to him. Papa would let me communicate with no one yesterday, and I could not think how to get word to you. Would your friend Monsieur Janvier consent to accompany me to the place? I will tell Papa that Monsieur Nogent has not been well—though he was in the court room this morning—and I beg you to come this evening and say that he wishes to see me again. I am distracted and do not know what to do. Yours, Célie.

"Interesting," said January. "It explains the way she looked at court this morning, but I wonder if it's a coincidence that the letter came the day before the trial." He sniffed at the paper. Imbued with a conglomerate stench of dirt, smoke, and turpentine, it held no scent obliging enough to be in any way distinctive or remarkable. "Cheap ink and a pen cut with something less sharp than a penknife by someone who hasn't had much practice in splitting the point: Look at the way the *h* in *Thursday* drags and smears, and the *m* and the *n* in *midnite*. Whatever Isaak's abilities to spell in English, I should imagine he knows at least how to cut a pen."

"Not to speak of spelling his own name," interjected Hannibal. "In other words, it's a trap."

"Looks like it." January held the paper to the light. "Now, who do we know who's small enough to pass for Madame Célie in the darkness of the *cipriere* at night?"

In the end they got Gabriel to do it, balanced perilously on a borrowed pair of pattens that added three inches to his height and wearing a dark-blue tignon stuffed and padded out to bring the top of his silhouette up another four. "Oh, M'sieu," he squeaked, holding out his arm to his uncle for balance as he minced around his mother's parlor in one of her borrowed dresses, "please lend me your arm! I feel faint!" And amid gales of laughter from his siblings he brought the back of his hand to his forehead in imitation of the frailer Creole belles. "Can't I wear at least a little rouge, Papa? I can't be a real belle without rouge."

"You're there to lure these people into the open, not seduce them," said January flatly. "It'll be so dark we'll be lucky to find the place, let alone have them find us." He checked the oil in the dark lantern that stood on the parlor table, then the load of the completely illegal pistol he'd brought to the house thrust through the waistband at the back of his trousers.

"I don't like this," said Paul. Like January, he had changed into his darkest calico shirt, and since no man of color was permitted to carry so much as a cane, let alone a rifle or the *colichemarde,* he had armed himself with the stoutest chunk of hardwood in his workshop, a mahogany chair leg whose carved top was as big around as his biceps. Quiet grimness had settled on his face, and January realized suddenly that he would very much not like to ever get on the wrong side of this man.

"Nor do I." January kept his voice low to exclude the boy, who was flirting and mugging with the Sunday-for-Church fan his older sister had no use for during the rest of the week. "But if we're to learn anything this man must be trapped. And there isn't a woman I know who I'd put in this position." According to Rose, who had visited Célie just after dinner, the girl had been dissuaded from accompanying them only by Rose's flat refusal to be party to getting her out of her father's house. At Rose's height it was out of the question for her to personate Célie, even had January been willing to let her, and Hannibal's extensive list of the gamer prostitutes of his acquaintance—both male and female—who would have undertaken the disguise had been useless in the face of January's utter inability to pay anyone to take the risk, even at the minimal rates that some of them charged for their time and services.

That left Gabriel.

A sharp rapping at the door drew Paul away into the front bedroom: "Are we ready?" January heard Augustus Mayerling ask, through the opened French door. "I received your message," added the fencing master, as he came through into the back parlor and handed January one of the two firearms he carried, an English shotgun. "I regret to say that Madame Mayerling is not yet returned from Mandeville. She should be here tomorrow. What is the affair tonight?"

As they set out along Rue des Ramparts toward the Bayou Road January filled the Prussian in on the events of the trial, including the note and his observations thereon. "It hasn't escaped me," he added, "that a mountain man like Killdevil Nash would cut quills with a skinning-knife and would barely remember how to do it into the bargain. It might be that this is a trap for me rather than for Madame Célie. But if that's the case there's definitely something deep going on, because Madame Célie identified that signet ring as her husband's."

At Rue de l'Hôpital they turned north, passing the dark brick bulk of the Orphanage as the trees around them grew thicker, and the leaden armadas of clouds from the Gulf sailed onward to assail the moon.

"The other thing that letter does," went on January in a low voice, "or almost does, is exonerate Mathurin Jumon—if the concern he expressed at the trial hasn't already. Why have Killdevil Ned send a note in clumsy English when Jumon could compose one in well-spelled French?"

"Why?" said Mayerling logically. "Because Madame Célie would almost certainly recognize Jumon's handwriting." Gabriel skipped and hurried along beside the men, skirts gathered in one hand and pattens swinging from the other; the dim slits and spots of light that leaked from January's lantern splashed the water in the ditches, and the sword master's scarred, beaky face, with fugitive gold. "And if this trap is for you instead of for her, my friend, you could not fail to do so."

"Maybe," murmured January.

"Or it may simply be that our friend Killdevil thought this up on his own. Jumon has been in Mandeville this past week, I believe, and only returned for the trial. Monsieur Nash may not have been able to get in touch with him. In either case," Mayerling went on, hefting the Manton rifle he carried over one bony shoulder, "I advise that you waste no time in hanging the lantern on a tree limb at the appointed place, and that both of you stand well back from it, and as far apart as you can and still be visible to one another."

January obeyed these instructions when they reached the northern end of the narrow tributary of Bayou St. John, which terminated in a sort of trench or basin surrounded by cypresses, hackberries, and long-leaved willows bending like princesses to trail their hair in the inky water. The prospective ambushees had taken the precaution of leaving the Corbier house at nine in the evening, so as to be at the rendezvous well before midnight; time enough for Gabriel to assume his pattens and totter into the clearer space a little inland from the basin amid the trees with the air of an ingenue playing Juliet. Paul stationed himself in a clump of palmettos just behind his son—having first cautiously prodded the spiny-leaved thicket and shone the light there to evict any snakes—and Augustus took up a position on the other side of the clearing in a stand of tall reeds. Clouds had covered the moon while the little party had been on the clamshell road along Bayou St. John, but now chinks and cracks of moonlight dappled down through the over-hanging trees to spangle the black still waters with pale light.

January checked his watch—it was barely eleven—and settled down to wait.

Gradually the frogs, which had fallen silent around them, set up their croaking again, bullfrog and tree frog and the tiny shrill *brill-brill* of the gray frog, the squeak of crickets and then the deep, metallic throb of the cicadas. Mosquitoes whined in January's ears. He slapped at them, fully aware that it was an exercise in futility—they'd only come back in thirty seconds, and they did. Something flickered in the dark-ness overhead; he saw moonlight silver the back of a flying squirrel, gliding silently down from the top of a white oak tree and out of sight into shadows.

The pale shape that was Gabriel, in his skirts and his tignon, fid-geted against the dark backdrop of the trees, and scratched his hip. January sighed. He'd warned the boy that no lady ever scratched herself under any circumstances but couldn't do so again without being over-heard, if there were anyone to overhear. Palmetto bugs the length of January's fingers roared around the light of the lantern, hanging from its limb, and crept across the bare ground beneath. Somewhere, distantly, January heard the *tap-tap-tap* of African drums.

They used to talk to each other, the plantations, January heard in his mind his father's voice, deep as it was in dreams, in a darkness like this, the dark of the *cipriere. And the villages where the runaways went to hide, out in the* desert, *out in the* cipriere, *where the whites couldn't go—they'd use the drums, too. The men who'd been priests, and wise men, back in Africa, they ran away and became wangateurs and voodoo doctors. They'd set traps for the foolish, made with snake venom and poisons. And they'd get the* loa *to watch the bounds of the village, too: Bosou and Ogu, Omulu the smallpox god and the Baron Cemetery. They'd give them rum and tobacco, and they'd tell them, "Kill anyone who comes near these places. . . ."*

In the dark beneath the trees it was easy to remember the stories his father and the other men of the plantation had told him, about Ogu with the lightning in his eyes, and Omulu, whose real name was Shapannan that you were never supposed to say, and the Platt-Eye Devil that gobbled up the unwary in the dark. Tales about the Damballah serpent, the rainbow serpent, that smelled like watermelon; tales about the lizards that would come on you when you slept and count your teeth so that you'd die; tales about witches who could change skins with the jackals or kill a man just by drawing a finger across the threshold of his house.

Like the chop of an ax the frogs fell silent, and January checked his watch. It was quarter to twelve.

He listened, straining every sense to concentrate, to pick apart the tiniest clues. Remembering the glisten of the knife slashing down on him, that pale furious face and filthy beard. *Gabriel,* he thought, *I shouldn't have brought you here. . . . This is absurd. This is absurd.*

No sound, save for the lapping of the bayou around the cypress knees. Sweat trickled down his cheeks and temples in the dense heat. *Do I call out? Do I let him know we know he's here?*

The night held its breath. Somewhere in the darkness there was a rustle, a startled movement that made January flinch, then stillness again. *A fox? Killdevil Nash? The Platt-Eye Devil?* The white eyeless thing that hunted him through the *cipriere* of his dreams?

Six feet away on the other side of the lantern's light Gabriel scratched again.

After some twenty minutes—January glanced at his watch twice, trying to appear casual—the frogs began their peeping again. How long had it taken, he wondered, for them to start up after he and his body-guard had arrived? He cursed himself for not taking note. Did this mean the ambusher had come and gone, or did it only mean Killdevil was a hunter, lying still? How long would it take for a skilled hunter's eyes to adjust, so that he could take aim at a black man in dark clothes, or a light-skinned boy, standing in the shadows among the trees?

Sweat crawled down his face. Mosquitoes sang in his ears and he dared not move to strike at them—a fear Gabriel evidently didn't share, but at least, thank God, the boy didn't speak. January checked his watch again.

At ten minutes to one, another sharp rustling nearly shot January out of his skin, but it was only Augustus emerging from the reeds. "The Devil fly away with it. He won't be back."

"You saw him?"

"I heard something, a little after midnight, coming and then going. Only morning can show us what the tracks have to tell."

Gabriel came running over, pattens in hand. "I thought somebody was gonna shoot at us." He sounded disappointed.

The fencing master sighed. "Stand over there," he instructed, pointing back at the tree near where Paul was collecting the lantern. *"I'll shoot at you, if that will make your evening complete."*

They walked back in silence through the woods and the marshy stands of hackberry and pussy willow, to the stone bridge where Bayou Metairie ran into Bayou St. John. A City Guard stopped them at the corner of the Bayou Road and Rue de l'Hôpital, but after one quick lantern flash over the sword master's pale cold narrow face and cropped fair hair, the man went away. Evidently men of color bearing weapons were acceptable if accompanied by a white, whose servants they were presumed to be.

"Will you come in for something?" said Paul, when they reached the house on Rue Douane once again. In direct contravention of the instructions he had left in parting, his daughters were both still wide awake, the parlor shutters left open to make a long rectangle of candle-light in the dense indigo dark. Nearly drowned by the stench of the gutters and the grit of plague smudges, a thread of coffee scent drifted on the air.

Mayerling shook his head. "You have your work to do in the morning. Me, I am off to meet that *geistesschwach* Vilhardouin and his seconds at the Café des Exilés, so that he and Herr Greenaway can take shots at one another over who shall fetch punch for Madame Redfern. It fills me with deep sorrow to contemplate the future of human civilization."

And he strolled jauntily away down Rue Douane, an angular figure with two rifles balanced easily over one shoulder. The light from the oil lamps that swung above the intersections glanced off the silky beaver of his high-crowned hat.

January waited for him until nine the following morning, but when he made no appearance—he had said he would come by eight—he and Hannibal set out to retrace the route of the previous night. January felt serious misgivings about dragging the fiddler into this, compounded by his conviction that Hannibal would be worse than useless in the event of an attack, but Shaw had not yet returned from Baton Rouge and he might need a white witness to anything he found. Clouds were gathering fast; at this season it rained most afternoons, and it was the walk of an hour and a half to Bayou Profite.

"Thorough brush, thorough brier," quoted Hannibal, pausing to dis-

entangle his coat skirts for the dozenth time from a tangle of hackberry thorns. "*Over park, over pale. . . .* My uncles never would take me shooting with them; I always would stop and ask questions about why mushrooms grew in circles and what kinds of birds nested in the tree hollows. I'd get the poachers to take me out at night with them to watch rabbits. *I know a bank where the wild thyme blows, where oxlips and the nodding violet grows. . . .* Of course there weren't any snakes in County Mayo," he added, stepping back rather quickly.

"King snake," said January, as the mottled brown-and-blue tail whipped away out of sight. "Mambo Jeanne on Bellefleur used to tell us that king snakes have powerful spines and can kill any other snake just by wrapping around it and crushing all its bones."

"I knew there was a reason I never went beyond Rampart Street." Hannibal looked around him at the still greennesses of cypress and loblolly pine, sweat already running down his face from the contained heat among the trees. "I didn't know all this was out here. Rather like discovering the maids' dormitory in my aunt Rowena's house."

"King snake's nothing to worry about." January scouted the knots and clumps of underbrush where Omulu and Baron Cemetery had lurked in wait last night. "You can tell a poison snake's trail because it's wavy; the safe ones leave a straight track like a ruler."

"Must be awkward for them when they come to a puddle. *Over flood, over fire. . . .*"

January found the deep print of Paul's big boots, and where the mahogany chair leg had scraped the willow trunk against which it had rested. In a clump of reeds, nearer than he'd thought it had been last night, he found the narrow neat marks of Mayerling's English boots.

On the other side of the bayou he found what he sought: broken twigs, and the soft brown leaves of last summer's oaks pressed down into the wet ground. Looking back through the trees across the narrow green water he saw Hannibal in the middle of the clearing, just where Gabriel had stood last night. The fiddler was blithely continuing with Act Two of *A Midsummer Night's Dream* as if he expected the spotted snakes with double tongue, thorny hedgehogs, newts, and blindworms to be listening in the deeper green silences of the *cipriere.*

Not long-legged spinners nor beetles black, thought January uneasily, turning to listen to that green invisibility. Bosou and Ogu and Agassu, watching with red ageless eyes; the demon Onzoncaire and the bleeding sheep-head sacrificed to Omulu; the rainbow serpent coiled under the reeds. And behind them the dimmer manitou spirits of the Choctaw and Chickasaw, exiled but still listening, angry at their people's dead and wanting blood.

Killdevil Ned Nash was here, thought January. Or someone was. And had decided not to try it.

Did he see us? Know there was more than one?

Or was there some other reason? Something else he saw?

He moved along closer to the edge of the water, picking his way carefully among the reeds. Gnats whirled up in clouds; wasps and dragonflies, hanging over the water, flickered away in eerie silence.

He found the marks of bare feet about four yards from the farthest signs of Killdevil's moccasin scuffs. Two men—one of them with enormous feet, larger than January's own—and someone who could have been either a boy or a woman. The marks came up out of the bayou itself, and hugged cover with the expert caution of those who knew the country well.

Thunder whispered overhead, low and close, a lion's growl. Wind whipped at the oak leaves and the long gray beards of moss. The cricket cries increased in the dense green air, as if the whole world were suddenly compressed by the coming of the rain.

January crossed back over the bayou on the rummage of deadfalls and cypress knees that had taken him, more or less dry shod, over the still green water in the first place. With the wind snaking in his long hair and his pale face skull-like with exhaustion and illness, Hannibal had the look of a wood-elf himself in the sudden dimming of the storm light.

> *Blow, winds, and crack your cheeks! Rage! Blow!*
> *You cataracts and hurricanoes, spout*
> *Till you have drenched our steeples, drowned the cocks!*
> *You sulfurous and thought-executing fires,*
> *Vaunt-couriers to oak-cleaving thunderbolts. . . .*

"Do you feel it?" He swung around as soon as January was near. "The watchers in the woods? *Be not afeared, the isle is full of noises. . . .*"

January nodded. Looking back across the bayou to where the reeds grew thick, he understood whole and suddenly why Ti Jon had lied to him, and where Isaak Jumon had been between the twenty-first of June and the twenty-third, and whom he had gone to meet beside the crooked tree near the Bayou Gravier. Oaks and willows, reeds and hackberries made matte walls of greens, dark and drenched with the rain; the beryl water was still, save for the growing and spreading circles of the falling drops. The air breathed the smoky odor of rot, and the waiting tension of the Congo drums.

"Indeed it is," he said softly. "Indeed it is."

Augustus and Madeleine Mayerling were sitting on the gallery steps outside the garçonnière when Hannibal and January returned. "I abase myself with chagrin at having failed you," said the fencing master, shedding his wasp-waisted coat and rolling up his fine linen sleeves as January helped Hannibal to lie down on Bella's bed. The fiddler had made it most of the way back from the *cipriere* in the rain, but exhaustion had claimed him as they'd passed the cemeteries; arms aching, January had half-dragged him up the stairs. Madeleine Mayerling, a full-bosomed, beautiful woman with dark hair wound into fanciful knots and ringlets, measured herbs into the little china pot of the veilleuse as her husband of six months went down to the cistern for water, and scratched a lucifer on the striking paper to kindle the flame underneath.

"Orell Greenaway put a bullet through Clément Vilhardouin this morning at six," Mayerling said, returning with the dripping pail and shaking the rain out of his hair. "Vilhardouin died an hour and a half ago."

"*Majnûn,*" said January, in Arabic—fool.

Mayerling's scarred face showed no change of expression, but the long upper lip pressed taut. "As you say. I'm told he spent all of yesterday evening in the woods at the end of Erato Street, shooting at playing cards nailed to the trees there: I am pleased to report the entire Court of Spades still enjoys excellent health. The surgeon Greenaway hired—that idiot Bernard over on Rue Bourbon—bled Vilhardouin and dosed him with calomel by the cupful, but I doubt he would have survived in any event. I hope he had a partner on Madame Célie's case?"

"None."

"Monsieur Trepagier—my first husband, as you know, Monsieur," said Madame Mayerling, "engaged in two duels while we were married." She crossed the little room in a rustle of claret-colored skirts, a steaming cup of herb tisane cradled in her hands. "This in spite of the fact that the next year's crop was already mortgaged and not yet in the ground, and in the event of his death I—and the children that I had then—would have been left destitute. The man he fought, and killed, was in a similar case, and I knew his wife. It was that which made me finally stop believing that he would ever offer me even the protection that the law demands."

"*I would not love thee, dear, so well,*" quoted Hannibal, cocking a sardonic glance up from his pillows, "*loved I not honor more.*"

"Goodness gracious me." Madame Mayerling widened her velvet-brown eyes and held the cup at arm's length above him, "I have accidentally spilled every drop of this scalding hot tisane over poor Monsieur Sefton's head."

Hannibal lifted his hands in surrender. "*Now mark me how I will undo myself.*"

"See that you do, then." She handed him the cup and settled in the chair that Mayerling held for her. Whatever could be said of her first husband, thought January, this second, odd marriage agreed with her. The haunted grimness of her widowhood had been replaced by a kind of zesty humor that he had not even seen in her girlhood. It was as if the subdued calm of her early years itself had been a facade, a defense against fate penetrated only by the ferocity with which she pursued her music. She wore now the look in her eyes comparable only to that of a young child presented with a large dish of Italian ice and a spoon: as if, at twenty-eight, she were finally permitted to be young.

"I spent Wednesday afternoon at tea with Madame Cordelia Jumon," she said a short time later, after January had gone down to the kitchen to fetch up the spirit kettle and remains of his mother's coffee beans. "We used to make jokes—my girlfriends and cousins and I—about how Monsieur Mathurin Jumon would never marry because he could never find a woman who would spoil him the way his mother spoiled him, calling him 'my lover' and 'my cabbage' and all those other things as if he were still in dresses. Years, as far back as I can remember. And now—poof!" She gestured as if drawing back from an explosion.

"A viper in her bosom; an adder; a beast who was always selfish, always cruel to her, always delighted in hurting her, even from the time he was a little child—this from a woman I heard with my own ears telling how he and his brother used to sleep in her bed with her, they loved her so much. Madame Cordelia would tell my father in detail about how she used to tell Monsieur Mathurin and his brother to pick out the most wretched little beggar child they saw, and she would give alms, saying that it was her gift to them so they would go to Heaven because of her. I remember she'd go on for hours—she saw my mother fairly often when I was a child—about what Monsieur Laurence and Monsieur Mathurin must be thinking about her when they were apart, and would ask them about what they'd been thinking about her at such-and-such a time."

Hannibal coughed. "Makes Monsieur Gérard sound positively Lear-like."

"I'd have run from home screaming," said Augustus Mayerling flatly.

A thought crossed January's mind: a black locked cupboard in an attic, a bloodied strip of sheet. "Maybe they tried," he said.

Hannibal's gaze crossed his, but the young woman went on, "In any case, now none of that has ever happened. Mathurin was always an unnatural brute. He never cared for her, always sought ways to hurt her and slight her—the *teacups* we were drinking out of were Sèvres ware, Louis XVI, fifty dollars apiece! She was wearing girandole earrings the size of chandeliers!"

"Did she say why he was selling up?"

Madame Mayerling shook her head. "But so far he's put on the market not only the carriages and horses and slaves that you heard of, but one of the properties that went to him in the settlement when they sold up Trianon, a warehouse at the foot of Julia Street. Madame Cordelia says he's given her some tale about investing in slaves to be let out, but he'd have to be buying an army of them. In any case what he *isn't* spending the money on is the black peau de soie she feels is critical to her standing in society—one can't be properly respectful to the dead, apparently, in plain paramatta—and getting her carriage reupholstered."

There was silence, save for the drumming of rain on the roof, and the muffled bubbling of the water over the spirit lamp. January measured out the ground coffee and added it to the water, nipped chunks of sugar from the loaf and arranged them neatly in a saucer on a folded napkin. "Mathurin can't be spending that much on rustic ware. It sounds as though he were being blackmailed."

"I thought of that," remarked Mayerling, who was, after the manner of fencing instructors, idly experimenting with Italianate redoubles with a coffee spoon. "If there'd been a run on a bank or a plunge in stocks, one would hear, and I've gambled with the man. He never plays beyond what one would spend on an evening's entertainment in some other pursuit."

"It's a shame," said his wife. "Because he has done a great deal of good."

"I've heard that," said January. "I've heard also that he has dealings with the voodoo doctors from time to time—over what, I don't know. What does his mother say of his charities?"

"Not much. They're usually people steered to him by the St. Margaret Society, or through Père Eugenius, though I think Mrs. Coughlin and her daughter, Abigail, came to him through a mutual friend."

"Coughlin?" Hannibal straightened from his pillows. "Lucinda Coughlin?"

"You know her?" Madame Mayerling regarded him in surprise. "A Philadelphia woman; her husband died of the fever last year. Monsieur Mathurin has been helping her find respectable employment, and giving money toward her daughter's schooling."

"Little girl about five years old?" Hannibal held out his hand to indicate a height of about three feet. "Honey-colored curls and big brown eyes? Looks like she came out from under a hill in Ireland somewhere?"

She nodded. "Abigail. I've met them over at Monsieur Mathurin's two or three times since Christmas."

"And Lucinda's a blond woman?" Hannibal coughed again, deep racking shudders, and groped under his pillow for the opium bottle. He sank back, white-faced, against the cushions, his breath stertorous, but a curious bright gleam in his dark-circled eyes. "Flax blond? Your height, but slim? About your age?"

"That's Mrs. Coughlin," said Madame Mayerling. She took the teacup from the bedside lest it spill. "A very sweet woman, from the little I saw of her. Maybe too strict with her daughter, who seemed a bit of a minx. Mrs. Coughlin had difficulty in finding employment of any kind in a shop, you understand, because she couldn't leave Abigail alone, but I understand they were arranging to have the girl put in the Ursulines convent during the day at school. She's a little young for it. . . ."

"And the first time she opened her mouth she'd probably blow the roof off the building," said Hannibal. He took another sip of opium. "I've heard that child swear. She could take the paint off a gate at fifty paces and make a muleskinner faint."

Madame Mayerling, Augustus, and January all regarded him in stunned silence.

"Lucinda Coughlin," said Hannibal, "is one of the most active—certainly one of the speediest—prostitutes on Girod Street, and if her daughter's still virgin I'll turn in my fiddle and become a monk. The pair of them got me drunk and turned my pockets out at the Brown Meg the day before Christmas and left me facedown in the gutter on Tchoupitoulas Street. Thank God it wasn't raining."

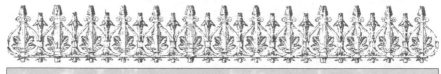

EIGHTEEN

"Are you sure we're talking about the same Lucinda Coughlin?"

"If we're not," said Hannibal, "there are not only two ladies by that name, but each has an adorable-looking little five-year-old daughter named Abigail. Possible, as Aristotle would say, but partaking of the improbable-possible rather than otherwise. Myself, I'd say our friend Uncle Mathurin is being set up." He coughed. Augustus, who was nearest him, caught his shoulders to steady him as the spasms doubled him over. He was a long way, thought January worriedly, from being out of the woods.

"You'd better rest," he said, as he and the sword master eased their friend back against the pillows.

A smile flicked at one corner of the graying mustache. "I don't seem to have any choice about that. *To sleep, perchance to dream.* . . ." Hannibal closed his eyes, and was asleep as if he'd been struck over the head.

January and Madeleine Mayerling walked out onto the gallery together, leaving her husband by the bed. "I don't suppose you know where this Madame Coughlin is supposed to live?" he asked.

She shook her head. "I only saw her twice, at Monsieur Mathurin's, when I went to call about the subscriptions for the St. Roche Society Ball." She worked her hands back into her gloves. "All he told me was that she was a woman he was helping, financially and in a business way.

He asked me whether any of my aunt Alicia's relatives were in need of a governess or a companion. The situation was complicated, he said, by Abigail's youth, as the child could not be left alone. But the very fact that he'd be seeking such a position for her—with his relatives and friends, I mean—tells me that he is ignorant of what she is, if in fact what Hannibal says is true. And in any case"—she made a wry grimace—"this *is* Monsieur Mathurin we're talking about."

"A model of rectitude," said January softly. "Impervious to Cupid's darts."

For a moment his eyes met those of the woman he had taught. Then because he had been trained from earliest childhood never to look into a white person's eyes—especially not those of a woman—he glanced aside. But the silence lay between them anyway, matters that were not discussed between women and men.

At length, gazing carefully out over the rain-pocked puddles of the yard, Madame Mayerling said, "If you're wondering whether Monsieur Mathurin's tastes are—unorthodox—I haven't heard it. Men of that persuasion often approach Augustus," she added, without irony. "But that doesn't mean there isn't something afoot. And if there is scandal broth brewing, should Isaak have seen something, or learned something . . ."

"Yes," said January. "The only problem is that if Isaak went where I think he went after he left the Turkey-Buzzard Saloon, there's no way that Lucinda Coughlin could have gotten anywhere near him."

January considered the matter through the rainy afternoon, between bouts of trying to capture some of Aristophanes' absurd lyricism and frame the worst of that playwright's jokes into something a publisher could print without fear of prosecution. Propped on his mound of pillows Hannibal slept, waxen and skeletal. Two or three times January produced his stethoscope from his desk drawer and listened to Hannibal's chest. But though the faint, wheezy rattle of consumption was always present, there was no sign of pneumonia, which given Hannibal's general state of health would almost certainly finish him. Useless to hope, however, that the fiddler would be in shape to make inquiries in the Swamp concerning the double life of Lucinda Coughlin anytime soon.

But to go into the Swamp himself would mean death. January

thought he had glimpsed Nash within the French town, watching him, and had begun to fancy that the market-women crossed over Rue Royale when they saw him coming. Shaw might possibly help him, but there had been no word from Shaw.

Far off a steamboat moaned, down at the foot of Canal Street. Otherwise the world was silent, save for the silvery voice of the rain. The downpour ended at sunset, and heat and blue twilight deepened in the room, and he went and dragged the mattress of his bed from his own room into a corner of Hannibal's, then went back and brought the mosquito-bar as well. Useless, maybe. The fiddler was too far gone now to provide him with anything in the way of protection. But January had dreamed last night of the demon Omulu, and of red eyes watching him from within a sheep skull clotted with dry blood and ants. Waking, he had had to fight the desperate urge to tear mattress and pillows and bedding to pieces lest there be feathers in them twisted into the shape of a rooster or a cat. Lying in the darkness he had tried to think of all the places in the room where balls of black wax and graveyard dust might be secreted.

And that way lay madness.

Coming out onto the gallery again, with the sky glowing lapis behind a streaky battlefield of leftover clouds, of smudge smoke and steamboat soot, he saw, far down at the end of Rue Burgundy, the white moon stand above the town's low roofs, a baroque pearl, only a day or two from full. And he remembered the big man with the cut-off stump of an arm, laughing with white teeth as he spoke to Mamzelle Marie in the heat and dust of Congo Square; the shine of sun and sweat on the bare ribs of the men in red loincloths, and the bare feet of the women beneath their short petticoats.

He left the shutters open for as long as he could into the evening, working on his Greek under the mosquito-bar by the light of candles. When at last he barred and barricaded them, and slept, he dreamed of dark ships beneath hot gibbous moons, spirits clinging in the rigging and watching the low green coast of the New World grow before them with flaming eyes.

In the morning Hannibal was still resting quietly. In gloom clear and still as blue topaz January dressed and went to Mass, where he encountered Mamzelle Marie just emerging from the confessional: He wondered what it was that she said to the priest. Coming out, January fell into step with a man named Natchez Jim, who had a wood boat on the levee and another, smaller craft in which he ferried people and goods back and forth across the lake.

The two men had coffee and gingerbread together on a bench outside the market; and Jim said, to January's request, "Whatever I can do that will help. Your sister's gris-gris has saved my life from the river, many a time."

From a market-woman January bought a fancy box of *estomac mulâtre,* and went home to change his clothes. Hannibal still slept peacefully. January found a piece of gilt paper and some ribbon, to wrap the ginger cakes, in his mother's storeroom and spent another ten minutes at his desk, with "Baron von Metzger's" cold-pressed parchment stationery, composing a note to Miss Abigail Coughlin "from your very dear uncle Charles." He made his way by circuitous detours to the line of oyster huts that fringed the levee where Jim waited with his boat; and though he never saw Killdevil Nash, he knew the man waited for him, watching in the half-deserted quiet of the streets. Only when he and Jim maneuvered Jim's lugger out from among the flatboats and keelboats tied in a tangle around the giant river queens did he relax, as the current took them in the open water and swept them fast downstream.

"It would be just about there, that General Jackson rode along to look at the upper line of his men," January said, pointing to the trees just beyond the white house and carefully laid gardens of one of the many Macarty plantations. "He came out of the fog, like a ghost in a dream on his gray horse, leaning from the saddle to shake this man's hand or that."

"It drove my papa wild, hearing about that fight," remembered Jim with a reminiscent grin. The river breeze stirred all the tattered pickaninny braids of his long hair. "He was all for the British, of course, saying they'd keep the Americans out." Gulls wheeled and yarked above the sunflash on the browned steel of the river; a line of pelicans swooped down low, precise as if they practiced the maneuver in their spare time. "Not that Papa had any use for Napoleon, either, you understand. *'What's that Italian ever done but make more curfews and more* code noir *and more taxes so that he can fight his boneheaded wars?'*" He imitated an old man's growling *mo kiri mo vini* French, and richly laughed; January laughed, too. " 'Pox on 'em all,' he'd say."

Clear and distant the Cathedral bells chimed for noon Mass, answered from among the trees farther downriver. A steamboat's whistle sounded, and the tiny chime of the Algiers ferry bell. The white bulk of steamboats had given way to the dark-hulled oceangoing vessels of the downstream quays and they in turn to scrubby trees and the wilderness of broken casks, boxes, and garbage along the batture. The levee crowds thinned. Only occasional carriages and horsemen could be seen passing on the shell road. Across the river dark poplars fringed the cane fields of the Verret and Marigny plantations, spotted by the red-and-blue flags on the mast of a keelboat, beating its way upstream close to the bank. Among the trees, buildings came into view, an open quadrangle fenced on the riverside with a wrought-iron gate. Natchez Jim put in at the little wharf there, where during the week flour and provisions, soap and gray cloth, ink and mail, and coffee were unloaded, and January thanked him, and walked up the shell path to the gate.

"Oh, I'm afraid Miss Abigail Coughlin did not come to us after all," said the lay sister, her brow furrowed a little under the broad white band of her veil. She spoke with the accent of Normandy; January wondered what she made of these flat green monotonous coasts, the bougainvillea and Spanish jasmine, after the late cold springs and bare Februarys of that land of apples.

January put on an expression of distress. "My master will be very sorry to hear that," he said, slipping back into his pocket the note from "Uncle Charles." "He understood that the child was to be placed here."

"And so she was." The woman's wide blue eyes smiled a little with tender reminiscence of what must have been a very pretty and well-spoken little girl. "We were so looking forward to having Abigail with us. But only three days before she was to have come to us we received a note from her sponsor—Monsieur Mathurin Jumon, a very respected gentleman in the city—saying that the health of the child's mother obliged her to leave New Orleans, and take Abigail with her. I do hope it was nothing serious," added the woman kindly. "Monsieur Mathurin has sponsored four of our pupils here in the past—in fact one of them, Danae Bonfils, is still among us, as a fourth-year, a most sweet and kindly girl. Monsieur Jumon is truly a guardian angel."

"My master will be most upset," repeated January. "At one time he was quite fond of Mademoiselle Abigail's mother, but lost track of her when he was called away to Paris. He hasn't seen Mademoiselle Abigail herself since she learned to walk. You wouldn't have a direction for Madame Coughlin herself, would you, M'am?"

The sister shook her head. "Though I'm sure Monsieur Jumon would be able to direct you. His house is on Rue St. Louis in town, a tall blue house on the upstream side between Rue Bourbon and Rue Dauphine."

Across the courtyard behind her January saw two gray-robed sisters shepherd two neat lines of girls, arranged oldest to youngest, like stair-steps: dark Creole curls and fair French locks modestly bonneted in uniform blue, white linen aprons, making the children look like a flock of hurrying birds. The breeze from the river cooled the court a little, and rustled the trees. Better they were here, he thought, than in the smoky and fever-ridden heat of the town.

From his pocket he took the box of cakes, and held it out. "Since I can't locate Mademoiselle Coughlin," he said, "perhaps the young ladies would like to divide these amongst themselves, Ma'm. They were fresh this morning, and they'll be stale tomorrow."

Her smile brightened. She was really little more than a girl herself. "They'll be very glad of it."

"You wouldn't happen to know the day Mademoiselle Abigail was supposed to come here, would you, M'am?" he asked, as she made to close the door. "Michie Charles is only in town for a day or two. We did ask at the house, but Michie Jumon is away in Mandeville, they said. Michie Charles may just ask at the steamboat offices for word of Madame Coughlin going upriver."

January wasn't entirely certain what he hoped to learn from that piece of information, if anything. And in fact the date of Mathurin Jumon's note to the Mother Superior, which the lay sister went and found out for him—the eighteenth of June—meant nothing to him. The day before Isaak Jumon's distrainment and over a week before the young man had died in his uncle's house.

Still, thought January, as he walked back to the wharf, there was something going on. Not a shred of evidence linked Mathurin Jumon's connection to the virtuous or not-so-virtuous Lucinda Coughlin, and the death of his nephew in his house. . . . Except that in each transaction a large sum of money was involved.

"You find what you sought, brother?" asked Natchez Jim, when the dark trees of the batture were drifting past them again and the smoke of the city dirtied the brazen air ahead. The day was hot now, even down here near the water. Turtles lined the half-sunk logs, blinking in the sun, largest to smallest with yet smaller ones perched on their backs; here and there the brown-and-cream zigzag of wet scales marked the passage of a water moccasin among the cypress knees.

"I'm not sure." January stroked the water with the oars a time or two, then both men slacked the left-hand sweeps, steering around a muddy point of land to hug the shore, seeking instinctively more sheltered water. His arms ached, but he found that by leaning his weight from his hips it was possible to put some strength behind the stroke, enough to be of use, which made him glad. On the other side of the point, only a little way into the river, a rusted smokestack reared green and dripping, where a steamboat had tried in the same place to avoid the big current. January hoped the wreck had taken place by day and not at too fearsome a speed.

"We can argue all we want, that Olympe was somewhere else on the night of Jumon's death, and Célie Jumon was in her room alone— though she can't prove it—but it won't matter to a jury. Especially now that the attorney defending Madame Célie is dead."

"Aarh," growled Jim, who had apparently been keeping up with the bones of the case through market gossip. "That wasn't that fool Vilhardouin that got himself shot in a duel? . . ."

"The very one."

"Imbecile. Row straight on here; there's a snag closer in."

"As you say," said January. "But until we prove who did poison the Jumon boy, I think they're going to hang the wife for it—and if they hang Madame Célie, they'll hang my sister. I need to find out where Jumon was during the days he was missing, and where he went on the night of his death. And I think," he went on, "the moon being full tonight, that the man who would know is going to be at the voodoo dancing."

Though he had passed many times by Congo Square during the slave dances on Sunday afternoons, and had two or three times—as he had the previous Sunday—mingled in the crowds there to find someone he sought, January had not been to a true voodoo dance since the night twenty-two years ago in the brickyard on Rue Dumaine. Lying under a black weight of tarpaulins in Natchez Jim's pirogue, January felt the small cold clutch of some emotion he could not name tightening behind his sternum, as if he expected the voodoo gods to know about the fix that had been put on his room.

They didn't exist, he knew. Old Papa Legba with his keys and his crutch and his smoldering pipe; Ogu the warrior; the rainbow serpent Damballah. . . . They were no more real than Moloch or Apollo. Juju balls were nothing more than dirt and wax and the feathers that came off chickens, like any other chickens in the French town . . .

But still he felt fear.

January had taken the long way to meet Jim in his pirogue where the canal crossed Rue Claiborne, glancing behind him for sight of Killdevil Ned all the way. He didn't think he'd been followed. It was a little more than a mile and a half, through a morass of pondlets, long grass, and cypress knees, to where the canal joined the bayou. From there perhaps another mile through the dark monotony of cypress, oaks, marsh laurel, and standing water, to where the channel split to make two islands, tucked and curled one around the other. When January put back the canvas that covered him from sight he smelled smoke, and by the dim glow of Jim's lantern he saw a three-foot gator slip from the bank and vanish into the opaque ink of the water. Dimly he heard singing:

> *Papa Legba, open the gate for me,*
> *Papa Legba, open the gate,*
>   *Ona pass through, ona pass through. . . .*

Into where? He remembered the darkness of his sister's eyes.

In a cleared space at the water's edge, guarded by a tangle of oaks drowned by the bayou's altered course, someone had kindled a bonfire. A pillar had been set up, and a sort of altar made from half a hogshead. Aromatic leaves covered it, tobacco and sassafras, and on top of them cut-paper doilies. Cigars and silver coins, dollops of rice and beans heaped on oak leaves or in gourds, pralines or pieces of pound cake on chipped earthenware plates. Beads and strange-shaped stones, a cat's skull, bunches of feathers, a bottle half-full of rum and another almost completely so, squat square English crystal. The man who'd sat on the big bamboula drum in Congo Square two Sundays ago was here tonight, thumping time with his heels; he'd shed his calico shirt and wore only a couple of bandannas tied around his loins. Someone brought him rum from the long pale shape of a dark house, barely visible on ground higher yet behind moss-curtained trees.

Dancers writhed and swayed around the fire. The chant of voices, weird and aching, lifted behind the slap of hands. Bach and Mozart, Beethoven and Rossini, January thought, were the flesh of his being, but this chanting, this rhythm—these were the bones they clothed.

He saw faces he remembered: a market-woman glimpsed at Mass only that morning; a young man who peddled paper and ink in the streets. The fat woman who'd danced close to Mamzelle Marie three weeks ago, all her flesh joyfully wobbling as she pirouetted, head rolling, lost in the joy of the movement; the thin-faced man who'd shoved the box of English tools off the quay. Firelight changed them, as did darkness and the gleam of sweat. Without their tignons most of the women seemed younger, wilder, shed of disguise. Mamzelle Marie swayed on top of Damballah's cage; the great king snake coiled and shifting as she raised him up, and her long hair was like a black waterfall of night. The force of her being—the radiance of Power—drew all eyes to her.

Beyond her, beyond the crowd, January glimpsed movement in the woods.

Men stepped cautiously, quietly out of the darkness, making their way toward the house. January couldn't be sure, but he thought one of them was very tall, and very black, and there were others, following behind. He edged his way through the dancers, back to where the trees grew thick, keeping himself half-hidden in the shadows. These were men who clearly did not wish to be seen.

Only when he drew close did he see these weren't the men he sought. Rather, he saw, they were those who'd shoved the boxes of tools from the quay the day he'd spoken to Ti Jon. And indeed, there was Dr. Yellowjack, as Hannibal had said, emerging from the dark house to meet them.

Works all the way up through Natchez. . . . Never lets himself come into view. . . .

At the wangateur's signal the black man—who was in fact only a porter—carried the bundle up onto the gallery that ran around three sides of the house, which was of the kind common in the marshes: three rooms, brick between posts, raised high against the rise of the river. Dr.

Yellowjack took down one of the lanterns that hung on the gallery's overhang to examine the goods, the shiny buckle of his heron-hackle aigrette catching the light. During this conference two or three white men emerged from the woods, as silently as the thieves had and keeping even more to the shadows.

But Yellowjack saw them, and gestured them up onto the gallery. One of them gave him something—probably money—and a couple of young women appeared, briefly, in the dark doorways of the house. They were clothed the way many of the girls at the dancing dressed, in bandannas knotted around their breasts and forming complicated, swirling skirts, like those in the Square on Sunday. Taking the girls by the arms, the white men disappeared into the house.

Disgusted, January turned to go back to the dancing again. But it occurred to him that whatever else could be said of this man, Dr. Yellowjack would certainly be aware of anything that went on here, on St. John's Eve. So he stepped from the darkness as the thieves were departing, and said, "Dr. Yellowjack," and the little man turned, regarding him with wet pebble eyes.

"I'm Ben Janvier."

"I know who you are." He had an astonishingly deep voice for so small a man, deeper than January's own. Like the echo of cold stones falling into the River Styx.

"Then you know my sister's in trouble, in prison." Of course a root doctor would know who he was, January thought. Like Mamzelle Marie, such men relied on information about everyone and everything to read fortunes, cast spells, predict the future—to astound the ignorant and peddle gris-gris in the Cathedral's very shadows. And evidently, to know who was in the market for English chisels and handsaws. "She was here, wasn't she, on St. John's Eve?"

"That she was." Yellowjack was like a coiled snake, or something carved out of polished black wood, watching and wary. A man who never let one sliver of advantage slip from his grip. *A man*, thought January, seeing the way he kept an instinctive distance, beyond arm-reach, *who trusted no one.*

"I'm looking for a maroon, a big man with one arm, nearly as big as me," he said. "You know him?"

The cold eyes narrowed under the brim of the leather hat. "I know him."

"Does he come here to the dancing? Will he be here tonight?"

"We never know about the future, do we?" said Yellowjack softly. "Why don't you—?"

From inside the house a woman shrieked, not in pain or in terror but in annoyance, and cried, "Let it be, pig! I told you . . ."

Above the little tuft of whiskers Yellowjack's lips pressed tight. "Excuse me." Like a snake he whipped up the steps and into the house; a moment later January heard the white man's voice lifted in protest.

"You said these gals'd do whatever . . ."

He turned away. Between the water and the fire the rhythm of the clapping had increased, drawing him to the bayou's bank. As he came near there was a shrill wild cry, cut short in a smell of blood, and January saw a stone-faced man of perhaps sixty hold up a decapitated chicken above the blaze. The black-feathered body still jerked and flapped, spraying the post, the altar, the man's naked chest with blood. When the chicken ceased to move, the priest—Dr. Brimstone—threw the carcass on the altar, then took a long swig of rum. This he spit at the post, and for good measure poured a stream of the liquor over the rice and candy and cigars. His handprints showed bloody on the crystal as he set the bottle down.

The pulse of the dancing had grown swift, maddening, like the hammer of a machine or the beating of a wild heart. A woman groaned and stumbled into the firelight, her eyes rolling in her head. Spectators reached to catch her, steady her, straighten her skirts as she collapsed to the ground. The drumbeat panted, a crazed insistent heart, and most of the dancers didn't even stop; January, watching, felt himself still moving as he watched. Someone picked her up, her long black brush of hair falling in a cloud around her shoulders, then she brought up her head and smiled, a flirt's lascivious smile in a middle-aged market-woman's face.

"Hé, li belle fame, li belle fame," Mamzelle Marie sang, and lifted up her arms. "Si Ezili!"

And smiling, twirling, the market-woman swung her hips and laughed. Blowing a kiss at one man, holding out her hands to another, her very face seemed transformed. She spoke to someone, too low to hear, but there was a clapping of hands, and people called out "Hé, li belle Ezili!"

"Lady Ezili to you, Michie Long-Feet," the woman retorted to a man near her. "You stay home with your wife more and you don't go chasin' around the wife of you-know-who. . . ." And the man drew back, genuine shock and alarm in his face, raising his hands in a gesture of silence. Her eyes were roguish, understanding, and she bumped him with her hip. "Hey, you, pretty girl. . . ." She spoke to another woman, and in the crowd across the fire another man cried out.

Romulus Valle, January saw, a man he had known for almost two years, the majordomo of the Orleans Ballroom. But when Valle rose from the ground, reeling and shaking his head, his face was no longer the face of the elderly and dignified servant. Its lines, its muscles— almost its very bones—shifted, until it resembled not only in expression but in its underpinnings the face half-remembered from nightmares: Olympe's face as it had been at the brickyard dance.

"Ogu!" voices cried out, and the name echoed back in January's heart: Ogu was what they had cried out twenty-three years ago. *Maître Ogu drinks, but never gets drunk. . . ."*

Valle snarled something incoherent, foul soldier's slang that never would have passed the old man's dignified lips. "Give me to drink. My balls are cold." He caught up a branch and slashed at those around him, clearing a space among the dancers. January shivered, remembering Olympe's face, and the way Olympe had moved. It was as if Paris and the Hôtel-Dieu, as if the apartment on the Rue de l'Aube and the woman he had loved and married there, had never existed. As if all those forty-one years had been spent among these people, in these hot fever-stinking nights.

Still Valle danced, leaped, and lunged to the music, and in the fire glare and the full moon's light his movements were a young man's, a warrior's, full of rage and strength. Passionate, and no man's slave. As Olympe had danced.

Dr. Brimstone held out a bottle of rum and a torch. Ogu stretched out his hands—Valle's hands—and Brimstone poured the rum from the bottle, touching the flame of the torch to it as he poured. Ogu caught the stream of fire in his hands, laved it from palm to palm, laughing. "Hey, you give me rum to warm my balls, not my hands," he teased, and the old root doctor laughed, too.

By the burning rum's blue light January saw Dr. Yellowjack making his way toward him, a cup of lemonade in one hand and a plate of congris in the other. He caught January's eye, nodded toward the edge of the crowd where they could talk.

But as January moved to follow, a voice called out, "Yo, Benjamin

Bones!"—a nasal voice, thin and shrill, like wind blowing through broken teeth.

January whirled, for the voice spoke right behind him, and the one who spoke mimed playing the piano with thin hands spread like spiders, like fleshless ivory twigs. January felt the hair prickle on his nape.

He didn't know why or how he knew who it was who possessed the speaker, a man he'd never seen before and was never to see again after that night. In any case he doubted he'd have recognized him in a normal state.

Face distorted in a rictus grin, teeth gleaming behind back-drawn lips—somewhere the speaker had gotten a pair of spectacles whose lenses caught the light, and January had the momentary sense that if he were to pull those off the nose where they rested, only empty sockets would lie behind. Someone had given the possessed one a top hat, the other symbol of the god that rode him.

January didn't know whether it was his imagination or some trick scent within the man's clothing, but for a moment his nostrils were choked with the damp charnel smell of cemetery earth.

"Bone fixer doctor man, you done cheated me many many times." The Baron Cemetery tilted his head, grin never changing, a skull's grin. His hand gestured. January could almost see the bones. "By all rights I should be mad at you, you take away this man and that man from me." He reached out without glancing beside him and, taking a clay flask of tafia rum from a woman, drained it in a gulp, and threw it over his shoulder into the fire. "But you know, I just kind of like a man what got a way with bones."

And he mimed playing the piano again, this time down his own chest, as if his fingers danced down the empty ribs of the animate skeleton that was the Baron's true form.

"So I tell you a little secret. The fellow you look for—lookin' here, lookin' there, how'd he die, who killed him, who hid his body . . ." He mimed searching through his pockets, then pirouetted with a shriek of laughter, throwing out long arms. "You lookin' all in the wrong place! I ain't got him! I ain't got him at all!"

And he spun around, tripping Dr. Yellowjack in a splatter of lemonade and chickpeas, and whirled, laughing at the mess, away into the crowd. January followed him, shocked and shaken, but dancers came between them: men gripping bandannas in either hand, women spinning on the other ends of the colored cloth. Closer and closer they danced around the fire, laughing and calling out: "Calinda! Dance the calinda!" Women caught his arms, spattered his back and shoulders with water painted in the form of a cross; struggling free, January found himself face-to-face with a woman possessed, eyes slitted, staring blank. She opened her mouth and let out a thin rattling stutter, between a hiss and a shriek, and flicked her tongue like a snake. The smell of rum soaked the air, fighting odors of smoke and scalded blood.

When at last he came on the man again, he was lying with his back against an oak trunk, sipping a little tafia out of a calabash held for him by a young girl. January was never really certain whether this was in fact the same man as had spoken to him, or someone else of similar height and build. The spectacles were gone, but the borrowed top hat lay in the weeds at the man's side. The man's thin ribs heaved with the drag of his breath, and when he looked up at January, standing between him and the firelight, his dark mild eyes held only a kind of exhausted inquiry.

"What did you mean?" asked January quietly. "You said you didn't have the man I was looking for. Who were you talking about?"

The girl at the lying man's side said, "He don't remember nuthin'."

"The *loa* had him," added the fat dancer, coming out of the crowd, sweat sticking her hair to her round cheeks. She'd lost most of her teeth to poor nutrition and childbirth. It aged her face, though there was no gray in her hair. "The Baron. He rid him and rid him, sayin' all sorts of things, but you know nobody remembers, what the *loa* make them say."

January looked down at him. Without the lunatic grin, with eyes instead of flaming circles of reflected firelight, he couldn't even be sure it was the same man.

"I'm sure sorry, brother," said the man in a voice deep and gentle, nothing like the Baron's shrill whistling tones. His clothing was soaked with rum. January wondered whether that had had anything to do with his "possession," and saw again the grinning death's-head pouring the contents of the bottle into its mouth. "I remember dancing, and feeling kind of light in my head. Did I say crazy things? I didn't mean no harm."

"Let him be, Michie," said the fat woman. She held a dripping branch of gladiolus, with which she'd blessed the other dancers. "What the god want to tell you, he told you. Don't do no good to ask questions of the horse when the rider done got down and went into the house."

January looked around him. The crowd was thinning out. A few still danced, or waited for one of the mambos to slop water on shoulders and back in blessing, but more and more they were pairing off, or departing in threes—a man and two women—into the darkness of the woods. The drum throbbed, but its note had changed: deeper and darker, the trip-hammer of pursuit changed to the rhythm of rut. In the woods somewhere close a man grunted and cried out with orgasm; elsewhere he heard a woman's throaty triumphant howl.

On the gallery of the shut dark house he saw Dr. Yellowjack watching still, a dark smudge against the pale stucco; then saw him turn and go inside.

There was no sign anywhere of Mamzelle Marie, or Cut-Arm, or any of those he had come here to seek.

"One thing about the powers of voodoo," chuckled a youth named Pedro from the bow of the now-overloaded pirogue, "it sure fires up the ladies. Oh my, yes."

"Now you don't go talkin'," chided another voice out of the lapis darkness—Saul, January thought he'd introduced himself when Natchez Jim had agreed to take him and Pedro and their cousin Clovis back to town. They were all cousins, more or less, of Jim's, all poor and all slightly drunk. January gathered that he himself was the only one leaving the island sober that night.

"What?" protested Pedro, flinging out his hands in an exaggerated gesture of innocence. "I was just thinkin' how fine a dancer that little gal of mine was."

"You see that tall gal with the gap in her teeth?" put in Clovis, and drew in a lungful of smoke from a forbidden cigar. "Now mmmm! That was some fine—dancin'."

Moonlight spangled the water, between the darknesses of clouds and cypress trees, blue ink and quicksilver. Frogs sang their chorus, bass to tiniest descant, and the water rippled where a fish bit at a firefly. January, weary to his bones and already heartily sick of the three cousins' banter, wondered whether fish slept, and thought, *Rose would know.*

The garçonnière that waited for him seemed an empty box of blackness. Rose, or Ayasha, or someone should be there, and he knew no one would be. He watched Pedro and Jim pole in silence from where he sat at the back of the pirogue, his mind moving this way and that, wishing only that he could be still and sleep.

"There many maroons at the dancing?" he asked after a time. "When I was a little boy they'd always come in from hiding out in the *cipriere,* even when the dancing was in town." None of them spoke of the *loa,* or of Romulus Valle bathing his hands in flaming rum. Had Olympe coupled with any of these men, nearly a month ago in that place on St. John's Eve, under the influence of the rum and the dancing. . . . Then, or at any time in the past twenty-three years?

Did that count as adultery? Did Paul know? Would he say anything if he did?

January tried to put the distasteful thoughts from his mind. It was none of his business. He rubbed his shoulders, which ached from helping Jim row upstream from the convent that afternoon, and tried to work the hard fibers of pain out of his upper back.

"Hell, maroons don't need to hide in the *cipriere.*" Cousin Clovis blew a smoke ring and grinned with owlish pride. "Half the runaways I know just hide out in town. Rent theirselves a place in somebody's attic or shed, there you are." He was a fat man, balding, and older than his two companions, like a rotund gargoyle in the moonlight. "Who wants to hide in the woods and dig yams when you can get good money workin' the cotton press or the levee? Who's gonna ask, if you take a little less than the next man? Pedro . . ." he turned his head to look up at the gangly form of his young cousin, "you got runaways down the levee workin' with you, don't you?"

"Hell, I got to," said the big youth with a shy grin. "But I don't ask. My mama say, 'Mind your business.' "

"Like your mama don't mind everybody else's business on—"

A shot cracked the darkness. Pedro flung up his arms and fell.

"Pedro!" Clovis heaved himself to the gunwale, grabbing at his cousin's body in the black water. Instinctively January flung himself back against the opposite gunwale to keep the pirogue from going over; Saul had joined Clovis, grabbing Pedro's arms, dragging his head up out of the water. January was aware of Jim beside him, leaning likewise on the gunwale but pressing a pistol into his hand.

"I got one," January told him softly and pulled it from the back of his waistband. The pirogue rocked desperately and there was a smell of blood as they pulled the wounded man from the bayou. "He's after me." *How the hell had Killdevil known?* Stupid to ask, the man was a tracker. . . . "When I dive, you kneel up and pole fast. Get Pedro to Charity Hospital, it's right near the basin, there'll be somebody who can care for him."

"You need help?" asked Jim.

"Not as much as Pedro does." Guilt ground him, every whimper of the wounded man's pain a knife blade in January's heart. The stink of waste was strong, telling him an intestine had been perforated—there was agony to come. *Damn you,* he thought bitterly, *damn you. . . .*

Every fiber of his heart told him to slip silently into the bayou unseen, but he knew that unless he was seen to leave the pirogue the others would be targets. So he lobbed his pistol to the blackest shadow he could see on the bank, then got to his feet in the moonlight (*Please blessed Mary let him miss . . .*) and flung himself off the end of the pirogue, thrashing fast for the place where the gun would be. *Blessed Virgin Mary let there be no alligators, let there be no snakes . . .*

A second shot snapped as his boots sank in the ooze of the shallows. For a heart-sickening moment he stuck, thigh-deep among the cypress knees and sedges, feeling like a mountain-sized black target in the dappled moonlight. Another gun cracked almost immediately—two rifles and a pistol, he thought, and how many more can the man have on him? . . .

He heaved himself free, flopped on the bank (*Please, no snakes . . .*) and rolled. *Blessed Mary get me out of this.*

Or should he pray to Zombi-Damballah, lord of snakes?

He thrust his hand into the sedges at the roots of the cypress tree. There was no snake there. Neither was there a pistol.

Silence across the bayou, save for the silken gurgle of the pirogue heading away as fast as Jim could wield the pole. January's mind followed the unseen hunter's movements: measure powder and ball by touch, load, wad, ram . . . rifle, rifle, pistol. . . . He let out a groan and rolled, to cover moving his arm in the sedges, sweeping to find the pistol by touch.

Then he lay still in the muck, his legs flung wide. No pistol. He made his breathing loud, whispering little moans as he'd all his life heard wounded men make, on the battlefield of Chalmette and later in the Parisian clinic when they brought in the night brawlers and the drunks. *Is that what Saul and Clovis are hearing now in the bottom of the boat as life leaks out of their cousin?*

He lay in the dense shadows of the cypress. Killdevil would have to wade the bayou and come to him, to kill.

Was that the whisper of water around a body? He couldn't tell, didn't dare move his head. He stilled his breath, drawing it thin and thready and silent into nearly motionless lungs. Absurdly he remembered a production of *Romeo and Juliet* he and Ayasha had attended in Paris, in which the deceased hero continued to visibly inhale and exhale throughout Juliet's suicidal paroxysms. Surely that was something they taught actors?

A faint, the faintest, soggy squeak on the bank, and the tap of a belt buckle against a gunlock.

Now. Now.

A squelch, and the drip of soaked clothing, and through his eyelashes he saw the loom of the man against the pale backdrop of moonlight, pistol pointing down.

With all his strength, January lunged and swept with both legs scissoring the trapper's legs at ankles and knees. The pistol went off and Killdevil yelled "Fuck me!" fell and rolled, hauling free a second pistol as January sprang to his feet and stomped the man's wrist, pinning hand and weapon in the muck. Killdevil made a left-handed grab at his belt and brought out a skinning-knife, came up on his elbow slashing at January's groin, and January kicked him with all his might in the chin.

It was a perfect blow. Killdevil's head snapped back, his body arching impossibly from the fulcrum of his prisoned shoulder, and January smelled feces and piss and knew the man was dead even before the body flopped to earth. He'd hoped to stun him if he could, to tie him up and get from him who'd paid him to stalk him, all these weeks, *But,* he thought, standing trembling over the body, *dead would do, too.*

Breathing hard, he knelt, and helped himself to the skinning-knife, the powder flask, and both pistols, which were strung on ribbons the way pirates used to carry them. Killdevil's pockets contained a flask of rum—January helped himself to that, too, drinking a greedy pull that went through him like violent sunlight—and a wash-leather sack that jingled. January was about to thrust it back when he remembered the men in the boat chatting about Pedro living with his mother and sisters. He put it in his own pocket instead.

Two hundred dollars, Hannibal had said. Given to Killdevil by a toff who didn't even stay for a drink. If the young man died, his family would need this—if he lived he would be unable to work for months.

There were matches in Killdevil's pocket, too, wrapped in waxed linen and stuffed in a tin box. January lit them, one after another, and searched the sedges—painstakingly, prodding and parting the long weeds with a stick—until he found his own pistol. Something slithered away, fast and angry. He caught only a glimpse of a thick tail, a zigzag of buff and brown. A water moccasin, close to four feet long. He'd have put his hand on it, finding the weapon.

He followed the bayou, picked up the canal and walked on the shell towpath, a mile and a quarter to where the grimy shacks began on the edge of the trees. Ahead of him lights still burned. Ramshackle saloons and warehouses clustered around the turning basin, and he heard drunken voices raised in altercation: "I don't take that kind of talk no way! Cut dirt or I'll bark you clean from the tip of your nose to the end of your tail!" Turning aside, he followed the sodden line of Rue Claiborne over a few streets, then down and into the French town.

In his room he lit the candle and counted the money: a hundred and fifty dollars, some of it in Mexican silver. The rest was a mingle of Dutch rix-dollars, American eagles, and English gold sovereigns, such as he had seen stacked so neatly on the edge of Mathurin Jumon's desk.

For the first time in many nights he slept soundly.

In the morning he returned to the Cabildo, to be told that Lieutenant Shaw had still not returned from Baton Rouge. "No, no message," said Guardsman Boechter, a short dark Bavarian on duty in the watch room. "But Shaw's not much one for writing. He'll be back when he's found what he seeks."

"M'sieu Janvier." Vachel Corcet came through the big double-doors from the arcade outside, clutching his slender brief of notes. "Did you learn anything?"

January shook his head. "I was prevented from speaking to the men I sought," he replied evenly. "But I did hear that Killdevil Ned is dead."

The lawyer's shoulders slumped with relief. "You're sure?"

January hesitated. "I spoke with a man who saw his body."

"Well, it's a small favor." Corcet patted his forehead with an immaculate linen kerchief. His pomaded curls were already wilting to limp gray corkscrews in the heat. "I'm afraid there's nothing for it but to move for another continuance. It won't be difficult, given M'sieu Vilhardouin's death. I'd be very surprised if M'sieu Gérard was able to locate another lawyer in two days. Not with the fever spreading the way it is. But we can't wait too long. I heard that Judge Canonge is leaving at the end of the month, and if the courts go entirely into recess it will be September before your sister's case is heard."

January glanced back at the closed wooden doors that now blocked all view into the courtyard of the jail. Smoke leaked through them, bearing on it the stench of burnt hooves and gunpowder. "I'll do what I can. If I can. . . ."

He looked past Corcet's shoulder and saw Fortune Gérard. The little man's face was grim and lined almost beyond recognition from the angry, blustering challenger of last week. Pale brown eyes, resentful, furious, scared, met his. Corcet felt the silence and turned.

"M'sieu Corcet." Gérard inclined his head. "If I may have a word with you?"

January excused himself with a bow and made his way out of the room. He wasn't sure what to say about what he thought the money told him—after all, with coinage short, everyone used whatever came their way. Rix-dollars and sovereigns were rare, but they weren't unknown.

He passed through the shadows of the arcade, into the sunlight of the Cathedral steps where merchants and laborers—prospective jurors—stood smoking and spitting and buying ginger beer from marketwomen, and slipped through the crowd to the Cathedral's doors. His footfalls echoed in that cavern of dim silence redolent of burning wax and mildew, and he knelt before the bright-colored statue of the Virgin in her sky-colored robes.

"Thank you for delivering me last night." A young girl who looked like a German shopkeeper's daughter knelt near him, whispering her own prayers; behind him a small group of nuns murmured softly, praying at the Stations of the Cross. "Please forgive me the death of the man Ned Nash, whom I killed in self-defense. Pray for his soul's salvation before God and His angels. Forgive me the danger I put Jim and his companions in last night. Send your healing to Pedro, spare him and his family from the danger in which I put them. Show me how to find the men I seek. Show me where I can find them, and get the answers I need. Help me deliver my sister from that pest hole, from the Valley of the Shadow where she's now imprisoned. I promise you when I have money again I'll buy a dozen Masses in Nash's name."

He crossed himself and counted out decades on his blue glass rosary, the words calming him as they always did, bringing him peace. *The Lord is with thee. . . . The Lord is with thee. . . . The Lord is with thee. Pray for us sinners. . . . Because most of us are sure in no shape to pray for ourselves and be heard.*

And he knew, rising from his knees, that he would indeed be prayed for by one free of sin. He used the last three cents of his own money to buy candles for Killdevil Ned, for Pedro, and as always for Olympe, and when he turned he saw his brother-in-law kneeling among the worshipers behind him, rosary in hand. Together they walked to the Court without speaking.

Two jurors were missing, and only three girls, not four, came in to take their places near Greenaway's chair. Anxious and irritated, Greenaway seemed to be questioning the others. Judge Canonge's lean jaw set as he tallied the absences from the bench. Monsieur Doussan the notary was gone, too, and when Canonge leaned over and whispered something to the Bailiff, January caught the words *yellow jack.*

Canonge banged his gavel. "It appears," the Judge said, "that due to the illnesses of Messires Templeton and Flügel, it will be necessary to reexamine some of the alternate jurors before these proceedings begin." He repeated the words in English, for the benefit of Greenaway and the American jurors. "I hereby order a recess of—"

"Your Honor." Vachel Corcet, who had entered quietly with Monsieur Gérard, rose to his feet. Beside them Célie sat, subdued, ill, and rigid with tension—as well she would be, thought January, with the matter of the signet ring unresolved. Corcet went on, "Due to the death of our esteemed colleague Clément Vilhardouin, we would like to request another continuance of this case until I can more fully marshal the defense of Madame Célie Jumon as well as that of Madame Corbier."

There was a pause, during which Mr. Barnes offered Mr. Shotwell his hip flask and demanded, "What'd he say?" And then, Rothstein the printer having translated, "God damn it, they gonna keep us hangin' around this town with the fever spreadin' like wildfire. . . . I got a wife and children."

"As does the husband of the accused, Mr. Barnes," said Judge Canonge grimly, and rapped his gavel. He switched from English to French with barely a drawn breath. "I'm afraid the Court calendar is full until the thirty-first, Monsieur Corcet, after which, in the absence of Judge Danville and Judge Gravier due to the contagion, the Court will be in recess until the fifteenth of September."

January's eyes cut to Olympe, where she sat at the other end of the table. Her jaw tightened and her eyes closed momentarily, but otherwise she gave no sign. Beside him, Paul lowered his forehead to his hand, a shiver going through his body. Corcet opened his mouth to speak, then closed it and made as if to sit down. Then he took a deep breath and straightened up again.

"If the Court please," he said, "I beg the Court to take into account the youth of the defendant's children, and the possibility that the delay of six weeks might well deprive them of their mother for good."

"Oh, for Chrissake," said Barnes loudly, and took another swig from his flask. "She's a goddam *voodoo*."

Canonge's dark eyes hardened, and he rapped his gavel again. "Very well," he said. "The Court will continue in special session the night after tomorrow, Wednesday the twenty-third of July, in order to accommodate the case, and members of this jury will present themselves at this courtroom at seven P.M. or will find themselves in contempt." He translated into English for the benefit of Mr. Barnes, who looked as if he might protest and then wisely thought better of it. Canonge looked back at Corcet. "Can you have your case in order by that time, Monsieur Corcet?"

Corcet glanced over at January, then said, "I can, Your Honor. Thank you."

"Goddam nigger pansy," said Barnes.

As an armed constable helped Olympe to her feet January made his way over to her through the milling of clerks, bailiffs, and the witnesses for the next case: "Snakebones," he called to her, throwing the slurry African twist to the words, and she turned her head, braced against the tug on her wrist chains.

"There a village in the woods, maroons, runaways?" January used the word some of the fieldhands had used back on Bellefleur for those who'd escaped to the woods, *afeerees,* and called the *cipriere igbé.*

"*En,*" she said, an African word the old men had used.

"Where? Do you know?"

She glanced beside her at the Guards and said, "No. They don't tell no one. Not even the voodoos, brother. . . ." She used the old word some of the slaves had used for the mambos and the wangateurs, as he and she had done as children, *idans.* "Too many *idans* be sellin' women to the white and buyin' stolen goods these days for Cut-Arm to trust. But they there."

Paul caught her hands, had barely time to thrust into them the bundle of food and clothing he carried, barely time to kiss her lips, before they pulled her away. Canonge was already striking his gavel and calling for order; January and his brother-in-law moved into the corridor, where not a breeze stirred and the air reeked with gutter smell and tobacco and smoke.

"Wednesday," said Paul. "I'll be back. . . ."

"Cut-Arm," said January quietly. "I knew it."

"Cut-Arm?" Corcet bobbed from the stream of men like a cork, dabbing his forehead with a handkerchief.

"The one-armed man who saved me from Killdevil Ned. He has a village in the *cipriere.* A lot of maroons used to. That's where Isaak was those three days, I'll take oath."

"Can you find it?"

"I can try."

It was twenty minutes' walk from his mother's house on Rue Burgundy—where he stopped to change his clothes—out of the French town and up Poydras Street to the near end of Gravier's drainage canal, and another three-quarters of a mile along its muddy banks to the little offshoot of Bayou St. John where Isaak Jumon had waited on Saturday night. Even so short a distance from the last houses of the town— broken-down shacks where Irish and German immigrants lived cheek by jowl with the cheapest of the taverns and bordellos in the New Cemetery's shadow—the trees grew thick. January picked his way along the root mounds of the oak trees to avoid the scummy standing pools, but nothing he did could keep the mosquitoes and gnats from him. Three times he saw the glistening brown-and-buff coils of water moccasins, sunning themselves on fallen logs.

He followed the bayou back to where the sluggish stream divided around its two islands. From a distance across the standing water he saw the clearing among the cypresses where the dancing had taken place less than eighteen hours before. The altar was gone, and the post that had stood before it. At this distance he couldn't even see evidence of where they had stood, but the ground was thick-covered by fallen oak leaves. He remembered then that Dr. Yellowjack had called him aside to talk to him, but when he crossed the bayou, and walked up to the house, it was shuttered tight.

From the gallery he looked back again to where the pillar and the altar had been. The air still carried a faint reek of smoke, and on the planks of the gallery there were stains of what might have been blood. He remembered with a shiver the Baron Cemetery, laughing hysterically as he searched the pockets of his clothing. *I ain't got the man you seek. . . .*

Well, at least I gave you somebody for all the ones I kept out of your hands.

Killdevil Ned might have been gathered to his fathers, but January knew that there was danger still. Whoever had hired the mountain man—be it Jumon or Granville or someone else—would know within a day or so that Ned was gone. There were many men in the Swamp who needed money and were good with knives and guns. Shifting his aching shoulders uneasily, January descended from the silent gallery, retreated into the green shadows of the cypresses, and crossed the island and the little channel of bayou beyond in silence.

Here was the true *cipriere.* Sheets of standing water alternated with knots of hickories, palmettos, and red oaks, and coarse gray triangles of moss formed continuous tapestries overhead on the oak limbs. Ibis and white egrets lifted in flapping clouds at his approach; turtles basked on the curves of logs above water the hue of puréed peas. The day was baking hot and the trees closed in that heat, as if he were wrapped in blankets. The drum of the cicadas, the whine of mosquitoes, the constant low hum of gnats, were the only sounds. He was only a mile or so, he knew, from the shell road that led out along Bayou Metairie, but beyond that bayou the *cipriere* resumed, a dark finger of swamp and woods between river and lake. Truly the *igbé* that the old men on Bellefleur had talked about, the forest that spoke to them of the greater forests of Africa. The alien realm of Ogu and Shango and Damballah-

Wedo, where such as Apollo and Zeus—and even Christ and Mary—
had never walked.

It took him over half an hour to reach Bayou Metairie, along the
oak roots where the ground was firm. In the open ground along the
road a little breeze drifted, but did nothing to cool the sweat that soaked
his blue calico shirt. The sun glared in his eyes and the feverish heat was
a nutcracker, clamped around his skull. He made a careful detour
through the fallow cane fields, then plunged back into the *cipriere* on
the bayou's other side.

For the rest of the day he quartered the maze of swampland and
cipriere west of Bayou St. John, searching for signs he wasn't sure he'd
recognize. The woodcraft he'd learned as a child came back to him, but
he wasn't entirely willing to trust it: He cut a staff, first thing, from a
hickory sapling and with it saved himself from two snakebites and half a
dozen duckings, prodding the cattails and oyster grass ahead of him.
Time after time he saw things that made him wonder if he were close to
the maroon village: catfish lines set in the marshes; cypress stumps that
looked as if they'd been cut without proper tools; once a white chicken,
far from anywhere. . . . But then, it wasn't more than a few miles to
the small plantations along the Bayou Sauvage. How far *could* a stray
chicken travel?

Slanting sunlight rimmed the hanging moss in blazing white. The
green gloom behind creeper and palmetto seemed to clot and grow
dark. *Not now!* he thought, desperately, straightening from examination
of what might have been a foot-broken twig and realizing how close
he'd had to bend to get clear sight of it. Like Gideon in the Bible, he
wanted to pray that the sun hold its place in the heavens until he had
accomplished what he needed to accomplish.

Another night—after how many nights?—that Olympe would
spend in the reeking hell of the jail, listening to the wailing of poor Mad
Solie. Mopping with filthy water the bodies of the sick. Waiting for the
sickness to touch her on the shoulder, for Bronze John to call her name.
Dear God, how many nights had it already been?

He called out, into the close-crowding green silence, "I know you're
there! Cut-Arm—Danny Pritchard—anyone! You have to help me! All I
need is help!"

Like cushions the creepers absorbed his voice. The dark in the green
aisles deepened. Somewhere close by, frogs began to croak.

Guardians of the way to Hades, Aristophanes had made frogs. Pale fat-bellied souls of the dead.

He found his way back to the Bayou Metairie and followed it east to the stone bridge of the Bayou Road. The white shell of the roadbed crunched beneath his boots as he walked back through the crying darkness to town, as if he trod a carpet of shattered bones. Twice he turned to look into the dark of the trees, positive someone followed and watched.

But there was no one there.

TWENTY

"Ah yes, they're out there." Marie Laveau turned a slice of yesterday's stale bread over in a yellow pottery bowl of batter, judging with an exact eye its state of saturation before she laid it in the frying pan. "Cut-Arm and his friends."

Morning light touched the heavy black curls of her hair where she'd pinned it carelessly on the top of her head; warmed the painted earthenware bowls lined around the table where her children sat, spoons in hand, waiting with eager expectancy for their breakfast. Someone had put yellow hibiscus and late-blooming magenta crape myrtle in a blue jug on the table, a splash of gaudy color. A dragonfly paused for an instant in the open windows, then flicked away.

"They've been out there for six months now, since he ran from General deBuys. I buy herbs now and then from them, and the snakes they trap and kill. I don't know where their village is." She dropped the bread into the pan, sizzling in the butter; the heat from the hearth where she sat was like a glowing yellow wall. "I haven't looked."

"I thought you knew everything," said January.

She glanced up at him, lazy eyes fathomless. "I know there have been free colored who've sold information to the police about Cut-Arm and his friends, for money to buy themselves a shop, or their children an education," Mamzelle Marie went on. "I know how some among the voodoos spy and creep and gather information, not knowing how to keep their mouths shut about what they learn. I know there are things that it's better for all I don't know." She forked slices and laid them on the plate. At the back of the hearth a small pot bubbled, its smell rank and gamy and tiny bones floating among the roiling scum of fat. On the hearth's edge seven or eight mouse pelts lay spread to dry on a folded piece of newspaper. The heads, tails, and feet, neatly severed, lay on another piece on the windowsill, surrounded by a ring of powdered red pepper to keep off ants. "Will you eat with us?"

January shook his head. "I'll have some coffee, though." He'd cooked up grits and molasses for Hannibal and himself before leaving the garçonnière that morning, all they could afford. Rose, who'd spent most of yesterday doing her translating in Hannibal's room to keep him company, had promised to return today, that the fiddler not be left by himself.

"Could you find out where the village is?" He drew a chair to the end of the table nearest the hearth. Mamzelle Marie continued to work as they talked, first finishing the lost bread, then checking the boiling mice, dipping a holed spoon into the broth and lifting clear tiny lumps of flesh, from which she picked the bones with her fingernails.

"I could, in time. But they trust me more, knowing I don't know and have not sought." She laid a tiny femur on a cheap pottery plate. "I meet them Sundays, as you saw, or sometimes if I need something special or if they're not at the dancing I'll leave a drawing of it—a snake or a ground puppy or a deer's foot—in the crook of a certain tree. Like as not two days later it'll be here on the step."

"Would Isaak have gone to Cut-Arm?"

"He might. Cut-Arm—Squire he was called back in those days— never had much use for the free colored. Ti Jon would have told him Isaak was a runaway, which of course was true. Cut-Arm's always willing to help those who'd be free."

"Will you come with me?" he asked. "Help me? We can make a case of some kind, Corcet and I, out of the fact that the body they buried as Isaak's had no arsenic in it, but Greenaway can argue around that in five minutes. Greenaway's thick as thieves with Geneviève Jumon's lover. Maybe the man truly believes Madame Célie actually did the murder. Maybe it's just what he wants to believe."

"They all believe," said Mamzelle Marie quietly, "that one who worships the *loa* will do murder. It's all one to them, Protestant or Catholic. You read that journalist's story. They hear the drums at night, they see the people dancing in the Square, and they get afraid. This lover of Madame Geneviève, this banker who uses her money at interest, he loves the Protestant God, and sees God only with one face, and that face white."

January remembered suddenly the woman in the Cathedral, looking around her nervously at the unfamiliar images and Stations of the Cross; the golden-haired child who supposed that nuns routinely kidnapped little girls.

"Granville mistrusts even Catholics, and won't promote them past a certain level in his bank."

She set down the last of the mouse-bones, rose and signed January to remain where he was. "I promised Dr. Ker I'd help him at the hospital today, but I'll send Marie with a note, that there's something else I must do." She nodded to her daughter, who was clearing off the dishes, silent as the Zombi serpent. "Maybe when Cut-Arm sees me with you he'll know you're to be trusted, for all you're a policeman's friend."

They walked out the Bayou Road, and along the path that skirted the Bayou Metairie on the lakeside, with the morning sun strong on their heads. After an hour's walk they left the path and plunged north into the *cipriere.*

Ahead of him, January watched Mamzelle Marie's straight slim shoulders, half-bared by her blouse of red-and-blue calico, sunlight filtering through the oak leaves to dapple the coppery skin. Her mother, he thought, or her mother's mother, had paid the price of freedom, as his own mother had, taking a white man into her bed and using whatever she had to use to buy that freedom for her child. Fortune Gérard's mother had beyond doubt done exactly the same thing, and why not? Who among the free colored wouldn't betray Cut-Arm to the whites for money to buy themselves a shop, and buy schooling for their children? If you're knee-deep in water on a sinking boat, you get your child and your child's children yet unborn onto shore—or at least onto a sounder vessel—at whatever price you and those in the doomed craft with you have to pay.

Mother, he thought, *I've done you an injustice*—not that Livia would ever have admitted to making any sacrifice for anyone. His hand sought the rosary in his pocket: *Virgin Mary, who understands women, forgive me.*

"See there?" Mamzelle Marie pointed to a bag of red flannel, hanging nearly hidden by beards of moss in the branches of a cypress tree. "That's Ti Bossu, that guards the paths. They move him from place to place, Cut-Arm and his friends. They know we're here."

Throughout the day they sought, working their way upstream. Ponds and marshes and sloughs crisscrossed the land among the trees, cut-off loops of old waterways that once had absorbed a high rise in the lake or one of the greater bayous or the river itself. Cypress and willow hung gray-trunked over the still water, cypress knees poking from the green sheets of duckweed like an army of submarine monsters frozen in the act of rising to invade the land. Palmetto and oak backed them, and thickets of loblolly pine, false harbingers of hope that the going would get easier—then suddenly they were in wet ground again, trying to find their way along root lines and ridges without getting soaked.

How Mamzelle Marie determined their route January didn't know. He was glad of her guidance as they strove patiently through the woods, coming out now among the pines of the lakeshore, now above the fallow cane fields along the Bayou Metairie. He was glad of her company, too, in the hot silences of the advancing day. Sometimes she would point out the faint prints of tortoises or snakes in the soft mud of the water verges, identifying water moccasin or garter snake or king snake by their traces; sometimes speak of the habits of the deer, or the possums, or this or that planter who lived along the River Road. She asked him about Paris, and his studies at the hospital there, and listened while he told of the balls given by members of Napoleon's lately come nobility to which members of the new King's diplomatic corps would not go.

He found himself speaking to her of things he hadn't remembered for years, or had put deliberately from his mind, and with them all the memories of that time of his life: walking with Ayasha along the Seine on summer mornings when the hay boats would come in from the countryside, or sitting in the window of their rooms in the Rue de l'Aube late at night, a balcony barely wider than a windowsill, hearing the voices from the café on the ground floor and seeing its lights reflected on the soot-black brick walls on the other side of the street, but unable to see the café itself because of the height of the building and the narrowness of the street.

All memory, it seemed to him, of Paris had been erased from his mind by those final, terrible months of the cholera, by Ayasha's death. Now Mamzelle Marie's quiet uninflected questions coaxed it forth again, gentle as if seen in candlelight. He understood then how she came to know everything, to fit all things together in a giant mosaic of intelligence. She listened, and she remembered, and she cared.

"Your sister, now," she said, as they stopped past noon and shared water from one of the bottles he carried slung over his shoulder. "She came to the voodoos first out of hatred, looking for the Power to fight those she believed turned her mother into a whore. All she saw was the hoodoo, the juju: Burn this candle and money will come to you and make you strong. Sprinkle graveyard dust on this man's floor and he will die. She made witch dolls against your stepfather for years, and buried bottles of beef gall and red pepper with St.-Denis Janvier's name written on them in the cemetery. And, of course, he did die. I never met a human being who didn't, in time."

"I remember when Mama found the makings of a hoodoo in Olympe's room." January unwrapped the packet of bread and cheese he'd brought along, handed the voodooienne some of each, and wondered a little that he'd be here, sitting on an oak root with this woman. Dangerous, they said. A poisoner or a procuress. Certainly, Granville would have added, an idolator. An enigma who danced with the serpent Damballah.

But then all women were enigmas, infinitely faceted. Rose like a many-petaled blossom of interleaved brilliance and pain, fear of men and love of gardening, knowledge of steam engines and chemical reactions and optics all woven together. Olympe, who spoke to spirits in bottles and then turned and played Juba-this and Juba-that with her children. You never knew them, thought January, and for some reason saw in his mind the pink-tinted portrait of a sixteen-year-old maid-in-waiting to a murdered French Queen.

"Sometimes you need to hate, until the hate's all gone," said Mamzelle Marie. "Until you see for yourself what a waste of time it is. The *loa* understand that, the way the saints sometimes don't." She plucked a purple blossom of marsh verbena, and turned it in the fawn-spotted light. "Your sister could have gone Dr. Yellowjack's way, all cleverness and skill and Power, with no more heart to him than a shrike. Or been like Mambo Oba, selling gris-gris and telling fortunes and reading the bones, seeing nothing but the money in the pot on the kitchen shelf. There's good and there's bad, in people and in the *loa* alike—saints and devils, light and dark, and sometimes the dark ain't so dark as you think."

January was silent, remembering Olympe in the King's arms.

"What was it your friend likes to say, about what the maggot said to the King of France? He told me once."

"ξ ὦμεν γὰρ οὐχ ὡς θέλομεν ἀλλ' ὡς δυνάμεθα," said January. "It's Greek, from the playwright Menander. *We live not how we wish to, but how we can.*"

"So," she said. "The *loa* help us do that, Michie Ben. Same way the saints help us do that. Sometimes God seems a long way off. I've seen you watch the voodoo dancing, and I've seen you light candles and pray for your sister's soul to be safe from Hell."

The day's heat and the constant movement had told on her, as it had on him; a line had settled between the corners of her nostrils and the side of her mouth, and another pinched, very slightly, the dark clear arch of her brows. "But so many are in Hell now. The *loa* come here— here to Hell, to us, to be with us as we dance. And they say, *We didn't get left behind in Africa. We're here with you, on the ships, on the ocean, in this land. We remember your names and what you care about, you and your parents and your children.* You judge your sister harshly."

January worked the cork back into their water bottle, and did not meet the woman's eyes. " 'Thou shalt have no other gods before me,' God said."

"Is that what you think they are? Ogu and Ezili and Bosou? Some other god other than the one that's in the Cathedral?" Her eyebrows lifted, gently mocking. "Ben, when you go see a white man, you put on your best black coat and your best high hat and you talk your best French that you learned in school, and he listens to you because of what you look like, as much as for what you say. If you could paint your face white you'd do that, too. But when you go see Ti Jon, or Natchez Jim, or the Widow Puy, you put on a calico shirt and talk gombo like the rest of them"—her voice slurred articles and pronouns in the Creole way—"so they'll listen to you and won't say, *Hah, there goes somebody who's like the whites.*

"You think you're smarter than God, Ben? You think God hasn't figured that one out, too? If a man's been beat, and his woman's been raped, by any man, white or black or purple, you think that man's going to see God's face the way the man who wronged him tells him it is? God finds all sorts of ways to speak to those that need Him, Ben. He's a man with a sword, to those that need a rod and staff to comfort them, whether that man's called Ogu or St. James. He's the man with the keys in his hand, to those that're in chains, and seeking a way through the door to Heaven. You're like your friend Granville, that only sees God's face like his own in the mirror."

Still January said nothing. But he remembered the leap of flame against the brickyard walls, and how it felt to surrender to the drums, to couple as gods couple, or animals, without grief or disappointment, laying all in the hand of God.

"It's not my way," he said at last. "And I don't see . . ." He shook his head. "I see men like Dr. Yellowjack, selling girls to whites; I see Mambo Oba peddling hexes to whoever will pay her. . . . Dead chickens and fortune-telling . . ." He broke off, remembering the tales of how this woman herself had stolen a powerful idol—or some said a gris-gris in a bottle—from the house of the Voodoo Queen who reigned before her.

"No one's asking you to follow it." The dark eyes flicked to him, smiling as Olympe sometimes smiled. "I never yet heard of voodoos burning a Christian at the stake for not following their gods. And you know, Ben, if a whore leans on the church door talking to men, that doesn't mean that Christ isn't still there on the altar."

She got to her feet, and shook out her blue calico skirts. "Come," she said. "There's a lot of ground yet to walk."

The sunlight turned, yellowed to saffron. The heat became unbearable and then quite suddenly eased, filling the green world with slanted bars of molten glass and the melancholy gentleness of change. Birds cried their territories before settling for the night. But the only person they met in all that wilderness was old Lucius Lacrîme, who had a shack somewhere in the *cipriere*. The wrinkled old Ewe—freedman or maroon January did not know—was out setting a fish line in Bayou Metairie. He had not, he said, seen anyone all day.

"Where are they?" January gazed around him at the twilight woods in despair. "They should have seen us by now."

"They've seen us." Mamzelle Marie leaned against the gray bole of a cypress, and mopped her face and neck with a kerchief pulled from her bosom. "You've been seen with a policeman too many times for Cut-Arm to come up to you and speak. He killed a white policeman that went looking for him in March, and another one in May. Not so very long ago there were laws on the books that said a black man who did such a thing would be burned alive."

January was silent, remembering the big laughing man who had not been afraid to save his life. "Her trial is tomorrow," he said softly.

"They know that. You think there's much that goes on, between the black folks and the white of the town, that Cut-Arm doesn't make it his business to know?"

She hitched her skirts, where they were girdled high around her knees like a fieldworker's, and started down the path. "I'll do what I can do, tonight. These girls of Greenaway's, that are in court to say that Olympe sold them poisons. . . . Them I will speak to, and conjure them dreams. For three nights now I've prayed to Papa Legba, and left pound cake and cigars at the feet of his statue at the back of the Chapel of St. Antoine. Judge Canonge, he's an upright man." January wondered if that meant Canonge wouldn't be influenced by the *loa* in his dreams, or whether Mamzelle Marie spoke of other influences—money, threats of exposure of some past peccadillo, a chicken foot on his bed. "Beyond that, all we can do is trust God."

Gabriel was sitting on the gallery outside the garçonnière when January returned to the house on Rue Burgundy, sharing out rice and beans from a pail with Rose and Hannibal. "It ain't much," said the boy, over January's protests. "Papa said he'll bring money when he comes back tomorrow."

January felt a pang of guilt at taking the food from his brother-in-law's family again but couldn't afford to refuse. Instead he grinned widely and said, "Gabriel, to show your papa how grateful I am for this, tell him I'll give every one of you children"—he pretended deep thought, then said, as if joyfully presenting a treasure—"two hours of piano lessons every single day!"

Gabriel hastily tried not to look aghast. "Oh, you don't have to do that, Uncle Ben. Really."

"I really want to," insisted January with somber eagerness, but the sight of the boy's darting eyes as he sought for some way of escape was too much for him, and he laughed out loud. Rose had brought bread, and lemons to make lemonade, and had rigged up smudges all along the gallery rail to keep the mosquitoes at bay; the smoky light glinted off her spectacles as she handed January a plate.

"You offer that sort of payment again," she warned, "and I expect it will be a hungry summer. Did you find anything?"

January shook his head.

"Cut-Arm and his men, they got *Power*," said Gabriel, settling down cross-legged beside the kitchen chair where Hannibal was propped with a blanket over his knees. "Bullets bounce off him—these Kaintucks, they went after him, and shot at him, and the musket balls bounced right off his chest and came back and whizzed close to the Kaintucks' heads, so they ran away, they were so scared!" He looked up at January, his dark eyes shining.

"If that's so, how did he lose his arm?" inquired Rose, in a tone of scientific interest.

"That was before he ran away. When he ran away, he found these herbs in the *cipriere,* Indian herbs, that made him invulnerable. When the patrols went after him, they disappeared in a cloud of mist, and were never seen again." He swallowed hard. "You just probably weren't looking in the right places, Uncle Ben. He's probably way away on the other side of the lake, and doesn't even know about Mama."

January, who had settled down on the gallery planking at Rose's side, looked across at his nephew's eager face, at the glow of pride as he spoke of a black man who could thumb his nose at the white police with their dogs and their bullets and the prison that held his mother, and said, "I think you're maybe right, Gabriel." He glanced at Rose. "We should probably get Corcet here."

"He sent a note saying he'd be over this evening," she replied. "Though what—" She broke off as the yard gate creaked, and by the filtered glare of the smudges January saw Vachel Corcet enter the yard, followed by two other forms: the short, stocky shape of Fortune Gérard, in his neat blue coat and beaver hat, and beside him his daughter, veiled and wrapped in a cloak that must have been like being rolled in a blanket.

"Monsieur Gérard!" January descended the gallery steps, holding out his hand in greeting and trying to keep his voice from sounding as if the next words were going to be *I never thought you'd deign to associate with us.* When a man surrenders his pride and admits he's wrong he generally doesn't want the fact underlined. "And Madame Jumon." He bowed. "My mother keeps the house locked up in her absence, but I have the key. We can . . ."

Fortune Gérard looked for a moment as though he'd insist on proper lighting and comfortable chairs as his right and his daughter's right, then shook his head wearily. "No, thank you. Unless . . ." He looked inquiringly at Madame Célie, who was gratefully putting back her veil now that they were out of the public view.

She shook her head. "Papa, I've seen the inside of a garçonnière before this." And a little smile lightened her face.

He sighed. "So have we all." Biting his lip, he turned back to January. "If you might just bring a chair for my daughter. . . ."

January fetched two from his mother's storeroom and handed them up to Corcet on the gallery, then climbed the stairs to join the little group. "Don't, please," Célie was saying as Hannibal made to rise. "Mademoiselle—Nogent"—she glanced quickly from her father to Rose—"tells me you've had lung-fever."

"Good Lord, no," added Gérard. "When I had pneumonia it was six weeks before I could walk from my bed to my desk." He made as if to take the second chair—which was why January had brought it—then stepped back, and offered it to Rose. Only when she'd shaken her head did he sit, folding his hands on his knees. "Monsieur Janvier, I owe you an apology for—for things I have said in anger. And when your sister is freed I shall tender her one as well. I have been . . ."

January held up his hand. "Least said is best," he said. "Thank you." He seated himself again on the planks, between Rose and the rather uncomfortable Vachel Corcet. "We think we may know where Isaak spent at least part of the three days prior to his death," he told them, and Célie's hand went quickly to her lips, hiding her quick indrawn breath at his words. "Tell me, Madame Jumon. How well did your husband know a woman named Lucinda Coughlin? You said you saw her at Monsieur Jumon's, but did Isaak ever speak with her?"

Madame Célie frowned, then shook her head. "Well, she thanked him for carving that little horse for Mademoiselle Abigail; the little mademoiselle thanked him very prettily, too. Uncle Mathurin introduced Isaak to her then. But, of course, beyond that they never spoke."

"Then a message from her would not have brought him out of hiding?"

"I don't think so." She shifted the cloak from her shoulders and dabbed her face with a handkerchief. "Not unless she was in some terrible danger."

"If it's the Lucinda Coughlin I know," said Hannibal, "she could easily have forged Mathurin Jumon's handwriting—helped herself to his signet ring, for that matter. And the keys to the house. I don't suppose there's any word from Shaw about Zoë?" He glanced at Corcet.

"I asked at the Cabildo this afternoon. Of course, the woman Zoë might have been resold, for all we know, and the Lieutenant followed the trail farther than Baton Rouge. In a way," the lawyer added, wiping the beads of sweat from his brow with a handkerchief scarcely less delicate than that held by Madame Célie, "the mere fact that Isaak was missing for five days can work in our favor. We don't have to prove who poisoned him—only that neither Madame Corbier nor Madame Jumon could have done so. You don't happen to know, M'sieu Gérard, anything about what M'sieu Greenaway's case is for the State? I understand that M'sieu Vilhardouin will have had information to which I have no access."

"Only that Greenaway had witnesses against Madame Corbier." Gérard's heavy face creased with anger. "Nothing to the point. Silly girls who'll swear she sold them spells, poisons. Against rats, belike. They'll swear she went to the voodoo dances, too, and . . ." He glanced at January, not wanting to deride the woman whose safety was so closely tied to that of his daughter. "And participated in them," he finished awkwardly.

"These girls claim," Vachel Corcet spoke carefully, producing a notebook from his pocket, "that your sister was sometimes possessed by Devils during these dances." He licked his finger, flipped the pages, peering in the dimness. "Marie-Noël Sauvignon, marchande . . . Alice McLeary, laundress . . . a woman named Philomène Louche apparently saw your sister on St. John's Eve itself, in the crowd at a voodoo dance on Bayou St. John."

January's eyes met Rose's, understanding as none of the others did the deadly workings of rumor.

"Now, this is ridiculous on the face of it." Corcet slapped the little leather folder shut. "We can contest this on the grounds that—"

"We may not be able to," interposed January evenly. "It is—part of the rite. Part of the dancing." He saw Corcet's eyes flinch aside, as his own had for so many years, and realized that this was the first time he'd spoken of that secret, that center of the voodoo rites, to anyone. And then, he could only say, "It isn't as it seems."

After a long moment Hannibal said, "Unfortunately, no good Protestant or Catholic juryman is going to make a decision on how things are. Only how they seem. Monsieur Corcet, maybe you'd better ask just what exactly this Mademoiselle Louche was doing at Bayou St. John herself."

It was close to ten when January helped Hannibal back to his bed in Bella's room. "Nobody looks out for the curfew," protested Gabriel, carrying the remains of the rice and beans down to the kitchen and covering it with a plate. "I go out at night lots of times, and I've never met the City Guards."

"All your father needs now is for you to get in trouble." January sighed, holding aloft his single tallow candle as his nephew led the way out of the kitchen again. Corcet and Rose stood together, lantern in hand—Rose lived near enough the wharves that no street lighting was provided; Gérard was shaking the lawyer's hand.

Tomorrow night, thought January. A curious long shiver passed through him as he watched them depart. *Tomorrow night.*

He turned wearily and climbed the garçonnière stair.

The heat was such that he left the doors of his little chamber open, but even the memory of Killdevil Ned, lying dead in the hackberry thickets along the bayou, was not enough to let him sleep. Whoever had hired one assassin—rix-dollars and sovereigns, gleaming in the afternoon sunlight along the edge of a desk—could hire another. So he lay awake, listening to the roar of the cicadas, and the crickets' cries; to Hannibal's breathing on the other side of the wall, the whining of mosquitoes outside the veiling of the bar, and to the scratch and scurry of geckos and mice across the floor. His legs ached from two days' tramping through the swampy ground of the *cipriere,* and when he did sleep he found himself there again, his heart in his throat, watching the white leprous shape of the dead thing flit from tree to tree.

He had just drifted off to sleep a third time when the soft creak of a foot on the stair brought him broad awake. His hand slid under the pillow for his pistol even as he was rolling out of bed, down under the mosquito-bar; his injured shoulders gave one great blaze of protesting pain as he half-crawled, half-slithered across the floor to the door. The outside air showed gray with the barest watering of dawn. Silently he rose to his feet, pistol in hand, waiting, and heard another stealthy creak of weight on the gallery.

This time, he thought, *I'll have a live man to ask.*

A dark shape poked its head around the jamb like a terrapin emerging from its shell. "Michie Janvier?" The dark eyes, barely visible in the gloom, blinked at him from pockets of wrinkles stitched across and across with old tribal scars; a hand was extended to him like a dry bundle of sticks. "Nuthing to be afraid of, hiding there by the door like a rabbit in the brush."

January recognized the voice as old Lucius Lacrîme's. He lowered the pistol. "Somebody comes calling at this hour of the morning," he said, "I'd sure rather be behind the door than in the bed."

The old swamp dweller chuckled creakily. "You may be right at that, Compair Lapin. Cut-Arm send me. He say he want to see you, out in the *cipriere.*"

TWENTY-ONE

The village was smaller than the slave quarters of January's childhood. The huts, too, were smaller, built of a species of wattle-and-daub, thatched with brush and banana-leaves, windowless for the most part and raised on stilts above where the bayou would flood. Their gardens came right up to their walls, and extended to the green eaves of the woods; beans, squash, yams, and gourds ripened bright in the hot sun. Chickens scratched in the dooryards, the baskets where they were caged at night for fear of rats dangling from the house-corners. A sow and her litter lay in the shade of a roof overhanging their pen.

"I hear you been looking for us," said Cut-Arm.

The voice came to January as his blindfold was taken off. Lucius Lacrîme had led him out of town as far as the stone bridge over Bayou St. John, then had turned off the shell road into the *cipriere,* as January himself had done yesterday in company with Mamzelle Marie. "I been told to cover your eyes," the old man had said, producing a big faded red bandanna, and January had put it on, and tied it tight. As he did so he heard the creepers behind him rustle, and men's hands had taken his arms, firmly but without roughness or anger, to lead him into the deeper woods.

He looked behind him now and saw little Dan Pritchard and the woman Kitta, beginning to show with child, and others, also runaways, whom he recognized from Congo Square. Then he turned back, where Cut-Arm stood before him in front of the largest hut.

"Thank you for trusting me," January said. "I swear to you no one will learn of this place through me."

"They always swears." Cut-Arm had a way of standing with his weight on one hip, his whole arm folded across his chest and his big hand closed around the stump of the other. "And somehow, the white man's Guards always finds out."

January said nothing, because he knew what this man said was true. He knew, too, that this village was doomed, this little scrap of the free memory of Africa tucked away in the woods. On still mornings like this one they must be able to hear the groan of the steamboats on the river, and in the winter fogs, to smell the burnt-sweet sugar of grinding time. There were only a half-dozen huts here, men and women, he guessed, who had family and friends here in Orleans or Jefferson Parish, who couldn't bring themselves to flee utterly into the West. Maybe they realized how hopeless it was to think they could completely escape.

"My nephew says bullets bounce off you," he said. " 'No white man ever going to catch Cut-Arm.' And his eyes shine."

The maroon leader laughed, and some of the tension went out of his big shoulders. "I wish he could come out here," he replied, "and see the way we live, apart from the towns of the whites. Your sister probably bringing him up to be a little white man."

"My sister and her husband are bringing him up to be a man," answered January. "Black or colored or even white, town or woodland, there's things that don't change."

Cut-Arm smiled. "Maybe." It was his voice January mostly remembered, deep as he had imagined the voice of Compair Lion to sound in tales he'd been told as a child. "Maybe. I hear you're looking for word of this Isaak Jumon."

"That I am." Cut-Arm's men had led January through the woods for what felt like hours. But, as when Antoine Jumon had taken a fiacre to see his brother, they could have spent the time going in circles. By the sun it was midmorning now, nearly noon. In any case it would be a difficult matter to get back to town by the time Olympe and Madame Célie had to appear in court. "Was he here?"

Cut-Arm nodded. "I heard tell about Isaak Jumon from Ti Jon," he said. "That his own mama had claimed him as her slave, to get her hands on a white man's money, and her lying like a harlot with a white man to get advice and help with these investments they put such store in—faugh! There were advertisements in the newspapers, and men in the Swamp would have known him, and taken him in. I sent him a map where to meet me, and we brought him here."

"How long was he here?"

"Till St. John's Eve. He went with us to Dr. Yellowjack's. He'd heard Dr. Yellowjack knew men in the City Council, did favors for folks sometimes. Dr. Yellowjack, he knows about the law. He knows what white men got secrets that can be used. *I'll promise him some of the money, when I get it,* he said. Isaak Jumon wanted to talk to the doctor about getting a lawyer himself, about getting some kind of order to get his mama off him."

"What happened at the dancing?"

Cut-Arm grinned. "What always happens?" There was a wry malicious mockery in his eyes, like an older boy speaking double to a child. "There was gumbo and there was rum; there was Mamzelle Marie, dancing with her snake. There was the calinda and the pilé congo, and there was girls ready to make jazz in the bushes, when the fire burned down low. You been to a dancing, Music-Master. You know what happens there."

"I thought I did," said January. "Now I'm not so sure. Did Isaak leave with you?"

Cut-Arm shook his head. "We looked around for him, when it was time to go. He didn't know his way back here. It's a long piece, to Dr. Yellowjack's house. Yellowjack, he said Isaak was going to head on back to town, to see his young wife. He asked us—Isaak asked us—to find him again at the same place where we'd met before, at the crooked tree by the head of the canal, at sunrise."

"And did he come?"

"No. I wasn't best pleased and neither were my boys, for it was close to sunrise already. I had a good mind to leave the boy there, givin' us orders like we was servants. Those yellow boys, they're all the same. Stuck-up. But we went. It might have been Isaak was drunk, when he said that to Dr. Yellowjack. We was all a little drunk. But he never came."

Because he was dying in his uncle's house, thought January, *in his brother's arms. Because he was poisoned.*

A woman came out of one of the huts, a child on her hip. A little boy, following her, uncovered the big iron pot that hung above the coals of the fire before the door. The mother stirred, and the strong smells of stewing meat, of rice and onions and peppers, billowed on the air. The boy, still holding the pot lid, looked up at his mother with laughter in his face and January recalled that it was legal to sell a child of that age— eight or ten—away from his mother. He knew, too, that even though it wasn't legal in Louisiana, children were sold away as young as five or six, and across the border, in Texas or in the new cotton lands of the Territories, where nobody cared anyway, and there was no such law.

"Would Isaak do that?" He pulled his gaze away. "Go see his wife, in spite of the danger?"

Cut-Arm shrugged. "Like I said, we was all drunk. You don't give yourself to the dancing, Music-Master. Try it some time, and you'll see. Crazy things look possible. Sometimes the *loa* give you the strength to do what you were afraid to do before. Isaak loved that girl."

The memory came back to January, sudden and agonizing, of Ayasha, combing her hair in the window of the single room above her dress shop, where she'd lived when he'd met her first. Ayasha at eighteen, thin-faced and agile, her every movement like a dancer's movement. . . . Would he have risked his freedom, to seek her out then?

He would risk it now, he thought, if he could. If anything but the widest and blackest of waters separated them. There had been a time when he'd even considered crossing those waters, to be with her again.

Cut-Arm went on, "It might have been he thought some god was with him. It leads you to great good or great harm, the strength of the god."

January looked back at Cut-Arm, at the village around him. Someone at least was stealing from town, or buying from those who did. Over the other fire a coffeepot was set, and the smell of the brewing liquid was smoky and delicious in the noon heat. On the wall of one hut tools hung neatly, hafts of whittled oak and hickory, heads of new German steel, and there was a pistol in Dan Pritchard's belt.

"Did Isaak get any messages when he was here?" he asked. "From Célie, from his uncle, from anyone?"

The white teeth glinted in a sarcastic grin. "We don't got postal service, Music-Master. If anyone gets a message that my boys don't bring in, it's time to burn the huts and move on."

All we have to do, thought January, *is prove that Olympe didn't poison Isaak Jumon. Prove that she couldn't have.*

But that was exactly what he wasn't able to do.

His heart beat hard at the thought that instead of clearing Olympe he had uncovered still greater peril. She was possessed by a Devil, Corcet had said. Had that woman who had seen Olympe here, seen Isaak Jumon as well? Olympe almost certainly hadn't seen him, not to remember anyway. It was easy to miss someone, January knew, in the crowd, the torchlight, the dancing. But even had this market-woman Louche not actually seen Isaak, how easy it would be to say that she had, if someone offered her money to do so.

To put Isaak and Olympe together, at the same place, at the same time.

Times were hard. January had seen how Paul had fought, leaving his wife in peril to save the children he loved, at the lure of money and work to be had. If this Philomène Louche was a strict Catholic, how easy it would be to say, *What's it matter? She worships Devils. If she didn't poison him she sure poisoned someone else, and my child is hungry.*

A white could not hang on evidence given by a free colored. But another colored could.

I'll speak to them, Mamzelle Marie had said, with a world of implied chicken foot in her enigmatic eyes.

Lucius Lacrîme left him near the turning basin at close to six in the evening. He reached the house on Rue Burgundy with barely time to bolt down what was left of the beans and rice Gabriel had brought last night, and change into his respectable garb of biscuit-colored trousers, linen shirt, and black coat. "Give your sister my regards," whispered Hannibal, lying waxen as a corpse under the tent of mosquito-bar. He'd been violently sick—January could see the signs of it in the ill-cleaned slop jar—and January thought, *Not the fever. Not now.*

He felt his friend's hands and face, and they were cool. But all the way through the streets to the Cabildo he remembered Ayasha, lying dead in their rooms on the Rue de l'Aube. Remembered the smell of the sickness as he climbed the stair. Remembered opening the door and seeing her.

Some part of him, he thought, would never recover from that. Some part of him would always be trapped in that moment, like a ghost returning to repeat endlessly one single action in the same corner of the same house forever: opening the door and finding her. Opening the door and finding her.

"Where've you been?" Corcet was waiting in the shadows of the Presbytère arcade, with Monsieur Gérard and Madame Célie. Shadows lengthened over the Place d'Armes. The fruit vendors had packed up their stands hours ago; the tables outside Bernadette Metoyer's chocolate shop stood half-deserted, moths dancing around the candles scattered on their tops. A few colored children played marbles in the dirt under the sycamore trees, and someone in the market café near the levee yelled obscenities at a woman who walked away from him. A little farther along the arcade January could see Hubert Granville, chubby and red-faced and sweating in his coat of gray superfine wool, deep in conversation with Geneviève Jumon. Antoine, nearby, fidgeted. January wondered if he'd had his opium for the day.

"Monsieur Corbier hasn't arrived," Corcet went on. "He's in town, I met him at the levee this afternoon. . . . Perhaps when this is over we'd better go there and see if they're all right. The fever takes one so suddenly."

January thought of Hannibal, lying still and spent in the darkening quarters above the kitchen, and shivered again. "If someone had been taken sick there, one of the children would have left me a note," he said. But he spoke without much conviction. He'd been too many times in the hospital when whole families had been brought in, parents, children, grandparents, and maiden aunts together, dead or dying.

Cholera, he thought, a whisper at the back of his mind. *Cholera. Please, God, no. Not again. Not them.*

"Let's get through this first."

Two of the jurymen were absent. "God bless it, I never signed on for this!" roared Mr. Shotwell, and Judge Canonge snapped back from the bench.

"You signed on for whatever takes place in the Court, Mr. Shotwell, during the term of your duties. Bailiff, call in replacements from the jury room."

"It's enough to make you catch the fever yourself," the saloonkeeper grumbled, and uncorked his flask.

"I spoke to the men with whom Isaak Jumon stayed between the twenty-first and the twenty-third of June," whispered January, while the new jurymen were filing in and a city lamplighter kindled the oil sconces around the courtroom's walls. "Maroons, runaways, hiding in the *cipriere*, no one who could testify in court. They say Jumon went to a voodoo dance the night of the twenty-third, at Dr. Yellowjack's. Is it possible to subpoena him?"

"Yellowjack?" breathed Corcet back. "And get what? Anything resembling the truth? Anything that would clear your sister of poisoning Isaak Jumon, or selling Célie the poison to do so? Yellowjack has his finger in so much crime his testimony would be likelier to hang Olympe than get her released."

. . . said he was going to head on back to town, to see his wife.

Célie, Isaak had whispered. *And died.*

January glanced at the slender girl sitting by her father, chin raised, face a porcelain mask. He started to speak but a wave of nausea gripped him. *Damn it,* he thought, as he rose and stumbled from the courtroom, *Damn it!*

No one noticed him as he fell to his knees and vomited in the gutter outside. Sweating, shaking, he leaned against the brick pillar of the arcade, cold terror gripping his heart. *Not the cholera. After all this, not the cholera. . . .*

He'd been gone all day, all yesterday and the day before. If Ker had sent him a message asking for his help at the hospital he might not have received it. Certainly if there were cholera cases being brought in, the Englishman wouldn't have said so in a note. But surely he'd have sent one saying, *Come in?*

And what if Ker had? he thought. Would he have seen it? How often had he been in the kitchen in the past three days? Or in the house? He hadn't entered his room in daylight in forty-eight hours, except to pelt in, change his clothes, dash out again. The whole town could be vomiting and purging its heart out and he wouldn't know.

Shakily, he climbed to his feet again and made his way back to the courtroom. He felt better for being sick—it might, he thought, merely be bad food of some kind, though as a rule a sausage or a bit of chicken that had gone off didn't affect him. As a slave child he'd learned to eat anything.

Olympe looked up as he came into the courtroom. She'd been brought in while he was out, and sat with her manacled hands in her lap. Her face was expressionless, but he could tell, by the way she turned her head, that she'd been hoping when the door opened to see Paul. A glance told him that Corbier was still not in the room.

Not them. Not them.

He took his seat. Olympe closed her eyes, breathing hard. Her face was a mask; and it came to him that if there was cholera in the city, it might have begun in the jail as well. He hadn't seen her, spoken to her, in three days. In the flare and smut of the oil lamps she seemed to have aged years.

Hubert Granville was up at the front of the court, speaking quietly to Greenaway. His gesture took in the two women seated in the front row, Irish or German by the look of them. Corcet whispered, "Two of his witnesses haven't shown up. Marie-Noël Sauvignon and the Louche woman."

January glanced across at the door, where Mamzelle Marie stood framed. Clothed in a dress of plain black wool made high to her throat, her seven-pointed tignon white as a death-lily against the gloom behind her, she scanned the courtroom, dark eyes seeking out the remaining witnesses. One of them, sandy-haired and freckled, met her gaze with cold defiance. The prettier one flushed, and looked hastily away. Greenaway walked to them protectively, but Mamzelle Marie had already moved to take a seat, her face the face of a woman who has never seen a chicken foot in her life.

In the back of his mind January heard Greenaway's voice: *Gentlemen of the jury, this woman Corbier is a voodoo, and accustomed to making threats against those who cross her. . . .*

He wondered if, like Dr. Yellowjack, Mamzelle Marie might have done her friend more harm than good.

Abishag Shaw was still absent. Constable LaBranche, trying hard not to meet Mamzelle Marie's gaze, had two clay pots and a candy tin on the table before him and didn't look happy. The poisons, guessed January, they'd found in Olympe's house.

No sign yet of Paul. Rose entered with Basile Nogent, and caught January's eye. Fortune Gérard took a seat beside January, almost as haggard as Olympe. The heat of the lamps was unbearable. January brought out his handkerchief and wiped his forehead, sweating though he felt strange and cold.

There was a protracted argument, in English and in French, over the selection of jurors, while the jurymen passed around hip flasks and looked at their watches, and darkness slowly overtook the windows of the room.

"It's the damned aristocracy running this country, that's what it is," declaimed Shotwell in English, and passed his flask to Barnes. "And them Creoles are in with 'em, tryin' to keep good men down."

"Seventy-six votes in Plaquemines Parish . . ."

In the front row, Burton Blodgett scribbled away on his notepad, soulful dark eyes darting from Olympe's face to Mamzelle Marie's. He rose and staggered toward Miss McLeary and her companion, and Canonge rapped hard with his gavel and switched from French jury instructions to English: "Leave that till after the trial, Mr. Blodgett."

"The Constitution of the United States declares . . ."

January's attention shifted, as if beyond his own volition: "It'll cost me ten dollars just to get the wagon painted up with my shop name," juryman Quigley was saying, "plus the repairs to the harness. . . ."

Juryman Seignoret looked at his watch. The Cathedral clock could be heard, striking nine.

And wretches hang, that jurymen may dine, thought January, and wondered how many of those in the box today would disappear tomorrow: Leaving town on business, or coming down "sick" in order to abandon New Orleans with its threat of coming plague. Only Olympe would be left, he thought, immured in the jail for the rest of the summer. . . .

"Are you Célie Jumon?" The Bailiff rapped his staff.

"I am." She looked like St. Agnes, facing the wheel and the knife.

"Célie Jumon, you stand accused of causing the death of your husband, Isaak Jumon, by poisoning. . . . All right, all right," the Bailiff added impatiently, and translated into English. "Having paid one Madame Olympe Corbier to either administer or cause to be administered, or sell to you the wherewithal to administer, poison to your husband. How do you plead?"

She lifted her chin, delicate and beautiful in her black gown and veil. "I am not guilty, sir." And she remained haughtily silent while the man translated again.

"Olympe Corbier, you stand accused of causing the death of one Isaak Jumon of this city by poisoning. . . ." He paused, then translated for the benefit of jurors Shotwell, Barnes, and Brennert. "Having been paid by one Madame Célie Jumon to administer or cause to be administered, or sell to her the wherewithal to administer, poison to the said Monsieur Jumon. How do you plead."

Olympe sighed, and stood up. There was defeat, and exhaustion, and an iron stillness in her face. "I plead guilty," she replied, in a clear, carrying voice. "Célie Jumon paid me fifty dollars to put arsenic into her husband's drink, when he came to see her that night. And this I did."

TWENTY-TWO

Once when he was twelve January had gone down to the Armory on Rue St. Peter with Olympe and Nicolas Gignac, on the day soldiers brought in a new shipment of gunpowder. Olympe, at ten, was already experimenting with spells, and she'd dared the boys to come with her. Nic and January faked a fight to draw the men away while Olympe slipped forth and helped herself to about a cupful from the open barrel. As payment she'd given each boy a generous spoonful, and Nic had used his to make a sort of bomb that he'd thrown into a hornet's nest—Nic had never been notable for his brains.

January still remembered the roaring cloud of insects, the split-second violence, the frenzy of terror and confusion and rage.

It all came to his mind now.

Corcet was on his feet, shouting "Madame Corbier! Madame Corbier!" while Monsieur Gérard lunged up, flung himself at that erect, manacled figure in the dock. Célie, too, was standing, crying "No! No, it isn't true!" and every juryman was giving tongue like six couple of hounds with a possum up a tree, gesturing and shouting with Mr. Shotwell's voice rising above all others: "If you did it, why the tarnation didn't you have the courtesy to say so three weeks ago?" Canonge slammed his gavel again and again, shouting for order and threatening to have the court cleared, while above all other sounds Olympe cried out, in a flat desperate voice, "I poisoned him. I poisoned him. Célie Jumon gave me fifty dollars and I poisoned him," without change of expression, as if she were some kind of horrible clockwork toy.

The Bailiff seized Gérard, dragged him back before he could reach Olympe. Other Guardsmen entered the courtroom, two of them pulling Olympe to her feet and another two closing in on Célie. The girl looked around her desperately, a deer ringed by hounds in a clearing; Gérard, seeing his daughter across the heads of the crowd, tried to force his way back to her but was held fast by the Guards, against whom he fought like a roped bull.

"I poisoned him," called out Olympe again, and someone in the jury box yelled, "Well, then, hang the bitch and let us out of here!"

"Order! Order or I'll have the court cleared!"

Rose and Basile Nogent were trying to struggle forward, swimmers in a heavy sea. Blodgett had leapt up on a bench, and from this vantage point was scribbling wildly; Geneviève Jumon clutched Hubert Gran-ville's sleeve and poured out words unheard over the tempest.

Mamzelle Marie had vanished.

"Olympe!" January waded through the press around the dock, thrusting men aside unheeding of the pain in his shoulders and arms, and for an instant caught his sister's arm.

She turned, dark eyes blank as a stranger's. "Don't meddle with it, brother," she said quietly.

"Papa!" Célie's scream drew January's attention, as the girl was pulled away through the door; Fortune Gérard's fist crashed into the jaw of the nearest Guardsman and the little man went down under a storm of clubs and blows. When January turned back, Olympe was gone. It took him some minutes to battle his way to the door. When he ran down the steps to the arcade it was to see Olympe and Célie led into the Cabildo. Célie turned desperately back as if she could catch a glimpse of what was taking place in the courtroom, but Olympe stared resolutely ahead of her, in the flare of the oil lamps, willing herself not to feel, not to know.

January stood for a time, panting in the dark arcade. He felt numbed, blind, as if he'd been struck over the head—then he turned, and strode as fast as his long legs could carry him up Rue St. Pierre, and over to Rue Douane, to the yellow stucco house where his sister lived.

The doors were closed, shuttered. The plank drawn up, which customarily led over the gutter from the banquette to the street. Traces of light burned in the jalousies of the front bedroom window. January pounded on the parlor shutters with his fist, and saw a shadow start and move behind the jalousies, but no one opened to him. He pounded again, harder, and called out "Paul! It's me, Ben!" to a silence like that of a house stricken by plague. "Paul, open up! Let me in!"

He went over and hammered on the bedroom shutters. "Paul, it's Ben!"

No sound. But the silence behind those shutters was pregnant with breath, furtive stirrings furtively stilled.

January stood for a long time on the pavement. Hot black silence pressed the Rue Douane, darkness absolute but for the oil lamp on its chain above the intersection nearby. A dog barked. A few houses away, a baby wailed. *What do I do now? What do I do?*

It was growing in his heart, why Olympe had lied. Why her husband had not appeared in court, why he would not now open the door. Cold knowledge and dread.

No, he thought.

Gabriel leaving the house last night. Crossing the yard in the lamplight, waving a jaunty good-bye at the gate into the passway that led to the street. *You watch how you go, now.*

No.

He closed his eyes. *What do I do?*

"You got business out this late?"

A City Guardsman stood at his elbow: blue uniform, brass buttons, cockade of black leather in his hat. Expression of wary neutrality.

January drew a deep breath. *The man's only doing his job.* "I've just come from being a witness at a court case at the Cabildo, sir. A special session convened by Judge Canonge on account of the crowding of the docket," he added, as the man opened his mouth in disbelief that the courts would still be sitting at ten at night. "I was charged with a message for my brother-in-law here. I'm on my way home now, sir."

"Mind if I see your papers?"

January produced them. The Guard held them up to the street-lamp's flare to study the signature, which happened to be one of Hannibal's better efforts.

"Best you get along home, Mr. January." The Guard handed them back with a mollified air. "It's after ten."

"Yes, sir." The man could arrest him, and that would be the doom of them all. "Thank you, sir." January walked away from the house, shivering all over with anger, panic, dread.

What do I do? What do I do?

The chicken foot on the bed—a warning.

Killdevil Ned Nash, paid off by a white man, a toff—who might not, January knew, even know why Lucinda Coughlin had said to him, "Go down to the Flesh and Blood and give Ned Nash two hundred dollars."

Never lets himself come into view. . . . Always uses a cat's-paw. . . . That's the way not to get caught. . . .

Dr. Yellowjack, coming toward him through the swaying dancers with a plate of chickpeas in one hand, a cup of lemonade in the other. And the signet ring that appeared so mysteriously on Célie Jumon's windowsill: He'd been a fool, to study paper and handwriting, to say, *This is a trap* and not think, *The juju ball, the graveyard dust, appeared in my room the same way this appeared in Célie's room.*

And he saw in his mind, whole and clear and suddenly, the blond woman, the angelic child, in the Cathedral the morning after Olympe's arrest. *It has to work,* the woman had said, and January had thought then she'd spoken of a gris-gris. But she meant, he understood now, whatever leverage they were using to obtain money from Mathurin Jumon.

What Yellowjack had given her that day had in all probability been steamboat tickets out of town, which she could not be seen to purchase herself for fear of being traced.

The nuns won't get me, the lovely child had asked, *will they?*

Lucinda Coughlin was at Yellowjack's on St. John's Eve. The packed earth of the banquette along Rue des Ramparts thudded under his feet as his pace quickened. *And Isaak saw her.* Of course she'd told Yellowjack—of course Yellowjack would get rid of Isaak, lest the boy speak to his uncle. And, when, after consuming the poison, Isaak left the place—*how? Why?*—of course she'd tell Yellowjack *get rid of Célie, too.*

The oily glare of the lamp above Rue Toulouse glimmered down the street as he passed over the sloppy intersection, the street close to his mother's house. He passed it by, prayed he wouldn't meet another Guard.

A cat's-paw . . . Mambo Oba. Someone who could deliver a warning, and a curse when the warning wasn't heeded, and then drop out of sight, so that Mamzelle Marie wouldn't recognize the hand of Dr. Yellowjack. *That's the way not to get caught.*

Mathurin Jumon, almost certainly turned into a cat's-paw against himself.

Candles burned behind the jalousies on Rue St. Anne. Mamzelle Marie's daughter opened the door to him, tall already, beautiful already, with her mother's secret ophidian eyes. "Maman hasn't yet come home."

Damn it, thought January. *Damn it, damn it.* He thought about going to the Cabildo in search of her, but nearly an hour had passed. Mamzelle Marie would certainly be gone by this time, the cells all locked, Olympe beyond his reach. The Guards would only send him home, if the Guard he'd spoken to wasn't there. If he was, January stood a good chance of a night in the cells.

"When she comes back, would you tell her I have to see her? Whenever that is, whatever the time. Tell her it's urgent, desperate."

"I'll tell her, sir." No inquiry, no shift of expression, but a kind of calculation behind the cold dark eyes, adding things together. January had the strange sensation that this young woman already knew what had happened in the Court. He was, he realized, talking to the woman who would be the city's next Voodoo Queen.

He returned home, through sullen gluey darkness and smoke of burning. So far the sickness was not as bad as it had been last year, nowhere near what it had been the year before. His heart shrank up inside him nevertheless. There was Bronze John, and there was Monsieur le Choléra, and the memory returned to him as he made his way down the passway to his mother's yard, of climbing the stair in that tall narrow building in Paris, of opening the door. . . .

The smell of sickness struck him like a blow.

Hannibal. . . .

He reached the second door along the gallery in three strides. It stood ajar. His friend had managed to get it open in his attempt to crawl out onto the gallery, but had collapsed just inside. One thin white hand lay over the threshold, fingers reaching.

January touched it. It was deathly cold. The smell from the room was overpowering.

Cholera.

His heart seemed to stop within him.

Then Hannibal whispered, "Water," from within the room and began to retch. January rolled him over in the darkness and held him so that he didn't choke, his mind stalling, chasing: *Is this when I catch it?* If he didn't have it already. And, *At least Bouille can't have me run out of town.* And, *That chicken foot seems to have finally come home to roost.*

As he clattered down the stairs a few minutes later to the kitchen a wave of nausea gripped him, an agony in his belly and the big muscles of his thighs, and he remembered his sickness at the courthouse. *Dear God, no!* Sweat came out all over him as he gripped the stair rail, trembling, retching himself now—

Please God!

The epidemic in Paris. Last summer's cases here in New Orleans. The explosive indecencies of the sickness, the dried pinched faces, the agonies of cramp and vomiting and purging.

. . . please God . . .

He stumbled into the kitchen, cracked his shins on a bench, groped in his pocket for lucifers and struck one on the scratch-paper. By its light he found a pitcher on the table by the wall, next to the emptied bowl Gabriel had brought last night. The match had burned down to his fingers and nearly out when he saw the rat.

He lit another lucifer, as a second spasm of nausea seized him. He fought it down, and looked again.

The rat lay close to the corner of the table, its back bent in a spasm of agony, its tail still thrashing in pain.

The lucifer went out. January cursed and scratched another, and looked around this time for a candle. The smell of tallow acrid in his nostrils, he walked around for a closer look at the rat. It lay beside the blue pottery bowl that had contained the beans and rice. The spoon he'd used to wolf down the leftovers before going to the trial was licked clean nearby. Bella would wear him out with a broom handle for that kind of untidiness. Another wave of nausea hit him and he clutched at the edge of the table, dread and cold and enlightenment all exploding in his mind at once as he thought,

Not cholera. Poison.

Dr. Yellowjack coming toward him through the dancers, congris and lemonade in his hands. He'd waited for a long time for January to slip up and eat something that had stood unwatched in the house. And in the end he had done so.

How long?

When he could stand again January filled one pocket with candles, the rest with whatever eggs Bella had left behind in the egg basket and staggered into the yard. Filling the largest bucket he could find from the cistern he hauled it up the stairs with an effort that made him weak. He stuck candles in every crack and on every level surface in Hannibal's room, then wobbled into his own for his medical bag and ipecac, iodine, medicinal salts, anything. . . . In the midst of administering as much of a stomach lavage as he could to his friend he was sick twice more, but didn't dare stop. There was no telling how much earlier Hannibal had eaten the poisoned food, how much of a margin he had.

Laboring in the heat, in growing pain and fear, racing to overtake a goal that was itself hidden in darkness, he was conscious of how very silent the night was. How isolated the garçonnière, tucked away back from the Rue Burgundy behind his mother's house. How isolated he was himself. If he cried out, would anyone hear? If he shouted, "I am dying—there's a dying man here!" would anyone come down the dark passway from the street? Or would they say, as he had, *Cholera?* And flee?

He mixed water with egg whites—throwing the yolks and shells on the floor in his fumbling haste, his vision starting to play tricks on him in the wavering candlelight—and gulped them down, heroic quantities. He gagged, then induced vomiting and purging, as he had done for Hannibal. The fiddler lay stretched now on a blanket on the floor, like a drowned elf dredged from a gutter, wet with sweat and spilled water and slime. In the jittering dimness January thought for a moment that he saw, not the bones staring through the skin, but the man's skeleton itself, a nest of snakes creeping in the cage of the ribs. . . .

He blinked, and jerked his head, and found himself lying on the floor with spilled saline solution and nastiness everywhere about him. Doggedly he prepared another draught for himself, fighting the pains in his belly, his thighs, his arms where they'd been twisted nearly from their sockets last spring. . . . Had old Mambo Jeanne at Bellefleur been right, all those years ago, about certain poisons making snakes and lizards grow under your skin? He looked down at his arms and found that the old woman had indeed spoken true: His skin was moving with them, bulging out or twisting in long tracks. He forgot the draught, stared fascinated, horrified. . . .

And then he was in Paris. It was late, past two, the dead slack leaden hour of exhaustion, and stars burned, opium-crazed diamonds in a sky black with the velvet abysses of infinity. Summer heat like boiling glue, and the stenches of Paris in the summer; and every light was quenched, in mansion, flat, attic, and hovel. Where he was coming from he didn't know—the Marais Quarter across the river, he thought. Someone's Christmas Ball. And he saw Death, skipping and dancing down the street. Death looking just like He should, with his black cloak draped over a raggedy mess of stained wool shroud, and bony feet clattering a little on the slippery cobbles. Death messier than engravings portrayed, Death the way January was familiar with him from years at the Hôtel-Dieu, shreddy flesh dribbling gobbets of black fluid and maggots.

Death with his attendant skeletons—revolting in their stained shroudless nakedness. They knocked on doors, climbed through windows where no one would open, came out of alleyways, dragging men and women by the wrists or arms or hair. Fat butchers and slender milkmaids, a nightshirted child clutching a carved wooden horse, stockbrokers digging through their pockets looking for coin to pay off those grinning Guédé. . . . The coins fell through the bony fingers and clattered ringing on the stones. Some people came dancing, skipping: Ayasha tossing her scented hair. A woman leaned out a garret window and called her son's name, frantic with weeping. The boy didn't hear.

Carts rolled behind them, heaped with bones. Baron Cemetery was driving one of them, tipped his hat to January, and winked behind his spectacles. "Care to come?" His voice was creaky, shrill and hoarse. "Free ride. Good to see an old friend from home."

"I can't." January's words came out harsh and whispery as the skeleton god's. "I have to find Olympe."

The boy who was dancing beside the cart turned, waved to January, and held out his hand. January saw it was Gabriel.

"Gabriel, come back!" He stepped off the curbstone, something he knew he should have known better than to do. His feet sank ankle-deep in the black mud of Paris. "Gabriel, don't go!"

Gabriel only waved again, with one hand. The other gripped the hand of a young man, dancing, too, a slim light-skinned youth with a black trace of mustache, whom January knew was Isaak Jumon. January tried to follow but the ooze held him fast. "Gabriel. . . ."

"He'll be all right," said Mamzelle Marie.

January shook his head. "The Baron," he tried to explain.

He climbed the stairs in the Paris house, put his hand on the door-knob. . . .

"Who?" asked Hannibal's voice.

"The Baron," explained Mamzelle Marie. January opened the door, and saw Ayasha sitting on the bed, sharing a glass of wine with the Baron Cemetery, who had one bony arm around her waist.

"Don't look at me," said the Baron. "I haven't got him in my pocket." And he dug in his pocket with one hand to prove it, coming up only with some shards of broken crockery, such as the slaves at Bellefleur had stuck around graves. Then he laughed and dragged Ayasha down onto the bed, lying on top of her while she giggled and squirmed, pulling up her skirts, her long hair trailing onto the floor.

"Baron Cemetery," explained Marie Laveau, unnecessarily, January thought. "The lord of the spirits of the dead." (*You don't have to tell me that!*) She touched January's hand.

He was lying in his own bed, he thought, and felt as if he were coming off a ten-month drunk.

Cholera?

The image returned to him, of a rat dying by candlelight on a table.

"I have snakes in my arms," he said.

He opened his eyes. The light in the room was gray. Mamzelle Marie sat on the edge of his bed, a damp sponge in her hand. Behind her stood Rose with a basin, and Hannibal, like a handful of fence pickets rolled in an undertaker's coat, slouched in the chair by the desk.

"I took them out," said Mamzelle Marie.

"Thank you." January drew in his breath, and let it out. His whole insides seemed to be raw and there was a curious quality to the room and to everything he saw: Mamzelle, Rose, Hannibal, the books piled on the desk. As if without warning they could mutate into other forms, or prophesy unknown events.

"Dr. Yellowjack kidnapped Gabriel," he said, as if he'd read it all in a book and needed only to relate it to these people for them to understand. "He got word to Olympe that unless she confessed the murder—and implicated Célie, I think—he'll kill him."

"If he hasn't done so already," said Rose. She still wore the neat dress of pink faille she'd had on in the courtroom, the sleeves rolled back over her arms and dark with wet.

"No," said Marie Laveau. "He wouldn't. Not unless he has to. Not until Olympe is hanged. She's a mother, and she has the Power. Olympe would know."

January sat up. The room darkened, then shivered with a kind of aerial fire, and it seemed for a moment that he saw two chicken feet gripping the end of his bed, as if an invisible chicken sat there. He rubbed his eyes, and they vanished.

"Where would they be?"

They looked at one another: Mamzelle, Hannibal, and Rose.

It was Mamzelle who replied. "The house by the bayou." She turned to Rose. "That policeman wasn't there yet?"

Rose shook her head. "He wasn't there two hours ago," she answered. "I'll go again."

"Two hours?" January blinked at the room around him. By the light it was only an hour or so after dawn.

"It's close to six." Hannibal's voice was the whisper of scar tissue. And, when January's brows pulled together, trying to calculate sunrise and time, "Six in the evening. You've been off your head for most of the day."

"Moon won't rise till near midnight," said Mamzelle Marie. "There's a mist in the air. It'll be bad later, by the bayou. Best we go now while there's some light. Can you stand?"

"I think so."

Rose modestly turned away and stepped through the door onto the gallery while January got up; Mamzelle merely handed him his shirt. As his mind cleared a little January realized it was indeed evening, but the equivocal light left him confused. He felt weak, and caught himself on the back of Hannibal's chair. On the narrow desk lay a newspaper, open to the second page. SENSATION IN THE COURT, announced the header at the top of the column. And, smaller, VOODOO CONFESSES HEINOUS CRIME.

"What was it?" He made a mental note to buy serious gris-gris from

Mamzelle, if she hadn't already put a fix on Burton Blodgett. "In the food, I mean?"

"The world's full of things it could have been." Marie Laveau set his boots down in front of him. The room, he saw, had been cleared and cleaned. It smelled of burned herbs now, and soap. "Maybe two or three together. *Fricasee,* they call it in Haiti, or *akee.* It was one of those they brought over from Africa. It takes time to act, so there'd be none to point and say, 'This man was poisoned.' They'd only say it was the cholera, and run away." She brought a cup over from the desk, and held it out to him. Sweetness and salt, soothing as it went down. Some of the strangeness seemed to go out of the room, as if a necessary ballast had been added to his brain.

"If I'd eaten as much of the stuff as you had, I'd probably have been dead when you got back," said Hannibal in his thread of a voice. "I still don't think I'll ever be able to look at beans and rice again, which is a pity, since some weeks that's all I live on. πόσων ἐγὼ χρείαν οὐκ ἔχω, and I suppose Socrates ought to know. Are you sure our friend didn't put a hex on Bella's room as well as yours?"

"Rose," said Mamzelle, as January dug under the mattress for the pistols and the powder flasks he'd taken from the corpse of Killdevil Ned. While he was checking the loads he heard her go on, "If you can't find this Shaw at the Cabildo, go to M'sieu Tremouille's house . . ."

January's hands shook as he thrust pistols and flasks through his belt, slung the spares around his neck on their long piratical ribbons.

". . . a child been kidnapped, held at Dr. Yellowjack's house on the bayou. Tell him Yellowjack will kill the boy . . ."

A skinning-knife in his boot and another in his belt. He'd be hanged, he reflected bitterly, if he was seen with this much weaponry on him. He could hear Cut-Arm's laughter now.

"Tremouille's a smart man, and he's no coward." Looking around, January saw that Mamzelle Marie had kilted her bright skirt high, as she had the previous afternoon to trek through the *cipriere.* "If this Shaw isn't there, Tremouille's the best we can do."

If Shaw wasn't there, thought January, the chances that any of the other Guardsmen would be bright enough—or have sufficient woodcraft—to rescue Gabriel before the wangateur killed him were slim.

The voodooienne turned back from the door as Rose's shoe heels clattered away down the steps. Her long coppery fingers curled around the crucifix at her breast. "Virgin Mary, Mother of God," she said softly, "take us there safely." Then she snapped her fingers and made a sign with her hands, and spit into the corner. "Papa Legba, who has the keys to all doors, we need your help, too."

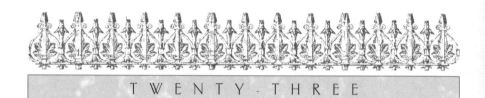

Mamzelle Marie took him by a different route into the *cipriere* this time. They passed through the Protestant cemetery where the smudge fires burned sullen in the dusk against the rising of the night miasma from the swamps, across the marshy verge of shacks and sheds and poverty-stricken immigrants, and straight into the trees. The failing light lent a weird cast to the gloom beneath the canopy of oaks and pines: Cypress trunks took on the appearance of men in that queer twilight, beards of moss the semblance of tree trunks or stands of laurel, water the look of solid land. The air felt close and thick in the lungs here, and mosquitoes swirled in stinging clouds.

"Judge Canonge spoke to your sister after the court was cleared, trying to get her to explain." Marie Laveau paused to get her bearings, then pressed through a stand of hackberry that hid a thread of game trail, pale in the dusk. "Even he smelled rotten fish. She said only she'd repented of her deed and of the lies she'd told."

January whispered, "Damn." He could see Olympe sitting there, with a face like a mechanical doll's, repeating over and over again, *I poisoned him. I poisoned him.*

"There's ways of getting messages into the jail, even though none from the outside are allowed in. It wouldn't have been hard."

"It wouldn't have been hard, either, to poison Célie in the jail," said January. "She has—we have—her father to thank there, for keeping her so close. And of course if Olympe had died in jail—Olympe the voodoo, Olympe the idolater—there would have been less of an outcry at the trial. Célie might have gotten off, and if Isaak had passed word to her somehow, spoken of what she'd heard."

From the edge of the trees to the island in the bayou it was only a mile or so, and the night was a still one. Mamzelle Marie led the way cautiously, and January flinched at each sound. While it was true that Dr. Yellowjack would hang on to his hostage as long as he could, it was also true that in kidnapping the boy he had provided a clinching witness to the existence of Lucinda Coughlin's plot, and to his own part in helping her.

They came on the house over the rear of the island, following the low ground, the wet ground, where they could. Mosquitoes and gnats swarmed around their ears and nostrils, but once Mamzelle touched January's arm, and pointed out to him a cluster of tin pans and tubs, dangling together in a spiderweb of fishing line, half-hidden among the beards of Spanish moss. January followed her gesture down, and saw where the line was stretched among the root ridges of the higher ground, where the insects were less. Between the creeper and fern, and the gathering mists, it would have been impossible to avoid giving the alarm.

"He has spells, too, that keep the snakes angry hereabouts," murmured Mamzelle Marie. "He says they'll call out to him, and tell him who's coming. But they won't speak of me. Or of you, if you're with me. Still it's best we be careful."

January wondered if the voodoo-man claimed the allegiance of the local alligator population as well. The light was going, and he probed each pool and reed tuft with his stick, poison-dreams still whispering and buzzing in his head. He felt at any moment that the white eyeless thing of his dreams would come sloshing up out of the depths. Red eyes seemed to watch from the shadows, eyes that were gone when he turned his head. Once he thought he saw a huge water moccasin curled on a log, and when he met the serpent's copper eyes it flicked its tongue at him and slipped down and into the cattails, hastening away toward the house. Maybe it did have a message to deliver.

In any case the house was dark—shuttered—when January and

Mamzelle Marie finally saw its pale bulk shimmer amid the trees. Woodsmoke lay thick on the clammy air. *Gone indoors?* wondered January. *Driven to stifling in the house by the mosquitoes?* They circled the house once, straining their eyes through the cinder-dark dusk to see if anyone watched from the gallery. It seemed to be true that snakes in the thickets behind the house were angrier, for a small one sank its fangs into January's boot, and a few minutes later a larger one struck at him from a hole under a log.

"You stop that," ordered Marie Laveau, her hand darting out and catching the serpent behind the head as it tried to retreat once more. The reptile lashed and struck at her wrist, scratching the copper skin, though January guessed it had spent its poison on his boot-leather. It was only a young one, too, barely the length of a biblical cubit.

Marie Laveau held it up, and stared into its yellow eyes. "You got no respect," she said softly, as the serpent's coils circled her arm. "You tell your friends Mamzelle Marie is here, Mamzelle Marie who walks on glass and golden spikes. You tell your friends Damballah-Wedo is my husband, and I have coffee with John the Revellator two afternoons a week, who drove off snakes out of his coffee cup when King Herod tried to poison him. You tell them, leave me and my friends alone."

She set the snake on the ground, and watched it as it slipped away. "It'll be a while," she said, "before they all get the word."

Carefully, they moved in toward the house. A boat was tied at the bayou, where the dancing had been. Heart hammering, January crept through the water and the reeds—this was the kind of place where alligators loved to lie—cut the line, and let it drift away. On the ground where the last light fell he could see the *vèvès* scratched into the dirt, sprinkled with rum and fresh blood. As soon as there was an inch of cover he crawled from the water and crept along the thickets to where Mamzelle Marie waited, probing always ahead of him with his stick. A turtle studied him from a log. He wondered if he should hand it a calling card to take in.

"I see no track around the house going away," she said in a breath. "He's in there."

January pulled on his shirt again, and looped the ribbons of the pistols once more over his neck. "Then let's have a closer look." He spotted where the carry-beams went, that bore the weight of the gallery's planking, gritted his teeth hard, then lifted Mamzelle Marie over the rail and onto one. She was a tall woman and built strong, but still her weight was a good sixty pounds less than his, less likely to make the boards creak. From the woodpile he handed her up thick shakes and bars cut from timbers, and these she used to bar the shutters from the outside. They were latched from within, but at the house's rear was a window where the shutters did not fit: Even from ground beyond the edge of the gallery, January could see the crack was big enough to get Killdevil's skinning-knife through and flip the catch. He waited until Mamzelle Marie came slipping back, then vaulted silently over the rail. He crossed the gallery in a stride, flipped the catch, hurled the shutters back, and stepped through, pistol in hand.

There was only the single room, and that room Hell-dark and choking. Smoke grabbed his throat, shoved hot coals up his nostrils, acrid, sweet, stinking. By the dim glow from the vents in an American iron stove he got an impression of chairs, and a table scattered with pots and jars, open as if in haste. A hole in the ceiling showed where a loft was, but there was no ladder beneath it. He stepped in, called out, "Yellowjack!" and behind him he heard Mamzelle Marie scream his name.

The shutters banged shut behind him and he heard the crash of a bar. The next moment a pistol bellowed, inches from the other side of the wall, and something fell on the gallery, and he knew he'd been trapped.

They'd been trapped.

Footsteps fled across the gallery, creak-creak-creak, and were gone. He shouted "Mamzelle!" but there was no sound, and dizziness broke over him, choking, swooning. *The smoke,* he thought. *Poison.*

He flung himself against the shutters, but the wood was stout. Images swirled in his mind, and he thought he heard laughter: thought he saw Death dancing a jig in the corner of the room, with his black cloak and his fiddle; thought the shutters rattled, where the white thing pawed and picked to get in. For a panicky moment he started to move the table, to block it out, then thought, *Don't be a fool!* and braced himself against the table, brought up his right leg and kicked with all the strength of his back and hips at where the bar would be.

He felt it jerk and give.

Voices whispered in his mind. Ayasha's laughter: *Eh, malik, you think you're stronger than oak beams and steel?* And the soft polite tones of Delphine Lalaurie, the most terrible woman he had ever known: *I'm afraid you haven't learned your lesson very well, M'sieu Janvier,* clear as if she stood with her whip in hand in the dark behind him still. Things crawled and crept and rustled among the pots on the table—he thought he saw a thousand tiny snakes wriggling toward him, each with a paper bearing his name in its mouth.

Big young Pedro, smiling shyly, *My mama say, "Mind your business."* Among the pots he saw a carved wooden horse, with flying mane and flowers whittled into it: As he looked the horse got to its feet and began to dance.

Olympe's voice: *"I poisoned him. I poisoned him. But he isn't dead, I know it. . . ."*

And another voice, *"Up here! Please, up here!"* Coughing.

It was the coughing that made January turn. Fighting panic, fighting terror, still he knew that hallucinations didn't cough. On the table the little snakes vanished. The carved horse lay again on its side, edged with the ruby reflection of the stove's hellish glare.

"Please! . . ."

He dragged the table over to the hole in the ceiling, sprang up onto it. The smoke was worse in the loft, roiling from the stove's broken-off pipe. The young man up there had managed to squirm his way over to the hole, despite the ropes that bound his hands and his feet, so that January nearly tripped over him in the burning dark. "Gabriel," gasped the young man, as January groped for the ropes, for his knife. "He took Gabriel—threw the powders in the fire. . . ."

January dragged him to the hole—the young man's weight was slight as a girl's—and dropped through, holding up his arms to catch him. There was pain, but nothing like the agony of a month ago, and January silently blessed Augustus Mayerling and his miserable scale weights and beams. "He was here?"

The young man's face was a skull, bare of flesh, save for a little black mustache. . . . Then the vision vanished and revealed in the dim red smolder of the stove the emaciated features of someone who was unmistakably Antoine Jumon's brother.

"Last night." Isaak coughed again, agonizingly, doubled over and pressed against the table. "Said his mother. . . . Accused. . . ."

"Save it." January was already beside the stove, but through the rolling smoke he could see the lock that clamped it shut. Dizziness flooded his brain, and it seemed to him that things had begun to crawl from the opened pots on the table, chicken feet scratching across the planks toward him, and every little foul juju ball that had been tucked into the corner of the room. The skin of his belly, his arms, his thighs crept and twitched with the tiny lizards and snakes growing within: He knew if he remained here they would feed on the smoke, grow, and devour him.

He returned to the shutters, dragging the table back to brace himself—and it seemed to him that the white thing from the swamp, the white thing from his nightmares, gripped it and tugged. *You owe me,* the thing hissed, looking at January with eyeless sockets, and grinned. *You still owe me, for Pedro's death.*

"Let me out," bargained January, panting, "and help me, and I'll pay you what I can. You tell Mamzelle Marie what payment you want—I'll pay."

But the creature only grinned.

January turned from it, braced his body against the table, and drove his leg again at the shutters. Once, twice, then the wood cracked and he threw himself up against the door, slipped his arm through and shoved the broken bolt aside. Isaak was unconscious already; January dragged him out, and left him propped against the side of the house.

"He'll head north across Bayou Metairie," said Papa Legba, leaning against the corner of the house with his keys in his belt and his pipe in his hand. He jerked with the pipe to show the direction. "Woods are thicker on the other side, between the bayou and the lake."

January remembered Cut-Arm's men, sheltering in the *cipriere* there.

"There's gators in the bayou. Yellowjack'll make for the bridge most likely. You can get him there if you hurry."

"Thank you," January gasped, and ran.

The mists that had drifted all evening among the trees seemed to thicken and coalesce, although that, decided January, might only be the effect of the poisons in his brain. It was difficult to tell what was real and what was not, but he knew it would be madness to try to find the wangateur's tracks in the woods. He grabbed one of the lanterns that hung on the side of the house, kindled it, and followed the bayou itself, which he knew would lead him eventually to the cleared ground of the Roquigni and Allard plantations, that lay along the Metairie Road. Even if Dr. Yellowjack didn't try for the bridge he might be more visible from that point, and Papa Legba was correct. There would be gators in the bayou. Snakes, too. The voodoo-man would be a fool, to try to cross.

I'll never make it, thought January, striding as fast as he dared through the creepers and reeds. *He has a start on me. . . .*

You'll make it, rasped Legba's voice in his mind. January thought he glimpsed the old man in the mists again, though now he looked more like the battered old statue of St. Peter at the back of St. Anthony's Chapel, Heaven's keys dangling from his belt. His face was black rather than white. *Might so be he's delayed in the woods. You hurry, though.*

January hurried. Sweat poured from him and the blood beat in his head, and around him the woods chittered with ghosts and *loa* and the twitching white leprous shape of the smallpox god. But the bayou lay always to his right. Sometimes there seemed to be something wrong and strange about the water; it glowed with blue light, or ran red like the Nile with blood. The cypress knees thrusting up through it stretched twisty gray hands to him. But he worked his way only a little inland to avoid being grabbed, and kept striding. And always the mist grew thicker, the silence pressing, and even the lantern's glow didn't help him much. *I can't,* he thought, gasping, his knees weak from the poison, and Legba whispered, *Not far. . . .*

Strength came into him. Sometimes he thought someone else ran with his legs, someone who carried a sword and whose eyes burned with fire.

A bayou ran in from the west that might have turned him aside. But from that point the lights near the second of the stone bridges was visible, guiding him forward. As he waded through the hip-deep waters under their blanket of fog he heard an alligator bellow, horrifyingly close, and the slip and whisper of water. He scrambled up the bank, stumbling, praying he wouldn't put his hand on a water moccasin, and ran forward again, toward the lights where the Bayou Road crossed the bridge. At the third bridge, where Bayou Metairie ran into Bayou St. John and the Metairie Road forked off, he stopped, gasping, leaning on the stone bridge's rail, the clammy fog thick in his lungs and, it seemed to him, the voices that had whispered all around him in the mists fading from his mind.

He knelt, and scanned the threshold of the bridge. If someone had crossed who'd come through the marshy lands to the west, they'd done so without leaving wet footprints. Shutting the lantern slide, January stepped down from the bridge, panting, and crouched in a clump of pine. In the stillness, and the black thick fog, his mind felt clearer. Had Isaak Jumon, like Papa Legba, been a figment of whatever had been dumped into the stove?

But the carved horse on the table . . . the child's toy that Isaak had carved. That told him those final few things he had not known.

That was what Isaak had seen in Dr. Yellowjack's house on St. John's Eve. He would not even have had to see Lucinda or Abigail Coughlin, although the woman had almost certainly seen him. Of course, he'd be horrified to see his uncle's two delicately protected protégées there. Of course he'd risk his own freedom, to go back to town and tell his uncle that the woman and her daughter were there, and in danger. . . .

But in that case, why wasn't Isaak dead? If in fact he hadn't been a hallucination? Had he been a prisoner there, all those weeks? The idea was surely even more absurd than incarceration in the Jumon town house. January remembered the emaciated face, the way the young man had clutched at the table. Surely Dr. Yellowjack would have been better off to kill him immediately? If . . . ?

A voice screamed in the darkness, "Let me alone!"

Hoarse panting breath, and the clash and rustle of young cane trampled. Water splashed. Dr. Yellowjack cried, "Get up and run you young bastard or I'll burn you! I swear I'll tear you to pieces with hot irons. . . ."

"I am," whispered Ben's nephew's voice, gasping in the last extremities of exhaustion and pain. "Please . . . don't. . . ."

The hissing rattle of cane, the slither of mucky earth. January forced himself to remain still. He knew that if he moved, if he went out into the wilderness of mist and darkness, Yellowjack would hear him, turn aside, and he'd be lost. Only if the wangateur thought the bridge was safe would he cross.

Papa Legba, lord of bridges. . . .

Virgin Mary, help us. . . .

"Come on!"

"Please . . ." A broken whimper that twisted January's soul to hear.

I'll kill him. For hurting that boy, I'll feed the cat with his heart.

"Come on!"

"I'm coming . . ."

He saw them in the mists. Yellowjack had a lantern, the glow of it bobbing, jerking in the choking vapors around them, glinting on the black heron-hackle in his hat. By its light January saw Gabriel, limping, staggering, falling, and trying to rise. His hands were tied behind him, and there was a rope around his neck, a rope that the voodoo-man jerked and dragged as a vicious child would drag at a puppy on a lead. Gabriel fell, sobbing, and braced himself, trying to keep from being strangled as Yellowjack dragged him along the shell path toward the bridge.

"Get up!" The voodoo-man turned back. January could see he had a knife in his hand. Yellowjack tried to haul the boy to his feet again, but Gabriel was clearly at the end of his strength. The boy half-rose, then, with a cry, collapsed as his left leg buckled beneath him.

"Please—my leg. . . ."

Yellowjack cursed him and stuck the knife in his belt, reached to grab his shoulders with both hands.

Gabriel writhed like a snake and rammed his head into the man's groin. At the same instant January sprang forward, yelling, "Gabriel! Roll clear!" and flung himself on Yellowjack's back. His weight slammed the smaller man to the ground; the lantern bounced away.

"He's got a poison sticker!" yelled Gabriel from the darkness, and January sprang back as he felt Yellowjack wriggle and lunge. Yellowjack twisted from beneath him and fled up onto the bridge, January ripping loose a pistol from his belt to follow. Yellowjack was yards ahead of him on the bridge, mists already closing around him, when he stopped, and threw up his hands.

"*No!*"

Just for an instant, January thought he saw clearly the silhouette in the darkness and the fog: thought he saw the outline of a top hat, the gleam of spectacles, the white glimmer of bones. What Yellowjack believed he saw—Baron Cemetery or something else—January never knew. But the wangateur veered from the end of the bridge where the dark form waited, and flung himself over the edge, into the water. The dark form vanished into the mist again, and January doubled back, sprinting to catch Yellowjack if he emerged from the water on this side of the bayou.

Mist and water roiled, and he heard another cry. He saw something heave itself from the water on the far side and snatched up the lantern in time to see Yellowjack scramble, stumbling, out of the bayou on the far side, and limp across the marshy ground for the trees, half a mile away.

He never made it. As January ran across the bridge he saw the man fall, and saw a dark shape stride from the mists toward him, a shape that resolved itself into a tall woman in a tignon with seven points. How either he or Yellowjack could have mistaken her for Baron Cemetery January didn't know—a final dream-shape born of poison and smoke— but when he reached Yellowjack's side, it was indeed Mamzelle Marie who knelt there.

The wangateur was gasping, clutching at the wet weeds in terror and pain. A knife gleamed in Mamzelle Marie's hand as she looked up at January in the lamplight. "Snake," she said. "In the water." She took January's lantern from him and held it close, and slashed an *X* in Yellowjack's already swelling arm.

"He thought you were Baron Cemetery," said January uncertainly. "He saw you in the fog on the bridge."

Mamzelle Marie looked up with blood on her lips where she'd sucked clean the wound of its poison. Dried blood crusted her temple where Yellowjack had struck her from the gallery of the house. "I was never on the bridge," she said. "I came around over the bayou a ways back, and through the *cipriere*."

January walked back the half-dozen paces required to shine a lucifer's dim quick flare on the bayou. He saw the sleek zigzagged backs, the arrowing ripples of wake as they swam away. Water moccasins, two of them, six feet long, the largest he had ever seen.

Footsteps crunched on the shells of the bridge. The rope still dangled from Gabriel's neck and his hands were still bound but he wasn't limping. In fact he walked with his usual jaunty stride.

"The Grand Zombi's her friend," said the boy, without a trace of the pitiful agony that had rent his voice only two minutes before. Without a trace of surprise, either. " 'Course all the snakes in the bayou would go after Yellowjack, once she told them to. He was really stupid to try and swim."

TWENTY-FOUR

Judge Canonge was not best pleased, after a day in the courtroom hearing all those cases left behind by ill or absconding colleagues, to be summoned from his own packing yet again to the Cabildo. Nevertheless, half an hour after Constable LaBranche left the watch room where January, Mamzelle Marie, Gabriel, and Isaak waited, the deep golden voice could be heard through the open doors in the arcade:

"Ridiculous? Of course it's ridiculous! If the man had had the sense God gave a goat he'd have seen there was something amiss in the confession. . . . What have we here?" The Judge squinted around the grimy semidark of the watch room, then touched his hat brim. "Madame Pâris."

Mamzelle Marie nodded like a queen.

"Your Honor." The young man got shakily to his feet, aided by the stick January had cut for him out by the bayou. "My name is Isaak Jumon. I understand you have convicted my wife, and this man's sister"—he gestured to January—"of my murder."

The Judge's dark eyes flicked from Isaak's face to January's, and he remarked, "You again." He looked back at the young marble carver. "You look like you've been buried, anyway. Sit down, for God's sake. LaBranche, get this boy some brandy. I never liked that jiggery-pokery with your brother and his mysterious carriage rides in the middle of the night. And I understand some poor bastard has been buried under your name. Where have you been?"

"In the care of a good couple named Weber." Jumon glanced self-consciously around him at the various Guards in the room, then sipped from the glass he'd been handed. "Germans, who spoke no English. They feared moreover they would be sent back to Bavaria if they spoke of my presence in their house. They found me, soaked to the skin and dying, close by the gates of the Old Cemetery, and took me in, though they believed me to be stricken with the cholera."

"Weber worked with me at Charity early in the month," January explained. He had not been asked to sit, and though his head had cleared considerably with the walk back to town he felt weak and a little shaky, and still half-expected to see snakes moving in the corners when he wasn't paying attention. "Members of the City Council were at pains to impress upon all of us there that there was no epidemic, and especially that no mention was to be made of cholera."

"That idiot Bouille," said Canonge. "As if the pilots of every steamboat on the river don't carry the news. Though with that imbecile Blodgett giving cry in the newspapers I don't blame the Council for acting like a parcel of ninnies. They'd arrest the Samaritan on the road from Jericho for operating an unlicensed hack service, belike. I take it," he added, studying Isaak's drawn face and emaciated shoulders by the glare of the oil lamp in its bracket above, "that cholera wasn't your problem."

Jumon shook his head. "As it happened, I had nursed Monsieur Nogent's wife during the cholera the summer before last. I know the symptoms, and I knew that, similar as my own were, I had been poisoned, I think with arsenic. I was lucky to survive."

"Do you know who administered the arsenic?"

Jumon was silent for a time. "I think now that it has to have been Dr. Yellowjack. At the time—and I am ashamed to say it—I thought that it was through some agency of my mother's. I was—I was upset, and very frightened, and I thought all sorts of things about her that cannot have been true. I went to Dr. Yellowjack's house, you understand, to ask his help against her. . . ."

"Thus putting yourself remarkably in accord with your good wife as to the proper way of dealing with the lady," remarked Canonge grimly.

"Far be it from me to speak ill of a man's mother to his face, but Madame Jumon makes Lady Macbeth appear doting by comparison, and amateurish to boot."

January stepped unobtrusively back to Abishag Shaw's desk, and leaned his weight on the corner of it, his knees abruptly weak. His body ached and although the mere thought of food was nauseating, he felt overwhelmed with a desperate craving for sweets. The air in the watch room felt stifling, like a dirty liquid in his lungs and throat, and he wondered if the hallucinations were returning. Everything seemed suddenly distant, like a Rembrandt painting—the Judge's craggy face in lamplight and shadow, the straggling curls of Jumon's hair, the buttons on Gabriel's shirt.

"I was naturally appalled—horrified—to see poor young Madame Coughlin in such a place," Jumon was saying. "And her daughter, too. She told me she had come there only to ask Dr. Yellowjack's help. I had not imagined she could be so superstitious as to believe that his potions and gris-gris would 'change her luck,' as she said. She swore that she was perfectly safe, but the more I thought of it, the more uneasy I became. I begged her to do nothing foolish, or without consulting my uncle. . . ."

Jumon's voice retreated from January's mind, distancing itself, like the disconnected images of lamplight and blackness. ". . . began to rain as I made my way toward my uncle's house . . . feared more than anything that that poor woman would be lured or forced into something which would cut her off utterly from the help of decent people. . . . Innocent child. . . ."

Innocent indeed.

"The symptoms struck me halfway there. I guessed at once what they were, from the metallic taste in my mouth, and from all I had heard of the voodoos. Had not Zoë been in the shop itself, sweeping up for my grandmother's new tenants, I doubt anyone within the courtyard would have heard me, for I did not have the strength to turn the gate key. I'm afraid I don't remember much, Your Honor, but I know that twice or three times she went out into the carriageway and listened, fearing that Grandmother would have heard something."

January listened with only a fragment of his mind to Jumon's account of Antoine's visit, reeling drunk on opium; of Zoë's growing panic and terror about what Grand-mère Jumon would do if she found her son's slave had admitted a man sick with the cholera to her home; of the bout of pneumonia that had kept Isaak bedfast and delirious for weeks after the Webers found him.

"As soon as I was a little recovered I sent a message to Dr. Yellowjack," Isaak was saying. "He replied that I must come to him at once, without notifying my wife or anyone else of my whereabouts. There must have been some evil going on at Yellowjack's house of which I was ignorant, for on my arrival I was overpowered—he had a gun, but he could have done it bare-handed, as weak as I was—and imprisoned in the attic, with this young man here." He nodded to Gabriel with a smile.

"That old man was snake-bit pretty bad," put in LaBranche. "That was smart work on January's part. . . ." He looked around for January, spotted him in the gloom by the wall, and nodded in his direction. "The sawbones here says January, and Mamzelle—er—M'am Laveau— sure enough saved his life. Yellowjack's one tough old nigger and that's for sure. His lawyer, he says. He wants to see his lawyer."

"I still don't understand what part the man played in the villainy." Young Jumon rubbed one thin hand over his face. "Unless—no harm came to poor Madame Coughlin, surely? Or to Mademoiselle Abigail?"

January said, "As far as I know, they're well." Canonge glanced over at him, as if he heard something in the quickness of that reply, but held his peace.

"He gave you food at the voodoo dance, then."

Isaak nodded. "He was one of half a dozen, really, sir. I gather there's always food at the dances. Mostly coarse fare, like congris and rice, or pralines, or sugar in the cane. Everyone seemed to be—"

"Isaak!"

Célie broke from between the Guards who had escorted her in, and threw herself into her husband's arms. "Isaak! Oh, God, oh, God! . . ."

The Guards released Olympe at the same time. She caught her son in her arms, holding him in tight ferocious silence, head bent over his. She breathed in, once, like the tearing loose of the foundations of her soul.

"Célie!" cried Isaak desperately, and clutched his wife close.

"I'm all right." Gabriel's voice was muffled by the circle of his mother's arms. "I wasn't scared. I knew Uncle Ben would come get me."

January shut his eyes, and couldn't help himself. He laughed.

At Olympe's house, later that night, he ate grits and syrup—the only things he wanted or could stomach—and slept for an hour or two on a truckle bed they rolled out for him in the children's room. But while dark still lay on the city he rose and made his way to the turning basin in quest of Natchez Jim. The bargees said Jim had gone downriver for wood, so January walked out along the Bayou Road, five miles through the insect-drumming scorch of the morning to Spanish Fort. There he inquired around the wharves for a skiff bound for Mandeville, and hired himself to help load and unload crates of champagne in trade for passage across the lake. His back and arms still hurt, and he knew he'd be stiff that night, but it was good beyond words to be able to do the work.

The power of the voodoos—of Mamzelle Marie, and John Bayou, and all the great ones of New Orleans—lay in secrets. January had seen how the nets of their intelligence lay like spiderweb over the town; had seen the look in Vachel Corcet's eyes, when the lawyer had offered his unwilling services to Olympe. To a greater or lesser extent, everyone played with secrets: his mother, Dominique, Madeleine Mayerling, his mother's gossiping friends. . . . Traded them like counters in a game of loo.

Shaw would be returning to town within a day or so. Dr. Yellowjack would be questioned before that, and would almost certainly tell where Lucinda Coughlin could be found.

And if I'm wrong about who was whose cat's-paw in this, thought January grimly, *I'm sure Olympe will see to it that my tombstone reads, What an Idiot.*

But once a secret was out, there was never any calling it back.

So he helped load crates in the blazing heat and sat in the stern while the boat's owner set and plied the sails across the flat steely waters. January had brought bread and honey and cheese from Olympe's house, but the boatman shared sausage and rice with him, and they talked of this and that—the boatman's white father had given him the craft, and set him up in the business, rather than pay for an education he would have been hard put to find a use for. January wasn't so sure that this wasn't a better course. In all of his life he'd made more money as a musician than as a surgeon. Yet he felt a kind of tired anger, insofar as he was capable just then of feeling anything, that this should be so.

In Mandeville they unloaded, and on the boatman's advice January sought out a grocery in town run by a woman of color. She let him bathe and change clothes in her shed. The long twilight was just beginning when he made his way, clothed in black coat and top hat and the respectability of the free colored, to the Jumon house.

An old house, perched like so many Creole houses on six-foot piers of brick and built in the shape of a U to trap the breezes from the lake. Gardens surrounded it, box hedges and topiary snipped neat as masonry walls. French doors and brisés stood open to show the honeyed candlelight within. January went around to the back and sent in his card with a boy who was scrubbing vegetables in the loggia by the kitchen. In time the graying butler who had admitted him to the town house came down the back steps.

"Monsieur Jumon is out for the evening, M'sieu." The butler inclined his head politely, but despite his calm he had a nervous look to him. As anyone would, thought January, whose master was selling up. "I doubt he will return before eleven."

"I'll wait, if it's all right," he replied. "I think he'll want to speak with me."

The butler brought paper and pen to the enclosed rear gallery, and a branch of candles, for the garden trees blocked out much of the fading evening light. January wrote,

Monsieur Jumon—
Please excuse this intrusion, and my rudeness in calling on you at such an hour, but the matter is one of gravest importance. Dr. Yellowjack has been arrested. I will await your convenience.
Benjamin Janvier

The butler brought him lemonade and, a little later, congris with bits of ham neatly arranged around it, which led January to deduce that whoever else had been sold off, Zeus still reigned in the kitchen. It was obvious to him that the household had been reduced: The same woman who stood at the table just outside the laundry room pressing napkins later fetched water from the cistern for the cook to soak red beans, and when the sun went down, January could see that there were only the two of them in the kitchen, which was lit from within by candles and the glow of the hearth.

A viper in her bosom, an adder, a beast who was always selfish. . . . Just how much had Mathurin Jumon told his mother, of why he had to sell those few servants who were his and not those of the family? *Always cruel to her, always delighted in hurting her. . . .*

Mathurin hastening from the room to assuage her pique. *"Now, Mama. . . ."*

Had Madame Cordelia become reconciled? Or was she still treating her son with frozen politeness tempered by martyred courage?

What could Mathurin possibly have given or promised or written to a woman like Lucinda Coughlin that would give her power to make him cross his mother's wishes? Zoë's sale argued a fearful desperation. Reaching into his coat pocket, January brought out the carved horse that had lain on the table in Dr. Yellowjack's house. He turned it to the candles, admiring again the carved roses in its mane and tail—no bigger than the straw flowers on Jumon's prized Palissy plates—and the flare of the little hooves. Of course the child would keep it with her.

The butler crossed through the gallery and out to the kitchen, to return a few minutes later with smudges against the mosquitoes, and a cup of chicory coffee. "You comfortable here, sir?"

January nodded. "Perfectly, thank you," he answered. "Might I trouble you for a few more candles, to read while I wait? Kitchen candles will do."

The butler smiled, relieved. "No trouble about that, sir. Kitchen candles is all I could let you have, Michie Jumon having gotten particular about economy, at least where it doesn't show. He even burns tallow in his study now, and his room, or else burns the ends of Madame's beeswax." He shook his head. "Madame never will have any but the best beeswax, and fresh every day: forty candles in her bedroom and a hundred in the drawing room, whether she has company or not. They're burning there tonight as we speak, sir, same as always, and both of them away at Madame St. Chinian's for supper."

"Sounds like your Madame won't have any but the best," January remarked, when the butler returned with two more branches of candles, and a packet of half-burned tallow work lights wrapped in a newspaper.

"Why, no, sir." The butler kindled the dozen or so wicks in a strong odor of sheep fat. "That's natural, her being the daughter of a

French Count, and raised in the palace of the old Kings, and maid-in-waiting to the old Queen. Why, even with Michie Mathurin having to sell up—his valet, and the woman that kept his books in order, and even the housekeeper he was . . . well, Michie Mathurin was fond of—he wouldn't even ask Madame if she could spare any of her servants. That's Madame's way."

Something changed in the man's eyes: old knowledge, old stories. January folded his hands and looked fascinated, which indeed he was.

"Madame is—a hard woman in some ways," the servant said. "You wouldn't think it to look at her, sir. Like a little china doll. But my daddy, who was butler to her back when M'am Cordelia first married Michie Hercule, he told me things of the way she treated the fieldhands out on Trianon Plantation that would make your hair stand up on end. Michie Laurence was terrified of her up till the day he died, and him a grown man fifty years old."

His fingers, rough-skinned from years of lending a hand with cleaning and swollen with arthritis, rested lightly on the ornate bronze candle holder: pseudo-Egyptian, January saw, like all the expensive and outmoded crocodile-footed furniture now consigned to Cordelia Jumon's attic.

"Poor M'am Noëmie, that was Michie Laurence's wife, she just got quieter and quieter every day, until she left—and even then she waited till M'am Cordelia was gone from home. Michie Laurence gave her the money for her passage, and I don't think his mother ever forgave him that. If you ask me, sir, Michie Mathurin still is afraid of her, for all he's always leaving flowers in her room and buying her gowns and diamonds and new sets of dishes every time a boat comes in from France."

January watched thoughtfully as the small, dapper man made his way back into the house. Then from his grip, which he had stowed on the floor at his feet, he brought out the octavo edition of *Hamlet* he'd brought with him to read:

> *Nay, but to live*
> *In the rank sweat of an enseaméd bed,*
> *Stewed in corruption, honeying and making love*
> *Over the nasty sty—*

And every word of it Hamlet's rage at the mother who had betrayed him by loving another than he.

The room in the attic returned to his mind. The blood on the sheets.

He was still reading when the clatter of hooves rang on the pavement of the carriageway, and a harness jangled in the dark. Rising, he descended the gallery steps, circled the corner of the house to watch them step to the block: Mathurin in the black of mourning, white shirt-front shiny as marble in the lights held aloft by the butler; Madame frail and exquisite in black satin du Barry, cut at the height of Paris fashion. More like a mistress, January thought, than a mother. The diamonds of her bracelet glittered outside the sable gloves. "You can go back if you wish," he heard her say. "I'll manage here somehow alone."

"Maman, don't be like that." Another man would have said it bracingly, or impatiently, or teasingly. Mathurin Jumon was coaxing, and behind the coaxing, just a hint of plea. This woman could hurt him still. As January's mother could hurt him, if he let her. "You know I'd never. . . ."

The pair passed inside. January returned to the gallery. A few minutes later the butler hurried through and out to the kitchen, to return with a tea tray: fresh white roses in a silver vase. "I gave Michie Jumon your note, sir, but no telling how long they'll be having tea before M'am goes up."

They have arrested Dr. Yellowjack. Mathurin had sold everything he could to raise money to keep Lucinda Coughlin and her partner silent—including a woman he was "fond of," Zoë. Yet he remained at his mother's side, drinking tea, until she was ready to let him go.

It was midnight when the rear door of the house opened, and Mathurin Jumon stepped out.

"Monsieur Janvier."

His face was an old man's. Dead, lined with exhaustion and defeat and despair. A fighter driven to his knees and looking at the spear. He held out a gloved hand as January rose.

"Please sit down." He brought up another wicker chair for himself. "I trust Télémaque made you comfortable?"

"Very. Yes, sir."

They sat in silence for a moment, face-to-face, the candles burning between, above the black-covered volume of *Hamlet.*

"Did you know it was me," said January at last, "whom Killdevil Ned was hired to kill?"

Jumon sighed. "I—I guessed. I saw him near the cemetery, on the day of Isaak's funeral. And I saw you there. I didn't—I didn't know for certain. Only that I was to take money to the Flesh and Blood and give it to him. But there was no one else at the funeral who—who was connected with—with the voodoos."

"Then it was Yellowjack who told you what to do."

Jumon looked a little surprised. "Of course. Who else? . . ."

"I thought maybe Madame Coughlin."

In candlelight even the most ashen pallor will appear rosy, but horror flared in the big man's eyes. "Madame—Madame Coughlin? . . ." He half-rose, then put a hand on the table's edge to steady himself, and sank again into his chair.

January took the carved horse from his pocket, and laid it on the black-bound book. "Your nephew met both Abigail and Lucinda Coughlin at the house of Dr. Yellowjack on St. John's Eve," he said. "Isaak was coming to you to tell you the child was in danger. . . ."

"Abigail?" Jumon's voice was barely a whisper. "Abi . . . she was alive?" His voice stumbled, fumbling for words. "Well? What evening . . . St. John's Eve?" His hands trembled, and looking at his eyes, January understood then that Lucinda Coughlin had not been Jumon's mistress.

Only his procuress.

There was no way he could keep that realization out of his face.

"Dear God." The big man shut his eyes. "Dear God." His words came out like a confession wrung through the tightening of an Inquisitorial garrote. "They—told me—she died. That she . . . That I . . ."

January was silent, filled with such a rush of comprehension, of enlightenment and revulsion and rage, that he could not sort what he felt into words.

Dr. Yellowjack will get anything a man wants.

Mademoiselle Coughlin would not be joining us after all . . .

The little horse lying on the table in the firelight.

And Antoine Jumon, hands trembling as he reached for the square black bottle of the only forgetfulness he could find. Eyes defeated as he whispered, *He's clever with investments;* and the look in his mother's face. *My uncle Mathurin is a consummately evil man, M'sieu.*

Antoine is . . . fanciful. . . .

January closed his fist very hard under the table, understanding why Geneviève had severed her ties with a protector who would have supported her for life.

Jumon was weeping, mouth pulled into a shape that no human mouth was meant to assume, struggling for silence as a drowning man struggles for breath. It was this that caused January to stay.

"Isaak is alive, you know," he said, more gently than he had thought he was going to speak. "He came to your house in town that night. Zoë thought he had the cholera and was so fearful of what your mother would say . . ."

"Oh, dear God." At the mention of his mother, January thought that the white man flinched.

"Zoë got a cab, we think, and fetched Antoine to be with him," continued January. "And cared for him in the empty shop until, as she thought, he died. Then she took his body away, probably using one of the wheelbarrows left by the movers. She may have tried to dump the body in the canal, or near the cemeteries; he was found by a couple on Basin Street just outside the Old Cemetery wall. They nursed him through the effects of the poisoning and the pneumonia he took that night from lying in the wet. Either Lucinda Coughlin or Dr. Yellowjack must have feared that Isaak might have reached his wife that night. Might have gotten word to her, or asked her to get word to you about Lucinda Coughlin being at Yellowjack's house. . . ."

"Yellowjack." Mathurin raised his head, and carefully blotted his eyes with a handkerchief of spotless linen. "It was Yellowjack. Madame Coughlin isn't—that is, I didn't think her very intelligent, but now I realize I don't know her, never knew her." He carefully refolded the linen, tucked it in his breast pocket, giving his whole attention to it so as to avoid January's eyes. "But Yellowjack . . ." His breath expelled in a whisper, like a bitter laugh or a sob.

"I don't know if you can understand," he said after a time. "Well, that's a foolish thing to say, because I know you *can't* understand—and I think I should be hard-put to keep from doing violence to any man who *could* understand. Who could do the things that I have done. *I* don't understand."

He raised his head, meeting January's eyes, and in the bloodshot irises, the broken veins that laced the man's nose, January saw the reflection of Antoine's Black Drop and Smyrna nepenthe. "I have tried—all my life I have tried to . . . to love normally. To love women. Or even young men. But every time I'd find myself . . . incapable. And telling myself that twelve wasn't really so different from fourteen. The girls on the levee, or down by the basin, do start at that age, you know, and younger. And ten wasn't really so different from twelve. I am an evil man, I know that, but I did try to atone. I always paid the children money they didn't have to show to Yellowjack, or to their parents if they had them."

"So you got them from Yellowjack?"

Jumon nodded. "He is—a devil. Looking back now I see he must have set it up from the start. With the Coughlin woman, that is, and . . . and Abigail. Not that he appeared to have a thing to do with either of them. Madame Coughlin came to me with impeccable letters of introduction, purporting to be newly widowed and desperately in need of assistance. I said I would do what I could for her, and that evening, about sunset, the child Abigail came—with some story about how she'd slipped away while her mother was resting—and pleaded with me to help her mother. . . ."

His eyes, his hands squeezed shut, thrusting the memory away. Or reliving it? January thought about Gabriel, and Chouchou. *White man or not*, he thought, *I would have killed him, if I had known this, and he had come near them. Killed him and taken the consequences.*

"God knows how I found the self-control to send her back home untouched," whispered Mathurin. "Because I did. She was so obviously sheltered, so obviously loved. What a jape! Because of course that only made me want her, which they must have known. And every time Madame Coughlin would come to my office, so that ways and means could be found for her to support herself, the child was always with her, asking to sit on my knee, calling me her favorite uncle and her dearest bel-ami. Have you seen her? Beautiful as an angel, sweet as cherries in cream."

January remembered the woman in the dimness of the Cathedral, the beautiful girl-child peeping around the side of her skirts. *It has to work.* "Yes," he said softly. "I've seen her."

Jumon's finger traced the flying caparisons of the dainty little horse, caressed the curlicues of mane. He did not look up. "And I dreamed of her at night," he went on, his voice almost a whisper. "Even now, much as I *know* that what I do is evil, I cannot *feel* that it is . . . so very bad.

At least not while I'm doing it. I see in your face how this disgusts you, but please believe that never at any time did I . . . did I want to be this way."

"Did Laurence know?"

Jumon shivered. For an eternity he did not reply, and into January's mind came that dark little cupboard below the roof-slates of the house on Rue St. Louis, the makeshift bonds and gags crusted with blood decades old.

"Laurence and I," said Jumon slowly, "went through . . . a great deal together, when we were children. Mother . . ." He couldn't finish. Only sat looking out into the darkness beyond the gallery railing, where even the lights of the kitchen had been quenched. One candle burned in the quarters above. January wondered which of the slaves would be awake so late, reading a newspaper, maybe, or mending a shirt.

Then Jumon shook his head, and said again, "Mother," in a soft defeated voice, as if that explained something, at least to his own heart.

He drew in his breath again, and let it go in a sigh. "I'm sorry," he said. "My brother . . . Laurence may have known. We never spoke about it. Once we were adults we never spoke of . . . certain things. And now that I think about it, it may be that Dr. Yellowjack held off putting his little scheme in train until after Laurence . . . died."

Because Laurence would have been more capable of scenting a fraud? wondered January. *Or because after his death you were lonelier than before? Robbed of the one who had been your companion in that bleak black prison-room upstairs, your only champion against the lover-demon of your childhood whose portrait still decorates every room in your house?*

We live not how we wish to, but how we can.

"In any case," said Jumon, "it's clear that Yellowjack has been behind this . . . this fraud . . . all along, pulling the strings like a puppeteer. He got opium for me, and arranged for me to bring the child to his house by the bayou."

"And when you were there," said January slowly, "something went wrong."

Jumon nodded. "The child must be a . . . a consummate actress. I . . ." He shook his head, shivering at the memory. "He asked for money, to cover things up. I gave it to him and he asked for more. You say—you say Isaak saw her on the night of the twenty-third?"

January inclined his head, thinking, *What of those who weren't 'consummate actresses'? What of those for whom you weren't a pigeon for plucking, but just the latest man their pimps made them pull up their skirts for?* He thought of Gabriel again and felt sick.

"And—my nephew is alive?"

"Yes. When he recovered from the pneumonia he communicated with Yellowjack, who evidently told him he'd be able to get his mother's order of distrainment canceled. Weber—the man who found him—was a doctor in Germany; another poisoning, there where he could see its onset and effects, could not have been passed off. Isaak went out to Bayou St. John Thursday night—he's lucky he was still alive when Madame Laveau and I arrived the next day, seeking my nephew."

"He's well?" There was a note of wistfulness in the man's voice.

"Yes. Thin and exhausted, but well. He—was at a loss," January went on carefully, "—as to why Mademoiselle Coughlin and her mother were in that place. He knew they were protégées of yours, but evidently he knew them only in their . . . respectable incarnations. And he knew nothing to your discredit." He couldn't have said why he tried not to hurt this big, clumsy man, who could love neither women nor men. Crippled from childhood by a woman who could find no other way to deal with her own terrors but to bind everything in her power, tighter and tighter, until they could not escape her control . . .

Jumon sighed. "Thank you for that discretion. Could I have had a son, I would have wanted him to be Isaak. Laurence was lucky there. Though God knows neither of us was ever very lucky with women. But of course if I'd had a son I'd have made a—a horror of raising him."

January was silent.

What were the first causes of wretchedness like this? he wondered. Maybe Isaak was right, to cut through the bloodied iron bands of the past and say, *You are still my father. You are still my uncle. I understand that you could not help what you did to my brother, my mother. . . .* Forgiveness is stronger than the graveyard dust of the past.

For Isaak it was, maybe, not knowing that his uncle's sins had gone far beyond Antoine. January knew that even had he himself been so ignorant in similar circumstances, it would have been beyond him.

He said, "Yellowjack was arrested yesterday, for kidnapping and attempting to murder my nephew and yours. It's only a matter of time, I think, until they find Madame Coughlin—she left New Orleans the day after Madame Célie's arrest. Once the City Guards start looking it will be easy to trace him as the man who hired Nash. You can do what you want about that, but Nash badly wounded a man in mistake for me, a young man named Pedro Lachaise, who had a mother and sisters to support."

"Dear God." Jumon passed a hand over his face. "I seem to have done nothing but ill." His jaw tightened. "I will make it good. I hope you believe me." He looked up at January, who said nothing. "I never set out to do wrong. That is . . . ." He hesitated. "I suppose I never set out to do anything. I have heard that . . . that Monsieur Gérard was arrested as well over an altercation. . . ."

"I've spoken to Judge Canonge about that," said January. "He agrees that in view of the mitigating circumstances the penalty can be commuted to a fine."

Jumon nodded. For another few minutes he sat quietly, his head in his hands, the candleflame glowing over the strong coarse fingers, the warm gold of his simple rings. The light in the quarters across the yard had been put out. In the trees the cicadas kept up their eerie throbbing cry, the frogs peeping a heavy bass-note line. By the stars, visible above the dark loom of the trees, it was very late, and morning would come soon, bringing with it all the matters of the day: justice, and movement, and the unveiling of the lethal secrets of the past.

Now was still the time of the *loa,* and dreams; stillness, and the dead, who see things differently than the living.

Jumon sighed. "Have you a place to stay for the remainder of the night, M'sieu Janvier? I doubt any boats are returning across the lake until daybreak and I understand that summer is not a good time for musicians. And I feel I owe you something for having warned me, in spite of all. If you have concerns about spending the night under the roof of a man who paid to have you killed, I understand them, and I'll gladly foot the bill at a lodging house of your choice."

"My sister would call me a fool," said January. "Mamzelle Marie as well, maybe. But I trust you."

Mathurin Jumon smiled, suddenly and with surprising sweetness, and stretched out his hand for the bell.

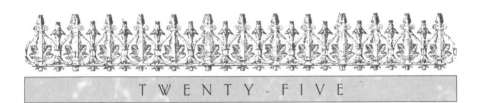

TWENTY FIVE

Mathurin Jumon walked with January down to the wharves first thing in the morning and paid his fee on the ferry; he stood waving on the dock as the flat-bottomed craft pulled away. Only later did January realize why the man performed this courtesy. Over a dozen people would afterward attest that Jumon had been alive and well when January left Mandeville. Returning home, Cordelia Jumon's surviving son put the barrel of one of his English dueling pistols into his mouth and pulled the trigger.

On the desk in his study his mother's footman found a holograph will leaving the sum of five hundred dollars to Pedro Lachaise's mother and sisters, with a further twelve hundred left in trust to Benjamin January to locate, purchase, and free Zoë Jumon. To Antoine Jumon, he left two thousand dollars in a trust to be administered by Isaak Jumon; to Isaak and Célie, three thousand, with the stipulation that if the said Isaak, or the said Antoine, were claimed as property by anyone, all the money would go to Célie absolutely. And to Benjamin January, Jumon left a rustic-ware platter and ewer wrought in the shape of seashells and crayfish, the work of Bernard Palissy.

Everything else of which he died possessed he willed to his mother, who did not attend his funeral.

January attended it, with Isaak and Célie. Black-bordered postings had been put up, not only in the city itself but in Milneburgh and Mandeville and Spanish Fort. A handful of the wealthy Creole businessmen who had taken refuge there for the summer appeared, sufficient at least to carry the coffin and to absorb some of the terrible echoing silence of the mortuary chapel as the priest read out the words of the service. Though not more than a dozen cases of yellow fever had occurred after the end of June, the graveyard was ringed with burning smudges, the stink of gunpowder and burning hooves almost drowning the charnel stench.

"Seven hundred and fifty dollars, Mathurin Jumon paid me to carve a trophy of arms for his brother," Basile Nogent said, coming out of the chapel's rear door beside January and watching the slim black-clothed pair follow the coffin at a respectful distance toward the oven tombs let into the cemetery wall. Afternoon sun hammered the sheets of standing water left by that morning's rain. Crayfish crept along their verges, making January remember with a shiver the young man entombed behind the slab from which Isaak Jumon's name had not even been eradicated yet. "Now the mother sends us word—in a letter from her solicitor, no less, as though Isaak were no kin of hers—saying just to add Mathurin's name to the block. A hard woman." He shook his head. "A hard woman."

January remembered the strips of blood-crusted sheet in the dark of the attic, the small circumference of the cut bonds. A child's head. A child's wrists. Maybe two children. Laurence, at least, when grown, had been able to take a mistress, and father children of his own, even if in the test he had sided against them—had sided with the man who had been his partner in that childhood nightmare of terror and adoration. January watched Nogent walk away, but did not join him. Since his childhood, he had never felt comfortable about funerals in the daylight.

"He really die of the cholera?" A tall, thin figure emerged from between the tombs, disreputable hat in hand and the filth of three days' travel crusted on his boots.

"I have no way of knowing." January had heard the truth from Isaak, and via letter from Dominique, who'd had it from Thérèse's second cousin Roul's lady friend, who was sister to Madame Cordelia Jumon's hairdresser, Hélène.

"Mighty auspicious timing, given what that Dr. Yellowjack's had to say of the man." Shaw spit, the tobacco disappearing into in the soupy brown muck of graveyard earth. "May not all be true, of course. And that gal Zoë, she swore up and down that Mathurin was good and kind to just about everyone he met, even if, as she said, there was an illness in his heart about 'certain things.' She didn't say which things."

"You found her, then."

The policeman nodded. "Clear up to Ouachita Parish, she was. Sold to a man name of Dedman. Nice enough feller, and seemed to treat her decent. Let me talk to her out in the kitchen. She didn't have a whole lot to add to what Isaak's told you. The cab feller had already left by the time she figured Isaak was gone, and Antoine was laid out colder'n a mackerel—bet he didn't mention he had a bottle of opium in his pocket that he was swiggin' right through his brother's mortal struggle. That Zoë's a big strappin' gal, and even in full health Isaak wasn't much heavier'n a flour-barrel. Like you guessed, there was a sort of cart or wheelbarrow in the shop, from bringin' in the floor mats. She used it twice, once to haul Isaak out'n there and again for Antoine. In the rain and the dark, and scared as she was about M'am Cordelia comin' down, she was kind of hurried over Isaak. She wept when she told me about it, said she'd never have done it, 'cept for bein' scared of what M'am Jumon would do."

January said dryly, "She had reason to be."

"Well now, by all I hear M'am Cordelia's mellowed some with age." Shaw spit again, at a roach the length of his finger, ambling down the side of a nearby tomb. "I understand when she was runnin' Trianon by herself, she kept discipline by bakin' the troublemakers in the brick ovens behind the house, or buryin' 'em up to their necks in the dirt for six, seven days. That kind of reputation buys you good service for a long time."

January remembered Mathurin Jumon's anxious, coaxing voice, *Now, Mother, don't be like that. . . .*

"That it does," he said softly. "That it does."

"But comin' back through Natchez," went on Shaw, scratching absently under the breast of his coat, "who should I see at the American Flag Hotel but them dear long-lost friends of mine, Lucinda and Abigail Coughlin. Turned out pretty as a pair of angels and actin' like little Abby hadn't never screamed and faked dead in her life."

January's glance cut sidelong, and met the chilly enigmatic gray eyes.

"They was waitin' for word from Yellowjack, seemingly." Shaw watched as the priest made the sign of the cross above the body, the men slid the shrouded form up into the rented holding-tomb—Laurence having a few months left to run before his year and a day's undisturbed occupancy of the family vault was up. "I understand now there was some certain amount of foolery with a pig's bladder full of blood, and the most heartrendin' death throes this side of a Bulwer-Lytton novel, and then somebody comin' around askin' somebody else for a whole lot of money not to say nuthin' about what had happened. I didn't speak to 'em—bein' shy of the ladies, you understand, and not knowin' at the time they was wanted for anything specific down here—but I sort of hinted to the Sheriff there to keep an eye on those two. I guess it's about time I headed back on up there again."

"Would it accomplish anything?" January thought with distaste of Blodgett and his notebook, of the elegant dark-haired gentleman amid his rustic ware and his books.

Shaw shrugged. "Might save the next man some grief."

The mourners were scattering, holding handkerchiefs before their noses as they hastened along the muddy paths. Lingering by the narrow hole in the cemetery wall to watch the sexton's men cement a marble square over the opening, the priest made the sign of the cross.

" 'In my father's house there are many mansions,' " quoted Abishag Shaw quietly, and folded his long arms. "And it may so be God has an understandin' that we don't, of how much a man can do with the hand he's dealt." He made his ambling way down the path between the tombs, hastening a little to catch up with Isaak and Célie.

Turning, January went quietly back into the church.

In my father's house there are many mansions. January lit a candle and set it before the feet of the Virgin, among the holocaust of waxlights always to be found there in the fever season. A handful of nuns from the Ursuline Convent grouped before the sixth Station of the Cross; their voices a soft murmuring in the gloom.

"Lead us not into temptation. . . . Deliver us from evil. . . ."

And what else, January wondered, was there to ask of God?

Quietly he walked to the rear, where the old statue of St. Peter stood, battered and shabby and soon to be replaced. An old man in a robe, with a beard and a bunch of keys. As January knelt at the rear bench, self-conscious and a little embarrassed, he noticed two or three pralines, a slice of pound cake, and a couple of cigars had been left on the base of the statue; another slice of pound cake and a dozen or more silver half-reale bits were tucked into the corners behind the railing.

To let those still in fear know prayers do get heard.

In my father's house there are many mansions. And in those many rooms, armoires containing, perhaps, many different suits of clothes. Maybe even a top hat and a pair of spectacles, for the benefit of those who didn't believe white men in long robes.

He saw in his mind Olympe in the darkness, swaying with silent ecstasy, the bride of the god of her understanding. Saw the hot yellow sun on the dust of Congo Square, and the stir and blend of life along its verges: the smell of gumbo and pralines, the laughter of flirtation, the murmur of talk as men sought healing or advice or just the money to make it through another day. Why wouldn't God like the smell of rum and cigars as well as that of incense?

Waiting for the nuns to finish and depart, he counted out the beads of his own rosary, and thought, *Blessed Virgin Mary, forgive me for my sins against my sister. You know—and Jesus Christ your son knows—more than I do about what lies in the human heart. Pray for me to be healed of my pride.*

When the sisters were finished and he was alone in the chapel, January got quietly to his feet. Reaching into the pocket of his black coat, he brought out a slice of pound cake, wrapped in a scrap of the *Louisiana Gazette*. This he opened up, and laid the whole at the feet of the old man with the beard and the keys.

"Thank you," he said, to the silence of the church.

Coming out of the chapel he glimpsed Marie Laveau in her seven-pointed tignon in the cemetery, kneeling beside a tomb. She might have been praying, but he suspected she was simply digging graveyard dust.

A second cortege arrived at the chapel as January left the cemetery gates, the undertaker's men going ahead bearing a black velvet pall and eight wax candles like ship's masts, flames pale in the hot still afternoon. Several dozen men followed, all those American businessmen who had not already fled the city, red-tipped wax tapers in their hands. Against the black of their coats the long white scarves of the pallbearers reminded January of bandages—where had he seen bandages, he wondered, wrapping skeletons who danced? He shook the thought away.

Carriage after carriage drew up, black plumes nodding on the heads of the horses. A black-lacquered coffin was taken down and borne past him, draped and padded in velvet and crêpe and trailed by Père Eugenius and a bevy of chanting choirboys. Only when the widow followed, supported by Elaine Destrehan and Manon Desdunes, did January realize who the dead man was.

It was Colonel Pritchard.

"It wasn't food poisoning, was it?" he asked the Sexton, who came out the cemetery gate beside him to watch the mourners file into the chapel.

"Heavens, no!" The official looked startled. "Whatever gave you that idea? The Colonel tripped on the front steps of the Union Bank, and struck his head on the granite carriage block. A dozen people saw it happen. A most sad and terrible accident."

January watched the floating darkness of the widow's veils disappear into the candle-starred gloom of the chapel vestibule: "It is terrible," he agreed quietly. The Colonel's slaves followed behind the widow, a long double file of them, trying very hard to look sad.

When the Supreme Court of the State of Louisiana reconvened following the fever season, it found in favor of Isaak Jumon against his mother's renewed claim that he was her slave. It likewise awarded Jumon the property from his father's will, and the three thousand dollars left him by his uncle, against the contest of his grandmother, Cordelia Jumon. That same month, Joseph Lafevre, also known as Dr. Yellowjack or Yellowjack Joe, was hanged for attempted murder and extortion.

After the ruling, Cordelia Jumon sold what remained of her sons' properties, and early the following year returned to Paris to live. She never returned to New Orleans.

AUTHOR'S NOTE

VOODOO

As usual when writing against a historical background, it required an effort of will on my part not to wander off and write a book about voodoo. Like most religions, including Christianity, voodoo has been used and misused, criminalized and politicized, trivialized, glamorized, and sensationalized, used to manipulate people's emotions and pick people's pockets. None of this alters the fact that it was a lifeline of comfort for generations of people in pain. I have tried to write about it as it must have appeared to the people at the time of my story: blacks, whites, and the free colored who were a class and a culture separate from either.

Historically, voodoo evolved from the tribal religions of West Africa, a complex interlocking of ancestor worship, reverence for the spirits of nature, and an overarching belief in a single deity who works through the various spirits—the *loa* or *lwa*—to aid humankind. The thousands of men and women who were kidnapped and enslaved by their tribal enemies, and sold to the whites, carried with them only what they had in their minds and in their hearts: skill at their trades, love of family, a rich heritage of music, and stories of animals and spirits. Among them were priests and herb doctors, priestesses and midwives, who carried the gods of their homeland, and the ways in which these gods might be petitioned for help—an invaluable treasure to people who needed help as desperately as any in the history of humankind.

As with most matters under slavery, how individual Africans or groups of Africans fared vis-à-vis religion depended largely on the personality and outlook of the individual white master. Many owners did not bother to convert their slaves to Christianity or were content with token baptism; others insisted on the show of belief. Given the brevity of the average slave's survival on a New World cane plantation, it may not have seemed worth the trouble. Anything that smacked of religious or any other organization among the slaves was, of course, severely punished, so the worship of the *loa*—always more or less a come-as-you-are, make-it-up-as-you-go-along proposition anyway—went underground, taking different forms, depending on where most of the slaves in any particular locale had come from and how strict a watch the local whites kept. It became a common practice to identify Christian saints with *loa,* either as a way to fool the whites while keeping integrity with one's own beliefs or out of instinctive syncretism, the belief that they really were the same entity by different names: like lenses of the same color, filtering the same Light.

In writing about voodoo in New Orleans in the middle 1830s, I have tried to extrapolate backward from the modern forms of voodoo found in Haiti and New Orleans. Even before the black revolution of 1804—in which it played a significant part—voodoo in Haiti was enormously strong, and remains close to its original African elements. Spellings and names of the *loa* vary in different accounts: Spirits and gods from several different African cultures were incorporated and, at different places and different times, Native American spirits (or what second-generation Africans perceived to be Native American spirits) as well. In most cases I have simplified and have used the modern Haitian spellings, names, and identification of the *loa.*

Reading nineteenth- or early-twentieth-century accounts of New Orleans voodoo—for the most part white finger-pointing at "barbaric superstition"—elements in common are clear: the priest and priestess (Hougan and Mambo, King and Queen), the worship of the serpent, animal sacrifice, dancing, possession by the *loa* in the course of the dance. Most agree that the *loa* like alcohol and tobacco—in fact, the *loa* like most of the things that people like: food, candy, bright colors, lights, pretty things, money, something to smoke. Voodoo altars are fantastic (and weirdly beautiful) accretions of whatever speaks to the worshiper of God or the gods, items dedicated to whichever *loa* is honored by that particular altar: Ezili likes certain types of perfume, the Guédé—the dark *loa*—like symbols of power and death. (I've seen a black plastic statue of Darth Vader on one such altar, and it's hard to see how that symbol of intergalactic power and evil could be considered out of place.)

Voodoo, both old and modern, is very much a religion of this world, of God or the gods acting in this world to help people attain success, health, help, or protection from a capricious and arbitrary universe.

Most accounts of New Orleans voodoo add that sexual excesses followed hard upon the dancing. This may be projection by whites who feared a more sexually liberated culture. But anyone who has gone to nightclubs and parties will be aware that the presence of *loa* is not required to connect the one with the other, particularly if this is the only time most of these people (a) get to see each other and (b) are able to enjoy a few hours in which they can forget they're someone else's property and aren't on call for some kind of work.

Voodoo has such an alien appearance to Westerners that, inevitably, it acquired an astonishing veneer of bizarre connotations. Nineteenth-century Christians regarded it as Devil worship (read nineteenth-century authors on the subject of the Buddhism of Chinese coolies working on the railroads and the Hinduism of most of the population of British India). Many French Creoles, brought up side by side with voodoo, went regularly to its practitioners for charms and gris-gris, something that would have deeply saddened their confessors but not surprised them. In the latter part of the century, half-understood practices coupled with the racism inherent in yellow journalism made voodoo a fertile source of sensationalistic plot elements in dime novels: zombies and voodoo dolls (and let's not forget those sexually degenerate dances) became staples of cheap thrillers, both printed and cinematic. Hoodoo—African-style sorcery and herbalism—was seen as part of the voodoo religion, although the closeness of the connection varied from place to place and from time to time.

In fact, the practice of voodoo varies even today. Some practitioners do it one way, some do it another, not to mention the plethora of tourist voodoo and of fakes and cheats to rip off the unwary and credulous. Even in Haiti, where voodoo is more or less an organized faith, it is a patchwork of personal interpretations of gods, rites, and emphasis.

All of the above—and the fact that nobody attempted anything remotely resembling an organized and unprejudiced study of voodoo until almost a hundred years after my story takes place—make it extremely difficult to present a picture of what voodoo was, or must have been like, in the summer of 1834.

I've done the best I can. I've tried to remain true to what sincere practitioners of voodoo have told me about ceremony and possession, but I am sure there are others who do it very differently. Excellent books exist about the history, and the current practices, both of voodoo as a religion and about African sorcery. There are voodoo shops—or shops catering to Santeria and other West African–based New World religions—in most big cities of the Western Hemisphere, and large segments of the population follow the practices of these faiths.

Likewise, it is difficult to get any kind of straight story about Marie Laveau—and the fact that her daughter was also named Marie Laveau, and also became "Voodoo Queen" of New Orleans (leading to tales of eternal youthfulness) does not make investigation any easier.

My goal, as always, has been simply to entertain without doing violence to the truth of former times. One can buy voodoo candles in nearly any supermarket or drugstore in New Orleans, and the priests of the Church of Our Lady of Guadeloupe—formerly the mortuary Chapel of St. Antoine—still regularly find slices of pound cake or bits of money at the feet of a certain statue in the back of the church.

"CREOLES"

One of the problems about writing a historical novel (or any other kind, for that matter) is that once you've said a thing, there it is in print for better or worse.

It's been pointed out to me by a research specialist in the Jacksonian period that my source for the way the word "Creole" was used in that time and place was incorrect (although the source seemed pretty authoritative at the time). In both *A Free Man of Color* and *Fever Season* I've said that in the 1830s "Creole" meant "white descendant of French or Spanish colonists" only; in fact, the word was used in contemporary documents to describe the free colored as well.

All I can do is apologize for my goof and promise to correct it in future Benjamin January novels, and future editions of the existing novels, should I be so fortunate as to have them. Thank you for your forgiveness and forbearance.

B.H.